MURDER IN ARUNDEL

Ruby Vitorino Moody

Timezone Publishing

This first edition published in Great Britain in
2024 by Timezone publishing of Highfield House,
189 Devizes Road, Salisbury, Wiltshire, SP2 7ls.

Copyright © Ruby Vitorino Moody 2024.

British Library Cataloguing in Publication Data.
A catalogue record for this book is available from
the British Library.

ISBN 978-1-3999-9826-0

Cover art and layout : Alex King

This book is dedicated to my parents,
David and Valerie King,
and my husband Frogg Moody.
Thank you for all your love and support.

This is a work of fiction. Names, characters and incidents are either imagined by the author or are used fictitiously. Any resemblance to actual persons, living or dead, or events, is purely coincidental.

While the author is aware that places and businesses described have changed since the 1930s, she has not felt obliged to be always historically accurate if in doing so she spoiled her plot or the enjoyment of her readers.

Acknowledgements

I would like to take the opportunity to thank the following fellow authors for their help and encouragement:

Michael Hambling
Elizabeth Keysian
Edward Stow (*The House of Lechmere.* YouTube.)
Annette J Beveridge
Dr Brad Gyori
Dr John Chandler
And readers:
Samantha Hulass
Maggie Burns
Maria Newton

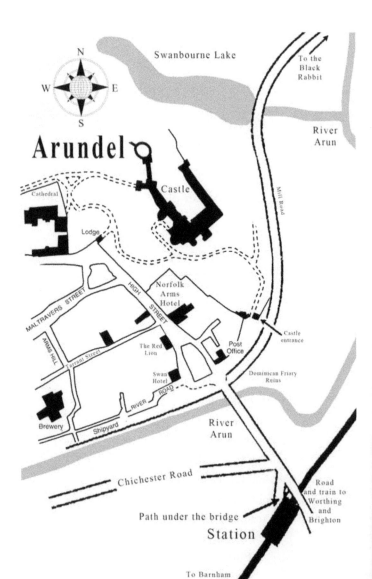

1935

CHAPTER 1

Looming above Arundel stood the massive castle, its pale grey crenellated walls dominating the skyline. Still higher, far above the battlements, soared a pair of buzzards, the ends of their wings like fingers stretching out into the spring sky as they swooped and dived.

Edith Kershaw turned off the main road, expertly steering the little green Austin as it rattled its way across the plain toward the river. Something about the buzzards attracted her attention and made her feel uneasy. It was an ominous, otherworldly feeling that something wretched was just around the corner.

Oh, no, she thought, *it's happening again.*

Unwilling to turn her head, she could only imagine the slight young man sitting in the passenger seat beside her. Michael was wearing overalls and a heavy leather sheepskin-lined jacket. He had a leather flying helmet on his head. She tried to visualise his lively blue eyes and blond wispy moustache. But, as she strived to feel him present in the car, there was no corresponding buzzing in her temple. She always felt that strange vibration in her head when a spirit was present so she knew, to her chagrin, that Michael remained resolutely elusive.

Edith tried to concentrate on driving, bouncing over the flag-stoned road and ignoring the queasy feeling in the pit of her stomach. She was supposed to be going to enjoy herself for a few days at a celebration of marriage in a comfortable hotel, with people dear to her, not trying to conjure up her dead fiancé and struggling with feelings of anxious foreboding.

Michael wouldn't have worn his work clothes to a wedding anyway, even though clad in his pilot's clothes was how she remembered him best. She mentally re-dressed him in a dark pinstripe suit with broad shoulders, a nipped waist, and wide trousers. Her imagination shaved off his moustache, too. It was a pity because she'd liked the moustache, but he'd thought he looked more like the film star Leslie Howard without it.

'Oh, Mick! You crazy, crazy man!' she whispered tenderly to the circling buzzards.

A gaggle of old men were sat on the bridge, enjoying the noise and activity of the town wharf, as she drove by. The salty air mingled with damp acrid smoke over that part of the river, and the sounds of machinery and seagulls drifted over the water.

A motorcycle and sidecar roared past her, backfiring loudly, as they started up the hill into the town, the many bicycles weaving up the street preventing her from taking her eyes off the road. She had to swerve as a weary young man - doubtlessly one of the many jobless looking for work - staggered slightly into the road under the weight of a cheap cardboard suitcase.

A char-a-banc was stopped on the cobbles of

the Town Square next to a brown and white country bus. Groups of spreeish tourists were milling about in front of the red brick façade of the Norfolk Arms hotel. She claxoned and carefully edged the car past them and through the archway at the front of the building, skirting the petrol pumps.

She'd arrived.

Parking behind the Hotel, Edith sat in the car for a minute, looking at the empty front seat and remembering her past happiness. However much she tried to see the ghost of Michael Callaghan, he never appeared, although the ghosts of others, who usually meant nothing to her, often seemed to linger at the sides of rooms or tell her things she hadn't asked to know.

Edith didn't look in the mirror as she freshened up her red lipstick and squeezed the bulb on her perfume spray. She didn't look in the mirror because she was beginning to notice a definite bitterness starting to creep around the set of her mouth lately.

It's so unfair, she thought. The irony wasn't lost on her that, as a Test Pilot, Mick had done one of the most dangerous jobs a man could have done yet had died cleaning out the guttering on his roof. Of course, she'd realised that Mick had less respect for heights than other people since he was used to flying flimsy biplanes, but that was beside the point. Mick was exciting; he always said it was his mother's Irish blood. He wrote wildly romantic poetry and sang lilting ballads from the Emerald Isle as he raised his beer mug and talked to her about James Joyce and Ulysses, and Dublin painters. He'd been a bit of a hell-raiser too, always riding his motorbike too fast, and had once spent a night in the cells for shinning up a flag pole and cutting down the German flag. The trouble was, for Edith, no other man was ever painted in such bright colours as Michael Callaghan.

Why hadn't she had any premonitions that Mick was going to die? She had experienced terrible fears when she knew he was flying an untested aeroplane, but nothing had warned her that he would have such a banal accident. She always asked herself if she might have changed things had she been able to warn him of what fate intended? Could one change the future - or was it already fixed?

Edith exchanged her sensible shoes for high heels and her leather driving gloves for pristine white ones. Then, bending slightly, she surreptitiously adjusted her thick silk stockings.

'You're not wearing that.' The man's voice seemed to come from high up, quiet and controlling. *It's coming from one of the bedrooms*, thought Edith. *I really shouldn't listen.*
She heard a woman start to sob as she walked to the boot.

'But why? I thought you liked it. I haven't brought anything else with me for the evening.'
'You look like a streetwalker in it. Men will be looking at your breasts. Is that what you want? Is it?
Answer me! Look at me, will you? And stop whining - I can't stand it.'

4

'It's a fashion. That's all. Please don't start. Don't let's ruin the weekend. I'll wear a scarf. There are shops here - I'll buy a scarf to match it and cover my shoulders if that's what you want.'

'And now you've wasted your money - my money - buying it. I shouldn't have to tell you.'

'But you liked it before.'

'Oh, shut up!'

The pair of buzzards mewed and cried as they wheeled overhead and disappeared over the ramparts toward the castle.

'The name is Kershaw. Miss Edith Kershaw,' she said, carefully putting down her small leather suitcase and the satchel containing thick paper and oil pastels in front of the reception desk. Painting was Edith's passion, although few people were as enthusiastic about her work as she was. Still, the paintings seemed to express how she felt, not what other people might think pretty, or even recognisable. She stood up straight. She was a fine-boned, slender woman with dark auburn wavy hair and grey eyes flecked with amber. The smiling hotel receptionist ran his finger down the register and - at the word 'miss' - looked at her appreciatively. Edith Kershaw was a little too old to be a 'miss' at thirty, almost on the shelf. However, she was still a pretty woman and looked sensible and respectable. Edith had style but was unassuming in her manner. She wore sombre navy blue and greys but you could see she was the sort of woman who might sing aloud in her motorcar when no one was looking.

Turning away from the mahogany desk, Mr Hinton took down a large key attached to a heavy brass fob and said 'Room Fifteen,' Miss Kershaw. The porter will take your case up.'

Somewhere in another room, a hollow-sounding Bakelite wireless played the BBC Empire Service.

'You should also have Mrs Clara Kershaw on the register - my mother. Has she arrived yet, d'you know?'

'No, Madam.' Hinton bowed his greying head slightly. 'The hotel is only receiving guests for tomorrow's wedding and you're one of the first to get here. I shall be sure to tell her that you are already here as soon as she arrives. We've booked her into the room next to yours.'

Edith found herself admiring the handsome red carpet and taking in the pungent beeswax and turpentine smell of furniture polish and brass, unsure if she was pleased about that, or not.

'And Mr and Mrs Denney? I don't suppose they've arrived yet?'

'As a matter of fact, they have,' Hinton said, brightening up. Shall I send a message up to their room for you?'

'Yes, please. I would rather like to drink a pot of tea in the snug before I go up. Could you have the porter take my case and bag? Please let Mr and Mrs Denney know where to find me. Thank you ever so much.'

Edith walked back to the cosy little sitting room she had seen on her way in. Another couple was sitting there, whom she didn't recognise. On the bridegroom's side? Although Edith would probably not recognise many of the guests on the bride's side either - the bride was only a second cousin after all. The elderly couple were deep in conversation, so she didn't want to interrupt them. She glanced at the pair of West Highland Terriers beside them, straining at their leads to reach her, wagging their tails, and sticking out pink tongues. She mouthed 'lovely dogs,' but the couple didn't notice her.

Perching in a leather club armchair on the opposite side of the room to the couple, next to a potted palm, she sipped tea poured by a waitress in a white starched hat and apron. She was enjoying the unfamiliarity of the place, and she put that distressing conversation overheard in the car park far aside; troubling as it had been, it had nothing to do with her - nor the Norfolk Arms. It had been a private matter, and she wouldn't let it dampen her first impressions. Her mind turned to Phillip and Hester Denney in eager anticipation. Hester Denney - Hester Kershaw, back then, was more than a cousin; she'd been a close childhood companion before the Great War, after which life had become less Renoir and more Munch for everyone.

Edith could remember Hester and herself long ago trying to run and jump while wearing heavy lace-up boots and, painful, stiffly starched collars and heavy petticoats. She smoothed her comfortable crepe skirt and blouse, bought ready-made from a department store, as she cast her mind back. The world had changed out of recognition since their childhood. Edith and Hester were nearly the same age. They'd even waltzed with each other at dances and did the Charleston behind their parents' backs because so many of the young men they might have danced with had been killed in the War. She hardly saw Hester since Hester married Phillip and then moved to Birmingham. Still, at least they both had telephones. They'd kept in touch. It had been a good idea of Hester's to extend this family wedding weekend into a holiday for just the three of them. *It should have been the four of us*, Edith thought sadly - if only Mick hadn't gone up to his roof on that bloody ladder.

Deep in her thoughts, part of her was aware of the large clock ticking rhythmically in the sudden heavy silence and the warmth of the room. Her mind seemed to slip deeper into itself; her legs were heavy as stone. Then, her arms and hands grew heavy and limp. The clock tick-tocked back and forth. She looked at the pink and white china teacup but couldn't reach for it. She felt drowsy - but expectant. She couldn't move. The tension left her neck, and the top of her head felt light. The room felt different. The air vibrated. There came a buzzing in her temple. Edith watched unsurprised as a man in a top hat and a frock coat with glinting brass buttons ushered a lady in a long green dress across the room. They seemed to move effortlessly on a surface lower than the carpet. She stared transfixed at the shiny buttons and listened to the rustle of taffeta on a wooden floor. The moment could only have lasted a few seconds, but it was so unhurried that Edith felt she had all the time she wanted to scrutinise the details. Time no longer had a meaning. The beaver texture of the man's hat with its grosgrain band, and the woman's tiny hands with kid gloves buttoned on the side, were sharp and clear, but when the man turned, his features were indistinct, blurred. He reached inside his waistcoat, drew out a bright gold watch on a thick rose gold chain with an amethyst swivel fob, and held it towards her. She knew that something was important, but there wasn't a clue as to what it was.

It was a dog barking that made her snap out of it. The terriers were cowering under a chair, growling, their hackles and fur raised.

'Brandy! What's the matter, daaarling? Dodo, sweetheart.' The elderly couple fussed about the dogs, stroking them and calming them down. Terribly sorry to disturb you,' they called across the room. 'I don't know what's got into them. They're usually so well-behaved. What side are you on? Brandy - stop whining!'

'Sorry? Oh. Of course. The bride.'

'We're on the bridegroom's side. The name is Potter. Old family friends.'

'I'm Edith Kershaw. Pleased to meet you.'

The couple soon turned away to start an animated conversation. I wonder how long they've been married that they still have so much to say to each other? Edith asked herself. But then came the unwelcome knowledge that she knew very well that the answer was fifty-two years. She drank the rest of her tea in increasing misery; the past and the future were bleeding into the present.

Hester saw Edith's unhappiness the second she and Phillip entered the snug. They'd all hugged and flapped around, gushing their joy in seeing each other again, with the prospect of a long weekend of parties and dancing, followed by long country walks under the castle walls and shared confidences. Perhaps even motoring trips to the seaside, or a trip into Chichester to go shopping when the wedding was over. But something was wrong all the same.

'What's your room like?' Edith asked Phillip politely. She liked him. He had an open face and wide baby blue eyes that tended to water; she knew he needed glasses but was too vain to wear them.

Hester interrupted. 'What an earth has happened, Edie? I only spoke to you on the blower yesterday. You're absolutely pale, and you look wiped out.'

Edith glanced across at the garrulous Mr and Mrs Potter. Brandy and Dodo were happily lying on the thick carpet beside them, and Hester was soon down on her haunches making a fuss of them as they lolled their tongues and panted contentedly.

'May I get them a bowl of water?' Hester addressed Mrs Potter, making it sound as if Mrs Potter would be doing her a great favour if she would say yes.

'Could we all go for a walk in the town? I don't want to be overheard by those people,' Edith said to Phillip in a low voice.

They fetched their coats and hats from their respective rooms and sauntered up the high street, the castle walls rising above them to the right and yet more battlements ahead. Edith and Hester linked arms so as not to trip up over an uneven flagstone, in their high court shoes, and willing their fashionable little hats to stay on in the breeze. You could tell Edith and Hester were related. They both had the same build and delicate features, although Hester's face was narrower, and she had long, thin, fingers. But there the resemblance ended; while Edith's hair was dark russet, Hester's hair was nut brown, and Edith's grey eyes were serious whereas Hester's were hazel and sparkling. They didn't take out their cigarettes, although they both smoked; ladies did not light up in the street.

Phillip, however, lit his pipe. He was eight years older than his sparky wife and looked permanently amused and bemused by her.
Edith told them about the ghosts.

'I haven't told you, Hess, but it's happened a few times since I lost Mick, and it's perfectly terrible.' It wasn't that she was frightened of ghosts, but it seemed an intrusion into some perfectly lovely days when some sad creature sought her out, trapped on this Earth, or returned to give her a message that she didn't understand for somebody she didn't want to get involved with. Phillip said nothing, but Edith could tell by his expression that he thought the two women were caught up in shared, over-active, imaginations and he had simply decided to humour them. Mick had believed in ghosts and Heaven and Hell - although Mick had even believed in leprechauns, so it probably didn't count.

'I told you before, darling?' Hester gave Phillip a warning look. 'Edie used to see ghosts and 'know' things when we were children - she was both a medium and clairvoyant, and she'd dream true. We didn't think anything of it at all; it just seemed perfectly natural. I felt it was something special that Edie could do, and I couldn't, the way I was good at tennis, and she wasn't. Later, we realised that the grown-ups didn't approve of it at all. That was a shock!'

Edith sighed. Then, momentarily distracted, she let go of Hester's arm, as she stared at an olde-worlde café advertising traditional luncheons and cream teas and made a note to go there. It looked rather similar to the one she ran in Cuckfield, and you had to look at what the competition was doing, after all.

'Yes,' Edith continued, 'I just thought that lots of people might be able to 'know' things like they could draw a picture or sew. But Mama and Papa were certain I wanted to be that dreadful little child who only wants to be the centre of attention, who everybody hates. So, they wouldn't entertain the thought of spirits; they'd bring out the martinet at a mere suggestion. And I stopped telling anyone - except Hester - anything about it.'

'You got thrashed, didn't you? Didn't you tell

your neighbour something?'

'I told Mr Wilson that Mrs Wilson was standing next to him - she was dead, you know, but *I* knew that *she* wanted him to know that their daughter was going to have a baby girl and she was going to be named after Mrs Wilson. I thought that it would make him very happy but it didn't. He was petrified and thought I was very 'odd.' Pa was alive then, and he was furious. Mr Wilson wouldn't talk to any of us after that.'

Phillip exhaled a cloud of smoke that dissolved slowly into the ether.

'And did she have a baby girl?' Phillip tried not to show his doubts. After all, there was a fifty percent chance that this Mrs Wilson would have a daughter.

'Yes,' said Edith. She tried to explain to him that she hadn't wanted the gift at all as she grew older. She'd known that so many people were hoping to talk to loved ones who'd died in the trenches, and horrible fake mediums were extracting money from the bereaved.

'I couldn't do it to order. Like the intuition - ESP, call it what you will - the ghosts came to me because they wanted to. And then I stopped them. I just managed to shut the whole strange thing off. I know it's a peculiar gift, and I don't want it. Truly, I don't. I didn't ask to see ghosts in the snug at the Norfolk Arms.'

There was a long silence as Phillip seemed to mull it over. Did he believe her? Many people didn't, which is why she wouldn't have told anybody except him and Hester. She wished they could have fun and enjoy the holiday without the company of dead people; she wanted to relax with the living and paint.

'So,' said Hester, 'the ghosts you saw in the Norfolk Arms... d'you think they were like a photograph from the past? The place was an old coaching inn after all. Look at that arch where the carriages came in! They probably didn't mean to contact you for any particular reason.'

'Oh, but I know they did,' Edith said. 'The man showed me a watch. I often see things in symbols - like a dream? He meant to say, 'Time is ticking down.' But I don't know to what. Or even if it's to something good or bad.'

Edith didn't often lie to Hester, but she remembered her feeling when she watched those buzzards circling and knew time was ticking down to something terrible. *Liar, liar, pants on fire*! The rhyme sprang into her head with an unsettling intensity.

'Where'd you get your coat, darling? I love the fur collar,' Edith said, trying to change the subject. 'Hanningtons, darling, Brighton. But your coat's lovely, too. Grey is so smart.'

'You said that the gift came back after Michael died? Do you think you've seen Michael?' asked Phillip. He was limping his way up the steep stone-lined hill. Phillip had been wounded rescuing men from No Man's Land in the Great War for which he'd received the Military Medal, although he'd never talked to anyone about what had happened that day. They had reached the top of the road and turned left onto the London Road, away from the entrance to the Castle and towards the Catholic Cathedral. Edith felt the emotion well up.

'No,' she said. 'Mick is the only ghost I'd really like to see, but instead I see people who have really nothing to do with me. I try to concentrate and imagine Mick is with me, but it never works.'
She supposed he was at rest. He was the one who'd moved on, and she - the living -
struggled.

Hester gave her a friendly push.

'I'm sure it's because he's at peace.' Hester always understood. 'I wish you'd meet someone else. Not to replace him, of course not, but to make you happy again.'

'Don't!' Edith said, 'You sound just like Ma! She won't stop trying to fix me up with the grimmest men - anyone single with a pulse...and money, of course.'

They had wended their way along the London Road at the top of the town and had got to the 'St Mary's Gate.' Still, Hester had looked at the steep, narrow streets leading back down the hill and then at their heels, suggesting they return the way they'd come, so they turned around and started walking back to the hotel.

'I've got some presents in my room for your children.' Edith smiled. Phillip and Hester's four children were her godchildren. They were staying at home with the Nanny so the adults could enjoy a holiday. Edith would have liked to have seen them. Now that her fiancé was dead and her own wedding called off, she supposed that she wouldn't ever be a mother, which is what she had always hoped to be. Eligible men in the right age group were very few and far between since the War, and somebody always snapped up the suitable ones. She was resigned to being a 'maiden aunt.' Not a literal aunt; her older brother, Martin, had died in Flanders without leaving any offspring. The thought that she, herself, would most likely never have children struck at the heart of her. Edith imagined a painting of herself as a barren medieval Queen, howling. She supposed that one day, everything she owned would go to her godchildren, who rarely saw her.

'Perhaps I should move to Birmingham?' Edith mused out loud.

'But what would your mother do, darling?' Hester gave an exasperated sigh. 'You're all she's got!' 'I think it might just be the cocktail hour at the hotel when we get back,' said Phillip.

'And time for a cigarette. I'm gasping.' Hester grimaced, as she took Edith's arm again. 'I won't be able to go into the snug now without imagining it with a wooden floor - probably still under the carpet - full of people in top hats and long dresses.'

Looking back from the top of the town the view was magnificent. The green fields and trees could be seen above the vivid red brick buildings and dark, mossy, tiled roofs, as the high street seemed to fall away vertiginously from the top of the town. People strolled in the Town Square or walked down to the river. It was a peaceful, quintessentially English town where, despite the prominent war memorial nearly opposite the Norfolk, you could be forgiven for forgetting that Flanders or Suvla Bay had ever existed. The air was sweet, and if the roads smelt of anything, it was fresh manure from the horses and carts that still trundled up the steep streets between the motor vehicles. Surrounded by the glorious countryside, the presence of the Dukes of Norfolk in their fairytale castle on the hill, granted the little town a quietly grand air that raised it above the ordinary and attracted a steady stream of visitors.

'I love Arundel,' said Hester, gazing out to the distance. 'What a romantic place for a wedding!'

'Look at that!' Phillip stopped suddenly. 'Up there on the wall!'

The two women looked up to where he was pointing.

'I don't suppose you've ever seen a buzzard so close and in the town,' he said.

An enormous brown bird sat on the castle wall, watching them with beady black eyes above a menacing umber beak, its talons just visible under its sturdy body.

'It looks like it's waiting,' said Hester, with a shiver, 'for what, I wonder?'

'Or who?' Edith did not expect an answer.

'It looks like it's waiting for a *mouse*, and it won't be long before it finds one.'

Hester sighed. 'You frighten me, darling. Perhaps the mouse is one of us? Come on, Phillip, lead me to a G&T!'

CHAPTER 2

Edith opened her eyes sluggishly, momentarily disorientated as unfamiliar dark shapes loomed in the darkness, silent and menacing. The hotel cotton sheets smelt of lavender and the pillows were firm and comfortable, but the excitement of the evening and the memory of the wild dancing made it hard to settle despite her extreme tiredness. She could only sleep fitfully. It had been the eve of the wedding, and so far, it had been fun; she'd been somewhat afraid that it might stir painful emotions of having to cancel her own wedding. However, spending time with Hester and Phillip again, and of course, the cocktails and champagne, had made it easy to dance to somebody's gramophone after they'd pushed the tables back in the dining room after supper. An old jazz fox-trot came back to her:

'Flamin' Mamie,
a sure-fire vamp
When it comes to Lovin'
She's a human oven.
Come on, you-futuristic-papas!
She's the hottest thing he's seen since the Chicago fire!

Her toes started moving to the music in her head, and then her feet jiggled to an imaginary beat. It was infectious but the black shapes in the room stayed static and immutable.

She's a hot scorcher (dah DAH dah-dah)
She loves torture (dah DAH dah-dah)
She's-the-hottest-babe-in-town
(wah Wah, wah waaaah)

When her eyes adjusted to the darkness, the room seemed cold and rigid. Everything was mute. It felt like the depths of the night, but it must be about three o'clock in the morning, she guessed. Nothing moved. There was no sign of life anywhere else on Earth. The fox-trot started again the moment she closed her eyes.

She's a human oven!
She's hotter than Chicago's FIRE!

It was useless; Edith couldn't sleep, and the thought of lying awake until daybreak with that tune banging insistently in her head was too horrible to contemplate. Of course, one thing always relaxed her - painting. After all, there was some compensation to being single; nobody was there to mind if the sudden urge to paint took her in the early morning hours. She turned on the weak electric light and, slipping a bedjacket over her cotton nightie, hair in a knot, she padded barefoot over to pull the oil pastels and paper from her satchel.

Flamin' Mamie.

Edith hummed absent mindedly as she rubbed the oil pastels thickly onto her paper: Vermillion; Crimson Lake; Scarlett; Rose Madder.

She's a human oven.

Cadmium Yellow; Lemon Yellow; Yellow Deep; Indian Yellow Orange. Edith took the bed jacket off again.

The fireman had to retire.

Old Holland Blue Deep; Cobalt Green Deep; Van Dyke Brown; Ivory Black; Mars Black.
Hurrying to the window in her thin pale nightie, Edith threw it wide open, the early morning breeze fanning the room and blowing the lacy curtains inwards.

She's the hottest thing he's seen since the Chicago fire!

Old Holland Yellow Light; Mixed White; Titanium White; Flake White.

Lost in thought about tomorrow's wedding and the happy holiday to come, Edith mopped the perspiration from her forehead without noticing. She began streaking the paper as the fancy took her. She wasn't an artist to worry about what she was painting and didn't care about realism. She was more like those Continental abstract painters who mainly cared about expressing emotion or stray thoughts, and whom she so admired. She wasn't as good, of course, or maybe people in Cuckfield didn't care too much for 'that sort of thing,' for despite hanging her work on the walls of her tearoom, she'd never sold a thing. The usual comment was, 'What is it?' and if she replied, 'the smell of freshly mown grass,' 'the taste of peaches and cream,' or 'folk music,' they looked perplexed and searched for something figurative that wasn't there. She had learnt people didn't like something that they didn't understand or couldn't measure or compare, rather than simply immersing themselves and experiencing spontaneous emotion.

The grey light was inching in, and the first birds started to sing when Edith became aware that she was stiff and freezing cold. Her feet were blue (*Greyish Blue Pale*, she thought.) Shutting the window, she looked at her painting with a fresh eye, satisfied. It was bright, vibrant even, with giant geometric red, orange, and yellow angular streaks, prisms and spikes. The garish colours clustered on a dark swirly background with a strange black abstract shape in the centre, lit with white.

I've painted that silly Mamie song, she thought, but she had already forgotten the tune. Drained and shivering, she crawled back into bed.

Phillip Denney looked rather green around the gills as he contemplated his kedgeree, in the hotel breakfast room.   Judging by the festivities in the hotel's restaurants, bars, and ballroom the night before, a good many guests at the wedding of Louise Matthews and Arthur Lamb that morning would be feeling under the weather - not least Louise Matthews and Arthur Lamb.

The high breakfast room was painted in cool shades of green with small square windows all around the top of the walls, under the coffered ceiling. An immense chandelier - worthy of Versailles - hung in the centre of the room. They sat at a table for four, Hester eyeing the waiter.

'Phillip! Cover your ears! Doesn't that waiter look terribly like those wonderful statuettes of Nijinsky, darling? Couldn't you just imagine him in ballet hose? Dance with me! I want my arms around you,' sang Hester in a stage whisper in the general direction of the Russian looking waiter, waving her hands around with a clanking row of bangles. 'The charms about you will carry me through to...'

Edith sang back, beating time on her milk jug, although in a rather quieter voice, and checking around them to make sure nobody on another table had noticed. She felt quite tired.
'Please stop it,' groaned Phillip, clutching his thinning grey hair.

'Heaven! I'm in heaven,' the women sang in unison, giggling.

'It was an awfully good evening, though,' said Edith, 'Cuckfield isn't very lively, and I don't have many friends there who enjoy going out. I adore the tea dances at Sherry's Dance Hall or Snows, in Brighton, but I'm afraid I don't get to go very often. We probably shouldn't have done it when we've got such a long day ahead of us though. There's a Catholic wedding, a formal luncheon, and the reception to get through...Not good when you start off with a headache, Phillip! Hester, - I'm sure you're still squiffy! Don't tell me you're not...'

'Well, we should enjoy ourselves, darling,' Hester said. 'Just think of the War, when people couldn't enjoy themselves. We're alive, and we really ought to have fun - for their sakes. I know how much you loved dear Michael, but it's been over three years now. You looked so happy after a few cocktails. I caught some of the chaps looking at you...'

'Oh, stop it. I don't know how I'm not tireder; I was up in the middle of the night painting. I couldn't sleep because the music kept going round and round in my head.'

'You look very well on it,' said Phillip. 'I feel rather liverish, myself. What did you paint?' He poured some weak coffee from a silver coffee pot.

'What was the tune-that-wouldn't-go-away? It was some old jazz thing we danced to last night. I'll show my picture to you sometime - I'm rather pleased with it; the colours are very warm. Oh! – there's Ma!'

Edith started waving to her mother across the breakfast room. Clara Kershaw was smartly clad in a flowery silk dress with a lace collar, and carrying a roomy handbag. She crossed the crowded dining room, nearly knocking over one of the aspidistras and plonked herself at their table, in the chair awaiting her.

'Good morning! I'm surprised you bright young people are up so early. Edith - I must have heard your door slam around one o'clock? I hope you're not too fatigued to enjoy the day.'

'I fear calling us 'bright young people' is a bit too late. Well - Hester seems bright enough. I didn't slam the door. Were you listening out?'

'There was a lot of noise in the hotel, and I couldn't sleep.'

Hester smiled at her aunt, whom she'd known forever and was genuinely fond of.

'The Lamb family put on a terrific do. Louise and Arthur's friends were pretty wild. One of them brought a gramophone and we were dancing in the restaurant after you went. The Wedding Breakfast and the reception will be more formal, never fear. It's unusual they've chosen a Sunday to get married, isn't it? Still, apparently, all the Saturdays were booked up, and they didn't want to wait. More people are coming from Chichester just for today. I'm glad they've got good weather.'

Clara started fussing that they weren't already dressed for the wedding, as she was. It was only nine o'clock, and the wedding wasn't until eleven, but she'd probably got up when Edith was going back to bed, her daughter mused. Clara was always presentable. She slept in metal curlers, slathered in ponds vanishing cream, and had the hotel press her wedding outfit soon after her arrival. She even dabbed 'Je

Reviens' on her cotton gloves.

Looking around the breakfast room, the guests seemed in varying states of readiness for the long day ahead. Clara Kershaw ordered her grapefruit juice, bacon, and eggs from the graceful although powerfully muscled waiter whom Hester had envisioned lifting Princess Odette in 'Swan Lake' ('his hand might have to be quite high on the inner thigh, darling, during a ballet lift').

Clara began observing the other invitees closely. '*Those* people are already dressed for the wedding.'

'That's Mr and Mrs Potter. I met them yesterday,' Edith said. 'They're on Arthur's side.'

'They've got a pair of adorable dogs,' Hester chipped in.

'And there's a very nice-looking man. He appears to be breakfasting alone.'

They all followed Clara's eyes across the room.

A tiny man with a pencil moustache and wide collar was playing in a finicky fashion with his teacup, his little finger with its heavy gold signet ring stuck at an angle. He smiled at the waitress as she passed and beamed at a couple on a neighbouring table as he put the teacup down and reached for the marmalade. He looked like a jovial, pleasant sort of fellow.

For an instant, Edith felt herself disconnect from the room. Her temple was buzzing. She could catch glimpses of a scene in her head. It must be a room in this hotel similar to hers. The atmosphere was tense and hopeless. Someone was sobbing somewhere, - a woman. *'You're not wearing that,'* a man's voice said. She recognised the voice; she'd heard it only yesterday. She saw in her mind's eye a tall attractive blond woman standing alone, looking at her white tear-stained face in the mirror on the dressing table. Her wrist was limp and hanging at an odd angle.

He twisted it, Edith knew, as she felt a brief burning pain. *And now it's sprained, she's thinking up a story to explain to people at the wedding. She's missing her breakfast and wondering if she can repair her face with Max Factor and compose herself enough to come down and have a cup of sugary tea.*

'He's the biggest bounder in the hotel. His wife is upstairs crying in their bedroom. He leads her a terrible life,' Edith said, forgetting her mother.

'How could you possibly know that, Edith? DO keep your voice down.' Clara paused. 'Have you hurt your wrist?'

Edith became aware that she was massaging her left arm in a passable imitation of the blond woman upstairs. The name 'Joan' popped into her head. Or perhaps 'Johanna.'

'Oh. Just a guess. We did see him and his wife last night though. They're friends of the Groom, I think.'

Phillip and Hester caught each other's eye, and Phillip raised an eyebrow. Edith had told them about the domestic scene she'd overheard.

'How crummy,' said Hester. 'His wife looks very nice, too.'

'There's another single man over there.'
Under her thin, arched brows, Clara's eyes had
already moved, undeterred, around the room. They
settled on a dark, very handsome man who looked
like an advertisement for a gentleman's outfitter.

'Far too young for me,' said Edith. 'He's
Arthur's friend. His Best Man, I think. He was
dancing with an awfully smart couple last night. He
did the tango with the wife, - she looks rather like
Louise Brooks.'

'Ooooh! He *is* nice, darling,' Hester cooed. 'I
can hardly believe that *he* hasn't been snapped up. I
noticed him last night, too.' She had a distinct twinkle
in her eye.

'I thought you preferred greying men with less
hair,' said Phillip. 'He looks like a confirmed bachelor
to me.'

But just then Clara spotted Alma Matthews,
the bride's mother and also her own cousin.

Alma made her way over to the table and
greeted everybody; a smart woman in her early fifties
swathed in pearls. She seemed so happy and excited
that it made Edith feel terribly guilty that Clara no
longer had her own daughter's wedding to look
forward to. She wondered for an instant, how she
would cope in the Cathedral standing next to her
mother as the happy couple said, 'I do.' Poor Clara
would have so loved to fuss over all the details of a
wedding: The dresses; the hats; the flowers; the
menus; the music; the guests. She would have been
in her element. She loved organising everybody and

everything. But now her son was dead, and her daughter was unmarried.

Already thirty years old with not much prospect of meeting anybody at all in tiny Cuckfield, Edith had already been fixed up by Clara with all the eligible men in the area. They were mostly ruddy faced farmers, whey faced office workers, or smarmy tradesmen who couldn't keep her attention very long. Edith supposed that she was just too fussy to fall in love again, and certainly too particular to willingly give up her independence.

'Louise is getting dressed - along with her bridesmaids - upstairs. She had a champagne breakfast in bed! It's all so exciting,' Alma gushed. 'Duke Bernard can't be here today, but he's sent Louise a gorgeous card and a gigantic bouquet. Louise has never met him, but Arthur's family know him of course. I believe he's said that he'll invite all the Lambs to a dance at the Castle for the King's Jubilee, in May, so Louise will be going...'

'I can't wait to see the dress,' said Clara. The blonde and languid Louise would be sure to look divine in anything she wore.

'It's ivory silk, with a veil held by a wreath of milk white silk roses and trailing ivy. It's all held by mother of pearl and diamante clasps. She has white moiré shoes.' Alma was pink with pride. If it wasn't the greatest day of her life, it was certainly one of them. 'We sent descriptions to Country Life and Vogue.'

Clara's face was a picture of awe and envy.

'Arthur must be a Catholic if they're getting married in the Catholic cathedral?'

Clara's family had always been stalwarts of the Church of England, until now.

'Oh, yes. But we don't mind. He's a very successful businessman you know.'

While Edith and Hester were undeniably attractive women, Cousin Louise was an exceptional beauty who people would turn around to stare at in the street and who had regularly refused offers to become a photographic model or an actress for the Picture Palace. She had always looked rather sniffily at those who wanted to paint her or put her on the stage, considering most of those professions as not quite respectable. Nobody expected less of Louise than that she would make a materially advantageous marriage and become feted by High Society. The Lambs were bankers who fluttered like butterflies around the flower of English nobility and might in due course come to expect a peerage; when they got it, Louise would be the exact woman to be painted in oils sitting next to Arthur, framed in gold leaf, and hung above the fireplace of their vast Neo-gothic home. If Helen of Troy was a woman to launch 1,000 ships, Louise Matthews was a woman who was just as beautiful but untroublesome and placid.

'When the stock market crashed in '30, and everybody was racing to sell before they were wiped out, Arthur was busy buying the right shares at rock-bottom prices. Do you know he was so clever; he saw it coming? So, he sold his own shares quite high -

and then bought them back a lot cheaper after the crash. He's doing very nicely despite all the problems the country's been having. He absolutely *adores* Louise. I couldn't be happier for her,' Alma said. She looked at all their faces, searching for approval. I'm hoping for lots of grandchildren and that they'll want to stay in Chichester so that I can see a good deal of them. Oh, Louise has done very well for herself. Her father would have been so proud...'

'*Grandchildren*' was not a word that Edith liked to hear. She felt it as a reproach and her face went stiff although Mick's death had hardly been her fault. Grandchildren must seem a remote possibility for her mother now, and fast disappearing. It was a thorny subject they didn't want to talk about. Alma looked around at the rest of the table.

'How is your tea shop doing, Edith? I just remembered that I had forgotten to ask you yesterday. Your mother's told me about it. And Hester - how are your children? They must be growing up fast.'

Alma was Clara's first cousin, widowed in the War, like so many of the older generation. It had been lucky that Clara and Alma had shared wealthy grandparents and could continue a middle-class lifestyle after their husbands were both killed. Only through family help had Edith been able to buy the picturesque building on the corner of Cuckfield high street, with the comfortable rooms above it that enabled her to live well, although not extravagantly. Besides regular local trade for the café, there was a flourishing through trade from London and Brighton, and she often let the three spare bedrooms on to tourists and travelling salesmen.

'The tearoom is doing very nicely, thank you,' Edith said. 'I have a couple of waitresses, and they'll hold the fort while I'm away. They know how to reach me if needed, and I have a motor car if I need to get back quickly.'

'Driving! You and Clara are both so clever,' Alma said. She turned to Hester. 'Do you drive, Hester? No? Me neither. Nor can Louise. But Clara and Edith were always so capable.'

Edith knew that Alma's sincere compliments would be cold comfort to her mother.

At precisely ten-fifteen, Arthur Lamb and his Best Man set off on foot for the Cathedral, wearing top hats, morning suits, and white gloves. They were followed by their guests, all in their finery, chattering excitedly in the spring morning as they set off up the steep hill, clutching their scented posies. A pair of constables from Arundel police station stood at either end of the route between the hotel and the Cathedral, to momentarily stop the rare motorcar which might try to get through, so that the wedding procession could walk straight up the middle of the road. The garage behind the hotel had moved the motorcars generally parked out front around to the back, and these were now replaced with those of wedding guests not staying in the hotel but coming only for the ceremony and the celebrations. Passing strangers had stopped to watch the straggly but picturesque crocodile wend its way up the hill. The people of Arundel were used to fancy weddings in the town; they took place nearly every weekend in the spring and summer. But they still wanted to see a beautiful radiant bride in a gorgeous dress, with lovely bridesmaids and sweet little page boys against the backdrop of the romantic castle. And Louise Mathews didn't disappoint them. If ever a bride was beautiful, she was. Her ivory silk dress was just short enough to show tiny feet clad in moiré shoes. The veil held by silk faux cabbage roses and ivy, framed her blond hair and pink and white skin, and her little attendants skipped beside her in high spirits kept in check by Alma, and Louise's sister, chief bridesmaid. The staff of the Norfolk had all left their jobs to see the bride set off for the Cathedral which stood black and darkly gothic, silhouetted against the sky.

The pair of buzzards were out enjoying the sunny morning, circling the town high above and, all around, blackbirds and thrushes scavenged beak loads of straw, scraps of wool, and twigs for their nests. In not too long a time, the songbirds would be regurgitating seeds and insects to their young, and the predators would be digging their talons into a rabbit or picking carrion off the road.

Later that evening, Edith, Hester, and Phillip entered the ballroom at the Norfolk Hotel nursing yet more champagne glasses. Phillip had already resorted to 'the hair of the dog' over the Wedding Breakfast luncheon and was feeling very much better.

'Thank goodness *that's* over,' the three of them said to each other in low voices. The ceremony had been quite long, and Edith had found it very painful. She was a generous person, so she couldn't begrudge Louise and Arthur their happiness, but the actual part when they said their vows had been so emotional that many of the guests were dabbing their eyes or looking misty. Edith had felt hot tears spring up and sting as her mascara ran, and knew they weren't sentimental tears but angry, bitter tears. She had felt tired and a bit overwrought at the Cathedral wedding mass, and the copious luncheon at the Norfolk which followed. However, after a lie down where her mind had been devoid of dreams and simply blank, Edith had risen to have a bath, get dressed, and go along the corridor to the evening reception. She was dressed in a simple navy shift and a striking emerald necklace, which complimented her freshly washed dark red hair.

A dance band was playing popular hits in the corner of the ballroom. Phillip didn't mind when his wife danced a Lindy Hop with Edith, as the two women had always done, since his damaged leg meant that he could only move to sedate 'slows.' He was quietly confident that Hester preferred the slows.

In Arundel high street, passers-by looked up at the electric lights shining from the big windows in the ballroom and the young men in dinner jackets leaning out over the ledges to smoke. The sound of laughter and chinking glasses echoed over the Town Square as the stars came out in the sky and the band struck up 'Red Sails in the Sunset.' Even the row of automobiles, parked bumper to bumper up the street, provided a sense of occasion.

'I never realised how long a wedding ceremony might be,' said Hester, 'I'm sure it was longer than usual. But Louise looked absolutely scrummy, and the bridesmaids were darling. Arthur was so handsome - tall, dark, and handsome. Well, tall, pale, balding, and fairly handsome. Still, they looked so in love. He couldn't take his eyes off her. I'm sure you've never looked like that at me, Phillip. Like a cow. A nice cow'.

'She sailed at the dawning, all day I've been blue,
  Red sails in the sunset, I'm trusting in you.'

Phillip leaned out of the window to look down at the high street.

'Did you see some of the presents? Somebody has bought them a lot of linen sheets all edged in Belgian lace and monogrammed, with matching pillowcases. They must have cost a pretty penny.'

'I think it's that couple over there,' said Edith. 'Don't you remember them from the tango last night? She looks like she's wearing Chanel and has a French haircut - frightfully chic, and they're obviously wealthy. Look at her jewellery - she's covered in diamonds. They must be friends of the groom, too. They're far too glamorous to be from our side of the family.'

'Well - thank you,' Hester said. 'Watch out! Louise is circulating ... do be nice...'

Mrs Louise Lamb, as she now was, made her way over. She was changed into a parma violet evening dress, her shoulder length blond hair marcel-waved and held with a thick diamond clip. Her accent when she spoke was cut-glass English, and her expression decidedly patrician now she had instantaneously moved up in society.

'I've come over to smoke a cigarette with you for a few minutes and thank you for being here for my big day, and for your gifts. I shall, of course, thank you formally with a note.'

She struck a Hollywood pose, head tilted back, eyes heavily lidded, with a wide radiant smile. Phillip held out his cigarette case.

'May I offer you one, Mrs Lamb?'
Louise smiled with pleasure at the name.

'No, thank you. I prefer these. She took out a box of gold-filtered, different coloured Sobranie cocktail cigarettes and a Bakelite cigarette holder. Hester? Edith?'

She stretched out her right hand to offer the box, and Edith noticed the huge diamond cluster engagement ring she wore on the other; Louise had indeed married into money.

'It's a wonderful wedding, Louise. The luncheon was magnificent. And I enjoyed the speeches,' said Hester, half truthfully. The speeches had seemed to go on forever. 'The Best Man was very amusing.'

'Oh, he is. Arthur says that Peter was always funny, even at school.'

'Are you going anywhere nice for your honeymoon?'

'Oh, yes. As the fancy takes us, we're motoring down through France to the Cote D'Azur. We're leaving after lunch tomorrow.'

She lit a pink Sobranie with cupped hands, looking up at Phillip with practiced guileless eyes as he offered her his lighter.

'I expect you'll want a long lie-in tomorrow,' said Hester, giggling.

Louise turned bright red, and Phillip looked away quickly.

'Thank you again,' said Louise, 'I really should be getting around the room.'

Alma Matthews was on the other side of the room. She lifted her skirt above her knees:

> 'Daddy wouldn't buy me a bow-wow,
> Bow-wow,
> Daddy wouldn't buy me a bow-wow,
> Bow-wow,
> I have a little cat,
> And I'm very fond of that,
> But I'd rather have a bow-wow-wow!'

The band had taken up a different type of song on the instructions of the bride's mother, who was leading all the older guests, including Clara Kershaw, into an enthusiastic sing-song.

Louise and Edith exchanged embarrassed grimaces of commiseration across the room even as

Hester began to join in with the singing, until a warning glance from Phillip stopped her.

'Why are old people so ghastly at weddings?' mouthed Louise, looking terribly sophisticated. 'I did ask the band to only play top tunes. I'm dreadfully sorry!'

'Well,' said Hester when she'd gone, 'I'm sure they'll have a very long and happy marriage and lots of children. They look so well suited.'

She nodded in the direction of an exuberant Arthur Lamb.

'They won't,' Edith said suddenly. 'It won't last. It's a shame that Louise met Arthur.'

She realised at once what she'd said. The others stood looking at her in horror. Edith felt the blood in her veins turn to ice and a stone at the bottom of her stomach.

'Oh, how hideous,' she said. 'It is a curse to know such things. It's ruined the day.'

'It's a shame that you can't tell things like that before people get married, and you could save them a lot of unhappiness,' said Phillip, 'as well as the expense.'

'Edith - have some more champagne and dance. Put it out of your mind. It's not your fault. Just enjoy yourself,' said Hester.

But Edith could no longer enjoy herself. A man she vaguely recognised tapped her on the shoulder.

'Are you Clara Kershaw's daughter? I'm her cousin who lives in Wales. I haven't seen you since the war,' he twinkled.

'You are my Lucky Star,' she sang along with the band. 'I saw you from afar...'

Clara was talking to some ladies her own age and beckoned her over.

'These ladies are relatives of my father.'

'So sorry to hear about your fiancé,' said one of them, who had greying hair and was very stout and still dressed like a '20s flapper.

Turning to the dance floor, she saw the bounder, from breakfast, smooching with his wife who towered over him although her shoes had no heels.

He's going to do something terrible to her,' thought Edith, *'unless I help her. But how could I change things for her? I don't know there's anything I could do that might change her fate...*

The long silk scarf draped around her shoulders covered the blond woman's left wrist. Waiting for the woman to powder her nose, Edith ambushed her in the Ladies Room with some small talk about the wedding ('Weren't the bridesmaids divine?').

'My name's Edith Kershaw,' she finished by saying. 'What's yours?'

The woman looked uncomfortable. *She's wary of strangers*, thought Edith, in *case they guess her secret.*

'Joanne Forsythe.' The woman looked towards the door. 'I'm terribly sorry. My husband is waiting for the next dance, and they're about to start playing...'

The band were singing while Edith had returned to the dance floor and taken a few turns with various distant relatives.

'Is quite my impossible scheme come true?
Imagine finding a dream like you!'

The band serenaded the room as half the lights were turned off.

'Maybe it's the champagne making you maudlin?' Hester had caught up with her a bit later and was being solicitous. I'll fetch you some sherry... That crooner's awfully good.'

'I can't shake it off,' Edith said. 'This dreadful cold feeling. We had such a good time last night, and the wedding went off so well, but I keep getting these...horrible thoughts. It's getting worse.' She tried to get the image of circling buzzards out of her mind.

'Perhaps you over-ate at the luncheon? I saw you - tucking into those junkets and jellies,' Phillip said, puffing on his pipe.

'It wasn't the food, Phillip. It's not the hotel, either; the hotel is lovely. It was the ghosts yesterday afternoon. They warned me something's going to happen. I don't know what. Is it that poor woman with the horrible husband? I don't know.'

'Perhaps the wedding has made you overwrought? - after all, weddings are terribly emotional. And with all you've been through in the last couple of years... '

'No. It feels as if the 'other side' is trying to break into my subconscious all the time. Something is trying to tell me something - and I'm trying to block it. I don't really want to know, because I can't see what I could do to change anything.'

Hester sighed.

'Then let's go into the courtyard and get some fresh air, this room is full of smoke, and I feel a bit woozy. Phillip, you can stay here if you want; we'll be back. Come along, Edie, let's get our coats.'

As they headed for the door, it opened, and they almost bumped into the Best Man striding into the room.

'Oh, well done on your super speech,' Hester gushed, but he barely glanced at her as he hurried over to where Arthur stood in the centre of a circle of admiring friends and family.

As the two women walked along the corridor towards their rooms, the woman with the French haute- couture wardrobe came hurrying up the broad staircase. Edith thought that she looked in shock. Her bobbed hair and almond eyes were very dark, but her skin seemed deathly white against her scarlet lipstick. Her hands shook as she pulled out a packet of tissues and dabbed at her eyes. Edith looked the woman in the face as they passed, but her eyes looked blank and unseeing.

I think I'm going to vomit, thought Edith, and started hurrying to her room. The vibration in her temple was excruciating; *that's what making me nauseous.* She felt cold, cold dark water. Green Umber. Payne's Grey. Ivory black. Terrible fear. Edith struggled for breath; gasping; then trying to empty her stomach; her lungs. *I don't know which way up I am*, she thought. The intense cold was on her scalp, in her eyes. Freezing sticky hair was plastered across her face. The pain in her lungs was terrible, but the fear was worse. *This can't be happening!*

'She gave me the most dreadful feeling,' Edith told Hester after eventually opening her door twenty minutes later. I've had my head over my wash bowl for the last five minutes. She's going to die; I know it. But it's *how* she's going to die...I felt her confusion, being unable to breathe, dark, cold... water. It was dreadful. She was fighting her way up...but she was going down.'

'Oh gosh, darling,' said Hester.' Are you certain? What on earth can we do? You've got to warn her.'

CHAPTER 3

Dawn was barely breaking when the chic dark-haired woman with the sharp-cut hair hurried out of the Norfolk Arms with a click of her heels, wrapping her couture coat around her and clutching her bag to her chest. Her face was taut and tear-stained as if she had hardly slept. She hadn't waited for breakfast. Studying her Swiss diamond wristwatch, she glanced behind her and walked purposefully into Town Square toward the bus stop.

The small town of Arundel was waking up on a Monday morning. The day had begun with the street sweepers and carried on with the sounds of men on foot or bicycles going toward the station, the fields, and even the castle. Later, the office workers and shopkeepers busied themselves with opening their premises for the day. At the bottom of the hill, the silver river snaked through green meadows dotted with the first flowers as the spring weather warmed up. Birds sang - probably the direct descendants of thousands of generations of the same sorts of birds which had always spiralled up from the reeds along the riverbank.

The new Mr and Mrs Arthur Lamb lay in each other's arms in the Norfolk Arms Hotel. They had listened to a far-off cock crow, then a distant tractor starting up and a blackbird warning off rivals from high up on a roof top. It was far too early for them to know, but Louise was already carrying the beginning of Arthur Lamb Junior.

It was half past eleven when Edith and Hester finally got to the shops and were busy trying on earrings in a tiny shop in Tarrant Street. Edith told Hester how she always had to buy a pair of earrings everywhere she visited, if only for sentimental reasons, and then Hester decided to do the same.

The shopkeeper was hovering.

'Please wrap them up' said Edith, fishing for her purse in her little shell-shaped handbag. The earrings were Tiger's Eye drops, golden and red brown.

'I love them!' Hester's eyes sparkled. She waited for the shopkeeper to go away and make little tissue-wrapped packets. 'I'm thrilled you can separate Arundel from that - episode last night. I only hope you're enjoying yourself despite it...Everybody else will be gone soon...'

'Oh, I am,' Edith said. 'It'll be better tomorrow when we can be just the three of us. And even Ma will be gone home! We just need to get luncheon over with today, see Louise and Arthur off on their honeymoon, and everybody else will start leaving. We'll be able to walk up to the lake, and I still hope to get to the beach. I've heard there's an inn called the Black Rabbit, or Black Coney? Where the pleasure boats stop. We could go there! And, of course, we've got to visit the State Rooms at the Castle. I'm really quite excited. We'll have a proper holiday.'

They started walking back slowly, arm in arm,

towards the village square, admiring the bright window displays. Arundel attracted plenty of day trippers in the season, visiting the Castle or taking a boat trip along the river. The quaint little shops were filled with inviting goods to tempt visitors in; sweet smelling soap wrapped in tissue, barley sugar, and postcard photographic views. There was even a bit of excitement when a large motorcar passed them on its way up to the castle, evidently carrying the Duke of Norfolk judging by the respectful reactions of the townspeople as the car went up the hill, although only one, very old, man actually took off his cap and stood with bowed head, as the Rolls Royce went on its way. They were about to pass under the arch at the Norfolk Arms when Edith glanced across the road. A single-decker brown and cream country bus was chugging into the Square below them, belching out fumes.

'I say...,' said Edith, 'I swear that woman is on the bus. I think I saw her at the window as the bus turned sideways. She's got that distinctive haircut and a tiny little sailor's hat that doesn't look as if she bought it anywhere near here.'

'The woman you think's going to die?'

'Yes. Look. The bus is going to stop. She's on it, I'm sure.'

The pair stood back into the hotel entrance as the vehicle, carrying knots of casual sightseers, struggled over the cobbles and then ground to a halt at the bus stop - disgorging the few passengers who had bothered to visit Arundel on a Monday morning.

'Quick!' Hester said. 'Into the snug! Let's

watch her! Should we talk to her while she's alone?'

The sultry brunette who had made Edith feel so ill the night before, was walking elegantly up the flag-stoned pavement towards the hotel, trying to balance several parcels wrapped in tissue and brown paper in her arms.

'Well, I never,' said Edith. 'She must have got up incredibly early to catch the bus to go shopping. What do you suppose she bought that was so important? She didn't even take a bag with her.'

'I've no idea. But the parcels look soft. Fabric? She probably didn't bring a shopping bag to a wedding.'

They kept their voices low.

'So, she decided to go on an unplanned shopping trip at the crack of dawn? She looks like a woman who only has her clothes made in Paris, - or London at a pinch. Does Chichester have such chic boutiques? That's the Chichester bus; it was written on a sign above the window,' said Edith. 'I can't believe she went shopping for clothes in a provincial town. Why would she go looking for fabric? Could it be towels or sheets?'

'I thought she would be leaving today or tomorrow, anyhow.' Hester's eyes followed the woman as she walked past the snug. 'Why did she need to go to Chichester today? Especially after last night's party, and the one the night before. I'd have thought she'd have got up late like the rest of us. She is very mysterious...like Mata Hari.'

'Don't stop her!' Edith said warningly, one

hand on Hester's arm to restrain her friend.

They waited until they heard the woman's voice greet the receptionist as she took her room key.

'Very well bred,' remarked Hester. 'Are you going to warn her about the danger she's in? You know - that something horrible is going to happen to her? *Stay away from water*? - for example?'

'No,' said Edith. I can only sense - sometimes - what the future already holds, or the past held, although sometimes they seem mixed up. I don't *think* I can change what will be. Maybe it's better if she doesn't know. Besides, I don't want to get involved in other people's bad...bad...what's-the-word?..'

'*I* think that you should warn her,' Hester cut in. 'You might be able to change things - for all you know.'

'Don't you think that Edith should tell that woman that she's in danger?' Hester insisted to Phillip at luncheon.

Phillip had spent the morning bird watching by the river, in the sun. He'd photographed some of the bustling activity on the Town Quay and had even managed to get a shot of the Duke's car with his box brownie.

Hester was obliged to whisper because the guests were seated at long tables. Louise and Arthur Lamb sat at the top table, laughing, with their parents on either side. The newlywed Louise looked glowing in a blue silk dress, hair piled on top of her head and her face soft shades of strawberries and cream.

'Look,' said Edith, 'I'm sure her new Husband has his hand on her knee under the table... it's a bit outrageous. Arthur can't keep his hands off her, even though his mother is sitting right there.'

'Remember when you used to be like that, Phillip? Love's young dream and all that.'

'Wait a few years 'til they have four children and a pile of bills to pay to keep the brood.' Phillip blinked and rubbed his eyes.

Edith felt a sharp stab of pain and was determined not to allow thoughts of Mick to creep in and alter her mood. *It's something I'll save for when I'm alone*, she told herself. *I'm happy for other people - really, I am.*

A waitress cleared away the remains of the prawn cocktails.

'Her 'Going Away' outfit is lovely, though,' Hester sighed. The blonde Louise was a vision in a capri blue silk dress.

'Oh, isn't it?' agreed a woman to her left as the waiter served her a slice of veal in aspic jelly from one side, and a wine waiter poured her some wine from the other. 'They're catching the train to Portsmouth after lunch. They're going to the South of France - I've always wanted to go; the Promenade des Anglais and all that. Poor Isadora! Have you read any Fitzgerald? A car is coming to collect them to take them to the station. We were stringing together some tin cans to tie to the bumper this morning. And making a placard.'

'I love weddings,' sighed Clara Kershaw, theatrically. 'It's such a shame that Edith...' she began to say but stopped precipitately as Hester glared at her. She looked down and toyed with her fork.

But Edith hadn't noticed. She was too busy gazing across the room and whispering to Hester.

'Look at that couple! you know, the mysterious rich woman with the dark hair, who got off the bus. She doesn't look very happy at all.'

The woman who had been on the bus that morning had evidently had a row with her husband; the pair each had a face like thunder and were ignoring each other.

Edith pointed subtly and whispered to Phillip.

'Perhaps he didn't like her going off alone like that and spending lots of money. I wonder if she's been crying?'

'I thought you could know everything and didn't need to 'wonder' anything?' His baby face looked owlish.

'I told you before - only sometimes. I don't know what her life is like, although it's true I'm sure it won't end well. But I don't want to hear anything more about it. They'll be leaving soon.'

Hester had turned back and followed their glance.

'Perhaps it's the husband who will murder her? I presume that it *is* her husband. How funny - she's so striking, but he looks so wishy-washy. But then, again - so did Dr Crippen. I want to tell her to be careful of him. In fact, I'm going to when I get the chance...if Edie refuses to...'

The glowering husband had a pale blonde German look, but despite his well-cut Saville Row, double-breasted, grey suit, he was still a man you would pass over in a crowd. He looked monied but discreet.

'Who mentioned murder?' Edith looked anxious.

'What on earth are you talking about?' Clara Kershaw asked, catching the tail end of the conversation.

Nobody answered.

The veal, the Dover Sole and the junkets finished, yet more toasts proposed, and the bride's father rose to his feet:

'If you can all wait downstairs, please, Mr and Mrs Lamb will come down, and we'll all see them off in style. You have a few minutes to powder your noses - don't worry. They've got to get their coats on, and luggage brought down, and the car has still to arrive. Three o'clock?'

There was a short smattering of uneven and well wined applause.

Edith's eyes searched the room for the tall and arty Joanne, and her short little husband, the bounder. The pair looked relaxed and happy chatting with their neighbours at the table, and in no hurry to go downstairs.

She noticed the Best Man picking up a large piece of cardboard from behind the curtains with 'Just Married ' painted on it, heading for the door. Smiling, she turned back to Hester and Phillip.

'Let's talk about tomorrow,' she said, 'Anyone want a cigarette?'

By three, the lobby was filled with people, and quite a few cases. Some of the guests seemed to be leaving that same afternoon, no doubt already thinking of work the next day after a long weekend of festivities and overindulgence.

Edith said goodbye to the Potters as Hester bent to stroke their little dogs, who exuded a comforting canine smell, Hester thought. Phillip had brought his brownie box camera down and raised it to take a snapshot of his wife.

'What an earth are you doing?' Phillip said, lowering it again.

'Posing,' Hester said, looking hurt. 'Like Joan Bennett!'

'You will never look cuter than those pooches. Just be yourself. Now...one with Edie?' Phillip suggested.

The two women stood together looking to the light from the window and smiling as Phillip took the shot; Edith relaxed and natural, Hester hands on her hips and her feet turned like a ballet dancer.

'The car's arrived!' Somebody shouted to the room and cleared the way for a large black Humber Snipe convertible which drew slowly through the arch and around to the rear of the hotel, driven by a chauffeur in a leather cap and goggles. The hotel porter picked up Louise and Arthur's cases and carried them all the way out to where the car was parked.

'Well,' said Hester, 'I'd be taking ten times as much luggage if I were going on my honeymoon to the South of France. Two small cases, is that all they've got?'

'Apparently, yes,' said Edith, 'I suppose they've got to get them on and off the train, the boat, and in and out of their hired car remember?'

'I'd just get porters to do it. But I suppose they'll spend most of the time in bed. They won't need clothes.'

A cheer went up as Louise and Arthur appeared on the staircase and stopped halfway down so that the assembled guests could admire them.

'Do you mind if I take a photograph?' asked Phillip.

Everybody clapped and cheered again as Arthur leaned in towards his wife, and she raised the spotted veil on her pretty navy hat to let him kiss her. Her sky-blue silk jacket matched her eyes. Arthur looked very stylish in a grey sports jacket and slacks. He tipped his fedora hat towards the camera with a grin.

'Cat got the cream,' said Hester, in raptures and transported by the general atmosphere of bonhomie in the room.

Waving goodbye and shaking hands, the newlyweds finally managed to get through the clusters of people, out of the hotel and into the courtyard, with Louise's friends clearing the way.

'Now, are you sure you've got everything?' the

wealthy brunette was asking the bride, solicitously.

'Louise was always so smart,' chattered Clara Kershaw. 'The South of France too...so glamorous.'

'Everybody out the front to wave them off! Keep the arch clear! Off the pavements! If we could all spread out in the Square... PLEASE...' the bridegroom's father shouted. Anybody with cameras? Apart from this gentleman?' He pointed at Phillip. 'Could you get a snapshot of us all waiting for the wedding car? Please? I should be very grateful.'

The guests posed in front of the hotel, self-consciously, on what was a balmy afternoon, although a sharp breeze was whipping up. The wedding car, when it returned through the arch, did so in a clatter of tin cans with the 'just married sign above it' - somebody had obviously managed to slip out and tie them on with lengths of white ribbons. The hood had been folded only half down so the bride and groom could wave without losing their hats, and the groom turned to kiss the bride as they went by. Pedestrians stopped what they were doing to give a whistle or wave back. Finally, the bridesmaids ran after the car for a little way but quickly gave up as the car picked up speed. Everyone watched for a bit until the back of the car receded out of view behind the buildings on the Town Square. Had they been able to watch it further, they would have seen the car turn left at the main road and after a short distance, turn right onto the station forecourt.

'Let's have a smoke.' Hester suggested, 'And a pot of tea. What do you say? I'm going to fetch a cardigan from my room. I'll freshen up while I'm there. Meet in the snug in ten minutes?'

Half an hour later, the three friends had finished their tea and walked back into the lobby. Most of the cases had gone, and a strange quiet was falling over the hotel as it emptied of many of the wedding guests and prepared to get back to normal. Clara Kershaw had already left. Edith noticed the glamorous brunette woman and her husband, seemingly now on better terms, bidding farewell to the bridegroom's family. To her surprise, the woman beckoned them over.

'Would you mind terribly if I asked you for a photograph of my husband and myself taken with Mr and Mrs Lamb senior? I expect you'll share photographs of the wedding with the newlyweds, so I'll surely get to see them... We're all frightfully good friends.'

The couple posed with Arthur's parents. 'I'm dreadfully sorry,' the chic dark woman was saying. 'I changed my clothes for a walk in the countryside. I'm afraid I'm rather letting the side down for your snapshots.'

'She doesn't look half as good today,' thought Edith. *'That tweed skirt and brogues outfit looks dreadfully drab, really. Take away the Chanel, and she looks rather frumpy.'*

It was as if the woman could read her thoughts.

'We thought that we'd take advantage of the beautiful countryside while we're here. I really couldn't walk in the mud in my patent court shoes.'

She smiled, although the smile didn't quite reach her eyes. She began to walk away and Hester started to run after her:

'Wait! My friend here is clairvoyant. All I'm asking is that you be very careful,' she said in a loud whisper. 'Don't trust your husband and stay away from water!'

The woman turned, and her eyes met Edith's. Both women stared at each other in equal horror for a fraction of a second. Then, the woman in the tight tweed skirt turned her back and began walking as quickly as she could up the stairs with a wiggle.

CHAPTER 4

The hotel dining room had been nearly empty at breakfast time. Most guests, including Clara Kershaw, had left the afternoon before or had made a very early start. The Bounder had been sitting there alone again and gave Edith a weak smile as she pushed away her empty teacup and got up to leave.

The hotel seemed full of chambermaids running back and forth with piles of sheets and towels, and the smell of fresh laundry, fresh flowers, and furniture wax filled the foyer as the place returned to normal and prepared itself to welcome new visitors.

The courtyard was almost empty of motorcars as Edith, Hester, and Phillip prepared for a walk along the river. The three of them had gone to the little Austin so that Edith could retrieve her flat driving shoes to walk in. They almost bumped into the Best Man in the carpark, carrying a box filled with wedding decorations.

'I'll give them to Arthur when he gets back in a couple of weeks,' he said after bidding them all good morning. Then, walking towards his own small car, he turned to give them a cheery salute before opening the boot and putting the box inside.

'He's quite a smasher,' said Hester, 'although Nijinsky has the edge.'

'A *fop* with that floppy fringe,' Edith said.

'He looks rather temperamental,' Phillip added, as they all gave the man a cheery wave before ambling off to the Highstreet and then wandering towards the bridge. They meandered through the knots of women out shopping for their daily provisions and circumnavigated the many delivery boys on their bicycles.

The three friends strolled along the tree-fringed Mill Road, allowing Phillip, with his cane and gammy leg, to keep pace.

'The map says that the hamlet's about twenty-five minutes away. We could walk up there and back easily while it's so early and then still visit the castle before lunch? There're lots of birds - water birds - good job Phillip brought his binoculars.'

Edith looked suddenly much younger. Her unhabitual flat walking shoes had made her shrink in stature, and the morning light showed up the slight freckles on her skin. Now that the wedding was over, she had abandoned the face powder, although her mouth was still covered in poppy red lipstick. She also felt much happier; the feeling of dark foreboding had dissipated, and she put it down to the chic brunette Mata Hari having departed Arundel. Hopefully, the Bounder would also be gone by the time they returned to the Norfolk Arms.

Edith almost danced along Mill Road, sometimes skipping sideways to chat with her friends. Passing the castle's lower gates, a cart slid by them, filled with milk, butter, eggs, and flowers destined for the Norfolk Arms, coming from Swanbourne Farm. Blackbirds sang in the trees. Apart from the rumbling farm cart and the horse's hooves, the only other noises were the distant sound of the London steam train, the chug of a small boat coming up from Littlehampton, and the far-off shouts of men on the wharf.

'We must take a boat trip,' they all agreed.

They decided to walk along the river to Ford in the afternoon, and they could, perhaps, return by boat.

Reaching Swanbourne Lake, the three paused to admire the unfamiliar view. The lake was covered in ducks and swans fishing, their upended tails like white flecks of foam across the still, dark water. Swanbourne Lodge, selling ice cream and cups of tea to the visitors, wasn't yet open, and the row boats for hire floated, strung together, near the road. One boat sat forlornly on its own, detached from the others. Their eyes followed the path as it wound its way around the lake and then took a sharp turn around the hillside and eventually led upwards to the back of the castle, hidden behind the trees.

At the far end of the lake rose a plume of thick black smoke, shot with yellow. Phillip raised his binoculars and pointed them in the direction of the fire.

'They must be burning branches or something, but it's quite an intense bonfire, and I can't see any people around. Good job that it's not too dry; otherwise, I'd be afraid of it getting out of hand.'

'Come on - let's get on,' Hester said, adjusting her hat. 'It looks bad, but I expect they know what they're doing.'

'I would say the fire's spread to some bushes and trees or something,' Phillip went on, moving the binoculars back to the billowing smoke. 'We should tell someone, I think. I expect they already know...but it's quite ferocious.'

'Let's go on our way. We'll tell them at the entrance to the castle if we don't see any activity on our way back. The people on that farm cart must have seen it too.'

Continuing their way up to the hamlet, they stopped again to look back along the river and admire the view beyond the bend, dominated once again by the castle standing proud above the town. The hamlet of Offham had once been a stop for barges when Arundel had been an inland port, and a long flint building sat on the waterfront called the Black Rabbit.

A woman was pegging out washing in a garden near an old chalk quarry, her flowery pinny and turban rather garish in the morning sun.

'Good morning. What a beautiful place. You're so lucky to live here.' Edith smiled, and then she asked, 'Do they often light fires at the lake so early in the morning and leave them to burn alone?'

'That would be the Castle Estate workers,' shrugged the woman, uninterested. 'Nothing to do with us.'

All three were somewhat happier when they came in sight of the lake and discovered a police motorcar parked by the closed lodge. The constables standing beside it looked rather unworried as Phillip questioned them.

'Somebody reported it this morning,' a police constable replied, gesturing towards the fire. There's a wooden boat shed there - or it *was* there.
Someone's set it on fire, is what it is, I think. Arson. Probably lads on a lark from Littlehampton.'

Phillip raised his binoculars again.

'They certainly made a good job of it. I can't see a shed at all. You don't think that somebody was inside the shed and set it alight by accident? There may be somebody injured over there. There's plenty of fellows on the tramp looking for work who'd be glad of shelter.'

One of the officers pointed to the lone rowboat.

'Looks like they rowed over in that boat and brought it back. I suppose that we'd better roll up our sleeves and row over ourselves. Quicker than walking around the lake, and you can't drive that far round. Some Estate workers are coming down from the castle on the other side of the park. Don't worry, Sir, Castle firemen will soon be there, and they won't lack water.'

'Well,' said Hester, fixing the younger constable with a twinkle, 'with those strong arms, I'm sure you'll have that boat across the lake in double quick time, Sergeant...'

Phillip looked rather as if he were trying to impersonate an un-amused Queen Victoria and Edith gave a nervous giggle.

The three companions relaxed and made their

way to the Castle gates, paying their admission fees and mounting the grand stairway. By the time they were struggling up to the top of the keep, they could hear a few more motorcars in the town than usual. Still, Arundel had generally been going about its business in the spring sunshine like any Tuesday. When they gazed from the top of the keep at the serene views across the grass flats and the peaceful river winding its way to the sea, it was easy to put the burning boat shed out of their minds.

'There's ever such a commotion at the lake,' the guide told them breathlessly as they dawdled through the staterooms, a bit later. The guide had not been able to resist telling them about the fire. It was evidently not often that sleepy Arundel had any excitement that didn't involve the duke. 'The police are here questioning all the staff.'

They stood in front of the dining room fireplace, which was surmounted by the arms of the Duke of Norfolk. Upon the pale, high walls, the duke's ancestors looked down their noses at them as they weaved their way through endless brocade sofas, armchairs, and walnut tables covered in studio photographic portraits of aristocrats.

'A lot of fuss about a fire, isn't it?' Edith asked. *But it's not just a fire,* popped into her head.

'Yes. Luckily, it didn't catch all the trees alight, though it had started spreading. It was arson. There were at least ten policemen here.'

'Good Lord, I shouldn't have thought you'd have that many in a small place like this,' said Phillip.

'No, we don't. They've brought some in from Chichester.'

Hester went to the window. 'I can hear police bells ringing. There must be a lot of police cars. *Something's* going on. It's only a boat house.'

'Arson!' Phillip was contemplative as they walked through the big dark library hung in crimson. They'd all had the same thought, though; what if somebody had been inside the wooden building? Somebody burned alive. Somebody somehow lured to the boathouse because it was a lonely spot where nobody could hear you struggle or notice the flames until it was too late.

'But I felt that woman was drowning, not burning,' Edith said.

'Perhaps her husband took her to the lake, drowned her, and then burned the body?' Hester was a devoted reader of Agatha Christie novels.

Edith thought about it. 'I drew a fire,' she said. *Flamin' Mamie* came into her mind but it was all so confusing.

It was while they were buying a guidebook for Littlehampton in the giftshop that Edith felt a light tap on the shoulder and turned around.

'Hello, I'm David Forsyth', said the bounder, stretching out his hand. 'I believe you were a guest at the Lamb wedding. So was I. Friend of the bridegroom. We did meet briefly the first evening. You were at breakfast. Everyone else seems to have gone.'

Edith looked around quickly for Hester and

Phillip to rescue her from the man's frankly lascivious gaze, but they seemed to be busy buying a miniature castle in a 'snowstorm' glass dome at the souvenir counter. There seemed nothing else to do except shake the proffered hand without being impolite.

Forsythe immediately grasped it tightly and didn't let it go. Edith felt a cold come over her. It started in the pit of her stomach and then worked its way over her skin up to her scalp. She felt a prickle at the back of her neck.

'I saw you over the weekend,' he said pleasantly. 'You're by yourself, aren't you?'

'I'm with friends,' she said, pulling her hand back quickly.

'I didn't mean that.' He gave a 'charming' smile under his pencil moustache, 'I mean, you haven't got a hubby. At least not here... I say!' He appeared to just think of it, 'My wife has had to leave before me. She doesn't like history anyhow - she'd rather waste her time reading slushy romances and playing with the children. What say *you* if I buy you dinner and take you to see the '39 Steps' in Littlehampton?'

'You should have seen that slug's face when I finished by being really quite rude to him. Still, he won't bother me again,' Edith told Hester. 'He said his wife had to return to their two children, but he wanted to visit the castle, and they had another night booked. I think he just wanted to be cut loose for the night.'

They had reached the Highstreet when a fleet

of cars could be heard coming up the hill as they walked back into the Norfolk Arms.

'It's like Victoria station in the rush hour here today.'

'Oh, gosh! *Something* very bad *has* happened. Wait here while I go and find out,' Hester said. 'I need to go to the post office, anyway. We'll have luncheon here at the hotel when I get back.'

'I'll go and ask them at the reception if they've heard any gossip,' said Edith. The staff will probably know before anyone.'

She walked out into the foyer, leaving Phillip in the snug.

A tall man aged around 40, with a big muscular build, was talking to the receptionist, and he turned to face her as she approached to wait behind him. He wore a navy pinstripe suit and raised his fedora hat to her, revealing sandy hair.

Edith thought *he looks like a Viking or a great big Scotsman.* As she noticed his pale blue eyes, turned down at the corners, her stomach did a somersault, and she found herself involuntarily grinning inanely, unable to look away. It was rather forward, as he was almost certainly married. However, he was looking at her with interest, and it was rather reassuring that an attractive man might still find her worth a second look. It was very rare that she ever saw a man who had the ability to give her butterflies. She gave her warmest smile.

Mr Hinton, who was in charge of the desk again, called her forward.

'This is Detective Inspector Stevens, Miss Kershaw,' Hinton said, indicating the stranger. 'I was just telling him you were at the wedding this weekend, and he would like to ask you and Mr and Mrs Denney a few questions.'

'Certainly.' Edith was rather curt. Of course, the man *hadn't* been looking at her with interest because he found her alluring, but because Mr Hinton had just pointed her out as a wedding guest. And embarrassingly, she had responded by making rather vain presumptions that he found her attractive - and worse - had made it clear she reciprocated. In fact, he looked tickled pink as he clearly thought she was giving him the eye.

'We'll be in the snug,' she said, red faced, marching off without waiting.

DI Stevens followed her through the hallway, the hotel register under an arm.

'CID,' he said, smiling. 'Plain clothes.' He took out his ID.

'You don't seem surprised that a detective wants to speak to you,' he said, more as a statement than a question.

'I hazard a guess it's because you've found a body at the site of that fire. May I ask if it's a woman?' Edith was rather curt, reimposing a distance between them in case he had got the wrong idea.

'I'm not at liberty to tell you, Madam, until the body has been formally identified - and that might take some time. A good guess, though, about there being a body. We haven't given it out yet.'

Phillip leaned forward to shake Stevens' hand from where he stood, puffing on his pipe.

'I'm Phillip Denney. I suppose you can't identify the body quickly because it's been badly burned?'

The pungent tobacco filled the little room.

Hester just caught the tail end of the question as she came in (she had not got as far as the post office after all.)

'Oh, it's far worse than that...' she said excitedly. But she saw the Detective Inspector's natural authority and reproving expression and fell silent.

'Detective Inspector Stevens. CID.'
The detective shook her hand as they made their introductions. Stevens removed his hat and placed it on his knee as he sat down. He opened the hotel register.

'We have, in effect, found a body which we can't identify at this time,' he started, 'however, I know this hotel had a wedding party at the weekend - so, naturally, I need to account for all the guests' safety. But my first question would be, why do you all think the body has something to do with the fire? I didn't say it had. And...' His eyes met Edith's, giving her butterflies again, 'Why do *you* think the body is that of a woman? *We* don't even know that yet.'

'You think the victim was a guest at the wedding?' Phillip puffed away on his pipe, thoughtfully.

DI Stevens adopted a patient tone. 'Not at all, Mr. Denney. The victim, whoever they were, might have been somebody staying in this hotel this weekend. Or, they might have been a local person. They might also have been a person from anywhere else - including abroad, given our proximity to the channel - either murdered here in Arundel or transported here after death. They might even have died of natural causes, and somebody decided on an amateur cremation. Or it could have been an accident whilst they were committing arson. I'm open minded until the police have finished our investigation. Please answer my questions. I'd like to know how you came to your own conclusions so quickly?'

'The town is crawling with policemen, and you're a Detective Inspector,' said Phillip, 'so it stands to reason it's more than a fire, and most likely you think it's a murder. If there is a fire after a murder, it's probably because the corpse has been set alight. Am I right?'

Stevens smiled at Edith with a somewhat amicable expression as he questioned her.

'Why do you think the body is that of a woman? Let's just take a look at the hotel register,' he finished, 'and see what you remember of the other guests to see if anything leaps out.'

Hester was struggling with a mixture of enthusiasm and self-importance, ignoring Edith kicking her hard under the table.

'Um. I think that *we* know who the body is,' Hester said, 'Or, rather, we don't know her name, but we could describe her.'

DI Stevens turned the register towards her and took a pad and pencil out of his pocket, considering each of the three friends in turn.

'I think I'll have a highball,' he said, taking out an engraved silver cigarette case. 'Anyone else?'

He offered the women a cigarette. They both took one, and Phillip tapped the ash from his pipe as Stevens proffered a light.

'She was a woman who was not very tall, of slim build, with dark bobbed hair and in her mid twenties. She was here with a man we took to be her husband, but he was rather insipid. Older than her. She made Edith feel sick,' Hester said, as the DI took it down in shorthand.

Stevens inhaled a Senior Service navy cut cigarette and thanked the friendly waitress who had set down cocktails. He was silent.

Phillip said, 'They were guests on the bridegroom's side, as far as we could tell, not family, but friends of the bride and groom. She was rather younger than me but formidable. I took some photographs while we were here. She'll be in the official wedding pictures, too.'

'May I trouble you for your film, Mr Denney? The Police photographer will develop it, and I'll give you back the negatives, of course. It may help us with our enquiries.'

'With pleasure.' Phillip left to fetch the film. '*Miss* Kershaw?'

Stevens sat back in his seat. Edith fumbled in

her bag for a tissue to avoid his pale blue gaze. *He's bound to be married*, she told herself gloomily.

'She stood out because she was so much richer and better dressed than anybody else at the wedding. Smarter. Except for yesterday, when she looked almost ordinary.'

Stevens said, 'so... what made you feel sick about her, Miss Kershaw?'

Edith considered for a moment. 'It was a sense of foreboding,' she said finally. 'I felt that she was going to die an unpleasant death.'

'Something about her was a bit 'off?' Stevens was impassive.

'Edith is psychic,' Hester said proudly.

'Well,' Stevens drained his glass, and shook his head in an exasperated way. 'Nothing more concrete than that? So, in fact, you don't know anything.'

'Something *was* off,' Edith said defensively. 'That woman didn't look happy at all at the wedding reception, and she'd obviously been rowing with her husband the next day – we thought she'd been crying. Although she was leaving early this morning, she must have got the first bus into Chichester to go shopping yesterday. The woman didn't look like she usually wore clothes from a country town. She didn't look her usually sophisticated self at the 'going away,' either. She wore a skirt and shoes for photographs, which might have come from Chichester - when she *had* been wearing Chanel. Those things are worth remarking, aren't they? And I don't believe that the body was dumped here from somewhere else, either.'

'I'm not interested in frocks, Miss Kershaw. And why don't *you* think this body was dumped from elsewhere? Another psychic intuition?'

Edith didn't like his tone.

'No. Somebody coming from elsewhere might have hidden a body where it could've stayed hidden for months or never been found. Why not at the bottom of a river? Or in the sea? Why draw attention to it by starting an enormous fire on the Duke of Norfolk's estate?'

DI Stevens looked at her rather coldly.

'So, what is the point of rendering the body unrecognisable if it's supposed to be found?'

'I don't know? Perhaps the murderer *means* you to find out who the murdered body is, only not very quickly, by which time *they* will be far away?'

'Oh, very good!' said Hester, clapping.

'Nobody else among the guests leaps out?' Stevens reasserted his authority.

'There is a lady called Mrs Joanne Forsythe whose husband David is a cad who brutalises her.' Edith added, 'she supposedly left Arundel on her own before her husband.'

'Much better!' The DI inclined his head in approval. 'Assuming you know about Mr Forsythe being violent as a fact and not some fantasy of yours.'

'But why would Mr Forsythe want you to find out his wife is dead? He could simply say she had left and didn't want to be found. He wouldn't point the finger at himself. But you could frighten him into stopping hitting her. Look for the husband of the dark-haired woman before you find he's fled the country. I have a feeling that's what he might do. I mean, that would be the logical thing for the murderer to do before you've had time to identify the body.'

Stevens stood up, picking up his coat and hat.

'I shall ask the hotel Reception about the ladies you've mentioned, of course, in order to eliminate them. I will also get your own details from Reception - if I need to speak to any of you again. And thank you all for your help.'

He didn't even glance at Edith as he strode off, almost walking straight into Phillip coming back. He put the roll of film into his trouser pocket, muttering his thanks.

'Hester! How *could* you? You can buy *me* another Bloody Mary - and *luncheon*! You know what most people think about psychics! Why would you tell him *that*? He simply thought I was some sort of charlatan,' Edith snarled.

'What an earth has happened while I've been gone?' Phillip asked. 'You two haven't fallen out, have you?'

'Never mind that,' Hester said. 'What about the news that a police constable told me? He wasn't supposed to, but I told him what beautiful eyes he'd got - and he had!'

'What was it then?' asked Phillip.

'You're not sulking?' Hester looked at Edith, who was pink and tight-lipped.

'Alright, I'll tell you: Not only they can't identify the body because it's so badly burnt, but it has no head, hands, or feet. So, the police are now dragging the lake and searching the riverbank for the missing body parts. Edie - you don't really care what that silly DI thinks of you, do you? Why are you looking at me like that? Don't tell me you...? You *do*!'

CHAPTER 5

Edith had a dreadful night, tossing and turning and barely sleeping. The first thing on her mind had been the oil pastel painting of a fire, which she'd propped up in her room. Edith still had 'Flamin' Mamie' going round and round in her head, and now that she looked at the picture, she could see that the odd black abstract shape at the picture's heart resembled a person. Edith hadn't recognised it before as representing a human figure because it was missing the head, hands, and feet; her picture had foretold of the mutilated body in the burning boat shed. She had very mixed feelings about her psychic side encroaching on her painting, which was her biggest joy in life. On the one hand, Edith felt her greatest happiness was now contaminated by the 'gift' she wanted to shut out. However, on the other hand, she was very interested in it, on an intellectual level. Edith had studied female painters like Georgiana Houghton, Margaret Watts and Hilma Af Klimt, who claimed to be psychic like her and did automatic painting. Her favourite artist was Kandinsky, who also allowed art to come out of the subconscious and was interested in spiritualism. As a creative, she knew that she often painted in a trance-like state, and she tussled with the idea of embracing her gift and letting it inform her painting. But if she did that, would she be opening the floodgates, so to speak, and become swamped with messages from the other side?

It was a dilemma. Edith lay awake thinking about it. Would it ruin her art, or would it become much better?

She had finally drifted off and found herself in a warm, comfortable dream. In it, she lay in DI Stevens's arms, kissing him deeply as she hugged her pillow. She'd woken with a jolt, filled with guilt, and whispered aloud to the dark, silent room, *Sorry, Mick! Mick, I love you!*

It wasn't only guilt that she'd been 'unfaithful' to her dead fiancé, but Edith also felt terribly bad at the thought that Stevens almost certainly had a wife, and it was against her upbringing to lust after a married man. However, as soon as she managed to fall asleep again, the detective's clear blue eyes and powerful body invaded her dreams once more. She awoke with a feeling of pervading sadness that she'd alienated him with her psychic intuitions. Since she would be in Littlehampton the next day and then returning to Cuckfield, she would probably never see the man again.

The next day's trip to Littlehampton was somewhat overshadowed by speculation about the murder. As Phillip's Hillman Minx took them out of the town, they looked over the bridge at the police officers walking along the riverbank or rowing up the river. When they left for the coast, the town seemed full of police motorcars.

They'd walked along the beach, paddled in the sea, eaten whelks from a newspaper cone, and had fish and chips in a seafront café. They'd caught the matinee performance of 'A 39 Steps'. The three companions had finished the afternoon with ice cream cornets, watching the fishermen on the quay casting their rods. But nothing seemed as interesting as the thought of the police hooking out a bag full of grisly contents from the river and confirming that Edith had been right about the victim's identity.

'Drive up to the lake,' Hester ordered Phillip when, eventually, they got back to Arundel.
They'd passed several police motorcars driving in the opposite direction as they'd entered the town. It was the early evening, and the search of the riverbank was evidently winding down. However, some policemen were still knocking on doors, hoping to catch people who were at work in the daytime. A couple of bobbies were guarding the boats at Swanbourne, and Hester wound down her window.

'Find anything?' she asked, batting her eyelashes at the muscular young constable - the same one who had stood there after the fire was discovered

'No, Madam,' the man replied without a smile.

'Honestly, Hester...' Edith said on the way back, 'You *are* a bit heartless. The poor woman is dead.'

DI Stevens was waiting for them at the hotel. He'd been chatting to Mr Hinton and broke off as they walked into the lobby, handing Phillip an envelope.

'The negatives,' he said. 'I understand that you're leaving the day after tomorrow? I'll contact you if necessary - I got your details from the register.

It's Miss Kershaw whom I need to talk to...alone, please.'

Hester *will* be frustrated, thought Edith, but secretly, she was rather pleased, although her face was flushed, and her hands shook slightly; bits of her erotic dreams about the detective were coming back to her.

Stevens ushered her into the snug. Some people were finishing drinks, but he took a card from his jacket and held it up.

'Police. I need to talk to this lady in private. Nothing to worry about. Would you mind taking your tea into the dining room please? I'll call a waiter,' he said to the room. He turned to Edith. 'May I offer you something? This is just an informal chat, you understand.'

A short while later, he had a whisky and soda in his large freckled hand, and Edith held a Bloody Mary. He leaned forward to light her cigarette, inhaled his Navy Cut deeply and exhaled, and then spread some photographs on the coffee table.

'I don't want to hear anything about mediums. I want facts please. The lady who you were talking about yesterday, is she here?'

'Yes,' said Edith, 'there she is on the wedding day - and there she is at the 'going away.' She gestured to the pictures.

'What about her husband?'

Edith pointed to him.

'They are Mr and Mrs Edward Wren. He's an international philatelist. He has a Holborn shop selling stamps by mail order, and he also sells at auction. The shop has been shut since yesterday morning, and Mr and Mrs Wren have yet to return home. Now that might not mean anything, but it might mean something. Apparently, they go away frequently, leaving an assistant in charge of the shop when they do. The assistant says they left by motorcar for Arundel, and he expected them back yesterday morning, but they didn't show. He would have expected a telephone call if they wanted him to work, but he didn't get one. He was amazed that the shop was shut and that there were no instructions for him to put a note on the door for potential customers. It's never happened before.'

'Oh. That *is* odd.'

'Yes.'

'I mean, it's odd that they were here with a motorcar, but Mrs Wren took the bus to Chichester? It was such an inconvenience; she wouldn't have needed to get up so early if her husband had driven her. Maybe that's the reason they had a row? I think they had definitely fallen out before that luncheon.'

Stevens scribbled in shorthand in his little notebook and gave her a guarded smile from limpid blue eyes.

He's got huge hands, Edith thought tenderly.

'So why did you pick out Caroline Wren to talk about? There were lots of people at the wedding. The others all returned safely home. Now, don't give me any mumbo jumbo. I'm only interested in facts.'

Edith thought carefully.

'She didn't look happy at the reception. People are usually delighted to see their friends get married, but she looked upset. She was rowing with her husband, so it was probably for that. And then we saw her getting off the bus on Monday morning with a pile of parcels. She must have got up really early to go shopping. She said that she'd bought things for walking in the countryside because Arundel is so lovely. But she was leaving Arundel the next day. And now you say they live in the centre of London.'

Edith took a drag of her cigarette. 'By the way, did Mrs Forsythe get home?'

'A constable visited the Forsythe house and apparently, she's staying with her mother. The constable rang the mother and Mrs Forsythe is alive and well.'

'Alright.'

The DI smiled and Edith smoothed her russet hair and smiled back, playing with her pearls.

'So, the Police have found nothing to indicate that the body's anyone else but Mrs Wren?' she asked.

'Did you see the newspapers or listen to the radio today?'

'We saw a newspaper in Littlehampton.'

'Everybody in the country must know about the murder by now. We told all the Press yesterday evening. Yet, nobody has reported anybody missing whom they suspect might have been the victim. Every police station has been notified to watch out for the Wrens, and appeals for them have been made on the radio this afternoon. Every paper will carry their picture on the front page tomorrow morning. If they don't make themselves available to the police very soon, we'll be working on the assumption the victim is Caroline Wren.'

'And you're sure the body is that of a woman?' *He's got lovely eyes,* thought Edith, *so blue. The colour of his suit brings them out.*

'There wasn't much of the body left. But the autopsy concluded that the corpse was most probably that of a woman, from the length of the bones.'

'It's common knowledge in the town that the body was minus its head, hands, and feet,' Edith said. What sort of husband could mutilate his wife like that?'

Stevens lit another Senior Service and drained his glass. 'One who knew he'd be the first suspect if the body was identified as his wife. I expect that he thought he'd lay low for a few weeks and then tell the neighbours that she'd gone off with some other fellow or something like that. He's done something unplanned and on the spur of the moment, I think, but he wouldn't just abandon his shop - many of those stamps are extremely valuable. I'm not expecting Mr Wren to go far but to resurface alone.'

'To cut a long story short,' Edith told Hester and Phillip later after Stevens had gone, 'we decided that since Edward Wren is very wealthy, with a good many extremely rare stamps, he didn't want to pay for an expensive divorce. Or perhaps Caroline *refused* to give him a divorce. It would have been very shameful after all. They didn't have any children.'

'You were a long time? Should he have been discussing his murder case with a member of the public? One who might eventually be called to the witness stand?' Phillip raised an eyebrow.

'Oh, he bought me a second Bloody Mary. I promised not to breathe a word about the case to anyone else, and you mustn't either.'

Edith didn't say how the cocktails had mellowed them, and how she was sure the DI liked her in the same way that she liked him at the bottom of it all. He probably wasn't single, but finally, all they had done was have a whispered chat about a case they were both involved in, in a public place. There could be no harm done if it didn't get out.

Hester looked knowing.

'I know what you're thinking.' Edith said, 'Stop it *now*. He was very grateful to *me* for picking out the Wrens as suspicious. Do you know? The Detective Inspector takes his orders directly from Scotland Yard, and he's in charge of the CID Chichester division? He said that he wouldn't have been able to narrow the murder down to the Wrens so quickly without me. And we didn't say a thing about 'second sight.' Your pictures are good, Phillip... the police are going to show them in court. I've agreed to appear as a witness on the prosecution's side. Let's ask to listen to the wireless after dinner - The Police are putting out an appeal all over the country. *Do let's* have a lovely holiday tomorrow and take that walk to Ford? There's nothing more we can do about the murder until Edward Wren is caught and put in the dock.'

Edith had a happy contented smile. She would definitely dream of DI Stevens tonight, and the cocktails might stop her feeling guilty. She had to accept that Michael was dead, but she was very much alive. Dreams were a private affair, and she wouldn't even confide hers to Hester.

CHAPTER 6

The Honeytree café seemed to have got along perfectly well without Edith when she eventually returned to Cuckfield without seeing the attractive DI again - to her great disappointment. Indeed, she got the feeling that the cook, Mrs Thompson, and the waitress, Doris, would much prefer it if she went away as often as possible and simply did the books and the ordering.

The tearoom - or café - was a large white building with a spacious interior on the corner of Cuckfield High Street, opposite the King's Head. Downstairs there were wheelback chairs and the barley twist tables were covered with snowy white tablecloths. Heavy damask curtains were held back with tasselled cords, and tables lined the back wall, which was laid with cold joints for carving, preserves, cheeses, cakes, and jellies. The smell of soup, vegetables, and coffee wafted out of the kitchen.

It seemed that the café was always busy with a mixture of local regulars and those travelling down to the coast on the London to Brighton route. Edith noticed that nobody had bought any of her paintings yet, although their prices were prominently displayed. Mrs Thompson and Doris made no secret that they thought the pictures were perfectly dreadful and would probably dissuade any potential customers who enquired, and Edith was almost resigned to never selling anything.

The Honeytree hadn't changed while she'd been absent, but Edith had. In some subtle ways, she was different from the person who had left for the wedding in Arundel.

Upstairs, her large apartment seemed very silent after the lively camaraderie of Hester and Phillip and the bustle of the hotel bar. Mrs Tutt, the cleaner, had been in, and Edith's red linoleum shone with Johnson's Glo-Coat, the bathroom smelling of ammonia and vinegar. All the wood smelled of wax furniture polish. Her cushions were plumped, her few ornaments dusted, and the large photographic portrait of Michael in his pilot's overalls and leather helmet smiled back at her. Edith felt like a heel, looking at Mick in his silver frame, always close to the arm of her plush winged armchair. She felt as if she'd been away for a cheap 'dirty weekend,' and she'd have to run to the florist to buy a single red rose to put in a vase next to his photograph.

She passed the following week in a feverish daze where nothing she could do seemed to calm her down, even rearranging her books on the bookshelf in order of size. She scoured the daily newspapers and tuned in her wireless incessantly in the hope that the Arundel body had been identified, and the murderer caught, and that there might be a mention, perhaps even a picture, of DI Stevens; but there never was.

Come sun or showers, Edith strode about the countryside, attempting to burn off the nervous energy that coursed through her body, and every evening, she poured herself a stiff drink in the hope that it would make her sleep, but it never did.

In the early morning, she awoke like clockwork, hugging her pillow and knowing she had dreamt of the rugged detective. She never remembered these dreams; except they were either pleasant and she wanted to plunge back into them, or sad and frustrating.

The guilt that Edith felt towards Mick tormented her. His memory, usually ever present inside her, was receding even as he was being replaced with the memory of a man who was a mere acquaintance whom she knew nothing about. It was not something that she wanted. In fact, she wanted to reconcile herself peacefully to the fact that she would die an old maid, given the shortage of eligible men for women of her age. She refused to compromise when choosing a husband, as so many women like her did, to become a mother (or to give her mother grandchildren.) The happy memory of being in love, loved by, and engaged to Michael ought to be enough for her; it was so much more than many other women had.

She couldn't even paint; Edith would sit down to let the beauty of a bowl of flowers seep into her and flow out of her brushes and only see the crenellations of a castle keep, almost vertically above her, with buzzards circling the ramparts; Arundel castle, of course, she recognised it. Invariably, she'd find herself sitting in an armchair by the window at three or four in the morning smoking and staring down at

Cuckfield high street, deserted in the moonlight. There were generally one or two motorcars parked, and very occasionally, a vehicle would sweep around the corner on its way to or from Brighton, raking the silent road with the beams from its headlamps, the echoing sound of its rattling engine waking up the village dogs. If she picked up a sketch pad and a pencil, it was motorcars she doodled absentmindedly.

Nothing Edith could do made her feel at peace. She played 'Stardust' on the gramophone incessantly.

One day, she'd even given in to this obsessive state which seemed to be taking her over and, deserting Hoagy Carmichael, and leaving Mrs Thompson in charge of the tearooms, Edith had driven to Arundel for the day, setting off in the green Austin across the countryside, after an early breakfast (Bolney! Henfield! Amberly!)

She arrived before lunch. Parking the car by the Arun River, Edith headed for Swanbourne Lake on foot, searching the sky in vain for the pair of stout winged fan tailed buzzards but spotting only blackbirds and sparrows flitting from branch to branch in the trees in Mill Road. The water sparkled, and the sun shone through the new green leaves. Everything seemed so quiet and ordinary; it was impossible to imagine that it had been just two weeks since the gruesome, mutilated, and carbonised body of an anonymous woman had been found close by.

At Swanbourne, day trippers rowed upon the lake in the sun, just as if nothing had happened. Edith had bought refreshments at the lodge and a bag of stale bread for the white ducks dotting the lake. She had waited until the motherly middle-aged lady manning the counter carried a china cup of steaming tea across to the wonky wrought iron table where she sat.

'I heard that there was a murder here?' Edith effected excitement.

The rosy-cheeked woman had stopped to smooth the flowery pinny which was tied around what should have been her waist, and replied in a conspiratorial whisper:

'They found a body t'other week. T'was up t'other end of the lake - you'll 'ave to take a boat up to see the place exact. You can't miss the spot 'cause the bushes be all burned black.'

But Edith had not been able to glean much more; when she'd asked who the victim was and if the murderer had been caught, the woman replied with a shake of the head.

'I can't answer 'ee fur that, Mum. It were a woman is all I know, and if the Po-lice know 'oo she was, they've not told me. All I can say is tis good for business! - it brought crowds up 'ere last weekend.'

Edith had thanked her and set off back to the Norfolk Arms for lunch. She was greeted at the hotel like an old friend before she settled at her table in the dining room. She asked the handsome waiter about the murder.

He was happy to chat.

'As far as the police have told *US*, Miss Kershaw, they believe the unfortunate victim was murdered by gangsters from somewhere big such as Portsmouth or Brighton and merely dumped here, possibly because the killers were en-route to somewhere else. Likely, neither the murderer nor the motive will ever be known unless an unknown witness or accomplice decides to tell someone. The cocktail bar has done very well out of it.'

'Was it Detective Inspector Stevens who told you about the gangsters?' Edith had asked the waiter, just for the pleasure of saying the detective's name out loud.

'As a matter of fact, it *was*,' the waiter had replied, elegantly balancing the plates on his arm, turning his slim, muscled body to glide away, but not before giving her a brooding smile from Slavic eyes.

After lunch was over, Edith walked out to the car park, even though her little car was still waiting by the river. She felt sad and unsettled in the car park, which made her think of Joanne Forsythe and the domestic scene she'd overheard.

It was a warm clear day, and the ghosts of the Norfolk Arms seemed far away now. The separation between this world and the next felt more like a thick velvet curtain across which it was impossible to see, rather than a gauzy veil.

Back home, she moped around for days, waiting constantly for news. Eventually she decided to telephone Chichester Police Headquarters and simply ask DI Stevens directly what had happened with the case.

Edith had requested the Switchboard for

Detective Inspector Stevens and was horrified to discover her heart beating wildly and mouth dry, when she was told he was in the building. Asked to wait, she held the wall-mounted, candle-stick style telephone in one hand, turning her back on the nosy Mrs Thompson, her forehead damp. Edith's face looked pinched and white above her simple grey dress; what would she say? She tried to rehearse something in her mind.

It felt like she was stood there for hours, waiting on tenterhooks until he came to the other end of the line.'

'Miss Kershaw?'

Edith recognised Stevens' voice with a thrill.

'Good morning,' she replied, trying to calm herself down.

'It's not very good for me. Not at all. Edward and Caroline Wren walked into a police station in the Scottish Borders some days ago, and they're not best pleased to have found themselves unwittingly the subject of so much unwelcome, public speculation.'

Edith gasped.

'But the radio and the papers have been calling for them to come forward for ages. If they were safe and sound then why an earth have they waited so long? *The Scottish Borders?*'

'They'd simply decided on the spur of the moment, to take a holiday in the Scottish Highlands and visit some of the remoter areas. They've apparently not been getting on so well recently and decided that a little romantic getaway, a deux, would be just the ticket. They didn't take a wireless with them, evidently, and they hired an out-of-the-way cottage and didn't see any newspapers until recently. So, Miss Kershaw, there is a perfectly logical explanation for Mrs Wren's early morning shopping trip to Chichester to buy country clothes...she hadn't packed any to take to the wedding, and she'd need them in Scotland.'

'But I was *sure*...' Edith resisted the urge to ask whether Scottish shops sold ordinary tweed skirts or not.

'Alas, I started to believe you; I never should've. My superiors are furious. The Wrens pride themselves on their discretion, and they're very embarrassed by this unwarranted attention through no fault of their own, apparently. They've friends in high places at Scotland Yard - and they've certainly been complaining!'

Edith shrank as Stevens continued his tirade.

'That body at Swanbourne Lake hadn't anything to do with either locals or that wedding - it was a body brought there from elsewhere and dumped and, thanks to you, I've neglected other enquiries, and now we're weeks behind. Scotland Yard are calling me incompetent and trying to take over. The Chief Constable has been leaning on the Super' to get the Yard to take me off the case, too. May I ask you to please keep out of this enquiry and not bother me with your mumbo jumbo *ever* again. Mrs Wren hasn't been murdered, I tell you; The Wrens have been interviewed and eliminated from our enquiries.'

For Edith, sitting smoking and sobbing in her bedroom over a vodka and tonic, it felt as if she'd lost Mick twice. He had receded in her emotions as she'd nursed dreams of the blue-eyed detective, but now DI Stevens was gone forever, it was impossible to bring the dreams of Michael back; she'd lost both of them and emptiness was all there was.

And that might have been the end of the affair, with Edith left to soldier on with only black clouds and listlessness to accompany her. However, the Thursday after her call to the detective, Clara Kershaw arrived at the Honeytree. It wasn't unusual for her mother to visit her in Cuckfield, and in fact it was a regular thing, but this time Clara came bearing news from Arundel; well, not Arundel exactly but rather, Chichester.

CHAPTER 7

Edith was expecting Clara but was still telephoning suppliers when her mother arrived. Clara was as chic and beautifully turned out as usual. She'd parked her car in front of the churchyard nearly opposite and click-clacked her way across the road in front of the King's Head Hotel in her block-heeled T-bar shoes, clutching her felt cloche hat and wearing spotless gloves.

They sat near the window at the front of the café, from where they could see the vicarage and the old courthouse. Doris was scurrying between the tables in her black dress, white lace cap and pinny. There were plenty of customers because the weather was fine, and motorists were passing through the village on their way to the seaside and Brighton promenade.

With the small talk out of the way... 'the weather has been so good for the season'... Clara began to gossip.

'I spoke to Cousin Alma yesterday,' she started.

'Oh yes?'

Edith was immediately interested because Alma and her daughter's wedding were another link to Arundel, the murder, the intense psychic phenomena she'd experienced and meeting DI Stevens - her attraction to whom had so sadly altered her connection to Michael.

'What did Louise say about France? I imagine they must be back from their honeymoon?'

'Well, they haven't come back yet' said Clara, pouring herself another cup of tea. 'Alma said that she got a couple of postcards from Aix-en-Provence and Nice saying what a jolly good time they were having - but they were meant to be back by now, and she's very worried that their hire car might have broken down somewhere between the South of France and England.'

'Couldn't they have simply come home by train? Or sent a telegram?'

'I don't know', said Clara, pulling a face, 'it is France, after all. They might be in the middle of nowhere, and people can't even speak English. Alma's frightfully worried.'

Edith felt tension between her eyes. She frowned as she gazed out the window at the man and his dog walking up Cuckfield High Street. *Old Tom from the cottages and Billy,* she thought.

'How late *are* they?'

'Three days, Alma says. I'll telephone her tonight to see if there's any news. I'm sure we'll hear all about it when they *do* get back.'

Clara looked up at the wall. A new painting hung there, still faintly smelling of linseed and turpentine and probably not dry. She gave a somewhat patronising smile.

'What an earth is *that* meant to be?'

Edith knew she shouldn't feel resentful, but

she did.

'Cars!' Her voice was unnaturally bright.

The painting had thick paint laid on with a spatula and was bright red, blue, and white. You couldn't really see that they were cars at first, but once you saw that the round spoked shapes were wheels and steering wheels and understood the strange perspectives, then you could.

'Honestly, darling,' Clara said, 'with the opportunity to hang your pictures on the wall here and all the passing trade, I'm sure you'd make a fortune selling watercolours of the church or scenes of the village and countryside. What about a pretty vase of flowers? - where you can tell what it is?' Clara went on, 'I'm just afraid that if a decent single man came in here, and he realised that you had painted *that,* then it might put him off. It's probably alright in *Paaaaris,* but we're more traditional here, especially in a nice place like Cuckfield. I'm afraid that a decent Englishman wouldn't understand it, which might make him think he wouldn't understand *you.* Besides - he might become afraid you'd want to put things like that on *his* walls if he married you. I would take it down if I were you.'

'She drove me mad,' Edith told Hester on the telephone that evening. She'd rung her cousin urgently as soon as she was able. 'But the fact is, it's not just the thing about Louise and Arthur that she got from Auntie Alma...Alma also told her something far more interesting... *it's about the murder,* and I think I...*we*...ought to go back to Arundel. The police have got somebody in custody for the Arundel murder.'

Edith glared at the candlestick handset as if to threaten it. 'There's an awful lot of crackling on this line! Alma's neighbour's son is a policeman who let the cat out of the bag. They haven't announced anything yet. No, I don't know *who*, but if they've arrested a gangster from another town...' she filled Hester in about her recent visit to Swanbourne Lake, '...then they've got it all wrong, haven't they? If I accept that the ghosts of the Norfolk Arms were trying to warn *me* about the murder, then surely this has got to be about the hotel and the wedding? Hasn't it? The body wasn't just dumped there. The murder happened in Arundel - I'm certain of it. What's more, the body was set on fire on the Arundel estate to draw attention to it. It wasn't hidden. It's not a gangland murder.'

'What do you think *we* could do?' Hester's voice trembled with excitement on the other end of the telephone wire at the prospect of playing detective.

'First of all, we need to see that Detective Inspector.'

Edith hoped that her cousin had not picked up on the fact that she might also have another motive for contacting DI Stevens.

'Aha! Well, he *is* rather attractive with that sandy hair. I wonder what he looked like in uniform? Just don't get hurt, darling. Find out if he's taken as soon as you can...'

'Sorry sweetie, what did you say? This line is terribly bad. We could spend a week there and soak up the atmosphere - and see if, well, those ghosts will send me a clue as to what has happened.'

'A week! I shall have to be especially nice to Phillip - and Nanny - if he agrees for me to spend a week with you. I thought you hated spirits contacting you?'

'I do! But you see, Hess, we must have met the poor woman who was murdered, at the wedding, and perhaps I could have saved her if I hadn't tried to shut out the warnings? I've been thinking a lot about fate and destiny recently. Maybe I've been wrong, and you were right, and we *can* change things? I mean what if the 'other side' were trying to give me messages that a train was going to crash and I met a person who had a ticket for the train, but I ignored the messages and didn't warn them? You see what I mean? The train crashed, and they died, but I may have been able to stop them from getting on the train in the first place. Perhaps I could have prevented this murder if I'd concentrated on letting the spirits in rather than pushing them away?' She paused. 'Besides, if the police arrest the wrong person for the murder, then the real culprit will get away scot-free. What if they hang an innocent man? Maybe *we* can prevent *that*.'

Three days later, Edith was drawing off the main Worthing to Chichester road and onto the forecourt of Arundel's pretty little station to pick up

Hester from the train. The spell of good weather had ended, and the freezing mizzle almost made her stay in the motorcar, but an idea suddenly struck her. Walking past the coach waiting for visitors to the Norfolk Arms and going into the main entrance, she enquired at the ticket office about the wedding day, nearly three weeks before. Edith had explained how she was related to the bride, who, together with her husband, had not returned from France. The pleasant blonde woman behind the desk remembered the newlyweds well and was pleased for the opportunity to gossip about the murder.

'The car what dropped them off had a load of tin cans tied to it - made a right racket when they arrived. I remember the lady had a beautiful blue coat and hat - it looked expensive like. They definitely caught the train. It was waiting on the other platform when they arrived, and they crossed the bridge. I told the policeman. The tickets were bought in advance, but I inspected them as they walked through.'

At the mention of a policeman, Edith's heart lurched.

She pulled her hat down and put the collar up on her beige raincoat, waiting for the London train to pull in. She could hear it well before it arrived, as the pistons slowed and the brakes applied, and the driver pulled the whistle to signal to the stationmaster that they were coming in. The smoke from the train's chimney hung low in the damp air. Coming out onto the platform, Edith could hear the doors slamming on the other side of the train, and then the sound of the ladies' wooden heels, and the metal on the men's shoes, coming over the bridge from the far platform.

She almost missed Hester when she arrived - her cousin walked straight off the bridge and onto the forecourt through the side entrance. Edith found her by the Austin shivering. They threw her little leather case onto the back seat and set off following the fleet of other cars come to ferry the passengers the short distance to the town.

'Louise and Arthur are still not back,' she told a worried Hester. 'Ma told me that Alma is frantic that they may have had a dreadful accident and are lying somewhere in a foreign hospital, unable to contact us in England. She's reported them missing to the police.'

'That *is* probably what's happened; how perfectly dreadful. Poor Alma - what a worry!'

The castle was silhouetted purple against a deep lavender sky, and mist swirled around its turrets. The rain would stop them from getting out of the hotel and enjoying a walk.

Edith was increasingly nervous as they neared the hotel. Her pleasure at spending a week on a girl's jaunt with Hester was overshadowed by her nerves at the first task she had to do - contact the DI. After they had booked in and had their luggage taken up to the room, they warmed themselves by the fire which had been lit for them in the snug and ordered a gin and tonic and a bloody mary, and Edith told Hester her plan:

'I'm going to tip the receptionist to ring

Chichester Police Station and leave a message simply saying that Mrs Hester Denney and Miss Edith Kershaw would like to inform Detective Inspector Stevens that they are staying at the Norfolk Arms in Arundel.' She swirled her drink around her glass, making the ice cubes clink.

Hester was dressed in a pastel golfing jumper and Edith in simple navy, but they both wore pearls and had their hair pulled to one side with a clip.

'Surely you could ring yourself and tell him that we want to see him about the murder?' Hester crinkled her nose and raised her glass, 'Here's to you, darling! And solving the crime!'

The logs crackled in the grate, sending sparks onto the fire guard.

'I can't do that,' said Edith. 'I've given it a lot of thought. He was furious last time I spoke to him - I got him into a lot of bother over that Caroline Wren business. He won't want me interfering...especially if he thinks he's already solved the case. He probably can't talk before they've charged someone. I can't leave the message myself, either, because the switchboard might put me through to him, and I don't want to talk to him on the telephone. He might send someone else to interview us if I mention the murder, too.' She paused. 'This way, it leaves it open for him to come to see us,' *come to see ME*, she thought, 'if he wants to. Of course, he might not want to.'

'Oh, he'll come alright,' Hester gave a wry smile and rolled her eyes.

'You seem very sure?' Edith sipped her drink unhappily; she wasn't sure at all.

'Simple curiosity. It's human nature. You've been cleverly enigmatic. He'll want to know *why* we're here and why we left that message. The only question is how quickly he arrives. If I were you, I'd give the receptionist an even bigger tip and tell him that if Detective Inspector Stevens ever rings back to speak to us, then to tell him each time that we are not available but that we generally have a pre-prandial snifter, and then supper, here in the evening.'

Edith got up. 'Here goes, then. Wish me luck. If I see the waiter, I'll order a refill. Then all we've got to do is wait.'

She set off in the direction of the hotel reception.

A day elapsed before DI Stevens arrived at the hotel. Edith had spent a restless night, and she took special care to dress in her prettiest grey day dress the next morning, pinning up her auburn hair with a velvet bow and patting perfume behind her ears. She spent the day shivering with cold and the continuing rain made her fresh mascara run, making her panic. In fact, to Hester's annoyance, Edith seemed on edge and distracted any time they left the hotel.

'He's making us stew!' Edith pulled a face and checked herself once again in the mirror.

'No. He has to work! For goodness' sake, put on something sensible and come for a walk in the castle grounds. I didn't come here to hang about the hotel all day. Arundel is a very small place; I'm sure he'll find us if he wants to. He *is* a detective, darling.'

It was the evening when Stevens finally turned up, and Edith and Hester were sitting in the snug smoking before going into supper. It was Edith who heard him come into the hotel above the hubbub of conversation around her, and then saw him hurry past the room in the direction of the reception. He looked quite nervous, even anxious; he didn't know he had been observed.

Edith nudged Hester and composed herself. She felt that her face was flushed red.

'He's here,' Edith said.

DI Stevens walked slowly back to the snug and into the room, taking off his fedora. When he saw them, his face broke into a natural, warm smile. Edith grinned back.

'Good evening, ladies! Mind if I join you?' He searched around for an armchair and dragged it up to the low table as they stood up to shake hands.'

It was a complete coincidence.that they were back in Arundel, where a body had been found after a recent family wedding, the pair assured him. Well, not entirely a coincidence because they had enjoyed both the hotel and the surrounding countryside so much that they'd decided to return for a holiday. They'd merely let him know of their presence as a courtesy in the light of his investigation. They hadn't expected him to go out of his way to come to the hotel, but now he was here, perhaps he would have supper with them?

Stevens' blue eyes met Edith's grey ones. *So,*

what if he knows I'm lying? Edith thought. *It'll let him know that I'm interested in him. Please don't let him be married...*

He took out a cigarette and cupped his hands to light it. The detective was perfectly friendly and seemed to have put the anger of his telephone call behind him, now he was here.

Edith and Hester's conversation naturally turned to the bride and groom missing in France and the family's worry concerning their continuing silence.

'Of course, we're all afraid they're ill or injured.' Edith was baffled by his apparent puzzlement. 'There were some postcards, but now nothing. I'm surprised you don't know? Mrs Lamb's mother lives in Chichester and she reported them missing at *your* station. I was hoping you might have some news for us.'

He scratched his head. 'No, I didn't know that. It's not my case - we've got many cases, and I don't know them all. All the same, I think that I should have been informed. I must tell you in confidence that we're on the point of bringing charges against somebody for the murder of his wife, and that couple were guests at Mr and Mrs Lamb's wedding. I'm sure that the Lambs have nothing at all to do with the murder, but even so, I think that I should have been informed, that's all. Someone's going to get a roasting for this.'

Hester and Edith stared at each other in surprise.

Hester was the first to speak, her hazel eyes wide and glittering.

'You didn't arrest a gangster?'

'But you said every guest was accounted for after the wedding?' Edith said, 'except for the Wrens?'

'Well, it seems the constable who checked on this gentleman should have asked to see his wife rather than taking other people's word for it that she was fine.'

'Shall we go into the dining room?' Edith looked for her patent handbag. The lovely waiter who looked like Nijinsky was hovering around the door of the snug, and little by little the other guests had all crossed the hall to sit in the dining room.

They stood up, and Stevens picked up his hat.

'Look, I won't join you for supper tonight,' he began, ' because my Police chauffeur is waiting in the car outside, and I dare say that his wife is back in Chichester fuming that he's not had his high tea. If you would allow me to take you both out to dinner tomorrow evening, I could show you somewhere different? I'll need to make some arrangements and get a cab back.'

'Don't you have a motor car?' Edith was rather surprised.

He hesitated only for a brief instant. 'It's off the road I'm afraid.'

Well, well, thought Edith. *This man can't drive, and he's not above fibbing about it. He has some machismo.*

'Don't worry,' said Hester when he'd gone. I'll be sure to develop a terrible headache tomorrow evening. Now don't you think the man they've arrested has got to be that bounder, David Forsyth?'

'But why...' asked Edith, '... didn't he get rid of the body where it would never be found and tell his family she'd run away? She certainly had reason to. And why did Joanne's mother say she was fine? There's something we're not getting.'

CHAPTER 8

Edith awoke early and lay in bed, drifting in and out of sleep. Listening to the rain drumming on the pavement outside, she was lulled by the rhythmic sound of Hester snoring in the other bed. The early morning light over Arundel made a grey line between the chintz curtains. It was so warm and comfortable under the pale green satin eiderdown; she felt limp and relaxed and let her mind empty, and suddenly she was floating; her head filled with bars of colour, cerise and violet, yellow, green, and pink and shiny gold that reflected the light.

In and out of consciousness, she tried to have a pleasant anticipatory dream about the coming evening's dinner alone with DI Stevens. Still, the intense pastel shades were vivid just behind her eyelids and, somewhere, an orchestra played 'Red Sails in the Sunset.'

There was a time, just recently, that she might have been afraid of lulling into a trance-like state because of the feeling that other worldly messages were trying to communicate themselves to her, and she would have fought to shut them out, even leaping out of bed and drinking some tea to make herself fully alert. However, Edith had persuaded her cousin to return to Arundel because she hoped that clues to solving the Arundel murder would be given to her if she opened her mind and allowed the spirits in.

Music appeared to be playing in the room.

It sounded real. She was surprised it didn't wake up Hester. But perhaps the orchestra was back at the wedding reception; there was a buzzing in her temple.

Red Sails in the Sunset,
Way out on the sea,
Oh, carry my loved one home safely to me
(She sailed at the dawning; all day, I've been blue)
Red sails in the sunset, I'm trusting in you.

There were the bars of colour again. An unusual combination of shades.

'She sailed at the dawning, all day I've been blue.'

When blue came into her imagination, a clear image of Arundel station popped into Edith's mind from nowhere.

She felt a strange compunction to paint the colours. Hester showed no sign of waking, and she didn't want to disturb her sleep, so Edith tiptoed to the old-fashioned mahogany chest of drawers and took out some thin cotton stockings, a pair of culottes and the navy sweater and got dressed in the bathroom. Splashing her face with cold water and pulling back her hair with a slide, she dabbed on some pink lipstick.

Taking up her sketch pad and a box of pastels, she slipped down the stairs to the green breakfast room and was pleased to see she was the first person up. The tables had been laid the day before, and the sounds of clattering pots and pans, running water, blasts of steam and loud voices could be heard from the kitchen through a door in the corner ('Lawks! Mr Dimmock! You 'aint 'arf frisky today!' together with cackles and shrieks of laughter.)

By the time Hester's thin face peered around the door, Edith was on her third pot of tea and second round of toast and marmalade. She was sitting in the corner at a large table, not at their usual place, and her sketch pad and colours lay to one side. Other hotel guests sat around the room, dressed in country clothes and making civilised conversation. Most of the guests appeared to have colour brochures for the castle or adverts for the attractions of Littlehampton, Chichester, or the pleasure boat rides. *They're out of luck with the rain,* Edith thought, *but that's tourism in the lovely green English countryside for you.*

Hester spotted her and gave a cheery wave. Coming over and glancing at the sketch pad, she asked, 'What did you feel *compelled* to draw this time?' She sat down and began to look for the waitress.

'I don't know. Just colours. Nothing. It's an abstract.'

'May I?' Hester picked up the sketchpad. 'Maybe it does mean something? Do you remember how you painted a fire? And then somebody burned that body, and we saw a fire?'

Edith nodded as her cousin pointed at the kippers on the menu, and the waitress scooted away for tea and bread and butter. There was a gentle rattle of bone-handled knives on china, and now and then, the potent smell of hyacinths would drift over from the arrangement of spring flowers on a stand and mingle with the aroma of crispy bacon.

Hester pointed at the bars of pigment in the picture, 'what are those yellow tips on the ends of the colours?'

'I don't know,' said Edith, trying to rub off a spot of yellow pastel that she had inadvertently got on the starched white tablecloth. 'I saw shiny metallic gold in my head - but I didn't have any gold pastels, so they had to be yellow. It doesn't look like anything, but I quite like it. You're right. It means something, but the trouble with this 'gift' is that it's not always clear what the message is. It feels like a dream I've got to interpret, and I don't understand it yet. But I got an image of the station, and we need to go there and see if we can spot anything resembling these colours.

'Detective work,' said Hester, 'Yippee!'

'Yes. I might try to trust these intuitions more and learn to go where they take me.'

The rest of the breakfast was passed in pleasant chatter about Hester's life in Birmingham, and her husband and children, and Edith's life in Cuckfield, which seemed so solitary by comparison; the café kept her busy, and she tried to fill her diary with social engagements, but still, the evenings were long with only the wireless for company.

They had discussed David Forsythe and speculated on whether his arrest had made the newspapers, when suddenly the Hotel receptionist appeared and beckoned the waitress over. His expression was grave as he tried to gesture towards Edith surreptitiously, and the waitress looked frightened.

'Look! They're talking about us!' Edith kicked Hester under the table. 'I don't like the look of that!'

The waitress was hurrying towards them with a serious air.

'Madam?' Her tone was concerned. 'There is an urgent telephone call for you from Mrs Kershaw, at the reception.'

No wonder the receptionist had reacted rather dramatically to Clara's call. Edith's mother was clearly in tears, and it was evident that this wasn't a social call.

'I thought you ought to know...,' she began, '... that the police have been in touch with Alma about Louise and Arthur. No one can understand yet what has happened, but they've contacted the customs at Portsmouth and their records show that Arthur Lamb travelled *alone* to France! The day *after* they were supposed to take the ferry together!'

'What? Calm down, Ma.'

'Yes. They missed the boat and Arthur transferred the ticket. He got the ferry alone, took the hire car a day late and abandoned it in Menton.' Alma's voice rose in panic. 'The French police are searching it for clues. Poor, poor Alma! She says now that the postcards that came were from both of them, but they were written by Arthur, *not* Louise. She thought it odd at the time, but not *this*!' Clara had started to sob again.

'Please don't cry, Mama! We don't know what's happened yet.'

'What *could* have happened?' Clara's voice dared Edith to reply. 'I didn't say to Alma, but I remembered that woman's body they found after the wedding. They've never discovered who it is, have they?'

'The police have actually arrested someone for the murder, but they're not saying who yet, as they haven't charged him. He was at the wedding, and apparently, he murdered his wife.'

'Then it could be Arthur!'

Edith remembered Stevens' surprise at the news of the missing bride and groom.

'No. Hester and I think it is an antique dealer who was a guest on the groom's side.' *I'll find out more about that this evening*, she thought but didn't say. 'Look, Ma, calm down. I checked with the lady at the station. She remembers Louise getting on the train. Whatever happened to her didn't happen to her in Arundel. She may still turn up alive and well - with Arthur.'

'What were you doing checking at the station if you didn't suspect that body could be Louise?' Clara might be hysterical, but she was not stupid. 'Alma says that the police didn't want to say it, but it's very, very, suspicious that Arthur drove that car to the Italian border and then dumped it.' Clara gave another sob, 'Please send a card to Alma. Don't go and see her yet - I know you're not far. She's in shock at the moment and waiting for news. She says the couple's friends are comforting her, although they're as worried as she is. I just thought you ought to know.'

Edith and Hester were in a glum mood when they put on their raincoats and set off to get some fresh air when there was a break in the weather. They walked to the station. The clamour of seagulls rose over the town as they crossed the bridge and passed the White Hart. You could smell the salt of the sea and the damp grass.

How was it that the newlyweds had set off for their honeymoon from the Norfolk Arms, boarded the train at Arundel, but had missed the ferry at Portsmouth?

Perhaps the answer *was* at the station.

They seemed to be at the main Worthing to Chichester road in no time. They were walking on the opposite side of the road to the station. The path soon passed behind some vegetation before going under the Victorian railway bridge. The bridge made a tunnel to the station under the main carriageway and was not visible from the road. Anyone driving on the road would not realise that they had passed over the railway and the pedestrian footpath.

The pair were very quickly at the station; not at the top of the large forecourt, but the footpath had brought them out directly at the station buildings, by the side entrance.

'The woman in the ticket hall told me she'd

inspected their tickets,' Edith said, as they surveyed the front of the building, looking for anything multicoloured. 'She had to have remembered them because they arrived in the wedding car with noisy tin cans and - she's a woman - she remembered Louise's 'going away' outfit. I believe her,' Edith said. 'What reason would she have to lie?'

Neither Hester nor Edith wanted to walk through the little ticket office without a ticket nor a train to meet, and so they naturally drifted back towards the footpath under the road and the way back to Arundel.

The side exit to the station gaped invitingly as they reached the passage under the road.

'Come on,' Edith said, walking freely onto the platform. There was no barrier, and no one was about.

The station was much bigger than anyone might have guessed from the outside, although the size of the forecourt should have given a clue as to its importance. Decorative cast iron columns held up the canopy, and the platforms were extremely long.

'The platform for the direction of Portsmouth is on the other side of that footbridge over the rails,' Hester said. It's the same platform I arrived on from London.'

'Yes...so, when the ticket lady saw them walk onto the platform, up there...' Edith gestured further up to where the ticket hall opened onto the railway '... it was perfectly natural that they should walk down to where we're standing now to cross the footbridge.'

'Hmmm. I follow you. They could easily have gone through the tunnel under the road instead.'

'Yes', said Edith. ' The ticket lady couldn't see down here from her lobby. You can't see anybody on the footbridge very well, once they're up the stairs, and people on the other side are masked by the train itself when it's in the station. The train was already in when their car arrived.'

'That ticket woman couldn't have seen them actually get onto the train,' said Hester as the penny dropped. 'Look at the path under the road! It's on an angle, and it's masked by the stairs. Anybody who took the footbridge or the tunnel would be out of view in seconds.' Her hazel eyes looked very worried now.

'I wonder if the Stationmaster saw them on the other platform? We could ask.' Edith looked around the long platform which was beginning to fill up with people wanting to go to London.'

However, when they found the man's office and questioned the rotund and bespectacled stationmaster inside, reading the newspaper, he looked at them as if they were soft in the head.

'Lummy! How many weeks ago, d'you say? D'you know how many trains stop here every day? T'was the Duke of Norfolk gave the money for this station - on condition that every single train stops here!' He pushed his little round wire-framed glasses back on his nose. 'There ain't many people lives in Arundel - but there sure are a lot of trains, Madam. How could I remember all the people what get on and off them? Lot of day-trippers, y'see, come to gawp at the castle.'

Hester leaned forward and said earnestly, 'the lady was wearing a blue coat a sort of cross between sky-blue and capri. Made of raw silk. She had a hat in french-navy' and matching heels, gloves, and a handbag. Personally, I'd have had the handbag in a different blue, but toning, or then again, a contrast. At any rate, you *must* remember her clothes!'

The Stationmaster was trained to be polite, so his look was only as withering as he thought he could get away with.

'We could ask a porter,' he suggested, '*they're* known to be experts in ladies' fashion.' But the porter had no memory either.

Edith thanked them, and the pair set off back to the tunnel.

'I know Phillip would say that we should rather have asked them about her embonpoint or her bottom, but fancy them not noticing Louise,' Hester remarked and Edith agreed; men tended to notice Louise.

They had started making their way along the footpath when Hester suddenly pointed. Further along the path, sitting on a fence post, its feathers ruffled against the damp miserable day, sat one of the buzzards. Its hooked beak was in silhouette, and its talons gripped the wood.

'Those birds are out again! They've come out to hunt now there's a break in the rain.'

Edith looked up and recognised the V-shape of the wings of the other buzzard circling up high in the grey blustery sky'.

'They're probably looking for carrion near the main road.'

The buzzard on the post sat almost unnaturally still while they approached. As they neared it, it turned its dark eyes towards Edith, spread its stout wings, and leaped into the sky, soaring up until it had joined its mate.

She stared ahead.

'Which post was it sitting on?' Edith asked Hester quickly, 'about the tenth post along?'

'I think so - yes.'

Edith sped up and, reaching the post before her cousin, bent down and began rooting around in the wet grass. Half under a large lump of chalky stone sticking up from the ground at the edge of the field, under the fence, she found what she was looking for.

'What have you spotted?' Hester caught up with her cousin.

Edith opened her hand to show her. The cigarette butt had been faded by the sun indeed, and the damp had made the paper go soggy, and the remaining tobacco was spilling out. Still, you could clearly see that it was the remains of a jade green Sobranie cocktail cigarette with a gold foil filter tip.

Edith ran her wet fingers through her damply curling hair.

'Do you remember? The orchestra had just played Red Sails and Louise came over and offered us one of these.' She looked down at the tattered bit of paper. 'They were all different colours, packed in gold foil; cerise, violet, yellow, green, and pink.'

'Your picture.' Hester raised her eyebrows. 'It's an unusual colour combination.'

The pair looked at each other uneasily.

'And when she offered us the cigarettes, I had a sudden 'insight' that she wouldn't have a long marriage,' Edith remembered.

'It may have been even shorter than *you* foresaw,' Hester said, with a shiver. 'Oh, I do hope that body isn't darling Louise!'

They walked up the path, shielded from the traffic by the bushes, and within twenty minutes were back at the hotel.

'I've got to work out what I'm going to tell DI Stevens tonight about the cigarette end,' Edith said.

She screwed up her face. 'I know he won't like it - how can I explain how I came to find this? But I've got to tell him. Louise Lamb didn't get on the train; she got out of the car and walked back down the path willingly, or she was forced to. Either way, she lit up a cigarette. I can tell she was very upset because Louise would never, normally, have smoked in the street. Or on a footpath. It's the biggest clue yet.'

CHAPTER 9

That evening, at supper, Edith fished through her handbag and tipped the forlorn cigarette end onto the table, under the light of a candle which sat between her and DI Stevens. She looked lovely in her pale grey dress, with her hair pinned up, as she gazed at him in some trepidation. Up until then, the evening had gone like a dream.

Edith had dressed herself up for the occasion with care, after a long soak in a hot bath and multiple checks in the mirror. Had she felt like this for Mick on their first outings together? She must have done, but it was a long time ago and she could hardly remember. She stopped for a minute, closed her eyes, and tried to conjure up Michael, but he was still elusive. Edith had not gone on many supper dates since Mick's death, and they were mainly with local men who were boring small-town solicitors or accountants, and other chinless wonders Clara met at the golf club or in church, for whom Edith had not felt the need to make too much of an effort. A plainclothes Detective Inspector was rather more exciting - especially a tall, athletic one.

Stevens had turned up on time, looking relaxed and clearly having taken some trouble himself to prepare for the evening, although his jazzy tie really didn't go with his suit, which irked Edith's artistic tastes. He'd changed out of his work suit and was dressed for supper, as the hour and circumstances required, but with a touch of informality suited to the country setting.

He didn't seem too disappointed at Hester being taken suddenly ill with a cracking headache. If he suspected Edith was lying about that, he was polite enough to show some concern but still look pleased to get her on her own

Edith had felt butterflies in the pit of her stomach beforehand, but that soon disappeared as the pair enjoyed cocktails in the Norfolk Arms and got on first name terms.

His name was Adrian, which she liked immensely because it reminded her of the Emperor Hadrian, although the DI had never heard of him.

It was drizzling as they stepped out from under the arch of the Norfolk Arms. Adrian put up an umbrella and gave her his arm to help her cross the road in her heels. His physical closeness under the umbrella made her breathe in deeply; he exuded cologne mingled with tobacco, wet dog, and horses. It was an unfamiliar smell, but more exciting for that; she inhaled it with pleasure.

Stevens confidently steered her across the cobbled square onto the far pavement and then led her down to the Swan Hotel.

Settling at their candlelit table, they soon fell into a natural intimacy as their oxtail soup was served. They both had tucked in their white starched napkins and leaning forward, avoiding the candle, chatted as they looked into each other's eyes. *The chemistry is clearly there,* Edith thought, her heart singing.

The Great War was a natural subject because it had changed everybody's experience of the world. 'What did you do during the war?' was the question that everybody always asked each other, if they were old enough to remember it.

The smell, sound, and power of horses seemed to take over the pretty little oak table with its barley sugar twist legs as Adrian recounted *his* War.

Edith's eyes were soft as she listened to his voice, which revealed an evident passion for the animals. She almost told him how she had fallen off a horse as a child and been kicked by her mount, leaving her with a fear of the beasts, but he was so emotional when he spoke of the animals that she kept quiet about it. Adrian had grown up a farmer's lad. The son of a line of yeoman farmers, certainly, but whose land had been slowly diminished - sold off by necessity. He was not born the eldest son who would eventually inherit the farm but the third son. He'd followed his second eldest brother into becoming a blacksmith because he had an affinity with horses and enjoyed the manual side of metalwork, besides. He'd been 19 when the War had broken out (Edith had merely been 9), but his expertise with horses had made him a valuable man, so Adrian Stevens had enlisted as a volunteer and was made a farrier. The horses, of course, were more valuable than the men, and so Adrian had been kept together with his precious four-legged charges well behind the lines. He'd never seen a trench, let alone lived in one. Even his brothers had survived; the eldest, now a farmer, had been wounded, but that was all.

'What made you join the police?' Edith was curious.

'There was a shortage of suitable men for the police force after the war,' Adrian told her, and since he came from a long line of farmers, he was well nourished, tall, and well built, and so he was exactly what the police force was looking for. Motorcars seemed to be taking over from horses. He had seen that whilst he might struggle in the future, as a blacksmith, he could go far in the police force.

By the time the roast meat had been carved and the new potatoes and spring vegetables served, the couple had been touching hands and confiding in increasingly low voices. Edith had been burning to ask him why he was still single - she trusted he was, judging by his body language, - but she thought that it was probably not a good idea to ask a man about marriage on a first date, lest he feel that she was going way too fast. Things were progressing so well that she was certain there would be other dates and they would learn more about each other naturally. She did try to subtly find out his home arrangements in other ways, though, as she told Hester later, asking him how he managed at home and whether he employed a cook or a maid. Her excuse was to chatter about Mrs Thompson, Doris, and Mrs Tutt.

'Mrs Brown does absolutely everything; she's a marvel,' the detective had confided in turn. 'She's been there for years, and she always has a fresh shirt laundered for me or makes my favourite jam roly poly. Do you know, I don't even employ a gardener because she enjoys doing the vegetable plot as well as cleaning the house?' He shook his head in wonderment. 'She's a treasure. I tell her she mothers me too much.' Mrs Brown was his housekeeper.

Edith knew that she had got to tell the DI about finding the cigarette end.

'Hester and I just found it by a pure fluke,' she'd attempted to tell Adrian. 'Louise Lamb smoked Sobranie cocktail cigarettes.'

'Have you been poking around?' Adrian sat back in his chair. He looked miffed. He was probably thinking of the Mrs Wren fiasco.

She tipped the paper bag out, which she'd found quickly in her tidy handbag. The faded pale green and foil cigarette end fell upon the table.

'We found it on the footpath leading to the station. Where the path's hidden from the road?' Edith explained how she had gone for a walk with Hester that had ended up at the station for no particular reason.

'It could've been smoked by anyone,' Adrian said. 'You went for a walk by the main road when we have all this beautiful countryside?'

He examined, with attention, the posy of spring flowers in a tiny vase which the pair had pushed to one side, because of the lack of room on the table. He was waiting to see what she would say.

'I don't think it could have been smoked by just anyone.' Edith replied, avoiding the question. 'These aren't sold in Arundel as far as I know. They're expensive, luxury cigarettes that women generally smoke in the evening. Louise had a carton of them because it was her wedding. Alma Matthews brought them from Chichester for her - I distinctly remember my mother mentioning it. What tourist would get off the train and light up one of these on a country footpath?'

Adrian refused to look up, so Edith continued. 'Besides, one is brought up to *not* smoke outdoors, if one is a lady, and it was on a public footpath. Louise must have been very shaken up to smoke it while walking along. And I don't believe she went to the station in the days before. The couple did not buy their own tickets - Alma told my mother.'

'How do you know that you can't buy Sobranies in Arundel?' Adrian replied after a long pause.

'Because Hester and I spent the afternoon visiting every place in town we could think of which might sell them,' confessed Edith. 'There aren't many places; they wouldn't sell them in an ordinary public house.' She went on to tell him about the side entrance and the passage under the   road at the station. 'We think Louise and Arthur only pretended to get on the train and then walked back to Arundel. She was wearing a very distinctive outfit. Someone probably saw her. There must have been other people coming and going on that footpath.'

'Are you going to eat a pudding?' He poured her another glass of wine. 'So - do you think our mysterious body is that of Louise Lamb? Or somebody else? I'll be frank with you. I'm going to release the gentleman we have in custody, without charges, on condition that he stays where we can find him. We have no evidence against him yet. Only the fact his wife is missing and his mother lied about it.'

'David Forsythe?' Edith asked.
Adrian gave her a filthy look. 'I never told you his name. How did you know that? I'm beginning to think that you're more involved in this case than you're admitting.'

She quickly told him about overhearing the Forsythes from the carpark, and meeting David visiting the castle, alone, on the day the body was found.

'Until Mrs Forsythe is found, the husband is still a suspect. He lied to the police about her whereabouts. But he didn't abscond. The *other* husband has run off and is most probably in Italy by now - his car was discovered parked on the border. French police have found Mrs Lamb's suitcase dumped in the French countryside.'

Adrian studied Edith's face. She looked distraught. 'It looks highly likely that Arthur Lamb murdered his bride,' he said.

'But *why* would Arthur murder Louise?' Edith moved back in her chair as steaming plates of rhubarb pie and custard were set in front of them.

'They were so in love! Arthur was clearly besotted. They'd only been married a day for heaven's sake!'

'Perhaps he regretted getting married? Who

knows? We can't know what goes on behind closed
doors.' The DI shrugged. 'But I *will* tell you one other
thing, I perhaps shouldn't. Arthur Lamb telephoned
the wedding car hire firm first thing on the morning
he supposedly left for his honeymoon, and cancelled
the car booked by the bride's mother. The car that
arrived was hired from a different firm.'

'How very strange...' Edith remembered the
newlyweds posing for photographs and the large and
rather grand wedding car leaving the courtyard as the
couple waved goodbye to their guests. The hood was
rolled half down, so that people could see them
without the wind whipping off their hats.

'What did the chauffeur, who drove them to
the station, say? They looked so happy together when
they left here. What happened inside that car
between the hotel and the station?'

'I've no idea,' Adrian said. 'We haven't traced
the other firm yet. But I daresay, we will.'

A thought struck Edith. 'Why are you fixated
on Arthur murdering Louise? Even if that body *is*
Louise, have you thought that she might have been
murdered by someone else?'

'Then why,' he replied, 'has Mr Lamb fled
abroad? We know he used his passport and collected
the French hire car.'

Edith looked down at her pudding. 'I don't
want to put you off your food. But Louise was
beautiful - like a Hollywood film star - and Arthur
was in love with her. How could he have cut off her
head and her hands and feet? He would have to be a

cold-blooded psychopath to do that. I don't believe he is.'

'He had a powerful motive,' Adrian said, getting up suddenly. 'It gave him a two week start on the police. Finish your pudding! I'll pay! Come on! Get your coat! We've got to get you back to the hotel! I've got a cab booked in twenty minutes to take me home. Mrs Brown will be waiting up for me. If I'm very late, she'll want to know why.'

'He didn't kiss me,' Edith told Hester when she went up to their hotel room, 'but honestly, Hess, it was such a wonderful evening!'

Hester was sitting in bed reading a detective novel.

'He didn't ask when he might see me again. But I'm sure he will. His name's Adrian.' Edith looked radiant. 'Will you stop reading? I'm so happy!'

Hester put her book down. Her face was plastered in ponds cold cream. 'Did you make sure he isn't married?'

'Well, he evidently isn't. He lives alone with his old housekeeper, and he is obviously taken with *me*.' She bounced up and down with excitement as she sat on the bed.

'Darling...seriously...' Hester said, 'don't fall in love with this fellow until you know him better.' She stopped. 'Alright, I see it's too late. I don't want to put a dampener on things, sweetie, but the reality is we live in an age where you see women advertising in the newspapers for a husband . I know it's hard. Why is this tall, attractive chap, with good health and a good job, unattached? Every single girl in the area must set her cap at him? How come he's never succumbed? Do you know some men are love rats and very plausible?'

'But you didn't know Phillip when you fell for him!' Edith continued happily, 'You told me you picked him up on a visit to London because you liked him in uniform and it was love at first sight!'

'Ah, yes,' said Hester, 'but *that* is different.'

The subject of conversation came back, as it always did, to the murder in Arundel and from there to their missing relative, Louise Lamb.

'Let's go over it again,' said Edith, 'the police are releasing the Bounder pending their investigations, but Joanne is still missing, and he tried to cover it up. Is she dead or alive? Can her disappearance be a coincidence? Where is Louise? And why did she only pretend to get on the train and walk back to Arundel? Arthur cancelled the wedding car and hired a different firm - why? Where is Arthur, and why did he go abroad alone? And why did I think that it was Caroline Wren who would die? And she's the only one definitely alive.'

'It's a difficult knot to undo,' said Hester. 'But you've got an edge over that policeman. He would never have found that cigarette end alone unless he'd ordered a fingertip search.

'Edith gave a huge sigh. 'I've never tried doing this before... I don't even know if I can...'

'Do what?' Hester's eyes stood out from her white-creamed face.

'Contact the dead, on purpose. I've always hated having this 'gift,' but maybe it'll be useful now. I want to find out what's happened, don't you? It feels like I'm meant to find out because I was involved right from the beginning.'

'How are you going to go about it?' Hester got up and searched for her dressing gown.

'We're going to hold a séance. You're not scared, are you?'

Hester looked a mixture of frightened and excited. 'When?' she asked.

'It's ten to twelve now.' Edith looked at her bedside clock.' Midnight seems as good a time as any. Promise you won't tell Phillip! Or Detective Inspector Adrian Stevens.'

CHAPTER 10

The pair watched Edith's little gold travel clock as midnight approached. For the séance, they had wrapped up warmly with blankets from the beds and dragged the desk chair opposite an armchair in the bedroom.

Edith draped a thin scarf over the bedside lampshade to lower the lighting, and the room was now bathed in a dull pink glow, which accentuated the deep shadows made by the furniture. She wanted the right atmosphere to make her feel relaxed.

Everything seemed eerily quiet in the hotel and the street outside as the two hands on the clock reached twelve.

'Give me your hands!' Edith was very serious. 'Listen to everything and try to remember it. I don't know what will happen; these things usually happen by accident. I've never tried to invite them in before. I'm going to try and induce a trance.'

Hester looked like a barn owl. She was all white, and her eyes looked huge in her face. She rested her long, thin, fingers in her cousin's warm hands.

'Whatever happens, don't wake me up. Don't make any sudden movements, and don't let go of my hands,' Edith said. 'Please don't look so frightened. Trust me!'

Edith breathed in and out as deeply as she could to a long, slow rhythm. Her eyes were shut, and she tried counting backwards very slowly, emptying her mind of any thoughts about anything at all. She let her neck go limp, and then her shoulders, and she felt the energy from Hester coursing into her through her hands, making her more powerful, like a battery charging. She was a beacon in a big dark void.

Edith could hear voices somewhere in the hotel, and they annoyed her. She was trying to concentrate on emptying her mind, but people were chattering, and they were difficult to ignore. Were they in the room next door? It sounded like a group of men. They were men having a party. They were too loud. Despite trying to ignore them, another part of Edith seemed to strain to hear what they were saying, and it was becoming easier. They were just a little way off, just on the edge of the bedroom. If she tried, she could hear the rattle of bone dice on a table and laughter. There was the sound of pottery mugs banging against heavy stoneware bottles. She could hear their voices but couldn't understand what they were saying. They seemed to have thick country accents, a Norfolk burr, and a Suffolk dialect, and they used words she was unfamiliar with. 'Soldiers' was the word that popped into her head. They were garrisoned here while waiting to go to France. Off to fight 'Old Boney.' Hester told Edith afterwards that her face had become totally blank and expressionless; it was petrifying to watch - as if she had died. At the same time, the temperature in the room had grown suddenly colder, and the low pink light had flickered. *I wonder if I can speak to them?* Edith thought.

'Hello! Is there anybody there?' She called out as she felt a familiar buzz in her temple.

Her head was still full of black emptiness, but she was aware that one of the soldiers had stopped what he was doing and was listening.

Edith tried to concentrate on that soldier alone.

'Is there anybody there?'

She heard the footsteps of someone in heavy boots break away from the other soldiers and edge closer to her.

Holding Edith's hands, Hester heard disembodied footsteps in the bedroom, too, and shuddered.

'Don't be afraid!' Edith said out loud. She wasn't talking to Hester.

She was aware of the mysterious soldier coming closer. She sensed his curiosity.

'Are you a soldier sent to fight Napoleon? If you are, rap once on the bedside table. If you're not, rap twice.'

Hester nearly jumped out of her chair as a single sharp rap sounded from the direction of the bed.

'Do you know why I'm here?' Edith's voice sounded eerily distant.

Again, there was a loud rap.

'Will you help me?'

Rap!

'Is Louise on the other side with you?'

Rap!

Edith paused. *Poor, beautiful, tragic Louise,*

married for only a day.

'Is Louise the body found at Swanbourne Lake?'

Rap!

She was really afraid of the next question, but it had to be asked; they had to know. She took a deep breath. 'Was Arthur murdered, too?'

Rap!

Hester welled up but kept holding Edith's hands.

'Is Joanne Forsythe with you?'

Rap! Rap!

Thank goodness for that.

Edith couldn't resist asking the next question, even though the response was evident. It felt reassuring to communicate with the other world about Mick. She felt it was some sort of contact between them.

'Is Michael with you?'

Rap! Rap!

Hester got up hurriedly, wiping her eyes, as Edith awoke abruptly from her trance. The *last* raps were actually *real* raps coming from the bedroom door. Hester opened it a crack.

'I say!' A man stood there in striped pyjamas and a silk dressing gown. 'Do you mind stopping that banging and stomping about, please? Some of us are trying to sleep, and that noise could wake the dead.'

Hester had been scared out of her wits by the strange manifestations in the bedroom, and her cousin's transformation when she was speaking to the dead in a deep trance. Edith had to reassure her that no unseen spirits were left in the room when they'd finally got into their beds and whispered to each other in the dark, exactly as they had as children.

'Please don't tell Phillip!' Edith reiterated as she fell asleep, just as the morning light was creeping between the curtains. 'Or Adrian Stevens. I don't want anyone to know we've been calling up spirits. Nobody would approve. I'm sure the hotel wouldn't.'

She fell asleep trying to dream of the DI Adrian Stevens but dreaming only of the redcoat soldier whom she'd asked for help. William. Willy was his name, she knew. Finally, tears seeped into her pillow as she remembered the radiant bride and groom, who's wedding she had so recently attended and who now lay cold, dead, and unburied.

CHAPTER 11

'The thing I regret is that I didn't ask if Arthur *murdered* his wife,' said Edith for the umpteenth time as She and Hester took the air; taking the air was something the two of them did every day. '*Why* didn't I think of it quick enough?'

They both agreed that even if Arthur was undoubtedly dead, the police's conclusion would be that he had killed his wife, tried to run far away, but realising it was futile had committed suicide. It was a logical conclusion for the police to make because they'd seen murder-suicides before, but neither Edith nor Hester believed he'd done it.

'I think that Arthur was murdered, too. At the same time as Louise probably, although it could be before or after,' said Edith. She had dark circles below her eyes. 'I just don't understand why there's only one body. Oh, wait a minute! Yes, I do. Arthur's body is hidden to frame him for the murder. I'm worried he was murdered in France; if he was, we'll never find him.'

They were walking near St Nicholas's church at the top of Arundel town. Linking arms as they walked, they enjoyed the windy morning, holding onto their hats. However, when Edith looked up to watch the clouds scudding across the heavens, she saw the buzzards low in the sky above the town. She pointed them out to Hester. They were real birds, but somehow, they seemed to signify for her when the natural world was about to overlap with the supernatural world. They were beautiful birds, but they looked so barbarous close up. They knew all about the cruelty of murder.

Edith couldn't stop her eyes following the birds circling and diving as the two women discussed how soon would be seemly to order a much-deserved G & T and light up some ciggies. They speculated on whether the police had traced the wedding-car hire firm yet.

The buzzards were above the Norfolk Arms as they walked down the hill, and Edith soon spotted why; leaning in the arch of the inn, creating a bright splash of scarlet in the street scene, was a hatless soldier in an old-fashioned uniform, smoking a clay pipe.

He was so solid and natural-looking that for a brief instant, Edith wondered if there was a play or a pageant in Arundel that day, and one of the actors had taken a break to smoke.

'Can you see that man in the red jacket in front of the hotel?' Edith asked Hester, who shook her head. She described the man to her cousin. He appeared to be waiting for them.

'I do hope we haven't woken up something, darling! I'll be too scared to sleep in that room. What happens if you can't get rid of him?' Hester pulled a face.

'I can feel that queer vibration in my head now...'

Edith could see the man in more detail as

they approached, although she couldn't make out his features, as his face seemed to be a blur. He wore a shiny white cross belt on his chest, painted with pipeclay, and his dark hair was fashioned with two little plaits dipped in tallow. She knew instinctively that he was the soldier who had come forward at the séance. She noticed his heavy, worn leather boots, and he turned to look at them as they drew near.

Edith was surprised that she wasn't in a trance and, equally, that he didn't fade away as her ghosts usually did. Instead, he suddenly walked to the edge of the pavement and headed across the road without warning, striding toward Tarrant Street.

She grabbed Hester's arm and started dragging her across the street, narrowly avoiding a baker's van, which claxoned loudly as it swerved to avoid them.

Hester shrieked. 'What on earth are you doing?'

'I can still see him on the other side of the road!' Edith said, raising her voice against the wind whipping up. 'He hasn't faded away. I can see him walking down the street. I think he means we should follow him. This could be important.'

Weaving amongst the shoppers trying to go about their daily business, Edith propelled Hester along the narrow pavement.

It was easy to see the soldier even though he was pretty far ahead of them because his red jacket stood out like a bright flag as he moved along the road.

'Sorry,' she apologised, after bumping into a woman in a tweed coat and felt hat as she propelled Hester along.

The soldier stopped in front of a shop display and turned to wait for them to catch up. They finally reached the window he was scrutinising, and as Edith's eyes followed, she noticed that he had no reflection. When she turned back to him, Willy, the soldier, had entirely disappeared.

The jewellers to which they had been led was a shop they had admired many times before, as it had a window hung with pads of earrings in gold and silver and laid out with trays of rings and brooches. Why the soldier had led them to this place was a mystery, but they both agreed it must hold some sort of clue.

'I asked him for help during the séance,' Edith reminded Hester. 'I don't think it's a coincidence that he's led us here.'

Neither of the women could think how the jewellers could be linked to the murders, and yet Edith felt that it *must* be connected in some way. 'You pretend to be interested in buying a dress ring,' she told Hester, '...and I'll try to get them talking. It might be difficult because we can't really ask direct questions.'

A bell sounded as they entered the little shop, which had a long glass counter that went around three sides of the room and protected the jeweller somewhat from physical assault. The counters held more jewellery trays, and through a little door to the left, the jeweller was visible in his workshop, bent over his bench, welding a broken gold bracelet. A woman, smartly dressed in a black frock, wearing a jeweller's loupe on a chain around her neck, greeted them warmly.

The shop was very tidy, the carpet well brushed, and the glass counters polished. Soon, a mat was placed on the counter by the woman, who turned out to be married to the jeweller. Hester was trying on cheap rings that all seemed to suit her long, slim hands. She'd gone for rings with semi-precious stones rather than diamonds and rubies so that the jeweller's wife could relax and not be too excited at the prospect of an important sale.

It turned out to be surprisingly easy to strike up a conversation, as the woman wanted her customers to feel at ease and stay in the shop as long as possible to look at the stock in the glass cabinets.

'I heard there was a murder in Arundel a few weeks ago?' Edith asked the shopkeeper, as Hester wiggled a silver and amethyst three-stone ring onto her finger.

'Oh, yes! The body of a woman was found up by the lake.' The woman shook her head sadly, although truth to tell, her business had also benefitted from the ghoulish sightseers who'd swelled the numbers of visitors to the town.

Hester held her hand up to the mirror, admiring the ring.

'That ring is a particularly lovely one.' The jeweller's wife was still watching Hester, but she seemed happy to chat about the murder just the same. 'They haven't identified the victim yet. I've heard that she was horribly mutilated.'

Hester took the amethysts off and tried on a dainty garnet ring in nine carat gold, which fit perfectly.

'That ring is even lovelier,' remarked the woman as Hester waved her hand around. The ring was somewhat more expensive than the first one.

'Have they caught anyone yet, for the murder?' Edith asked.

'They haven't charged anyone, but I hear on the grapevine that the police have a good idea who it is.'

She means David Forsythe, Edith, and Hester both thought to themselves. *But the police are wrong because Joanne is still alive.*

However, the pair nearly fell over when the woman behind the counter suddenly began talking spontaneously about Arthur and Louise Lamb.

'I do hope the police are wrong. I really do.' She lowered her voice as if frightened of being overheard. 'The man they suspect is ever such a nice man - I've known him ever since he was a child. We both worship at the Cathedral. I know all the family. He was here just a couple of days before that body was found, just before he got married. I can't believe it.'

She hadn't been talking about David Forsythe after all, but about Arthur Lamb. Hester asked, 'He was in *here*?' She gestured around the shop.

'Perhaps Madam would like to try on this ring? I'm sure it would suit you.'

The jeweller's wife had picked out an even more costly gold ring with citrine and peridot. She was evidently happy to talk to Edith but didn't want Hester distracted from a potential purchase. 'Who do the police think he murdered?' Edith asked quickly, as Hester went back to trying on rings.

'His new wife - but I can't believe *that*. They were in here together, and you could tell how happy they were.'

'Oh?' Edith looked at her encouragingly.

'They were telling me all about their new house and how they couldn't wait to start a family? His wife was...is so beautiful. And such a nice girl. He's brought her in here before, and they always end up buying something. Even if it's little.'

'And what did they buy when they came in before the wedding? Edith asked, adding, 'Oh, I *am* sorry. I shouldn't ask - but I'm so nosy!'
'Just some little gold hoops for one of their bridesmaids. But they didn't really come in to buy anything...'

There was a long pause as the jeweller's

wife wrestled with her professional conscience at giving away a customer's secrets and her urge to divulge some interesting gossip.

'I'm going to try those three rings again,' said Hester. 'I just need some time to think about my finances - I may be tempted to buy two of them.' She turned her head away to hide the fact that her face had drained of colour.'

'They came in to enquire about *selling* something,' the woman confided, 'and it was extraordinary. I know I shouldn't say, but you don't know them, and I'm sure it's of no interest to anybody important.'

CHAPTER 12

Edith stood there staring at the excited face of the jeweller's wife; she had an air of someone with something important to impart while Hester made a great show of being engrossed in the jewellery on the counter.

Edith was suddenly aware that there were lots of ticking clocks in the shop, mostly little carriage clocks for sale, and sat on a shelf next to them. She held her breath; she realised that she was about to discover what the ghostly soldier wanted her to know.

'The gentleman in question showed me the engagement ring his fiancée was wearing, and he asked me how much they might get for it, selling it second hand. They wanted to know whether I might be interested in buying it because they both trusted me to give them an honest price.'

Edith had a sudden flashback to the wedding reception and Louise coming over with the Sobranie cocktail cigarettes. On her left hand, she'd been wearing a large diamond cluster ring with a huge central stone surrounded by many smaller stones. Edith remembered how it had sparkled softly by the light of the chandeliers. Why on earth had Louise wanted to sell it? It was a beautiful ring, and besides it was her engagement ring?

'That *is* a strange thing, isn't it? To want to sell your engagement ring when you're just about to marry the man who gave it to you?'

'Perhaps. But the lady said that it weighed her hand down, and she found it rather ostentatious. It was too big for her liking, and she said she would prefer something more discreet. They would put the price difference towards some nice furniture for their new home.

The woman made a face and continued,

'There's no accounting for taste. She was extremely lucky to have an exceptional ring like that. You don't see them every day. Well, perhaps in a bigger town. Not around here.'

'Is that what was strange? That she wanted to sell it? Why didn't you buy it if you liked it so much?'

'I probably would have, if I'd have known in advance what the gentleman told me *after* I'd *already* given him a valuation! Perhaps I could've sold it to the Dowager Duchess of Norfolk at a *huge* profit. But as it was, I told him that I don't really get much trade for that sort of jewellery around here. I get a lot of visitors in here, and this was not a piece one buys on a whim.'

She glanced at Hester, who said, 'Don't mind me. Finish the story, and I'll make my choice afterwards. I shall take one of them.'

'Go on,' said Edith, 'What did he tell you that would have made you change your mind about buying it?' She was dying to know.

'I looked at it under the loupe for flaws, and my husband looked at it too, under his microscope. We measured it and weighed it for the carat, graded it for colour and clarity and looked at the cut, but when we wrote down a valuation and the sort of money they could expect to get for the ring, this gentleman was totally astonished. He told me that he'd bought it new from a reputable jeweller who works in Hatton Garden. He told me that he'd paid for it about a quarter of what I suggested it was worth and that the paperwork it came with, for insurance purposes, said something entirely different to what I'd told him.'

Edith looked bewildered. 'How could either you or the other jeweller have made such an enormous mistake about the ring?'

The woman drew herself up, looking extremely aggrieved.

'My husband and I have been in this business well over thirty years. We've a great deal of experience. This was not a new English ring at all. It looked like French workmanship to me, and it had a bit of age. The cut of the stones was excellent. The centre stone, alone, was over four carats and had twelve stones around it. The big stone was getting on for colourless, although the smaller ones had the slightest yellowish tinge under the loupe. They weren't flawless but the inclusions were very slight, and it had personality and class. You would overlook the imperfections unless you were a professional; they weren't visible to the naked eye. The diamonds were set in 22ct gold. It was an extremely valuable ring.'

'But the paperwork said differently?'

'The paperwork he had, downgraded the colour, clarity, carat, cut - everything, apparently.

That alters the value enormously. I told the gentleman to take it to Sotheby's auction house, as he'd probably get the best price at auction there. I wrote him out a new insurance valuation to present with the ring. He said he'd telephone as soon as he got back to the hotel, for an appointment when he returned from his honeymoon.'

'I expect he was pleased?'

The jeweller's wife shrugged her shoulders fatalistically.

'*He* was pleased, but when I realised how much less he *believed* it was worth, I wished he'd told me first. I'd have certainly made him an offer for about a third of his figure, factoring in my expenses and my profit. Anyhow, I think the police have made a mistake about him murdering his wife. I don't believe he has it in him to do a thing like that. He's a good catholic, too.'

'I'll take the garnet,' said Hester, interrupting. 'Please, can you put it aside for a day or two? My husband is coming down this weekend, and he'll come in and pay for it then.'

It had been no use trying to talk in the street - the wind was too strong, and there were too many pedestrians, so Edith and Hester hurried back to the hotel, eager to get out of the gale. A tall but decidedly skinny young policeman was almost blown into the archway of the Norfolk Arms at the same time as them. He looked down ruefully at the tulip petals on the ground and the bunch of colourful spring flowers he held in his hand.

'Oooh, thank you! Are those for me?' Asked Hester with a seductive smile. She always had a weakness for young men in uniform.

The constable, who would not have looked out of place behind a school desk, flushed pink at the attention of this elegant older woman with glossy brown hair and a perky little hat.

'I'm sorry, Madam,' he said, but then had a thought, 'unless you're Miss Edith Kershaw, that is?' It was Edith's turn to blush.

'*I'm* Miss Kershaw,' she said. 'Are those for me?' Her hand trembled as she took the bouquet, full of emotion. A card was also in an envelope with the flowers.

'Do the police run a floral delivery service on the side now?' Hester gave a cheeky grin. She was enjoying the constable's awkwardness, and he was a nice looking lad.

'Oh no, Madam. I've been sent to make enquiries in the tobacconists in Arundel, and CID told me to bring these over while I was about it.'

'Well, do thank him,' said Edith. It was incredible how a bunch of flowers could completely change one's outlook on life. Just maybe, her fate would not be to die a childless old maid after all? Once inside the warm hallway, she ripped open the note, eager to read the message, and her face changed.

'Darling! Whatever's the matter?' Hester's expression changed from flirtatious to one of surprised concern.

Edith couldn't speak. She was doing her best not to cry. Wordlessly, she handed her cousin the card that had come with the flowers.

Hester read the first lines out loud,

'To Edith, thank you for your pleasant company at supper yesterday evening, and we must do it again someday. I trust Mrs Denney has fully recovered from her bad head. I shall certainly follow your lead about the Sobranie cigarette, and I hope you enjoy the flowers as a thank you for it. Enjoy the rest of your holiday.'

It was signed *'Detective Inspector A. Stevens.'*

Hester was generally a person who was a resolute optimist in life, but she was momentarily floored by the note.

'...But he sent you beautiful flowers,' she said gamely after a VERY long pause.

Lunch was a miserable affair. Try as either of them might to get on to the subject of the Arundel murder and the new mystery surrounding Louise's engagement ring, the conversation just came back in a circle to Adrian Stevens, and Edith's disappointment.

'I don't understand it,' Edith said. 'We got on really well. I didn't even tell him I don't like horses. You can tell when someone's attracted to you, can't you? I could see that he 'liked me.' I know he rushed off at the end, but it wasn't meant to be a proper romantic date in the first place; he'd expected you to be there. I simply assumed that he would arrange to see me alone again while I was in Arundel, and we'd take it from there. I shouldn't have built things up in my mind. But ...' she went on,'... there's another problem.'

'The ring?'

'Yes. He doesn't like me interfering in the case, and he certainly wouldn't accept that we'd held a séance to ask for clues, so I don't know how to tell him about the ring? I'm certain it's a huge clue. The trouble is the police will never find it by themselves.' 'D'you think Louise was murdered for the ring? Why didn't somebody just steal it? They didn't have to murder two people for it.' Hester shook her head in disbelief.

'They were leaving to travel around a foreign country on their honeymoon - the bride and groom were just going to stop where the fancy took them,' Edith said. 'How could the murderer steal the ring once the honeymoon couple had left the country? The police need to find out if Arthur really did ring Sotheby's as soon as he returned from that jeweller's shop. And where did he buy that ring? I've heard of people inflating prices for insurance valuations but not under-selling a ring by such a huge amount of money. Why would you do that? Hatton Garden, the woman said. It all sounds very unlikely. Cousin Alma might know something about it.'

After they had laid down their knives and forks and had enjoyed a cup of tea in the snug, Edith asked Hester if she would mind if she took a nap, after the broken sleep the pair had experienced the night before.

'Fine,' said Hester, although she was tired herself. 'I have to pop to the post office,' she said, 'to buy some postcards for the children, and stamps. I'll be up at the end of the afternoon.' Intuitively, Hester knew that her cousin needed time alone to weep by herself over Adrian Stevens. 'I can amuse myself,' she said, 'writing all those wretched cards.'
Edith gave a pale smile.

The post office was not far from the hotel, in a picturesque building opposite the bridge. After choosing a selection of both monochrome and tinted pictures of Arundel, which mostly comprised of views of the castle, the lake, Town Square, or the riverbanks, Hester suddenly found her resolve; she asked the postmaster if she might send an urgent telegram, which must be marked Priority and guaranteed to be delivered as soon as humanly possible. Dictating the words for the telegram slip, sent to Detective Inspector Adrian Stevens at Chichester Police Headquarters, from Mrs. Hester Denney, she said 'WE HAVE DISCOVERED CRUCIAL INFORMATION TO SOLVE THE ARUNDEL CASE (*stop.*) PLEASE COME TO THE NORFOLK ARMS, ARUNDEL, AT 6 o'clock THIS EVENING (*stop.*) ORDER TAXI FOR LATE (*stop.*) TIME IS OF THE ESSENCE. (*stop.*) YOU MUST COME TODAY. (*stop.*) REPEAT (*stop.*) COME TO THE NORFOLK ARMS AT 6 O'CLOCK (*stop.*) SUPPER IS ON ME (*stop.*)

Hester looked around for a magazine to buy,

because Edith certainly wouldn't welcome her in their room, and she would have to spend the afternoon reading downstairs. There was nothing of interest to be had except a very old dusty copy of January's 'Britannia and Eve,' which somebody had failed to collect. Identifying with the cover, which showed an attractive girl with red lips, and white hands with red nails grasped around a large glass of champagne, she supposed that she could make do with all the short stories since the magazine did have a 'Complete Home and Fashion section.'

Hester eventually went upstairs to wake up her cousin around five thirty. She'd reserved their favourite table in the snug for 6pm. Edith's eyes were swollen and red, but she had slept, and she was hungry. She was still downcast, though, and simply wanted to go discreetly down the back stairs and collapse in an armchair.

Hester tried to persuade Edith to put on a pretty dress, powder, and lipstick, but her cousin was so depressed that she couldn't even rouse herself to brush her hair, let alone dress up for supper. Edith was a naturally fine boned, pretty woman, with lovely warm russet hair, but after an afternoon of quietly sobbing alone, she looked terrible. The thin skin under her pink rimmed eyes looked blue and the tension showed in her clenched forehead.

When they got into the snug, DI Stevens was already there. He'd arrived early, and the handsome 'Nijinsky' had shown him to the table Hester had reserved in advance, with three seats.

Adrian stood up from his leather armchair, expressionless, and proffered his hand.

The absolute rotter, thought Edith. She was none too keen on Hester, either, at this precise minute. It was obvious that her cousin had known that the detective was going to be there but hadn't warned her. She would certainly have refused to come downstairs had she known - looking, and feeling, as she did.

The conversation quickly got to the reason for Hester's telegram, over drinks. Stevens offered them a cigarette and lit up, cupping his hand around the lighter as he did so.

'So, there you have it,' Hester finished. She'd been recounting to him how her desire to buy a new ring had led them by, 'coincidence,' to find out the strange story about Louise's engagement ring.

'And you think that this ring might provide a motive for the murder?' Adrian was thoughtful.

He isn't accusing HER of interfering in his case! Edith tried not to feel bitter.

'The ring is worth an awful lot of money,' replied Hester, 'And money is often the motive for murder.'

Adrian Stevens shook his head slowly. 'I don't see why the changed value of the ring would make Arthur Lamb murder his new wife and run off with it. He owned the ring already, in a manner of speaking. His wife was happy for him to sell it, and he'd benefit from the money. Unless of course, he had a secret life and needed the money for a reason that he couldn't tell Mrs Lamb? He must have taken the ring with him when he disappeared into Italy.'

Edith was sat looking down at the table, sucking on her cigarette.

'We don't believe Arthur murdered his wife. Maybe somebody else found out the real value of the ring?' Hester looked very serious. 'And decided to murder Louise for it?'

To Edith's surprise, Adrian actually seemed to consider this when Hester came out with the idea. *He respects her opinion more than mine*, she thought angrily.

'Alright, let's think about this. I still think that the husband is the most likely suspect in a wife's murder, though...and there is the fact that we know he travelled abroad, and he's either gone into hiding or done away with himself. 'He paused, then went on, 'but there are some strange details to the case, I grant you. Let's look at it all from the beginning. When did Mr Lamb buy this engagement ring?'

'They got engaged two years ago,' said Hester. 'I presume that he bought the ring then. Louise's mother will know when she had it exactly.'

'And it was bought from a reputable jeweller, with paperwork, and it was properly insured, you say?'

'Yes. In Hatton Garden,' Hester said. 'You know? The area in London famous for jewellery? It's in Holborn, I think. Only there was a mistake, and Arthur paid a lot less for it than it was worth because the jeweller who sold it hadn't graded it correctly.

Diamonds are graded, you know. The woman in the shop will explain it to you.'

Adrian had taken out a little notepad with a gold propelling pencil attached to it and was taking notes, writing shorthand.

'You say that Mrs Lamb didn't particularly like this ring?' He asked, 'Did she usually wear it? Or was it kept in a box, d'you know?'

'Well, she was wearing it when they went to the jeweller's shop and at the wedding reception,' Hester said.

Edith made a mental note to suggest to Hester that they speak to Alma themselves, but she didn't say anything.

'I would imagine that her friends and family had all seen her wear it out on occasion, but she probably didn't wear it on trips to the post office or suchlike. That would make sense,' Hester continued.

The DI nodded appreciatively and made a note.

'So, the ring wasn't new to anybody close to her who was at her wedding. I doubt she'd be shouting from the rooftops how much it was worth. Especially not before the ring had been sold at auction...You're very quiet?' Adrian looked at Edith. *Oh, he HAS noticed then!* Edith felt her pink rimmed eyes burning.

'It would be interesting to know if Arthur Lamb telephoned Sotheby's for an appointment immediately, as he said he would, and if so, where from, and what he said during the conversation.

Perhaps someone listened in?' Edith answered grudgingly.

'Very good!' The detective replied, scribbling in his book. 'I'll get on to that. You're thinking like a proper detective now!'

Patronising so-and-so! Hester and I have found all the important clues for you, Edith thought.

'To sum up the ring: If Louise Lamb was murdered for it, then it had to be by somebody at the wedding reception who discovered the value of the piece. They were aware that Mrs Lamb was leaving for her honeymoon the next day, and they had to act quickly. But...' Adrian went on, '...why didn't the murderer wait until her return, to draw the police away from the wedding guests?'

'Whoever did it mutilated the body so you wouldn't know who the victim was for at least two weeks,' said Hester. She told him the theories that Edith and she had been discussing privately. 'It's given them time to hide their tracks. It was very convenient, Mrs Forsythe going missing at the same time. Have you found her yet?'

'No.' Said Adrian, 'Shall we go to supper? Don't worry about treating me; I'll get it on expenses. And the cab as well. After all, we're working on the case, and it's very helpful.'

'I shall just go and powder my nose,' said Hester, 'I'll see you two in the dining room.'

Adrian waited until Hester had disappeared out of sight before he spoke. 'Have I upset you in some way?' He looked genuinely perplexed. 'It's not like you to let Mrs Denney do all the talking.'

He must know why! Thought Edith.

'No?' She didn't like the petulant sound in her voice as she avoided his gaze.

'Look, I'm sorry I had to rush off yesterday evening. Tomorrow is Saturday and my day off. Perhaps we could do something then? Before you go home. It's going to be sunny tomorrow. I hope you're enjoying the flowers?'

'How do you know it'll be sunny? Are you psychic?' Edith immediately hoped she didn't sound sarcastic because she was starting to unbend.

'No. The wind has blown the rain clouds out to sea. It's generally sunny weather afterwards. Can I take you into the dining room?' He took her arm and steered her across the hallway.

By the time Hester returned to the dining room, she was thrilled to see Edith looking a whole lot happier and Adrian pouring her some wine. Edith looked quite pretty, although fragile, by the light of the candle on the table. Adrian Stevens was eager to continue to chat about the murder.

'The police should get their money's worth don't you think? If they're paying for our dinner,' he said by way of excuse.

'Have you found the wedding car hire firm yet?' Edith patted his arm naturally, without thinking.

'No,' said the detective, 'and that's another oddity. I've had every firm contacted for miles around, and nobody appears to have supplied the car for the Lamb's wedding. The family didn't even know that the first car was cancelled. Now, why did Mr Lamb cancel the car that was originally booked? And who did he hire instead?'

The waiter pulled out Hester's chair, as the detective poured her a glass. A pianist was playing classical music very quietly in the corner of the room. The low tinkling melody and the sound of silver cutlery and chinking glasses, made the room feel more sophisticated than the Swan Inn, although still cosy.

'The car certainly took them to the station,' the DI continued. 'The lady in the ticket office is adamant about the chauffeur dropping them off, and then parking the car and cutting off the noisy tin cans and placards, before driving away. The car then appears to have disappeared entirely. My men have not been able to find a hire car like that, unaccounted for.'

'We wouldn't be able to identify the chauffeur now,' mused Hester. 'He was wearing goggles, I remember, and a chauffeur's uniform and cap. The glass was thick. I was looking at the bride and groom. Besides, it's ages ago now.'

'What made Louise and Arthur, walk back to Arundel by the footpath instead of catching the train?' Edith asked. 'That Sobranie cocktail cigarette! I just know it was hers. Where did they go when they got back to the town? It's so strange - the town was full of their friends and family, who'd only just waved them off. How could they be hidden?'

They carried on talking, over the soup. Edith

had begun to look animated. Her freckled face had got back something of its bloom, and her eyes looked less swollen.

'There are a few possibilities then,' said Adrian, getting out his notebook again. 'Mr and Mrs Lamb secretly came back to Arundel of their own accord by mutual agreement for a common purpose we don't yet know. Or, Mr Lamb tricked Mrs Lamb into walking back to Arundel; he might even have forced her along the path. She was upset enough to smoke that cigarette while walking along, and she was allowed to do so. That's why I'm not so taken with the idea that a third person forced both of them along the path at gunpoint, say. Of course, Mrs Lamb might have smoked that cigarette before the wedding. How do we know they didn't walk along that route at some other time?'

'I can't understand why no witnesses saw them on the footpath,' said Edith. 'There must have been people coming and going to the station. The London train was either about to arrive or was about to depart for the coast. Louise's outfit stood out anywhere, but especially on a country footpath. They must have been carrying cases.'

'Quite a few people might have been carrying cases to and from the station,' said the DI, reasonably.

'Mrs Lamb's suitcase was found in a lay-by in France, by the way.' Hester sighed.

'I think the case was left where it would be found, otherwise why not throw it into a deep ravine? Someone had the time to set a trail,' Edith remarked.

'Perhaps the Lambs returned to Arundel to try to get help?' Asked DI Stevens. 'Have you considered that? And why did Arthur Lamb flee the country the next day, probably at least as far as Italy? If he didn't murder his wife, what or who did he fear?'

'And what happened to the ring?' Asked Edith. 'Perhaps if we find who has that ring, we can find our murderer.'

Adrian seemed in no hurry to rush off after supper. His cab was being hired from the Norfolk Arms, which also ran a taxi service, and he had asked them to make sure that one would be available to him when he was ready.

'Won't Mrs Brown be annoyed?' Edith asked tartly.

The DI ignored her tone. 'I warned her that my meeting might finish very late.'

They had returned to the snug for a cigarette after their supper, and the chat had turned once again to the ring and its possible role in the murder.

'We need to find out where it came from,' said Edith. 'Cousin Alma and Arthur's parents might know. Please don't send a policeman again. Hester and I are family, I'm sure that we'll find out a lot more than the police could.'

'I agree we need to find that ring,' said Adrian.

'You couldn't sell it openly if it had been recently stolen from a murdered corpse. Trouble is - it could be anywhere by now.'

'Not just *anywhere,*' Hester murmured, remembering what the jeweller's wife had said. 'Not every jewellery shop would have a market for a ring like that. And it needs a place where they won't ask too many questions about its provenance.'

'Brighton.' The name just popped into Edith's head without bidding.

'Brighton would certainly be the sort of place to fence a ring like that. Brighton is famous for buying art objects, no questions asked. I know!' Adrian looked from one to the other. 'We could have a lovely day at the seaside tomorrow? It's my day off. We could look around Brighton's jewellers and antique shops and see if we spot the ring for sale?'

He ran his fingers through thick, sandy hair.

There was a folded bit of paper on the table, which none of them remembered seeing when they sat down. The others didn't think it odd that they hadn't noticed it before; they had been engrossed in their conversation. Edith picked it up and turned it over and immediately felt a vibration behind her eye. She saw she was holding a tourist brochure for Brighton. *That is certainly the right place* she thought.

'Just the same,' said Hester later, when she'd finished putting in her curlers and had piled on the Ponds, 'that ring is so valuable that whoever that murderer is, they wouldn't get a fortune for it from a dodgy Brighton second hand jeweller. It's not a motive for murder.'

Edith slipped on a black velvet sleep mask. 'Maybe this isn't about how much you could get for that ring...' she suggested, from the twin divan.

'Perhaps it was to stop Arthur keeping that appointment with Sotheby's?'

CHAPTER 13

The next morning felt fresh and bright, and you could feel the warmth from the sun even as early as breakfast. DI Adrian Stevens had been correct; the wind had blown the rain clouds far away.

Edith and Hester set off for Arundel Station before eight o'clock, waving a cheery bye-bye to Nijinsky before crossing the bridge over the Arun on foot. A slight haze hung over the river and a blackbird sang down on the wharf, as they headed for the main road and the footpath to the station. They were both excited at the prospect of a day out by the seaside at what felt like the beginning of summer.

Hester felt very guilty at playing gooseberry for the day, particularly as Phillip would be arriving by car in Arundel that afternoon; he had come to collect her but would stay a couple of days. She had secretly become frightened to stay in her bedroom alone because she felt that the ghostly William, the Napoleonic soldier, might be watching her or hiding under the divan ready to grab her ankles. She was looking forward to changing rooms for a double bed with her husband that evening.

Edith was very happy to be travelling to Brighton by train. It was something she rarely did, usually taking the little Austin. Still, the rhythm of the train's pistons, the high-pitched whistle, and the smell of smoke and cinders from the chimney as they raced through the countryside, thrilled her.

They made the short journey to Barnham to change lines, admiring the view of the castle as they left. It was silhouetted against a blue cloudless sky, and if the buzzards were out hunting, they were hidden on the other side of the park.

The sound of the birds, who were out in force on such a glorious morning, was momentarily drowned out by the puffing of the engine as their train chugged into the station. Adrian had already boarded at Chichester, and he stuck his head out of the window as the train drew in, and then helped them up the steep steps into the closed compartment and slammed the door behind them.

Edith had a silly grin on her face as she smiled at Adrian. It was the first time she'd ever seen him dressed in casual clothes for a day at a beach resort and he looked rather extraordinary. His long legs were draped in high waisted baggy slacks, held up with braces as was the fashion, over a thin knitted polo shirt. Unfortunately, he had somehow added both a bright fair isle sleeveless jumper and a spotted cravat. His straw trilby, with its striped hatband, sat in the luggage rack above his seat, and his beige sports jacket hung on a peg provided for that purpose. *'I'll have to dress him',* Edith started to think fondly, but then stopped; she was going too fast again.

Adrian in turn grinned back at Edith and Hester. It was a welcome day away from his responsibilities at Chichester police headquarters, to be travelling to the seaside on a warm sunny day, with two attractive women. Hester looked so pretty in her ruffled floral summer dress, and Edith in her simple grey frock, both adorned with white gloves, hats, and pearls.

He pointed at a flowery fabric bag on the seat next to him.

'Mrs Brown has been very kind. She made us some ham and pickle sandwiches, and cucumber ones with peanut butter dressing, and some fruit cake. And she's put in some bottles of ginger beer.'

'Oh,' said Hester. 'Edith and I wanted to eat fish n'chips at the end of the pier. Edith says there's a lovely palm court restaurant there, where you have a simply marvellous view of the sea.'

'Yes,' said Edith. 'It's divine! There's an orchestra that plays tea dances, and a barman of colour who shakes up cocktails like it's an american speakeasy.'

The detective frowned, embarrassed. 'I did tell Mrs Brown that we'd find somewhere to eat, but she pointed out that they charge way over the normal prices in a place like Brighton, to catch all the Londoners coming down to the seaside. When I got up this morning, she'd gone to all the trouble to make a picnic especially for us, to save us all wasting our money. Cucumber and peanut butter are my absolute favourite, too.'

'With ginger beer?' Hester wrinkled up her nose.

'Mrs Brown says that if it's too hot, or too windy on the beach, we can probably find a shelter on the promenade to eat the sandwiches in.'

'Maybe we can eat the sandwiches on the front, and just have a cocktail at the Palm Court?'

Edith tried to be tactful, although she had rather hoped for Sole Mornay at an elegant restaurant with white tablecloths and French waiters. She imagined with horror crumbs or a dollop of pickle falling in her lap. She supposed that many people her mother's age had lived through rationing after the Great War and couldn't get over being parsimonious. That wasn't Clara's case of course; Edith knew very well that Clara would never have eaten peanut butter sandwiches in a public shelter. Clara would have wanted afternoon tea at the 'Grand', or the 'Metropole', or one of the other comfortable sea front hotels with their luxurious powder rooms. Afterall, where could you powder your nose when eating sandwiches on the seafront? She had no idea, and she was sure Hester hadn't either. Edith glanced at their white gloves and wondered how you might wash your hands if you had to take your gloves off and didn't have a powder room? It all sounded too ghastly.

The journey passed quickly in excited chatter. They had started off by talking about the case, while they were alone in the compartment. However, they had very soon passed Worthing and the nearer they got to their destination, the faster the train filled up with day trippers, and they had changed the subject.

The conversation was easy and unforced, and it was a welcome change of mood for all of them.

Adrian told them about his dog, Monty, of whom he was evidently very fond. Edith had never had any pets, because Clara had never particularly liked animals, but she tried to imagine trying to bond with a small dog and thought that she would certainly try to like it for Adrian's sake. It would have been easier if she were more like Hester who was already cooing over the detective's description of the cuddly creature.

They came into Hove station, with the DuBarry Perfumery Company and its beautiful new mosaic panels sat behind the platform, and the crammed train slowed to a crawl as it puffed its way the short distance to Brighton station. To their left the South Downs were visible, littered with terraced houses all the way up to the racetrack.

The train chugged into the vast blackened-glass covered terminal, still belching smoke.

Hester wasted no time in buying a 'kiss me quick' hat from a souvenir seller, come to greet the weekend crowds at the barrier before they even had time to leave the station. There was a Tourist Information kiosk on the concourse, and they soon had a list of jewellers located in the town. The jewellers were mostly to be found in the Lanes area of tiny narrow old streets, which formed the original Brighton.

Although the town was busy on this sunny Saturday, it wasn't the holiday season yet, and nor was it a race day, so there was plenty of room on the open top deck of the little tram which carried them down from the station to the Aquarium, on the seafront. The tourists sauntered up and down the straight road between the station and the sea, on foot, by motor car, and by tram, unaware of the slum streets close by.

Hester, high spirited, started to sing 'What Shall We Do With The Drunken Sailor,' making Adrian pull his hat down over his face - although underneath it, he had a grin.

The sea shimmered with silver which matched the silver metal railings along the promenade. They found a café overlooking the cobbled beach and began to decide on a plan over a cup of tea.

'Do let's have fish n' chips on the pier later!' Hester pleaded with them.

'After we've done what we came for,' Edith said, firmly. The mysterious appearance of the Brighton brochure in the snug had made her feel, intuitively, that Louise's ring was in Brighton; Edith was sure she was being led to find it. Increasingly, she trusted her instincts and the spirit world to help her, although she wasn't sure how they would find the exact shop. They couldn't hold a séance and she hadn't drawing materials, and she felt that Willy's spirit was bound to the Norfolk Arms. Nevertheless, she was sure that she could find the ring and that it would lead them to the murderer. She didn't dare mention anything psychic to Adrian, though.

'We'll visit all the jewellers that we can,' suggested Adrian, 'starting with this list.' He gestured at the list the woman in the kiosk had given him. He might have been on a day off, but he was still going to approach their task like a policeman. 'We'll all check out the windows, and Edith and I will pretend to be a couple shopping for an engagement ring.'

'Aye, Aye, Sir!' Hester said, giving a playful salute which knocked her hat over one eye.

Edith stood up and leaned over Adrian taking off his spotted cravat in a rather familiar manner. He suppressed a giggle mid-way between embarrassment and pleasure at having a woman fussing over him in such a proprietary manner.

'I'm not pretending to be engaged to a man in a fair isle jumper and spotted cravat,' she said.

They began walking back along the esplanade, enjoying the weather and the colourful crowds, Hester in her lilac flowery dress with its puffed sleeves, and her Kiss Me Quick hat. A brass band on the band stand played 'Ta-ra-ra Boom de ay' for a crowd of pensioners sitting in striped deckchairs on the cobbles.

Crossing the road, they entered the lanes, and soon found the first Jewellers shop on the list. The rings were laid out in trays in the window. There were trays of diamonds, and trays of rubies and sapphires. The more expensive rings were in boxes, but nothing resembled Louise's ring.

'Are you certain you would recognise it?' Adrian asked Edith.

'Yes.' She had only seen the ring once, but the size of it, the cluster design, and the particular soft glitter of the way it had reflected the light stood out in her memory.

'The jeweller's wife in Arundel told us the details about it,' said Hester.

'Shall we go in and ask?' Adrian looked at Edith. 'Hester - wait outside.'

They pushed open the door of the shop and crossed the plush carpet, both enjoying the novelty of acting like an official couple; a couple making a commitment to marriage. It felt like a rehearsal.

The detective took her arm, at first shyly, but then said with confidence to the assistant., 'We're looking for an engagement ring.'

The man in a frock coat and old-fashioned wing collar, who was standing behind a high mahogany counter smiled and licked his lips.

'Diamonds?'

Adrian looked at Edith appreciatively in her simple grey dress and at her russet hair.
'Certainly,' he replied. 'Big diamonds! The biggest you've got.'

The assistant swallowed, but after summing up Adrian's sartorial taste, appeared slightly wary.

'Does Sir have a budget? If Sir would prefer to write this down discreetly, then he can do so.'
Edith turned her limpid grey eyes on Adrian and smiled at him adoringly.

'No budget,' he said authoritatively.

The assistant came back with a tray of expensive diamond solitaires and placed them on a black velvet lined tray. He picked up his loupe.

Edith pursed her lips and made a show of gazing into Adrian's blue eyes. She ignored the rings on the table.

The assistant hopped a bit from foot to foot and, enjoying his discomfiture and Adrian's eyes even more, Edith lowered her eyelashes and gazed lovingly up at the detective. Who cared if she was overacting? *But I'm not acting*, she thought.

'Those diamonds aren't nearly big enough,' she told her pretend betrothed, ignoring the assistant. 'Besides, I'm looking for a cluster. A *big* centre stone and twelve small stones.'

The man in the frock coat whisked away the solitaires and was back in an instant with some boxes of diamond cluster rings.

'If Madam would like to try some on?' He gave a half bow and placed a mirror in front of her. Edith swept the tray with a glance.

'Any of these?' Adrian searched her face for a reaction.

She shook her head.

'Is this all you've got?'

The assistant looked as if he might cry.

'Perhaps, if Madam were to try some on? They look totally different on the hand to how they look in the box, Sir. Are there any *you* like, Sir?'

'No, I'm sorry,' the detective said. 'The lady can't see exactly what she's looking for. I'm afraid we'll have to carry on searching elsewhere.'

Edith and Adrian didn't look at each other when they were back on the pavement outside, but rather made a big thing of asking Hester what *she'd* been doing whilst they'd been inside the shop.

Something had definitely passed between them inside the jewellers, and they both felt it. The pair had both enjoyed their role play and were quite eager to continue to pose as an engaged couple for the next couple of hours as they grew emotionally closer and physically comfortable, against a backdrop of seagulls, shop assistants, and diamond rings.

It was Hester who started getting agitated first. It was not so much that she was increasingly feeling like a lemon while her two companions became more and more absorbed in each other as she waited for them outside the shops, but she knew that her husband was arriving in Arundel that afternoon. Hester wanted to eat fish n' chips on Brighton Palace Pier, drink a gin and tonic, and have a paddle along the waterfront before she went home, and time was going on without the diamond ring being found. She was beginning to doubt the ring was in Brighton at all. Surely that Brighton brochure on the table in the snug had been there all along, put down by one of the many tourists who passed through the Norfolk Arms? It was after they had visited all the jeweller's shops on their list, and a handful more besides, without finding Louise's elusive ring, that Edith was surprised to spot an antique shop and gallery selling the sort of Art she had concluded that nobody liked except herself. The shop had an attractive burgundy, cream, and gold exterior and was on a street which they must have passed multiple times, without noticing it because they had been focused on something totally different. Edith recognised various abstract paintings as being by a local artist she admired, but also small artworks which looked to be by European artists and interested her enormously.

'Do you mind if I have a browse in here?' Edith asked her companions.

Hester pulled a face. 'Must you darling? Have we got time? I want to powder my nose, and I can hardly walk into any of these hostelries, a respectable woman on my own. I'm starving hungry, too. And I don't mean for curling sandwiches...well, they must be curling now, if they were made hours ago.'

She could see that Adrian wasn't interested in the paintings either and wanted to get away, but Edith was determined to go in. She hadn't known this shop was here although she often visited Brighton, and perhaps the owner might be interested in her own work?

'Why don't you two go quickly to the Old Ship hotel on the front and have a glass of something and a cigarette? Then Hess can use the Ladies powder room to freshen up. I'm perfectly fine on my own for a bit.'

Both Hester and Adrian looked relieved and hurried off in the direction of the sea.

Edith pushed open the dark red door and beat her way through the potted palms to the back of the shop where a man was arranging some antique candlesticks with cream candles, on a black lacquer table. He turned around to greet her, and it was with a shock that they both recognised each other at the same time; the man was David Forsythe.

I'm not supposed to know that his wife's missing and he's under police surveillance she thought quickly. The Bounder greeted her with an oily smile.

'Miss Kershaw, from the wedding in Arundel.' He looked at her admiringly. 'You're looking very well, I must say. Dressed for the splendid weather.'

CHAPTER 14

Hester's fake diamond ring was undoubtedly a quality copy of a fine, platinum, three-stone ring with elegant baguette cut stones on either side of a square central stone. It suited her long, tapered fingers.

'It actually cost a lot less than the garnet ring because it's copper with a thin cover of gold, and the stones are glass - well, french paste, but apparently that's just pulverised glass. The assistant told me that they sell absolutely loads of them, darling. You can't don them every day, but they're perfect for wearing on holiday when you don't want to worry about the chambermaids stealing your diamonds from your hotel room. The man who makes them is a real artist; he also makes whopping big rings to impress everybody at Brighton tea dances.'

Talk of diamonds led them back to the Bounder, although they had waited until they were passed Worthing, and had the train compartment to themselves again, before they discussed the case.

'It can't be a coincidence that he directed us to the very shop where the ring from the Arundel murder has ended up,' said Edith. 'I mean David Forsythe was at the wedding where Louise was last seen wearing that ring. Heck! - He's even the police suspect for her murder, and he recommended that jewellers to me, yet he appears to be totally innocent of the crime.'

DI Adrian Stevens mused. 'Yes... why would

he direct us to important evidence that would create a link between himself and the murder?'

Edith thought about it.

'Because the ring has had stones swapped out, and he thought we wouldn't be able to recognise it?'

'I was watching the assistant's face,' said Adrian. 'We were holding the two parts of the same stolen ring - if you're right - but the man's eyes didn't even blink when we mentioned Forsythe. He didn't associate the two. I've got enough experience of police interrogations to pick up on minute reactions.'

'Well, maybe we'll find out next week...' Edith said.

She was referring to the telephone call Adrian had made to the East Sussex police headquarters at nearby Lewes, whilst she and Hester had weaved their way through the colourful deckchairs to paddle in the sea after their fish and chips.

Frazer's, the jeweller's shop, would soon have a couple of constables guarding it, front and back, until the premises could be emptied of stock and the staff interviewed. The police would start by going through the paperwork and the jewellery in the secondhand window.

In the meantime, they all agreed that Edith, Hester, and Phillip would pay a visit to Cousin Alma to find out more about the ring's provenance. Adrian had been worried about getting into trouble for discussing the case with the two women. However, he agreed that visiting the seaside on his day off, with two attractive companions, wasn't breaking any rules.

Hester had decided to buy a costume ring and he had stumbled across evidence by chance, he would write in his report; the cousins merely helped to identify the diamonds with which they were familiar. He really couldn't stop the two young women from visiting Alma, their own relative, whilst in the area, suggested the Detective Inspector, relaxed.

It was Phillip who drove to Chichester the next afternoon after lunch, blinking his eyes at the sunlight. Edith hadn't rung Clara to tell her about the visit since she knew that her mother would try to dissuade her from bothering her cousin. There hadn't even been time to warn Alma of their visit, but Edith and Hester decided that the best thing they could do for her was to solve the mystery of Louise's murder, and for that, they would need her help.

With some trepidation, they knocked at the door of Oakdene, a pretty Edwardian detached house in a wide, tree-lined avenue. They were uncertain of their reception, not knowing what to expect from Alma's state of mind, and aware that they might have called at a bad time. It was, therefore, a surprise that Alma welcomed them in with a smile. She appeared almost normal as she sent the teenage maid hurrying off for pots of tea and plates of biscuits.

I shouldn't be surprised, thought Edith. *This generation of women were tough old birds who had lived through a world war and all its deprivations. They had been used to loss and bereavement and had stuck on their lipstick and jet brooches, rolled up their sleeves and jolly well got on with it.*

Alma showed them into the front parlour, and they sat around the large walnut table on heavy, carved wooden chairs.

Photographs of Louise in silver frames adorned the sideboard, sitting in the shade of an enormous aspidistra. Edith noticed that there were none of the ravishing young woman on her wedding day, and none of her with Arthur.

Edith's eyes scoured the pictures quickly and soon found what she was looking for; there was a beautiful portrait of Louise posed in an armchair with her hands at the forefront of the picture. Her left hand stroked the head of a lovely white Persian cat, and the enormous diamond ring was sharply in focus. It clearly wasn't an accident; Louise had wanted to show off her valuable new engagement ring.

They exchanged niceties as the maid poured their tea into bone china cups, but it was inevitable that the conversation would soon turn to Louise.

'The worst thing,' said Alma as she raised her cup, her little finger stuck out at an odd angle, 'is that I can't hold a funeral as the body is not yet able to be formally identified as Louise. I'm sure that it *is* her, and the police think it is, but there's no proof that it definitely is. We hope the police can find the evidence to resume the inquest. Apparently, another woman is missing after the wedding.'

'But *you* think that it's her?'

Edith knew the body *was* Louise but couldn't tell Alma about the séance and the ghostly soldier.

'I can feel it in my bones,' Alma said. 'Louise

would never stay away willingly and cause me, and her sister, this upset. Besides, the police say she didn't use her passport to get on the ferry; Arthur picked up the hire car alone, and he threw Louise's suitcase into a lay-by in the middle of France. It's quite clear to me that he's murdered her all right.'

Edith was astonished how, like David Forsythe, Alma had seemingly no trouble laying the murder at Arthur's door. She thought back to the wedding and how besotted and in love the bridegroom had looked. How was it that people were so ready to jump to the worst conclusions about him with no proof?

'Did you know Arthur well?' Hester asked, thinking a similar thing.

Phillip blinked his watery eyes and had another biscuit. The big fluffy white cat in the photo had come to sit upon his lap and was now raking his claws down Phillip's new flannel trousers, but he didn't want to interrupt except to mutter, 'You didn't want to have any more offspring, did you dear?' in his wife's general direction.

'I *thought* I knew Arthur well,' replied Alma. 'I met him so many times over the last couple of years, and I *thought* he was *wonderful*. He was such a good catch for Louise. But I realise now that I was taken in by him, and I didn't know any of the things being told to me now. It appears that Louise *did* have an inkling that something was wrong with Arthur, but she didn't confide in *me*. One's mother's always the last to know.'

Edith sipped her tea carefully, 'What have you found out about him since the couple went missing?' Alma gave a look, dramatically rolling her eyes and acting for all the world like a silent movie star, and it was suddenly apparent from where Louise had got her good looks.

'It appears that Arthur had a terrible temper on the quiet. He was very controlling, and he tended to be jealous. Caroline says that Louise had a few misgivings before the wedding, but she thought that it was too late to call everything off. She was too ashamed to confide in her sister. If only she had!' *Caroline.* The name rang a bell somewhere but neither Edith, Hester, nor Phillip were able to place it.

'Who's Caroline?' Edith knew she had heard the name somewhere.

'One of Louise's oldest friends. She's been ever so good to me since this all happened. She seems as much upset by it all as I am. She told me that she feels dreadfully guilty; She introduced them, you see.'

Alma passed round the plate of biscuits while everybody's eyes turned to the silver frames on the sideboard.

Edith gave a start. She hadn't noticed it at first, but there was a photograph of a group of fashion-conscious teenage flappers in too-short skirts and cloche hats. In the centre of the picture was an adolescent Louise with blonde bobbed hair and a long bead necklace, but standing next to her, shorter by a head, was the mysterious dark woman from the wedding, who had given Edith such a queasy feeling. Her big brown eyes stood out, like dark almonds, from under the brim of her hat. Although much younger, she was easily recognisable.

Caroline! Mrs Caroline Wren. They had rather forgotten about her after the embarrassment of causing Detective Inspector Stevens so much trouble by wrongly insisting that she was the murder victim. Edith pointed to the frame and heard Hester inhale and Phillip mutter something.

'We all remember her from the wedding. That's Caroline, isn't it? On Louise's right? A striking woman. Ever so well dressed.'

'More tea?' Alma picked up the china pot.

'Yes, she *is* well dressed. She wears the Parisian fashions you know? She came and helped Louise pick her trousseau and going away outfit before the wedding; they went shopping in Chichester. She's very, very, rich. Her husband's a philatelist, you know. You wouldn't think there could be so much money in rare stamps, but there is. He travels around the world to auction houses buying and selling stamps. I believe they have a shop in London. Holborn, I think. But she told me that he sells most of his finds to private clients by correspondence.'

Hester waited until everybody had a fresh cup poured. Her thin face looked pink and excited, but she tried to appear casual.

'Caroline introduced Louise to Arthur, you said?'

'Yes. Caroline's husband, Edward, was at school with Arthur. There's a gang of them. They all went to Lancing College - the public school near Shoreham. Caroline met Eddie at a country club dance down Worthing way, I believe, and introduced Louise to his friend. They actually started courting after Caroline and Eddie's wedding.'

The white cat suddenly hissed, raised its fur, and dug its claws into Phillip's leg, making him yelp and repress some choice vocabulary. He had tried to surreptitiously give the feline the heave-ho, hidden by the tablecloth, but the cat was having none of it.

'Do be quiet Phillip,' Hester said. 'Alma's talking.'

'How long did they know each other before they got engaged?' Edith wondered. 'You don't mind us asking, do you? I expect the police have been asking you all sorts of questions.'

'It's on my mind the whole time, so I'm happy to have the opportunity to talk,' said Alma. 'The neighbours try and avoid the subject. I only wish I knew what made him suddenly snap - and so quickly after the wedding! I suppose they knew each other around four years before they got married, and they were engaged a couple of years ago.'

'Quite long enough to get to know someone.'

'We were thrilled because Arthur was very ambitious and from a good family. He was a banker. Yes, we were very pleased. We didn't see that other side to him...but of course, he *would* hide it from *us*.'

'Louise had a beautiful engagement ring,' said

Hester encouragingly.

Alma pulled another face. 'It was, but she never really liked it. She said it was too big and heavy and caught on everything. Arthur surprised her with it, and I think she'd rather have chosen her own. She was proud to wear it to get engaged, and for special occasions, but they were going to sell it and buy a smaller one to wear with the wedding band...she told me at the wedding. The police have never found it.'

'Do you know where Arthur bought the ring?' The answer was important to them, and she crossed her fingers under the table.

'Louise said that he had contacts in the jewellery business and somebody did him an excellent deal,' Alma said. She shrugged, 'I expect *his* family know, but they're not talking to *me*. I don't think I could bear to talk to *them* anyway.'

They met up with Adrian Stevens at a hotel cocktail bar in Chichester when he had finished work.
The excuse was so they could tell him everything they had discovered that the police hadn't, although Edith simply wanted to see him. She had spent the night throwing off the bed covers as her temperature soared at the thought of his pale blue eyes twinkling, sighing heavily, and constantly turning over. She was sorry that Hester had moved into another room with Phillip, and she couldn't spend the night talking about Adrian and how divine he was.

'I'm surprised our beau Detective Inspector agreed to meet us in such a swanky place,' said

Hester, as Phillip steered the Minx over to the meeting place,' and motherly Mrs Brown didn't pack him off with a flask of ginger beer to save pennies.'

'What a good idea!' Phillip was still reeling at Hester's bar bill at the Norfolk Arms, which he would have to pick up.

'Alma Matthews was bound to be less guarded with us than with a policeman,' Edith reassured Adrian after they'd recounted the information they'd extracted from Louise's mother. 'She probably didn't want the body to be her daughter's when you first interviewed her. She's resigned to it now, and she just wants Louise to be formally identified and the inquest to resume so she can hold a funeral. She's afraid the police will bury her as a Jane Doe.'

They were drinking highballs in the lounge bar of the hotel after a wander around the outside of the nearby cathedral, and a look at the market cross. Edith and Hester were both hoping that Adrian and Phillip would bond and that they might spend some time together as a foursome in the future. Edith and Adrian were also happy that Hester was no longer a gooseberry because they hoped to get some time on their own together. The trip to Brighton seemed to have cemented their mutual attraction and dispelled the detective's doubts.

'It's Caroline and Edward Wren you need to re-interview,' Edith told him. 'I know people aren't always how they appear on the surface, but I can't believe Arthur was the person the Wrens have convinced Alma, he was. Why would the Wrens be so certain that he murdered Louise, and tell Alma all sorts of stories? Arthur was one of their closest friends. Why would they be friends with him if he was so dangerous?'

'Yes,' agreed Hester. 'We don't believe Louise courted with Arthur for four years and never let slip that she was scared of him or had doubts about marrying him. We can't speak to Mrs Wren because we don't know her - but the police can.'

'I'm staying out of it,' said Phillip, stuffing his pipe with shag, 'all I can say is that I wouldn't have blamed Arthur Lamb if he'd truncated the life of that Persian pussy and had it stuffed; bloody saintly psychopath - if he was one.'

'But let's face it,' said the detective, 'none of you know Mr Lamb. There's no proof he's dead and isn't half the way around the world by now. It appears that the people who knew him well, thought he was capable of the crime and had already shown behavioural warning signs towards our potential victim.' He went on, 'by the way - Frazer's is shut and the police at Lewes, who are in charge down that way, have seized the rings you identified and are trying to see if that big diamond is on record as stolen. That is a hard job. They're also going through the second - hand display. They're conducting interviews with staff down there.'

It took Adrian Stevens a couple of whisky and sodas to pluck up the courage to invite Edith outside to take the air, as he sensed she was waiting for him to make a move; the atmosphere between the two was electric. He knew that he was expected to kiss her, and that expectation had led to him not making an ironic comment when the name of Caroline Wren came up, nor raising an objection when Edith announced that she would be interfering even further in his case by visiting the Lamb family the next day.

Edith and Adrian had turned to each other the minute they had got outside, and he steered her purposefully behind a wall and out of sight before kissing her as she had dreamed he might. Afterwards, she leaned against him, drifting, her head on his chest.

Above the red brick walls and parked roadsters gleaming with wax and polish in the low electric light, the black sky shone with stars, and the Milky Way spiralled across the universe.

'I can't stay late.' He was stroking her dark auburn hair. 'I've been out late a few times recently, and Mrs Brown is cross because my daughters are getting fed up, and I promised my wife I'd always try to get home before they went to bed.'

CHAPTER 15

'Your *wife*?' Edith was stunned. It felt as if the world turned black. She didn't know how she would be able to walk back into the hotel lounge after making such a first-class fool of herself. She stood up straight, disorientated, trying consciously to look proud - and then she turned to go.

She regretted her reticence in not questioning Adrian about his past sooner. Edith hadn't wanted to interrogate him about his present romantic situation; it had seemed rather presumptuous that it was any of her business. The Brighton trip had appeared to confirm that he was a bachelor - even Hester assumed he was, after spending a whole day in his company and seeing how the pair interacted. He didn't act like a shifty cheat.

Adrian could see her distressed reaction and gave a low laugh, full of pleasure.

'I'm a widower,' he said, pinching her teasingly. 'What about you? We've never discussed how two such people as ourselves,' he laughed again,' came to be single? You *are* single, too, I take it? You don't have a secret beau?'

Edith told him about Michael, and how her fiancé, the brave test pilot, had died in a banal domestic accident falling off a ladder while clearing out the guttering on his house.

'I used to jokingly call him 'Biggles,' she said. Have you read The White Fokker? But the thing is he didn't just enjoy dangerous things; he liked nature and poetry, too. He always supported my painting, and of course, art can be dangerous too. Perhaps we both liked dangerous art?'

'Eh??'

Adrian filled her in quickly on how his beloved wife, Minty, had died of breast cancer around the same time as Mick, leaving him to bring up two young teenage daughters with the help of the live-in housekeeper, Mrs Brown.

'Minty was a wonderful person, too. I knew her all her life; she grew up on the farm next door and we used to hunt together as children, even. We got married when I was only eighteen, and she was sixteen. I suppose that the Great War happened almost straight away...and then we lost a couple of babies. John, the first one, was three.' He looked off into the distance and said, rather rapidly, 'Sophie, our eldest, wasn't born until 1920 when I came home, and Annabella ...Bella ...three years later. It's been a struggle with the girls, but Mrs Brown has stepped in and brought them up for me, really. You know, it's been incredibly tough sometimes... my job's very demanding. It's Minty who employed Mrs Brown, and Bella was only two at the time. So, the girls have always known her. She looked after Minty when she was bed-ridden; it was a dreadful time! I'll always be grateful to her. You'll like her. She'll always have a home with my family.'

'Has she no children of her own?'

'Good lord, no! I don't know if she ever had a

suitor. The 'Mrs' Is a courtesy title. You know, to give her more status. I insisted on it because she runs the house. I think my children are her children now, and that seems to be enough for her.'

They hugged each other in silence, with a warm complicity. They had things in common now that they would be able to each understand, and sympathise with, in the future. Bereavement would be a bond.

'Why didn't you mention your children before?'

'Because I wasn't certain I was ready for... someone else...and it didn't seem right.'
Adrian kissed her again, more tenderly this time.

'Alright...I was afraid it would put you off. But you'll have to meet them...if our 'friendship' develops. We come as a package.'

'Shall we go back in? The others will be asking questions,' Edith said, squeezing his hand. He already had children! It was something she'd never considered. She had always wanted to be a mother though, and here was a ready-made family. It certainly didn't put her off.

The next day, Phillip brought his car round to stop on the round driveway in front of the spacious detached country house which nestled between West Worthing and Arundel. The mansion was made of Victorian red brick and flint. Vast banks of rhododendrons guarded the front of the building. They were just coming into bloom and reflected in the mullioned windows staring out from the smart frontage. It was clearly inspired by an earlier, mythical, romantic age.

Edith suggested that Hester and Phillip sit in the motorcar whilst she walked up to the black front door and used the heavy brass knocker to try and gain an invite inside, unsure of the reception they might get. They had no obviously good reason to intrude on private grief.

The servant who answered the door was dressed in uniform and evidently not a local girl who came in to 'do' for the day, as Cousin Alma's maid had been, but was a live-in member of the household, in service. She regarded Edith with a suspicious air after Edith introduced herself as a relative of Louise's and quickly came back with the master of the house, who didn't invite her in but stood on the doorstep as if barring her route. He stood there silently, waiting to hear what she had to say, his arms folded and his expression defensive. He wore an old-fashioned walrus moustache and held his back straight with a military air; one wouldn't need to ask what sort of a war *he'd* had.

It struck Edith that if it was a terrible tragedy to bear, your daughter probably murdered and mutilated out of recognition, it was even worse if your son was missing and accused of doing the murdering and mutilating.

'*We* don't believe that Arthur is a murderer,' Edith said firmly, gesturing towards the car after introducing herself. 'Please, may we come in?'

Although he remained wary, Mr Lamb's

expression softened a little, and he kept his arms folded.

'You're the only ones then. The police think he's done away with her. Even his own friends think he's capable of it. But they haven't got definite proof that Louise is even dead, and they haven't the foggiest where Arthur is. It's preposterous that everybody is fixed on this theory and they're not seriously investigating alternatives.'

'Maybe I could help persuade the police to look at other theories?' Edith smiled, trying to exude compassion. 'Hester and I are relatives, after all. We were at the wedding... don't you remember us? No? Well, there were a lot of people there. We were still in Arundel when the body was found. In fact, we were the first people to be interviewed by the police. Alma Matthews is distraught, and she's not thinking clearly. She's always been very fond of Arthur, but she's been influenced by other people. Do let us talk with you... we only want to help. Please.'

A short time later, Edith, Hester, and Phillip were ensconced in William Lamb's front room, which was much more spacious and luxurious than Alma's, and they had been joined by Mrs Lamb. Arthur's mother perched on the edge of a mahogany dining chair as the others sank into leather club armchairs and a Chesterfield sofa. A large red chalk drawing of Arthur as a teenage boy hung over the fireplace.

'Why are you so interested in defending our son's reputation?' Mrs Lamb was clearly suspicious.

'You didn't know him. Louise's mother made

it clear to us that she thought Arthur murdered her daughter. *Why don't you think the same?*'

Edith and Hester exchanged a glance. They couldn't mention the séance.

'They were clearly so devoted at their wedding,' Edith said.

Mrs Lamb got up and rang the bell. 'Tea?'

'Or something stronger?' Mr Lamb was thawing.

Hester perked up, but it became clear that Mr Lamb was only addressing Phillip. She sank back down into her armchair.

'We already thought of Louise as our daughter,' said Mr Lamb, as he poured Phillip and himself a generous scotch. 'She was ideal for Arthur. She was very beautiful but also charming, and she would have been a wonderful hostess. Might still be, for all we know at the moment. She was the type to go down very well at the golf club and the bank.'

'She was a good egg. She would have signed up for all the committees,' Mrs Lamb added as the tea arrived.

'She was a picture of health. A strong-looking girl. Good teeth. She'd have given him hardy children.' Mr Lamb paused. 'We were delighted with her, and I could see she was always working to fit in with us. She might not have been the top drawer... Oh, sorry...' He glanced at Edith and Hester, 'but she could pass for it.'

'She wasn't rebellious,' said Mrs Lamb as a butler poured the tea and waited to be dismissed.

They can afford the wages of a male servant, Edith thought, although she didn't really need more proof of the Lamb family's prosperity. She was glad she'd worn her smartest navy and rust ensemble.

'I don't believe a word of what Arthur's own friends tried to tell us just last week.'

'What did they try to tell you?' asked Hester. Once again, Phillip was silent because he felt that this concerned Edith and Hester's family especially, and he didn't want to butt in.

'Do you mind if I smoke?' was all he asked. Mr Lamb fetched a drum of cigarettes to offer the ladies and proffered a flame from a lighter made from a Great War shell case. He took a cigar from a box as Phillip stuffed his pipe.

'They tried to tell us that, secretly, Arthur had a very nasty side to his personality, in a nutshell, and that Louise was scared of him,' said Mr Lamb, indignant.

'We don't believe one single word of it. We've never known Arthur to display the least malice towards anyone. *They* said that Arthur was jealous and aggressive with women but kept it well hidden...' said Arthur's mother. She went on, '...so I telephoned his two previous young ladies, and they said they had never known him to be any such thing. Our son was raised to be a gentleman.'

'Pack of lies!' Mr Lamb raised his voice. 'And you know? It hurts! Arthur has been best friends with Edward and Peter since Lancing. I'd have thought *they'd* have stood up for him. I can only imagine that they've been got at by the police and swallowed the official theory, hook, line, and sinker.'

'Is that Edward Wren, the philatelist?' Edith looked at him expectantly.

'Yes. Know him, do you? We've known him since he was knee high to a gnat. Done spectacularly well for himself.'

'I saw him and his wife at the wedding.' Edith didn't know how to steer the conversation around to the diamond ring and so, finally, she just waded in. 'I couldn't help but notice that Louise was wearing a spectacular engagement ring? Arthur must have paid a lot for it.'

Both of the Lambs looked momentarily imbued with pride.

'Arthur was - is - extremely astute when it comes to money,' said his father, taking a sip of whisky, and becoming rather pompous. 'He did his homework when it came to buying the ring. He realised that diamonds - *many* diamonds - lose value, like cars. He decided to invest in a ring that would become a family heirloom. He wanted to put his money in diamonds that he could pass to his grandchildren and great-grandchildren and would continue to increase in value.'

'Did he discuss this with Louise?' Hester said. Her lively hazel eyes were lit up.
Phillip blinked and gave her a nudge, to which she could not be seen to react.

'More scotch?' Mr Lamb got up and went over to the cut-glass decanter...

'Yes please,' said Hester, 'Oh, sorry. No, Phillip won't want any. No, thank you.'

'I will, please,' said Phillip. 'And I think these ladies would love a gin and tonic. Am I right?'

Hester nodded as Edith drank down her tea very quickly. Both the Lambs looked rather reproving, but Mr Lamb dutifully poured some gin. Whilst the Lambs might have been snooty about women drinking, they did not consider the fact that Phillip was driving.

Edith asked, 'What sort of diamonds increase in value?'

'Like anything else; something unusual. The quality, of course. The size. The colour. The cut. The artistic style in the setting. The provenance.'

'Arthur got a lot of advice before he bought the ring,' said his mother proudly. 'He explained it to us.'

'He seems incredibly clever,' Edith said. 'Where did he get advice?'

'He was so lucky that his best friend was a jeweller with important connections, so he could get expert advice and help with the purchase,' replied Mrs Lamb.

'That best friend must have been at Arthur's wedding, then?' Edith asked, trying to stay calm and collected.

'Yes, of course, he was the 'Best Man.' Arthur's father said. 'Arthur was just really lucky to be close to Peter Laine. Which is why we're so hurt that Peter is smearing Arthur's reputation.'

'Of course, I asked Arthur's parents about he and Louise wanting to sell the ring,' Edith told Adrian Stevens back at the Norfolk Arms that evening. Hester and Phillip were upstairs in their room packing since Phillip was driving Hester home the next day. They were taking a long time about it, too.

'The Lambs told us that the ring was bought from Peter Laine at a special price. When Arthur told Peter at the wedding that he meant to sell it, Peter offered to buy the ring back at the same price he'd sold it for in the first place and even a bit more. Arthur's parents seemed very proud indeed that he had decided to get an independent valuation in Arundel; it proved he was a good businessman. Hester said '*greedy*' when we were back in the car; she doesn't think he should have tried to make a profit from his best friend's good will, but sold it back to him.'

'I follow you.' Adrian was beginning to understand what Edith was trying to tell him. 'That's when Arthur discovered that the ring was worth far, far, more than Laine sold it for and refused to sell it back. He really *had* made an appointment with Sotheby's for the day after he returned from honeymoon, you know? I had it checked.'

'His parents knew, too,' said Edith. 'I don't think that Arthur let on to Peter Laine that he knew the ring was worth far more than Peter was offering to buy it back for - otherwise Laine might have proposed to pay him more - but he definitely told him that he had an appointment with Sotheby's.

He wanted as much as he could possibly get. Perhaps he was showing off a bit?'
Adrian mused out loud, smiling into Edith's earnest grey eyes.

'I see what you're getting at, but I'm afraid the profit on a diamond ring doesn't seem enough motive to murder two people for. Especially if they're your best friends. There must be more to it than that. I'm guessing the ring was stolen.'

'Agreed. We're on the right track,' said Edith. 'I'm sure. I mean, why otherwise would Peter give Arthur paperwork making the ring out to be less exceptional than it actually was? He obviously wanted to hide its identity and sell it at a price Arthur could afford. Arthur was looking for something to keep for generations, not to sell. By the way,' she added, almost as an afterthought,' I asked Arthur's father if he knew David Forsythe. He said, *Wiggy? Of course I do*. It appears that Forsythe was also a Lancing boy. Apparently, he was bullied mercilessly because his mother had alopecia and wore a bright orange bob, which was obviously a wig. Laine evidently thinks he's useful, though, because he deals in antiques and fine art.'

The detective was noting everything down in shorthand in his notebook.

'Are you going to tell Scotland Yard? What are you going to do about Laine?' Edith stroked his arm affectionately.

'Nothing until I have more on the Brighton shop,' Adrian took her hand. 'I wanted to ask you something? I have to go to Lewes police station tomorrow to collect those rings and to find out what they've discovered about them. You're going home, aren't you? Would you like to drive me over if you're going back in that direction tomorrow? You could show me your teashop and drop me off at Haywards Heath station later. I could buy you lunch in Lewes?' Edith smiled at him adoringly in answer. She had been half afraid that the distance between their homes might prove to be a hindrance to their burgeoning relationship, but tomorrow's trip would be an opportunity to test the practicalities of the journey and involve herself even more in the ongoing investigation.

'I'm sure Hester and Phillip are taking the opportunity to canoodle in the bedroom since it's the last evening,' Edith said.

Adrian took the hint. 'Maybe they're leaving *us* the time to canoodle too. Fancy sneaking off to the Swan Inn on our own? Mrs Brown will probably give me the sharp end of her tongue because I'm late in... but it'll be worth it.'

CHAPTER 16

She pulled her motorcar over into the first place where she could safely stop after Worthing.

'I've had enough!' Edith scowled at Adrian Stevens. 'If you don't be quiet, you can bally well walk to Lewes!' Adrian might not have held a driving license, but he had turned out to be a vociferous backseat driver.

'How ever does your police chauffeur manage to chauffeur you?' She stared out of the window with a stony face. The man was exasperating...but still rather handsome with that dark blond thatch and slight freckles.

'*He* can drive very well. *He's* had police training,' said Adrian.
She told herself to stay calm.

Edith had picked him up at Arundel station after breakfast, and after hugging Hester and Phillip rather tearfully as they all said goodbye, without knowing when they might meet again, she had sped along the coast on the Brighton road before turning up over the south downs to Lewes. She dropped him at the police headquarters mid-morning and browsed the smart little shops in the town centre before joining him for lunch near the Courthouse.

'Well, it's a complicated mess!' Detective Inspector Adrian Stevens pulled a face, sliding his rather bulky frame behind the little restaurant table and trying not to catch the white tablecloth or knock over the tall-stemmed wine glasses. By the looks of it, the other clientele were mainly lawyers and clerks from the Crown Court or businessmen enjoying an intimate tete-a-tete with their secretaries.

'Tell all! have they found out about the ring?'

'I shouldn't really tell you *everything* about the case,' he teased.

'Oh, don't be a chump! Come on!'

'Louise Lamb's engagement ring turned out to be the easiest part of it. It's the rest of the jewellery in that shop that is the nightmare... Wait until we've ordered our lunch, and I'll tell you.'

'Go on then!' Edith said as the waitress fetched the mock turtle soup. She crossed her legs and had to furtively sort out the suspenders on her silk stockings which had got in a twist under the table.

'It's remarkable,' said Adrian, that you would recognise that ring from the two bits in the shop because it might never have been found. Luckily, the jeweller in Arundel kept a carbon copy of their report on the ring for Mr Lamb. It's incredibly fortunate that you happened to visit that shop.'

It's a shame I daren't mention my help from the spirit world, thought Edith. *How many times will he believe in coincidences? We're going to have to talk about it one day if we're going to have honesty in our relationship.*

'The rings both had fake buying slips but when the police went to the addresses on the paperwork, no such clients existed, so we couldn't prove how it ended up in two parts in that shop.'

'Peter Laine has something to do with it.'

'Laine's name certainly came up in connection
with the shop, although not in any illegal capacity.
He does jewellery repairs for them and their
customers, as he does for other shops, including one
in Hatton Garden. He also writes reports and
supplies paper valuations for insurance purposes.'

The waitress came back, balancing a tureen of
hot soup, and they both leaned back as she expertly
ladled the broth into their dishes from over their
shoulders. They sighed with relief at not being
scalded and bent towards each other, drowning in
each other's eyes. The meaty smell of calf's head
wafted up from the broth, making them both hungry.

'So, Mr Laine is ideally placed to legally order
in precious stones, new settings, and buy and sell
gold,' Edith mused. She reached out a hand and
tenderly stroked his hair.

'Yes,' said Adrian,' He can also supply
paperwork. By the way, he also makes the costume
jewellery - that ring Hester bought? Although I
wonder why he'd bother; it's a nice sideline for him I
suppose.' He blew on his soup. 'But the whole thing's
a nightmare to unravel.'

'What's the nightmare?'

'The nightmare is that there was a lot of stolen
jewellery in the second-hand window, but sorting it
out from the legally bought second-hand jewellery
will be difficult. Firstly, the stones have been
swapped around, and pendants made into brooches,
and vice versa, and rings into earrings and so forth. It

means that the stolen jewellery doesn't match the description circulated. Remember that we must have people trawling through all the file cards and international correspondence to match up these items. There are other complications, such as the fake paperwork not necessarily corresponding to the value of the item. In most cases, the insurance valuation is given as much more than the customer would actually pay for the item.'

'So, a customer might well arrange to have their jewellery stolen back and make a profit from the insurance if they needed money?

'I imagine that they could, if they were that way inclined.'

'That doesn't make sense for the ring Arthur bought, though,' said Edith. 'The jeweller in Arundel said that Arthur had papers saying that the ring was valued at a lot *less* than it was worth in reality, not more. What's been going on?'

They ate their soup in silence for a bit.

'Do you want to know about the engagement ring then?' Adrian asked, his voice almost a whisper so that she had to lean in close to hear what he was saying. He put his left hand on her knee...

'Please.' Her breathing slowed, and she made a great deal of blowing on her soup and ignoring that hand.

'Thanks to your detective work, they identified the diamond ring fairly rapidly on a list circulated by the International Criminal Police Organisation, of jewellery stolen abroad. From the jewellers in

Arundel, we knew it was French, and we could match the description on the French lists. We had a timespan for the theft - we thought it was stolen just before the Lambs got engaged...'

'Yes, I see.'

He hadn't taken his hand away, and his warmth seemed to travel up her leg...

'...An identical ring was stolen from a Jewellers in Avignon, France, just over two years ago.'

'I'm beginning to see a few things,' said Edith.

'Peter Laine didn't bother to swap the diamonds out on the cluster ring because Arthur never intended to sell it. But then Arthur told Laine that he had an appointment at Sotheby's. Laine must have known that Sotheby's check the lists of internationally stolen jewellery and would then question Arthur as to where he'd bought it. I'm sure Arthur didn't know it was stolen, but he was soon going to find out. I bet you that engagement ring was only the tip of the iceberg. What about the other stolen items in the Brighton shop? And the other shops Laine works for?'

'Hmm.'

'Arthur must have had no idea that Peter Laine was involved in criminal activities, but unwittingly he was going to expose him. If only Arthur had simply allowed Laine to buy the ring back from him at the same price he had sold it! But Arthur had a new valuation and thought he could make a huge profit.'

Adrian took away his hand, scanning her rosy

excited face and grey eyes with their huge pupils.

They sat thinking about the situation, in front of their soup plates.

'D'you know? I think that Laine sold that ring so cheaply to Arthur in the first place, merely because that was the best Arthur's budget would stretch to. He was probably only doing his old school friend a favour that horribly backfired.'

The waitress brought their roast meat and potatoes.

'The trouble is,' said Adrian,' nothing in that Brighton shop proves that Peter Laine is knowingly involved in the owner's criminal affairs. He's just a jeweller paid to do work who also supplies some perfectly legal costume jewellery. There's nothing to charge him with. There's certainly nothing at all to link him to the murder, apart from the circumstantial evidence of the engagement ring being found there. How do I know that Mr Laine was aware that the ring was stolen when he sold it to Mr Lamb? How do I know that Mr Lamb didn't sell it back to him after all? That's what a defense lawyer would say. I'm not going to make a false move and arrest Laine too fast until I know we can *prove* him guilty - if he is. I'll make sure he's watched... doesn't scarper when he knows Frazer's is under investigation.'

'I'd like to know how that ring was stolen from the Avignon Jewellers and how it got into Laine's hands. Also - where is Arthur Lamb's body hidden?'

'We don't know Lamb is dead.' Adrian said.

Oh, we do, thought Edith.

'And how was Louise Lamb made to walk back down the path to Arundel - if that is her cigarette end - and why murder her in Arundel?' Adrian sighed. 'You know we're nowhere near solving this case yet. Still, I'm glad I've got you on my side.' He smiled. 'Fancy a pudding? And then...are you going to take me home? Will we be alone?'

After lunch, Edith drove Adrian Stevens back to Cuckfield, pottering along and allowing him to enjoy the countryside. She wasn't in any hurry for him to be going back to Chichester and wanted to show off her business and her home. She was quick to shut him down, though, every time he told her to break, look in the mirror, indicate or advised her to change gear. It was a habit she'd have to get him out of in the future, she thought fondly.

The village of Cuckfield had a rural picturesque side, but also a bustling high street with several fairly grand buildings, and some expensive looking motorcars parked by the kerb. Drivers often raced down the steep road from the direction of Crawley, heading for the coast. The place seemed to have more than its fair share of tearooms, a pub, and the smart King's Head public house opposite her tea room, as well as busy shops and the pale stone, Victorian, Queen's Hall with its mass of mullioned windows.

'*Very* nice,' said Adrian, but he seemed more interested in the horse pulling Mr Freeman's coal delivery cart. 'A pretty little piebald...my daughter, Sophie, would want to feed her sugar lumps. Needs re-shoeing, though.'

The Honey Tree café stood on a corner, whitewashed, and with an attractive black painted door and window frames, and Adrian crossed the road to stand back and get a good look at the whole of the building. Cake stands full of scones, current buns, and Victoria sponges stood in the windows together with gift-wrapped soaps, eau de cologne and postcards of the village.

'It's bigger than I imagined,' he remarked. 'Is that entire building yours?'

'Yes,' was all she said.

However, Edith felt a terrible sinking feeling as she walked through the front door. It was apparent that her staff always felt her absence as a sort of holiday. Mrs Thompson had evidently enjoyed being in charge though, and the café looked clean and tidy and bustling with activity. It smelt of baking and flowers. She did find her kitchen office had some neatly arranged bills for her to pay, but it was obvious once again that she had not been missed.

Edith ordered a pot of tea for herself and Adrian. He had carried her luggage from the car for her, and she showed him the stairs to her rooms above the café. She was acutely aware of two sets of eyes upon them as she self-consciously ushered him upwards, knowing that his presence was soon to be reported to all the Cuckfield gossips. Especially if they took some time before they came back downstairs.

The char lady, Mrs Tutt, had cleaned for her

while she'd been away, and the red linoleum floor of the sitting room was spotless and gleaming. Her armchair was drawn up at an angle in front of the gas fire under a standard lamp and next to a little oak table on which a photograph of Michael sat. There were other chairs in the apartment, but it was painfully obvious that she spent her evenings by herself, reading or listening to the wireless under a single electric bulb.

There were several bookshelves, with books all neatly lined up in order of size, and all facing the right direction. Automatically, Edith went to a drawer and, taking out some scissors, cut a few dead leaves off her red Kalanchoe potted plant.

She said, 'Make yourself at home!'

The tall, sandy-haired detective stood about awkwardly. 'You don't have a cat or anything?' The question appeared to trouble him. 'For company?' Adrian crossed to the little table and before Edith could stop him, he'd picked up her favourite picture of Michael in a leather flying helmet and sheepskin jacket, leaning against the body of an aeroplane. 'Is this your fiancé?'

Mick had slim, almost pretty features. The red rose she'd put in the little vase by the portrait had dropped its petals, and she saw Adrian looking at them reflectively.

'Yes,' Edith replied, disliking the fact that Adrian had picked Michael's photograph up uninvited and was now considering him with attention. It seemed like an intrusion into her private life and her past. It was quite unreasonable she knew since she would have been just as curious to see a photograph of Minty Stevens, the detective's dead wife.

She cleared away the browning rose and the dropped petals.

The doors to the four bedrooms were shut, as was the door to the bathroom, and Edith didn't invite him for a tour of the apartment. The place no longer seemed like home to her but a place where she'd spent too many nights crying in loneliness and fighting her spiritual nature and psychic intuition. In just a few weeks, Edith had grown used to Hester's lively company, the warmth and comfort of the Norfolk Arms, and cosy dinners out with Adrian Stevens - she didn't want to return here.

Adrian was staring at what he probably imagined was a bedroom door, and Edith knew that she had only to invite him through that door and...but she didn't; the moment of desire and temptation she'd felt in the restaurant was lost. She had been reminded of Michael.

Sadly, she led him back downstairs. Edith could see the staff observing the two of them surreptitiously and whispering slyly, as the pair drank their tea. He wolfed down an enormous slab of cake, even though he had not finished dinner long. The smell of fresh hot scones hung in the air.

'Did you paint those?'

Edith could see his eyes looking at her canvasses hanging on the wall.

'Yes,' she said. 'Do you like them?'

'Not really. I'm sorry...but I'm sure you would rather I was honest. What is that one meant to be, for example?'

He'd picked out the painting which she'd felt compelled to make of cars. A car but from different angles. All at once, the familiar, strange, dreamlike buzzing state began flooding her body. Looking at the painting, she remembered how automatically her hand had traced the harsh lines as she sat in reverie and tried to block the feelings out. She hadn't wanted to listen to what her intuition told her back then, but she trusted herself now.

'You never found the mysterious wedding car hire firm, nor that chauffeur, did you?' Edith asked Adrian.

'No. Nor any traces of that car. Why do you ask now?'

'Oh, it's just that the painting is of a car, and it reminded me. What if there wasn't ever another car hire firm, and the chauffeur of that wedding car was actually Peter Laine?'

Adrian looked at her. 'Is that even possible?' He was clearly sceptical. 'The Best Man? '

'Everyone saw the chauffeur but he was wearing a motoring helmet, goggles and a muffler, behind a thick windscreen. We were all looking at the bride and groom to be honest, not the driver. There was such a crowd of us to see them off, I wouldn't have noticed if anyone was missing from the crowd.' She went on, 'even if I'd have noticed he wasn't there, I'd have assumed he was inside the hotel and forgotten about him.'

'It's actually not crazy...' began Adrian.

'Thanks!'

'It would explain why we couldn't find the chauffeur and also start to explain how somebody might get the Lambs to walk back down the path. It explains why the *abductor*, as it were, let Mrs Lamb smoke a Sobranie cigarette. They all knew each other well.' Adrian lit up a cigarette himself and blew a smoke ring pensively.

An elderly couple at the next table glared as smoke drifted across their table as they ate.

'Trouble is,' said Edith, 'the lady in the ticket office at Arundel station remembers that the chauffeur parked up somewhere on the forecourt, cut the tin cans and placards off the car, and then drove away. She saw him leave.'

'What if he had an accomplice waiting by the footbridge to force them down the tunnel, and he picked them up again on the main road? Suppose the accomplice was somebody they also knew? Edward Wren, for example?'

'It can't have been Edward Wren,' said Edith. 'The Wrens were definitely at the hotel because they asked Phillip to take their photo. I remember Mrs Wren looked really rather frumpy - for her.'

'Perhaps it was David 'Wiggy' Forsythe, your bounder?' Having finished his tea, Adrian took out his pocket watch.

It was the minute that Edith had been dreading. She would have to drive him to the station without knowing when she would see him again. It would be too far for him to just pop over for supper, especially without a car.

'How's your French?' Adrian asked her.
'Passable?'
'Suppose I hire you as my translator?'
Edith nearly purred.

Adrian continued, 'I'm taking the ring to the Arundel jewellers so that they can put it back into one piece and confirm that it's the same ring Arthur Lamb showed them. Then, I'm personally delivering it back to its rightful owners in Avignon. You're not the only one with hunches.' he looked at her. 'I think it might be instructive to find out how it was stolen in the first place, and how it got into the hands of Mr Laine. I also think,' he went on, 'that we should pay a visit to the car hire place in Le Havre and confirm that it really *was* Arthur Lamb who picked up the car in France. The gendarmes insist it was, but we need to double-check.' He paused. 'Is there a Travel Agent in Haywards Heath? I'll get our tickets.'

'But you were always perfectly useless at French,' Hester objected, when Edith told her excitedly on the phone about the trip to France they had already booked.

'I'll buy a French to English translation book tomorrow. There's nearly a week, and if I spend every day reading it, I could learn a lot off by heart,' Edith said hopefully. 'At least, *something* will surely sink in. Besides I have a reserve plan.'

'What's that?'

'I can always hire my own translator in Avignon. But, oh, Hess! He's taking me for a night in Paris, and then on the overnight sleeper train to Avignon. We're going for a trip on the Seine, up the Eiffel Tower, and for lunch on the Champs-Elysees!'

'Phillip can overhear this conversation, and he says...what?... how will more canoodling help you solve the murder?'

'Tell him we won't discuss anything but the crime.'

'Well, be on your best behaviour, darling, and keep your legs crossed! Bottoms up!'

CHAPTER 17

The journey to Avignon had been idyllic as far as Edith was concerned. They took the 9am crossing from Portsmouth, having met for breakfast at the port, and arrived in Le Havre mid-afternoon. The crossing was smooth, and although the skies were steely grey, they spent most of their time on the deck leaning on the rail, watching the seagulls following the fishing boats, and breathing in the bracing sea air, which smelt salty and fresh. They gazed into each other's eyes as much as the strong breeze allowed, hair sticking across their faces and grasping cold hands, hot with ardour.

It was only when they could make out the cluster of French custom officers in their dark capes and kepis waiting on the quay that Adrian kissed her at last, and neither of them wanted to finish.

'Where's the accordion?' Adrian finally stopped; his blue eyes sleepy.

The car hire firm was within walking distance of the ferry, and the staff spoke English as most of their customers were English, straight off the boat. However, there was no hope of anybody remembering exactly what the gentleman looked like, who had hired the car later found abandoned near the Italian border. By the time the gendarmes arrived asking questions, several weeks had passed, and many other English drivers had picked up or dropped off vehicles at the large garage. The proprietor had simply shrugged his shoulders and told them the gentleman looked 'typically English' and had been dressed like a 'typical Englishman.' He had been shown a passport and a driving license in the name of Arthur Lamb, which they probably hadn't examined too closely since the gentleman in question had just been through passport control, after all, and was 'obviously who he said he was.'

'It doesn't prove anything at all.' Edith shook her head, frustrated. 'I don't believe it was him.'

By the evening, Adrian and Edith were in Paris, booked into a modest but comfortable little hotel, in adjoining rooms. They were soon sat on the terrace of a pavement café sipping red wine under a red and white striped awning to the sound of a gypsy guitar. It felt very daring to be travelling alone together, far from the constraints and social mores of stuffy England. This was France - the country of lovers - after all, but Adrian didn't attempt to persuade her to make love with him. He might be a Scotland Yard detective on a murder enquiry, but at heart, he was an English country farmer and not a wild Irish poet and daredevil. The moment in Cuckfield when he might have entered her bedroom was lost. Yet it was clear Adrian was in love with her. It would certainly not be Edith who would make a first move; she thought of Hester's parting advice. *These things are so complicated*, she thought sadly.

The next day, they visited some tourist sites and wandered hand-in-hand along the Champs

Elysee. Actually, Edith would have *really* preferred to visit Montmartre and its jazz clubs, and especially the famous Art supply shop 'Maison du Pastel' in the Rue Rambuteau, but she quickly realised that Adrian would not appreciate spending his one day in Paris missing out the Arc de Triomphe and the Eiffel Tower and the touristy things she could have happily missed. There was no time to fit everything in.

Still, Edith was in raptures. She hadn't imagined such a short time ago that she could meet a man and fall in love with him after her happy relationship with her adored Michael. Adrian Stevens didn't look anything like Mick, but she was bowled over by his tall frame, sandy hair, and chubby freckled hands.

The pair spent a lot of time gazing into each other's eyes and kissing. Paris was the most romantic city in the world, after all. The only worry was the valuable ring which Adrian carried in his inside jacket pocket; he was continuously patting his chest - an unwitting signal to pickpockets. His tall sturdy bulk made would-be thieves keep their distance, however.

The next evening, they had taken the sleeper train from the Gare de Lyon and dined in the restaurant coach, watching the French countryside slip by as the night fell and the table lamps in the Pullman coach lit up the carriage.

They slept, separately of course, to the sound of the pistons and the chug-chug of the engine as the smoke from the chimney drifted past the windows.

The sky was bright blue and clear when they left the

train at Avignon station after croissants, black coffee, and cigarettes in the buffet car, with its snow-white tablecloths.

The shadows on the ground in front of the station were sharp, as they looked around for a taxi to take them to their hotel. It drove them straight up the principal street, Rue de la Republique, and they both noticed the very smart jeweller's shop they had come to see at the top of the road on the left-hand side.

They booked into their hotel in the Rue Joseph Vernet and enquired about an English-speaking guide. To their delight, they found that the hotel proprietor's daughter was a guide and was happy to accompany them straight to the shop. Adrian was anxious to return the ring as soon as possible.

'Can you imagine if it was stolen? Or I lost it?'

Joallerie de la Republique stood nearly at the top of the broad, tree-lined boulevard, almost at the large square over which presided the Town Hall. It was much smarter than the little Arundel jewellers or the quaint Brighton shop. Its imposing façade was decorated in the modern style, and its thick windows had steep shelving with opulent, and chic, gold and platinum jewellery immaculately displayed and lit. There was not a speck of dust to be seen.

'Look at some of the prices!' Edith whispered to Adrian.

It wasn't possible to simply push the door and walk in, and they were obliged to ring a bell and wait. The Owner, who opened the door, wore pinstripe trousers and a frock coat and looked snootily down his nose at them until Brigitte explained why they had come, whereupon he and an assistant - who turned out to be his wife - were all smiles.

They were soon all seated at one of the walnut tables which sat upon the plush carpet with its geometric design in the *jazz modern* style.
Adrian placed the box with Louise's ring upon the table and the pair of jewellers cooed in delight.

'Yes, Monsieur, this is our ring that was stolen! It was two or three years ago,' they said through Brigitte. 'It is engraved upon our memory. Besides - here is our paperwork.'

They had put the description of the diamonds in a safe, ready for the detective's arrival, and looked at the ring with their loupes.

'Can you explain to us how it was stolen?' Adrian was speaking loudly and very, very, slowly - and gesturing - although there was no need to as Brigitte was fluent in both languages.

The man in the frock coat, who was obviously in charge, introduced himself as Monsieur Tardy. He recounted the story in French with a heavy Provençal accent.

'One day, an English gentleman came here. He wanted to see about an engagement ring for his young lady. He appeared to be a businessman, although he didn't specify what business, only that it was international. He spoke good French. He spoke of homes on the Cote D'Azur and in Switzerland.' M. Tardy coughed. 'Yes. I do find it odd now that the gentleman would not simply buy a ring in Nice or in Geneva. However, the monsieur was very plausible. He was very well dressed and had manicured nails and a heavy gold signet. I remember that. I can't describe exactly what his face looked like.'

The man paused to give Adrian time to write it down. He had his notebook out and was scribbling in shorthand.

'Go on!' Adrian lifted his head.

Monsieur Tardy, and Brigitte, continued:

'The Englishman picked out five rings. He wanted me to write down the exact information on the measurements, cut, colour and clarity of the stones and the dimensions and style of the settings, which I did. He also wanted photographs and promised to call back for them at the end of the afternoon.' He shrugged. 'It's normal to want these details if you are going to spend a good deal of money on a diamond ring. You wouldn't buy a house without knowing as much about it as possible, and a careful person would do the same when comparing rings. It didn't worry me. It would have worried me if he hadn't wanted this information; I would not have believed that he intended to spend the money.'

'So, there was nothing at all about this man that made you worried?'

'Nothing at all.' Monsieur Tardy said firmly.

'The gentleman wanted to negotiate on the prices. That's also normal. He appeared to have done his homework on the value of diamonds. I would expect nothing less from a businessman. He said he was shopping around and would decide in several weeks. That's also normal. It's not a purchase you make on a whim.'

'He telephoned three or four weeks later and reminded us of his previous visit,' the second assistant chipped in. She was frighteningly chic to Edith's eyes, with jet-black hair, scarlet nails, and lipstick. She looked terribly thin, and her tailored black suit was evidently made to measure to accentuate this.

'Did he give a name?' Detective Inspector Stevens' pencil was poised.

'Mr Sachs,' the man said with a weak smile.

'He wanted to make an appointment to bring his fiancée to see the rings so that she could make a final decision. He reminded me of his selection so that I could have the rings waiting. He put the cluster ring in the middle of the list and did not show any more interest in that ring rather than another.' Monsieur Tardy paused, forcing Brigitte to pause too. 'On the day of the appointment, we put a couple of bottles of champagne on ice to drink during the viewing, and we had a tiny box of luxury chocolates on the table here. And a bouquet of hothouse flowers in a bucket. By the way...' he looked at Edith, 'would you like some champagne? We always have champagne on ice to celebrate an important purchase with our customers.'

'Jewellery is very emotional, you know,' explained his wife. 'Men usually buy it for engagements, weddings, births, birthdays, anniversaries, and for their mistresses. People perceive it as an advertisement by the buyer to show how much a man esteems the person to whom he is offering these gems. Or a lady esteems her gigolo. It is primeval. It is very rare for a woman to buy jewellery such as this for herself, because it is a symbol of possession.' The woman raised one of her perfectly arched, pencil-thin eyebrows. 'Champagne makes the day special. Besides, it generally makes the customers think 'to devil with the money' and buy whatever the lady likes most.'

'I should love champagne,' Edith smiled. 'Thank you, yes,' said Adrian.

'Cherie, please bring five glasses.' The jeweller ordered. He cleared a place on the table for the ice bucket and glasses. 'Madame is my wife. We own this shop, and so the loss of this ring was a big financial blow to us. I never thought we would see it again, so we certainly have something to celebrate with you English police.'

'Let's continue,' Adrian said, pencil poised as Madame Tardy finished setting out the glasses, and the champagne had been poured, and polite toasts given. The diamond ring sat glittering under the table-light, placed between them.

It's got blood on it. It's the reason that two people were murdered, thought Edith, sadly.

Madame Tardy took up the story now, as Brigitte continued to translate.

'We locked the door so that other customers would not interrupt us, and because we had five rings out of the window - where they are not accessible -

those rings were now sitting on the table.'
She laughed, dryly.

'It was for security reasons,' her husband said.
'A thief cannot ask for an expensive ring from the
window and then run out the door with it.'

'The young lady was charmante. *Charmante*.
She was introduced to us as Mademoiselle
Aberconway.'

'A description, please?' Adrian acted firmly in
his role as Detective Inspector.

'She was dressed in Chanel,' said Madame
Tardy. 'And she smelled subtly of Chanel No. 5
perfume. She had exquisite taste. French taste.'

Ouch! Thought Edith.

'She had beautifully cut dark hair.'

Edith knew she meant a French haircut.

'But in fact, I don't really know what her hair
was like since the gendarmes told us later that she
wears all sorts of wigs when she visits jewellers. Her
hair looked real to me, but perhaps I was wrong. The
Mademoiselle was very confident and very at ease,
and she put us at ease. She asked us all about our
children and our house, and we were flattered that
these wealthy English people treated us like personal
friends. She admired our new carpet very much and
she confided that she would decorate her London
house all in the French Jazz Modern style.'

'Mr Sachs was talking to me about his yacht
on the Mediterranean,' said Monsieur Tardy. 'He
was, perhaps, more distant. His fiancée practically
invited my wife to look them up, if we visited Antibes,

and have lunch on their cruiser. With a French chef, of course.'

Of course! Edith thought.

'Naturally, whilst I was standing there sipping champagne and making small talk with Mr Sachs, I was watching the Mademoiselle trying on the jewellery and making sure that the rings were all there. Never did the young lady look particularly interested in that cluster ring. She certainly tried it on, but she appeared more taken with two of the other rings. At one point, she leaned over to my wife and whispered something to her, and my wife got up and led me to one side.'

'What did she say?'

Madame Tardy took a deep gulp of champagne.

'She insinuated that my husband was breathing down her neck, and she was beginning to feel ill at ease with him watching her like a hawk, and so I asked him to move further away. Of course, it was at that moment that she switched the rings quite comfortably because nobody was watching her for quite a few seconds, and Mr Sachs went and spoke to her, blocking our view.'

'What happened then?'

'Mr Sachs told my husband that Miss Aberconway had narrowed her choice down to two rings, and he could put the other three back in the window.' Madame Tardy looked furious; Monsieur Tardy looked rueful.

'I was still so shocked that I had been rather

intrusive watching over the jewellery. One is supposed to be subtle. It's unprofessional to make a rich customer feel as if they are being regarded as a potential thief. I put the three rings back in the window with only a cursory look -and, of course, one of those rings was now a replica. I was more concerned that I might have ruined the sale.'

He poured out the rest of the champagne.

'They were very clever. They stayed there with us for maybe another three-quarters of an hour, chatting and drinking champagne, until Mademoiselle finally made her choice. We took the size of her finger, and Mr Sachs agreed to have the money for the ring wired from his bank in Switzerland to a bank in Avignon. We would have the ring made smaller, the diamonds cleaned, and the ring put in a new box.'

'He was to collect the ring and pay for it the following day. He gave us the address of their hotel,' said Madame Tardy.

'We were so confident that even when Mr Sachs didn't return the next day, we were not seriously worried. We thought the money transfer was simply taking longer because of the large sum involved. That does happen. Even when it became obvious that they were not going to buy the ring, for any number of reasons we didn't know, we merely thought that they had been too embarrassed, or too rude, to tell us. We didn't realise we had been robbed until over a week later.'

'I was cleaning that shelf of rings in the

window when I saw that the cluster ring did not reflect the light as diamonds do. It was a paste copy.'
Edith and Adrian exchanged a look; Peter Laine and his costume jewellery made of pulverised glass.

'Have you still got the fake ring?' Adrian asked.

'Oh yes! We kept it as a symbol of our stupidity.'
Monsieur Tardy got up and fetched the glass copy, placing it next to the original on the table. To an untrained eye, the two rings looked identical.

'We talked to all the other jewellers in Avignon,' his wife said. 'They had visited every single one. When we spoke to them, some jewellers had not even noticed the copies sitting in their window. Only at one of them had they not succeeded in making the switch. The pair of thieves had made appointments to show glass costume jewellery to the cheapest jewellers, although they never turned up for the appointments. That's a mystery. '

M. Tardy shrugged in that particularly gallic way. 'By the time we found out we'd been robbed, they were in Spain, the French detectives told us later. In the same week they had visited Avignon, they had also visited Arles, Aix en Provence, Nimes, and Marseilles as well. They then got a ship from Marseilles to Barcelona and disappeared into Spain. Of course, they use many different names, and the lady wears wigs, so we were told. It is difficult to warn every jeweller in every town - no one knows to where they will go. We are always hoping for customers such as they appear to be - so it is easy for them,' he shrugged again in a world-weary fashion.

'May I take that glass ring, please?' Adrian stretched out his hand.

'Oh, I think so,' said Monsieur Tardy, 'It's an exchange I'm happy to make! Now, another bottle of the best champagne to celebrate that?'

They both agreed that the audacious pair of international jewel thieves fit Edward and Caroline Wren's description.

That afternoon, Edith and Adrian were holding hands under the table, sat in the shade from the sun, on the Place du Palais opposite the medieval Pope's palace. The Plane trees looked dusty, and the shadows were navy blue and violet as they looked out from under the yellow awning of a café, across a vast cobbled square, smoking and sipping pastis.

'Edward Wren is an international stamp dealer,' Edith pointed out. 'He travels to auction houses worldwide, so he has plenty of legitimate excuses to visit different cities and towns looking for likely jewellers.'

'Hmm,' agreed Adrian.' It's also an excellent way to launder the money from the stolen jewellery. Everybody simply assumes that Wren is incredibly rich from trading in stamps. But he can afford to buy valuable stamps with his ill-gotten gains, and then resell them.'

'And he must be wealthy if the rings they're stealing are all high-value. That cluster ring alone is worth a house. More. How many rings did the couple get from that trip alone to Provence? Several in each town. How many trips a year do they do?' Edith addressed her glass of Ricard.

'Even if Peter Laine has to work hard to swap stones around and the rings can't be sold at their real value because they're 'hot,' it still adds up to a fantastic amount of money coming in. No wonder they were in a panic when Arthur Lamb told them he was taking the ring to Sotheby's. Sotheby's must be aware of the existence of these English jewel thieves. Whatever the friendship between them all, Lamb signed his own death warrant, and his wife's, when he unwittingly threatened to bring the whole crooked business crashing down.'

Adrian took a minute to enjoy watching the tourists wandering across the grand square towards the public gardens on the Rocher des Doms, and the Petit Palais beyond.

He squeezed Edith's hand. He looked as if he might say '*we could come back to France for our honeymoon*,' but something held him back. He hadn't introduced her to his daughters yet. Edith shivered despite the heat; that would be a decisive moment to come.

'I don't quite understand why they made appointments to sell costume jewellery they didn't keep, though?'

'Oh, I do!' Edith looked at him with such fondness. 'Nobody noticed a glass ring amongst all the diamonds, so what better way to smuggle a real diamond ring back to England than amongst a hundred glass costume rings? They probably kept a list of jewellers they had appointments with to show costume jewellery, in case a customs officer questioned them about their baggage. But Caroline Wren is so 'charmante,' I don't suppose that any officers ever did question them.'

The most difficult thing, Adrian and Edith agreed on, would be proving that Peter Laine and the Wrens had murdered Louise and Arthur Lamb. While they had discovered what was certainly the motive, they undoubtedly did not have the slightest proof of the deed.

I'm going to have to use my psychic abilities, thought Edith, *but I can't ever let Adrian know that. I'll have to talk it over with Hester. We might have to hold another séance. Perhaps it's time I tried to contact Louise on the other side...*

CHAPTER 18

'Hester! Please! It'll be the last time I'll ask you to come to Sussex for this investigation. You can tell Phillip that. I promise! Please...'

Edith had been back from France for a week now and the pressure was on to find the proof to charge Peter Laine, and Edward and Caroline Wren, with the murders of Louise and Arthur Lamb. Edith was certain they were guilty, but she had no idea of how they had carried out the crime. She also had the idea that the mysterious disappearance of Joanne Forsythe wasn't a coincidence, and she was sure Joanne was alive - but where was she?

Edith hadn't seen Adrian Stevens since their return to England, but they had chatted on the telephone and by letter, and he was under increasing demands from Scotland Yard to make an arrest after he had filed his report on the trip to Avignon. The trouble was, the arrest would only be for jewellery theft and not for murder. Adrian told her that his superiors were still of the opinion that the bridegroom was the most likely suspect, since the French police were adamant that he had entered France at Le Havre and travelled through the country to the Italian border. It had been detected that 'Arthur' had left a trail along his route, including several nights in hotels and Louise's suitcase dumped in a layby.

'And they could still be right,' Adrian had pointed out. 'There's no body for Arthur Lamb, and you heard what the man at the French garage said, the gentleman who said he was Arthur showed his passport to customs officers. Perhaps we should accept that it really *was* him.'

'I don't believe it was him. You didn't either when we were in France,' Edith said. 'It was probably Peter Laine using Arthur's passport. He's a man who does very delicate work on jewellery...he could easily change a passport photograph - those photographs are dreadful anyhow.'

'Well, Scotland Yard has complete confidence in the French detectives who say that 'Mr Lamb' showed his passport to hotels, chatted with staff about details of his life, forgot a monogrammed handkerchief in one hotel room and physically resembled Arthur Lamb - they showed witnesses another snapshot of Arthur.'

'But it's ridiculous!' Edith was beside herself. 'No man on the run after murdering somebody is going to leave such a trail! It was a trail left on purpose! I'd love to know how the French detectives worded their questions...if they didn't just send the local gendarme round ...and the snapshot they showed staff? - Arthur was very thin on top and tall, and Peter is slight with floppy dark hair. They probably showed a picture of Arthur sat down with a hat on! Anyhow, the staff are most likely to remember that the man was English, and little more. It was weeks after the murder. How many people do they see in a hotel?'

'Be that as it may,' Adrian said patiently,

'Scotland Yard are never going to call their French counterpart incompetent. They accept that Arthur Lamb fled to France and then to Italy and presume the reason he did that is because he had murdered his bride in Arundel. This can't be proved with a trial, but we're not looking for anybody else in connection with the murder. Case closed.'

The inquest was to be quietly resumed, and with no definite proof that the headless body *was* Louise, the Coroner would have to order her body to be that of Jane Doe, and Alma wouldn't even get to hold a proper funeral for her daughter.

Adrian Stevens had then informed Edith that the uniformed police were also eager to announce some arrests in the press, even if CID got the credit, so that they could bask in the reflected glory of solving a major crime ring. The capture of international jewel thieves, pursued across France, would get many favourable column inches and the police hoped that some of the glamour of the crimes would rub off on themselves. The arrest of the charming, Chanel-clad Caroline Wren was eagerly anticipated as photographs would surely make the front pages of all the national newspapers, and Chichester police were thrilled. The Chief Constable was looking forward to a Press Conference.

DI Stevens was tickled pink that his sleuthing down a valuable diamond ring and his dramatic chase of crooks from Paris to the South of France would make him the toast of Scotland Yard - who were now muttering about promotion. He was the Golden Boy of the force at the moment, and Mrs Brown, Sophie and Annabella were very proud.

Edith recounted all the conversations with her cousin during their telephone call.

'Chase across France? And you know Arthur Lamb is also a murder victim, Hester. You remember the séance? Laine and the Wrens won't be charged with murder, only theft. Caroline will use her famous charm and they might only get a few years. Are the jury allowed to even know the extent of the jewellery scams? They might only be charged with one or two counts of theft which are easy to prove. They're getting away with it! I am so sorry for Arthur's parents and I'm sure his spirit is not at rest; it can't be.'

'But why do you need *me*?' Hester asked.

Edith had thought that Phillip might show some resistance to her cousin returning to Arundel, but she hadn't foreseen that Hester herself might not want to come.

'I need you to be with me to conduct another séance. I don't know if I have enough energy to bring forward a spirit that doesn't appear spontaneously. Besides, I don't know what might happen when I'm in a trance? I need you to watch over me. We ought to be at the Norfolk Arms because Arundel is where the murder occurred. We need to go back to what happened at the wedding up until we saw the flames at Swanbourne Lake. If we don't nail the case this week, then Adrian will be forced to do as his bosses at The Yard want. Please come back, Hess! You're my

Dr Watson, darling.'

'Phillip complained about my bar bill and the rings,' said Hester. 'I told him you're a bad influence.'

'Did he believe you?'

'No. He said it was probably the other way around. What about my children?'

'Phillip and Nanny can hold the fort. It's *only* another *week*. If we don't manage to get those murderers this time, then the case is all over anyway.'

'It's the Tourist Season. The Norfolk Arms is probably booked up. You know how popular it gets.'

'Good try, Hess. I already booked us into a twin double starting the day after tomorrow. Tell Phillip that I'll pay it *and* your bar bill. By the way, we're both invited to luncheon at Adrian's house on Sunday - I've never seen it before. I need you there for moral support. I'm going to meet his daughters, *and* Mrs Brown, the housekeeper - I can't face that battleaxe alone. It'll be worse than meeting his parents.'

Hester had, of course, capitulated, as Edith knew she would. Edith was almost sick with excitement at the thought of returning to Arundel. Her neatly arranged little rooms, with the polished linoleum and carefully dusted and arranged shelves felt like a prison cell when she had to spend all day, and night, there by herself with only a book and the radio for company. More worryingly, she felt unwanted in her own tea rooms downstairs. Of course, she was grateful that she was able to go away and leave the business in capable hands, but she simply didn't like coming back here anymore. She started to think about the possibility of selling up and starting anew.

Edith looked at the portrait of Michael with his aeroplane. The Honeytree had been a distraction for her immediately after his death, and her room was a haven to curl up in and lick her wounds. However, without realising the transition, she'd moved on emotionally; perhaps it was time to move on physically.

Sunday lunch at Detective Inspector Adrian Stevens' Chichester home led her to a rapid about-face. Hester had arrived in Arundel by train and the next day they had driven over to Adrian's in the little green Austin. Taking Hester's advice, she had brought gifts for Mrs Brown of lavender water and a pot of homemade jam from the Honeytree.

'Don't think of her as a battleaxe darling, is my advice. Get her on your side. She's bound to appreciate your consideration.'

It was the first time that Edith would have seen Adrian since they'd got back from France, and she had butterflies in her stomach all the journey. Excitedly, she told Hester what she knew about his family: There were two daughters; Sophie, the eldest, was fifteen and the scholar. Her father described her proudly as a bluestocking and said that she'd been most affected by the death of her mother when she'd been thirteen. Bella, the youngest, was twelve now and lived for animals. The girls were cared for by Mrs

Brown, of whom they were apparently, extremely fond.

'Adrian told me he doesn't know what he'd do without her, as she keeps the home going and the children happy. It takes the worry away from him, you see.' Edith explained once again to Hester.

She was certainly nervous about the meeting because the housekeeper came across as a protective mother figure. If her relationship with the detective panned out as she hoped, she might end up living in his house and giving her own directions for the household. It was vital that they could all get along together.

Edith had taken special care to look demure in her grey dress, when getting ready, and she had left off the face powder and chosen a discreet lipstick and one strand of pearls. She made sure her gloves were spotless and her perfume light.

'You look a bit like a nun, darling.' Hester had said. 'Just be yourself. The most important thing is to let her know that you're not going to upset the apple cart. She can continue to run things as she always has. I mean you can change things, darling, but very slowly...'

They found the house fairly easily following Adrian's directions, and despite Hester's attempts at map reading. The house was a bit of a surprise. It was a modern peach pebble-dashed, half-timbered house at the end of a row on a wide, leafy, suburban road. Although not too far from the city centre, it backed onto paddock land, which also took up the side of the house and had a metal five-bar gate, and a second one onto the road. Beside the paddock, the house had a large garden in front of it with unmown grass and brambles. A broken swing dangled from an apple tree, but a large vegetable patch was clearly well cared for and laid out in immaculate rows.

Four horses stuck their heads over the paddock gate as they drew up and parked the little car. There was a carriage parked on the driveway, which although fairly dilapidated, looked as if it had recently been in use.

'Adrian was a blacksmith and a farrier before he was a policeman,' Edith reminded Hester.

Hester looked at her from under the brim of her hat. 'Are you still scared of horses?'

'No!' Edith said. 'I mean, I wouldn't get on one, but I don't mind them.' She suddenly remembered the conversation in the Swan Inn.

'Adrian loves riding,' she said, sadly. 'I knew he had horses, but I assumed they were stabled elsewhere because he lives in town. Gosh - the garden needs some work. And fancy putting the veggies in the front.'

'That's because the back is a field, sweetie. Now, don't forget - if you're going to smarten it up... do it slowly. It looks like you'll be going for rides in a horse and carriage. How delightfully romantic!'

Edith pulled a face.

They walked up the drive, carefully navigating the rutted gravel path, grass seeds sticking to their silk stockings, and paused.

There was a sound of girlish voices, interspersed with giggles, coming from the paddock and through the wire fence; glimpsed between the tan and the white flanks of the horses who had moved back down the field, were two slim figures: one reasonably tall, and the other relatively tiny.

'Sophie and Annabella,' Edith said. Her heart gave a lurch, and she felt her hands shake slightly with nerves. She was determined to like the two girls and wanted *them* to like *her* back. She wasn't the type to be a wicked stepmother. She was already sympathetic towards them - they had lost their mother at a young age, as she had lost her father.

The two girls were obviously walking towards the garden gate, followed by the horses, and Edith and Hester waited to greet them - Edith practising what she hoped was a warm, welcoming smile. The pair had progressed quickly up the uneven grass of the field, affording a better view of them, and both Edith and Hester caught their breath at the same time.

Something was very odd about the scene. The girls had reached the gate, and the horses began to snicker and lower their heads as they were patted and gently pushed aside.

'Out the way, Star!' said the tall girl as she began climbing over the gate. She wore jodhpurs and long leather boots. Her sandy hair was shoulder length and waved, and her eyebrows plucked thin. She wore perfectly applied makeup, which would not have been out of place for an evening on a London,

West End, dance floor. She also wore a thin, tightly buttoned white blouse, bursting at the seams, although since she had small, neat breasts, she admittedly didn't look vulgar.

The girl caught sight of Edith and Hester, and her expression changed to defensive sullenness.

Why - she is *fifteen!* Edith thought as she tried to compose her face into a smile. It was not how she had imagined the sporty blue stocking described to her, at all, but now she looked at the girl, she could recognise the resemblance to her father. It was undoubtedly Sophie Stevens.

'Hello...' Hester started to speak but stopped as the second figure started climbing gracefully over the gate, also clad in jodhpurs, long boots, and a tight low-cut blouse.

The 'girl' was under five foot but still managed to have extremely long legs. Unlike Sophie, she had rather large breasts, which were made more prominent by her very tiny waist. She also had fashionably thin brows and perfect makeup, and her loose bubble curl platinum hair was cut off in a bob. *She looks like a blond Betty Boop.* Edith stood there, uncomprehending. *Betty Boop* clearly wasn't twelve-years-old. She decided it must be Sophie's friend, but the 'girl' walked confidently towards her with a polite smile.

'Good morning! Is it still morning? You must be Miss Kershaw and Mrs Denney? We *are* expecting you, and lunch is in the oven, but Sophie and I have taken far too long mucking out the stables,

I'm afraid. Do come in. Mr Stevens is about somewhere.'

She gave them a frank appraisal with her huge, very round blue eyes.

'Oh, I forgot to introduce myself. I'm Gwendoline Brown, and I'm officially the housekeeper, but I seem to do most things around here. I'm also the stable lad, as you can see. Sophie! Say hello to your guests!'

Edith felt the lavender water in her pocket and decided to keep it there. She thrust the jam towards Sophie,

'This is for you and your sister. I made it. I'm Edith Kershaw, and this is Hester Denney. Very pleased to meet you at last. Your father has often spoken of you.'

'Thank you very much,' the young girl said grudgingly. She didn't look like a person for whom jam was a thrilling present.

Hester looked at Edith and raised her eyebrows as they followed the two young women up the long path to the front door, their heels sinking in the gravel.

Edith thought it was a fairly new house, probably built just after the war, with a nod to the Tudorbethan style, despite the pebbledash. There were large diamond pane leaded windows on either side of the porch, around which grew a yellow rose, and four more windows looking out from the upper story, which were bedrooms judging by the chintz curtains and nick knacks on the window ledges.

Edith was quite shocked to notice some shiny satin feminine lingerie in tea rose and nile green which had obviously been rinsed out and hung up to dry at a bedroom window.

Surely it couldn't belong to the fifteen-year-old schoolgirl? But paid staff couldn't own such ravishing undergarments and hang them where their male employer might easily see them?

Hester followed Edith's gaze and raised her eyebrows again, as Mrs Brown pushed open the big yellow front door and invited them into the short, brown linoleum covered, hallway.

They're walking into the house in the boots they wore in the stables and paddock, thought Edith. It was not something she could imagine doing. *Sophie ought to be taught not to do it either. They must have manure on those boots.*

The hallway smelt faintly of cat pee, which somebody had tried to cover by hurriedly passing wax polish over the hall stand. Reproduction Renoirs and Stubbs paintings hung in gilt plaster frames in the narrow passage. Hester nearly stood on a large black kitten which hissed and promptly clawed her leg. A little scarlet spot appeared on her silk stocking.

'I am *so* sorry!' Mrs Brown said, picking up the cat and cuddling it. 'It's Bella's cat. There's a litter of them - they're a bit wild. Sophie...go and find Bella and tell her to come and get Satan. And tell your father his guests are here.' She looked at Hester without any embarrassment.

'Mrs Denney...? Please let me show you the

bathroom upstairs. There's a first aid kit in the bathroom cabinet. I think we need to put some antiseptic on that.'

Sophie had disappeared into the depths of the house, and a minute later, a slight child with dark hair had appeared in the hallway and, glaring at them, snatched the kitten out of Mrs Brown's arms. She looked as if she was going to go without greeting them, but the housekeeper bellowed at her.

'Annabella! Be polite! Say hello to Miss Kershaw and Mrs Denney. They've come for lunch, and I want you to take Miss Kershaw into the sitting room - and find your father, please. I've got to show Mrs Denney the big bathroom because Satan attacked her leg.'

'Do you like cats?' Bella was looking at Hester's leg with its torn stocking and scarlet stain.

'Yes,' said Hester pleasantly. 'I've got a Tabby Tom called Valentino. Don't worry about my leg. Satan didn't mean to do it - I didn't see him and I almost trod on him. He was scared.'

Bella's face broke into a smile. 'Satan is a girl. I'm sorry about your leg. Gwen will put some iodine on it, won't you Gwen?'

Mrs Brown led Hester out of the hall, and Bella gestured at Edith to follow her.

The hallway had been gloomy, and Edith had failed to see the young girl's face properly, but to her bewilderment, once in the brightly lit sitting room, she was able to see that the child's hair had been crimped into waves and, like her older sister, her eyebrows were plucked thin, and she had a full face of very professionally applied make up. Edith had never actually seen a twelve-year-old look like this before, and she was quite taken aback.

'Does Annabella always do her hair and face that way,' she asked Adrian when he'd appeared and they were installed on the sofa close together and he'd taken her hand and kissed her hair, taking advantage of them being momentarily alone. Edith tried hard not to sound critical.

'Good Lord, no,' Adrian said. 'The girls were looking at some magazines this morning with Mrs Brown and Mrs Brown was seeing how she and Sophie would look if they did their hair and faces like Jean Harlow. They don't usually look like that - they were just experimenting. I think they're going to put their best frocks on for lunch. Bella doesn't like to be left out, so Mrs Brown did her, too. It's just a bit of fun. A gin and tonic? I'm sure Hester will have one.'

'A Bloody Mary if you've got any vodka. Otherwise, a gin'll do fine. Please. Are Sophie and Mrs Brown very close?'

'Well, yes. Sophie was five when she started here - Bella was two - and now that they've lost their mother, Mrs Brown has to help them with all the... women's side of things. The girls are growing up, and they need feminine advice and guidance, which I can't really give. I'm hoping that, perhaps, the girls might also be able to turn to *you* one day?'
He patted her knee fondly.

Edith smiled but moved slightly away as

Hester and Mrs Brown came back into the room accompanied by Sophie, watching her father and Edith with a cool expression. Sophie had evidently noticed how close the pair were sitting on the sofa, but she was not giving any indications of whether she approved or not.

Probably not, Edith thought, *but that's natural. I'll need to reassure them that I won't take their father away from them.*

A smallish black dog with big eyes and long ears had followed the women into the room and had bounded across to his master, with evident joy, to have his head stroked.

'This is Monty,' said Adrian, reaching in his pocket to fish out a piece of sausage for him. Edith had already heard all about Monty when they were in Paris. He was a silky black-furred mongrel - a cross between a cavalier spaniel and a poodle - 'but so good-tempered that someone ought to start a breed,' the detective had said, 'although he will chase all the cats if he gets half a chance. Luckily, they're too fast for him and can climb.'

All the cats, Edith noted, as she reached over to pat Monty's rump. The dog ignored her.
Adrian handed a G&T each to Edith and Hester.

'Sorry - no vodka, I'm afraid. Cigarette?'

There was a large party drum of Camel on the table nest.

Edith noticed that Mrs Brown and Sophie were now wearing identical cotton tea dresses in different shades and similar shoes.

'I shall finish off in the kitchen, Mr Stevens, and Sophie will set the table. If you give me five minutes, you may go into the Dining Room. Perhaps you would like to call Bella down,' said Mrs Brown.

Adrian obediently got up and went to the bottom of the stairs to holler for his youngest daughter.

Monty followed Mrs Brown towards the kitchen.

'You were a long time?' Edith whispered to Hester with an interrogatory expression.

'Gwen Brown was cleaning my 'wound' and giving me a tour of the house. She's very chatty. I've lots to tell you - wait 'til we're in the car...Oh, look at that!' Hester pointed to a framed picture of a woman in a wedding dress who looked remarkably like an older version of Annabella. 'It must be the late Mrs Stevens.'

The picture was placed next to one of many house plants which were dropping leaves. But before Edith could reply, the detective returned to usher them into the dining room.

The dining room was spacious and high-ceilinged, as the sitting room had been, with a large diamond-paned window at one end, which gave onto the front of the house, and a smaller window at the back near the table, which was laid for five.
Adrian looked at the table momentarily and then pulled out two chairs.

'Please sit down. I won't be a minute.'
And then he was gone through a door which neither

of them had noticed but which obviously gave directly onto the kitchen.

Edith looked around the room curiously. It was strange sitting for the first time in the house of the man she was in love with and with whom she hoped she might marry and have her own children. Everything looked so different to her own home. There were no bookshelves, for one thing, neither in the sitting room nor this dining room, although there were piles of board games. She tried to imagine herself playing Monopoly with Sophie and Annabella and couldn't manage it. The pictures on the walls were all reproductions and distinctly twee, and furthermore, the frames didn't go together. Come to think of it, the cushions didn't either; they were tapestry cottage scenes or flowery chintz like the curtains, covered in cat hairs, and the springs had definitely gone on the old sitting room sofa, which had gone saggy in the middle. There were a lot of dusty ornaments in both the rooms - Minty Stevens had obviously collected china dogs and horses. Edith imagined that Adrian's late wife had chosen the décor with him.

Adrian had never known how to dress though, so he presumably didn't mind nothing matching. She probably could redecorate slowly, but it was evident that the place was none too clean and nobody minded in the least.

There were an awful lot of framed family snapshots on a sideboard in the dining room; photographs of Adrian in official police photos - he'd obviously started as a uniformed constable before transferring to the plain clothes CID - and there were many of the children at various ages, usually posed with a horse or holding Monty or different cats.

There were also some pictures of the girls which included Gwen Brown. In one, she sat on a rug at a family picnic, looking like a child herself as she cuddled a dark-haired toddler, her other arm protectively around a laughing blond Sophie with jam on her face. In another, she sat on horseback between Sophie and Bella following a smiling Minty, who was mounted on a Grey, and leading a riderless horse which was obviously Adrian's; he must have jumped down to take the picture.

'Buck up!' said Hester, and Edith realised that she must look rather glum.

The window near them had been left slightly ajar, and the kitchen window was definitely open, too, because the conversation in the other room could be heard embarrassingly loud and clear.

'Sophie! Lay another place at the table, please, and then could you leave us? I want to have a word with Gwendoline - alone,' came Adrian's voice.

There was a loud rattling noise of metal on metal, which was obviously the cutlery drawer being opened and knives and forks being taken out of it. There was another sound of cupboard doors being opened and closed, and finally, the door into the dining room opened, and Sophie appeared. However, neither Edith nor Hester paid her any attention, glued, as they were, to the private conversation.

What was so secretive between Adrian and his curvaceous housekeeper?

'Gwen? Why did Sophie only set the table for five?'

'Because I asked her to.'

'Why? Who's not eating with us?'

'Me, of course. I can eat in the kitchen.'

'Don't be silly - I wouldn't hear of it.'

From the clicking heels and clattering of saucepans, it sounded like Mrs Brown was walking around, preparing to dish up.

'I don't feel it would be proper for me to eat at the dining table when you have guests. They might not like it.'

'That's ridiculous. You always eat at the table with us. Why should it be any different if I have friends here? You've never said anything about eating with my other friends. You even made up a foursome at cards the other week...'

There came the sound of the oven door opening.

'Here! Let me help you lift the trays out of the oven - that's far too heavy!' Came Adrian's voice.

'The other people who visit here are policemen and their wives, and they all know my father, though he might be only a constable. The police are like one family, Sir, you know it. These ladies are rather proper, and I think they might not want to eat with the staff. I'm trying to be correct. I know my place. It's different when it's just us.'

'Well, you're more than staff. You're part of

this family. I won't have you sat alone in the kitchen. Miss Kershaw and Mrs Denney are very nice people, and they won't mind at all. I've told Miss Kershaw all about you. I always refer to you as *Mrs* Brown, to give you some status -they don't imagine you're our skivvy.'

Edith pulled a face involuntarily and then realised that Sophie Stevens was standing silently in the room, watching her closely. She must be aware that they were eavesdropping.

'I really want you and Miss Kershaw to be firm friends,' Adrian's disembodied voice continued. 'As you were with Mrs Stevens. I hope you'll like her - and you have some influence on the girls. After everything we've all been through these last years, you've managed to make this a happy house again for us all, and I don't want that to change. Gwen...' his voice dropped, and the clattering kitchen sounds stopped, '... I'm quite serious about Miss Kershaw, and I'm thinking that one day I might ask her to marry me, and if I do, then I suppose she'll be coming to live here. I'm counting on you to help her fit in.' His voice returned to normal. 'Now - let's do this as a team. I'll carry the roast through and carve; you can bring the vegetables and hand them around. Mmm - that smells so good. You really are the best cook, you know.'

Sophie hurried to sit down at the table with a secretive smile.

'Where do *you* live?' she asked Hester pleasantly as her father entered by the dining room door.

'Isn't Bella down yet?' Adrian asked Sophie, 'can you serve the wine? Glad to see you gals are getting on...'

The afternoon over, Edith drove the motorcar out of Chichester in silence, steering the little Austin through the beautiful countryside without seeing it. Hester sat beside her not knowing what to say; she knew her cousin well enough to know what was wrong, but she didn't know how to begin a conversation that wouldn't be easy.

The sound of a loud klaxon broke the ice. Edith had driven out of a turning without paying attention and had incurred the wrath of a delivery van, which had been obliged to break sharply.

'Pay attention, darling! I know you're in a stew, but you're just going to have to get on with it - if you still intend to be Mrs Edie Stevens, that is; it sounds like he wants you to be. His daughters are great fun. And Gwen Brown is very pleasant. You won't have to be a surrogate mother because she's like a big sister to them and does everything for them.'

'Why do you assume Mrs Brown will still be there - if I were to marry Adrian? I might want a fresh start with my own household arrangements? Did you see how dirty the house was? She's meant to be in charge of the housework! And she really shouldn't have plucked the eyebrows of a twelve-year-old and a fifteen-year-old to look like Jean Harlow. And she should have sorted out the cat problem.'

Edith had been horrified when, during lunch a

gigantic, evil-looking, tom cat had tried to enter by the half open window. It had yellow eyes in a thin tabby face, one fang hanging over the uneven lip and a ragged ear and you could smell its fetid breath across the room.

Monty threw his head back and gave a mournful bark at the sight of the cat.

'Brutus,' said Gwen Brown, jumping up from the table to shut the window. 'Excuse me,' she apologised, pushing aside her plate, which was still half full, walking towards the kitchen. 'I'd better go and give him something to eat. He usually arrives here because he's hungry,' she said to Hester.

'Brutus is a stray we've adopted,' Bella explained. 'He comes to see our black cat, Maisie. He's the father of Satan, Lucifer, and Nick.'

'Won't you keep getting more kittens if you encourage him around by feeding him?' Edith had asked.

'I hope so,' said Bella. 'You can never have too many kittens.'

'The cats go down to the stables to hunt,' is all Adrian had said. 'It keeps the rats down. And out of our vegetable garden.'

The trouble was certainly Mrs Brown, from Edith's perspective.

She didn't know what she had expected 'Brown' to be like from Adrian's description. She supposed she had automatically thought of a rotund, twinkly-eyed, maternal, middle-aged woman who scrubbed the house (or directed the maid to do so).

She had expected a faithful family retainer who ruled the girls, and Adrian, with a kindly authority and kept them looking smart and tidy. She hadn't expected Mrs Brown to be what they called a 'pocket Venus,' younger than herself.

'Besides...Mrs Brown is far too familiar with Adrian. She definitely *doesn't know* her place - whatever she might say. She was teasing him about his bad dress sense *and* finishing off his sentences for him.'

Edith put the car in the wrong gear and inadvertently revved the engine as they passed a cyclist, nearly forcing him into the hedge.

'Gwen has been with the family since she was fourteen. She came straight from school...' Hester said.

'Oh? Gwen, is it? *Very* chummy...'

Hester ignored her irritated crack and continued, '...She told me upstairs that her father was a police constable, and her mother a dairymaid, and they had twelve children who all lived. Most of the boys go into the police force as soon as they're able, and most of the girls have been placed into service to lighten the costs at home. Her father is based at Chichester police station and arranged things with the Stevens's. She didn't want to go into service - she loved studying at school - but she was given no alternative. That's why she loves encouraging the girls with schoolwork.'

'She's been very chatty, I see!'

'Well, I asked her questions I thought you'd

like to know...Do be careful!'

Edith was driving quite erratically.

'It must have been absolutely dreadful when Mrs Stevens got ill and died. Until then, it was quite fun when the children were small. Mrs Stevens taught her to ride and sew - they made all the home furnishings together. She already knew how to grow food and cook. Mrs Stevens was in decline for a long time, you know. She had cancer, and it spread. She died upstairs in total agony, and Gwen had to step up and take over the household. She says Adrian was out of his mind with worry...He must have confided a lot in her because she was so fond of Mrs Stevens.

Edith didn't reply. She didn't want to be uncharitable.

Hester said, 'you must be pleased to hear that Adrian's contemplating marrying you! - that's what you want, isn't it? Gwen is nearly half his age, and I think he looks at her almost like a daughter. I think that you're going to have become big friends with her if you *do* want to marry him - and make a real effort with the girls.'

'So, my relationship with Adrian depends on his staff, does it?' Edith didn't mean to sound so bitter, but it just slipped out.

'Oh, don't worry,' said Hester, and rather naughtily added, 'looking like *that*, she's bound to find a husband and leave - sooner rather than later. She probably looks upon Adrian as an old man. She's been there ten years, you know, living under the same roof. If ever there was going to be anything romantic between them, it would have happened by now. Wouldn't it?'

I just want to solve the Arundel murder case and go back to Cuckfield, Edith thought. *We'll take it from there, but maybe I'm destined to die an old maid after all.*

She couldn't imagine herself ever moving into that house. She really could cry.

'I think we're going to have to have another séance,' she said to Hester, abruptly changing the subject.

'When?'

'Tonight. Midnight, like the last time. When the spirits are closest. I want to concentrate on clearing Arthur Lamb's name and seeing justice served for that poor murdered couple and their families. Time is nearly run out. I'll decide about Adrian afterwards.'

CHAPTER 19

The evening had seemed interminable as they waited for midnight. They'd eaten so much at luncheon that they skipped supper and even passed up on the cocktails, preferring a long stroll along the river bank enjoying the wildflowers and river traffic. The buzzards were nowhere to be seen, and they supposed they were hunting on the other side of the castle, but as the twilight drew in, bats could be seen flitting over the town and hunting insects in the light of the street lamps.

Hester was nervous as the hour drew nearer; she remembered only too well how the rapping sounds and the stomping boots had woken up the guests in the neighbouring bedroom the last time around. She had also had the unwelcome sense of not being alone, every time she had to be in the bedroom by herself afterwards. Nevertheless, the thought of a séance held a certain fascination for her, for although she had always believed in her cousin's psychic abilities, she had never before experienced anything herself until she had heard the disembodied sounds coming from the Napoleonic soldier - or so Edith told her they did.

'At midnight, I get the feeling that the veil between this world and the next is thinnest,' Edith said. 'I want to see if I can reach Louise or Arthur. I'm sure they want their killers caught, so perhaps they'll help us find the proof we need.'

They prepared the room as before and sat warmly wrapped up, ready for a sudden temperature drop, facing each other with Hester's hands lightly resting in Edith's upturned palms, so as to share her energy.

As the clock reached twelve, Edith began: 'Louise - can you hear me? Hester - think of Louise. I'm imagining Louise. Try to think of Louise in her blue jacket. Louise, are you here?'

The atmosphere in the room seemed heightened, Hester thought. She could see the wardrobe, two beds, and the window clearly in the dim light of the covered lamp. The ticking of the little clock seemed louder.

'If you are here, Louise, make yourself known.'

The lamp suddenly started flickering wildly, making Hester's hair stand up on the back of her neck as something freezing cold brushed past her.

'Louise - please rap once if you're with us in the room.'

Edith's eyes were closed, and her face had gone an eerie blank, but Hester's heart was pounding as she waited for the loud rap on the wooden table. But the room remained silent.

'Is there anybody there?' Edith asked.

The room stayed silent, although Hester's heart still raced in fear and anticipation. The lamp flickered crazily again, and an unnatural cold was still circling the room.

'Is that Louise?' Edith asked, 'Louise, if you are with us, please rap on the table once. Louise - we are here to help, but *you* must help *us* bring those who murdered you to justice. Louise, please rap once.'

Suddenly, Hester nearly gagged; the room was filled with a foul and acrid odour comprising of a male body unwashed for months, unwashed clothes mixed with tallow hair pomade, leather, rotten stumpy teeth and bad breath, pipe tobacco, and faeces.

It wasn't the fragrant Louise Lamb who had come through but William, the redcoat soldier, again.

'Ugggh...can you smell that stink?' Hester whispered, but Edith was still blank and unmoved and appeared to be concentrating.

'Are you Willy?' She asked.

RAP.

Hester jumped. She was dying to hold her nose but didn't dare take her hands away from Edith's.

'Willy - is Louise in the room with you?' Edith asked, but the room remained silent, although she could feel that strange vibration in her head. Hester could sense somebody moving around the room, even though she couldn't hear his boots this time. The foul smell made her feel ill, and the unnatural chill in the room gave her goosebumps.

'Willy, have you come to help us solve the murders?' Edith asked him.

RAP

Hester's eyes were wide open, and she tried to see anything moving on the bedside tables, but everything was still. She whispered, 'I think he's attached himself to you, darling. If things don't work out with Adrian Stevens, then there's always Willy!'

BUMP

The temperature in the room returned to normal.

Edith awoke abruptly from her trance.
'It's no use,' she said. 'Stop larking about. He's gone now. I tried to concentrate on Louise, but I couldn't reach her. My mind kept emptying. I couldn't even see William - just everything was going blue.'

'I could certainly smell him,' Hester said. 'No wonder the Norfolk Arms complained about whole regiments of soldiers billeted here. Can you imagine the stink in the place?'

'He did say he'd help us, so maybe we just need to wait for him to lead us to another clue like he did with the ring? There's one more thing I could try, though...If I get my pastels out, maybe I could do an automatic drawing? You get into bed and warm up - and keep quiet!'

Edith put the open box of pastels on the table next to a blank sheet of paper and closed her eyes. She tried to ignore Hester and concentrated on relaxing her body - first her head, next her neck, then each arm, her spine and finally her legs. All the while, she emptied her mind of any thought except Louise as she had been when she saw her standing on the stairs next to her new husband.

Still with her eyes closed, she allowed her hand to lightly grasp a pastel and move as it wanted across the paper. The hand didn't want to take another pastel, and after a moment or two of sitting quietly, she gradually returned to the world and opened her eyes.

The only sound in the room was Hester's rhythmic breathing; her cousin was sound asleep.

Looking at the paper eagerly, Edith saw with great disappointment that she'd only drawn unintelligible scribbles, all in a shade of blue. It seemed that the colour blue was blocking all attempts to find out anything useful. Perhaps it was because she had been visualising Louise, and Louise had been wearing blue, the same shade in fact. But there was nothing beyond the colour. The thought struck her that Louise was probably wearing that blue when she walked back to Arundel to be murdered, but why had nobody seen her on the footpath?

Both women only slept in fits and starts in the end. Hester because she was afraid of the ghostly soldier appearing next to her bed or hiding under it, and Edith because her mind kept going back to Adrian Stevens and the lunch the previous day that had shattered so many of her illusions. Falling in love with Adrian seemed so complicated, bliss one minute and pain the next. It had never been like that with Michael; it had been effortless, apart from a constant fear about his dangerous job. That was probably because she and Mick had been very well suited with similar interests and outlooks on life, and there was nothing to come between them. It had been glaringly obvious today that whilst she was happiest with her paintings and books, Adrian enjoyed riding, playing board games with his children and socialising with police colleagues over card games - all things he could enjoy doing with Gwendoline Brown but which did not excite Edith. And then there was the fact that while she had now accepted that being psychic was a huge part of her life, and it was something that singled her out from most other people, she had to keep it hidden from Adrian, who didn't even countenance the idea that mediums existed. She was also worried that his daughters would never accept her as a stepmother; they obviously hoped they could continue as a family of four with Mrs Brown.

At daybreak, Edith crept to the window to smoke a cigarette and watch Arundel come awake. She imagined Hester was still dozing, but to her surprise, her cousin joined her at the window, wrapped in a blanket, and began slathering her face with face cream.

Suddenly, Edith pointed at the sky. The buzzards were up early and hunting, circling above the High Street, their fan tails silhouetted against the heavens. It was very faint, but her head began to feel odd as she watched them.

'Those birds again. Is it a sign, I wonder? Get dressed, Hess. We can take a walk before breakfast.' Hester gave a groan.

'Give me time. I've got to do my face. I didn't sleep easily.'

'I hope there are some bathrooms free. You get yourself together - we don't need to make up. I don't want those birds to go.'

Twenty minutes later, Edith was outside with a moaning Hester. She shaded her eyes, looking up at the morning sky, searching for the buzzards. They were still there, flying low and circling above the Town Square.

'You see, they can't find any prey here - there are too many people about,' Edith said.

The street was full of men, and some women, hurrying to work or catching the bus to a bigger town to shop. The brown and cream bus was parked in the square, and Edith could see the notice on the front - Chichester. The sides of it shook as the motor turned over, and the uniformed conductor leaned against the side, selling tickets from a machine strung around his neck. A steady stream of people were getting on; female shoppers with wicker baskets or fabric bags and some businessmen in suits with leather briefcases and bowler hats. Most of the crowd were in dark colours and looking smart for a visit to the cathedral city, but Edith suddenly spotted a flash of scarlet moving down the interior of the bus and looking very out of place. There seemed to be a little flurry as some of the passengers looked anxiously around them, pulled their coats closer, or grimaced and held their noses, before relaxing again.

'It's William - I saw him on the bus for Chichester. It's the clue. It's the early bus. It must be the one Caroline Wren got on the day Arthur and Louise set off for their honeymoon, and Louise was murdered.'

'We don't have to get the bus, do we?' Hester

asked, crestfallen. 'They stink of petrol, are noisy and drafty, and this one must stop off in several villages before it gets to Chichester.'

'No,' said Edith, 'I'll drive us after breakfast'.

Edith waited until the bleary-eyed pair were seated in the cheerful green breakfast room, sipping their tea, before she started thinking over the soldier's message again.

'Willy means us to go to Chichester,' she said after they had ordered their eggs and bacon from the exotically handsome Nijinsky. 'Hester, stop eyeing up that waiter! We saw Mrs Wren returning with her shopping, and she told the police that she had bought country clothes to wear in Scotland. Ergo she went shopping for clothes. But she had also accompanied Louise shopping for clothes in Chichester, before the wedding, according to Alma. They bought Louise's blue outfit together - the one she wore when she set off for the station. And during the séance and the automatic drawing session, I couldn't 'get' anything but that blue. Maybe we need to investigate the place where we know Caroline Wren went with Louise, first - and then where she bought that dull skirt. It could well be the same shop. Why else would Willy tell me first the colour blue, and then to go to Chichester?'

'Does that mean we're going clothes shopping?' Hester brightened considerably as she buttered her toast and patted her brown curls all at the same time.

'I'm afraid so,' Edith said. 'Leave your purse behind; I shall buy your luncheon. I promised Phillip you'd be good. We'll have to get ourselves rigged up to look as swanky as we can manage, though.'

Hester started humming Puttin' on the Ritz, and gave the waiter a playful wink.

CHAPTER 20

Edith parked the car and, after a quick look up and down South Street, led Hester almost straight away to an expensive-looking Ladies' dress shop.

'I must say, your psychic gifts are awfully useful,' Hester said. 'Can you find lovely shops in *any* city?'

'It wasn't my psychic intuition that found this shop...' Edith already had her hand on the long, vertical, brass door handle.'...but I'm sure Louise must have bought her jacket here, and it's pure deduction.'

'I say!' Hester looked at her from under the coquettishly angled brim of her fawn felt titfer.

'Whatever could make you convinced that this is the right place?'

'Elementary, my dear Hess!' Edith continued,

'Alma mentioned that Louise went shopping in Chichester town to buy her 'going away' outfit with Caroline Wren. Louise was so well dressed that, if she didn't buy her jacket tailored from her dressmaker, she had to have bought it from the best address in the city, which would be found in the most expensive shopping street. Judging by the window displays around here - this is the most expensive street. And this is the most Louise-like shop. Willy can't help us, I'm afraid, because he can't go far from the Norfolk Arms. We wouldn't want to go shopping accompanied by that pong, anyhow. Let's go in!'

They stood before a bow-fronted glass window with gold lettering and a greyish-green painted wooden surround. There was only one bronze silk taffeta dress in the window, displayed with a sable fur draped over one shoulder, a gold and sherry topaz brooch, and an exquisite little hat with dyed coloured feathers which complimented the whole look admirably. A huge antique vase stood beside the mannequin, filled with an enormous bouquet of hothouse flowers.

Edith pushed the door open.

The lady proprietor of the shop had been watching them hovering outside, and had maneuvered herself closer to the front of the shop, pretending to be engrossed in something and entirely unconcerned with them. In fact, the elegant shopkeeper was so eager to entice them in, that the black silk-clad woman was spinning around to adjust tempting displays, her tape measure draped over one shoulder. She rapidly ran an expert eye over their handbags and shoes as they entered, and evidently decided that they passed muster since she gave a professional smile and welcomed them over the plush carpet into the perfumed depths of her shop. It held only three rails of expensive clothing, a row of gorgeous hats, and some displays of modern satin bags and gloves. A glass cabinet held select gemstone brooches and enamel geometric necklaces.

'Modom? May I be of assistance?' The woman smelt of a refined scent. She looked from Edith to Hester and back again, unsure which woman was her potential customer.

Edith took the lead. 'I'm looking for a blue jacket,' she said. She was correct that they'd come to the right shop. It was surprisingly easy to get the shop's owner to talk about the beautiful young woman who had been a regular purchaser of her pricey wares, and had gone missing in such mysterious circumstances so soon after her wedding. Gossip had quickly gone around the shopkeepers of Chichester, a tight-knit community.

'We're not from around here,' Edith told the proprietress as Hester breathed in deeply the aroma of rose water, powder, leather, and fresh flowers that pervaded the air. 'But our cousin, Miss Louise Matthews, recommended your establishment to us.'
'Miss Matthews! Or Mrs Lamb, I suppose she is now. Have they found her alive then? I do hope she's well.'

The woman had a distinct Hampshire burr that could be detected beneath her rather snooty accent - even though they were in Sussex.

'Not yet,' said Edith. 'But she had told us before that she bought her beautiful blue jacket here. The one she wore to leave for her honeymoon. It was so lovely! I wondered if you had the same jacket in a different colour?'

'I know the jacket Modom is referring to,' the woman replied straight away as she walked over to a rail against the grey-green wall and began sorting through the jackets hanging there. Edith took the opportunity to shoot a reproving look at Hester, who was showing too much interest in a grey straw hat that looked Italian and very expensive.

'This is the one,' the shopkeeper declared, holding the jacket in front of her body with a practised flourish and smoothing the raw silk with her left hand as she did so.

'That certainly is the jacket!' chipped in Hester. 'I must say, it is yummy,' she sighed. 'Would you have it in my size, d'you think?'
Edith gave her another warning look.

'This one looks to be your size, but I can alter it to be tailored to fit you perfectly. I have a machine in a room behind the shop, and I could have the jacket finished in an hour or two, depending on the amount of work I have.'

She called to a young assistant who suddenly appeared through a door on the far wall.

'Maud, slip this on to show these ladies the style.'

Maud disappeared behind some grand velvet curtains and reappeared in the silk jacket, her rather sulky pout replaced with a professional sultry smile as she walked elegantly the length of the shop and gave a twirl before strolling back. The black-clad shopkeeper plucked an identical jacket from the same rail in sea green and showed it to Edith this time.

'This jacket would be perfect in green to go with Modom's splendid colouring. Maud!' She handed the green jacket to her trim assistant to model.

Soon, Edith herself was clad in the beautiful

raw silk jacket, admiring herself in the full-length wooden and gold leaf framed mirror. The jacket looked very glamorous, and the sea green colour with Edith's russet hair looked so entirely wonderful that, for a moment, she considered buying it. However, it was far more expensive than any jacket she had owned so far. She thought sadly that it was a jacket to wear to dinner with Adrian on trips like the one to Paris, and it was totally inappropriate to wear out to lunch in Cuckfield or Haywards Heath with the sort of person who usually invited her.

Edith realised that she was no longer so optimistic about her future. This was definitely not the sort of jacket in which you perched on chairs covered in cat hairs and allowed to be kneaded by sharp claws - but nor was anything she already owned. She suspected that Adrian might prefer it if she wore tatty jodhpurs.

'You *must* buy it!' Hester gave a generous smile. 'That style looks so much better on you than it does on me. I can quite see how Louise managed to look like an American film star from that Hollywood place if she shopped here.'

The shop owner smiled politely and gave the faintest bow, with a slight inclination of her head and an expansive movement of her hands.

'You look absolutely splendid in it, Modom,' said the spiderish proprietress, fingering her tape measure hopefully. 'Quite a number of people have looked at it, but one needs to have style, character, and personality, such as you have, to carry it off successfully.'

But Edith was now thinking about the reason she and Hester had arrived at this shop in the first place. Why had her psychic intuition - helped by the ghostly red coat, who appeared to have become her spirit guide in Arundel - sent her searching for the shop where Louise had bought her blue silk jacket?

'I love the jacket but let me think about it for a bit,' she told the woman as she gave another twirl in front of the mirror.

'Tell me,' Edith asked, 'there was another friend of ours who was with Cousin Louise when she bought the blue jacket. A petite, elegant, dark-haired woman? I expect she bought many things here; Mrs Caroline Wren is always so well dressed.'

The shop owner laughed graciously. 'Oh, yes, I do remember her. An absolutely delightful woman. Is she a friend of yours? A lovely lady. She'd visited with Miss Matthews before. She did buy something, yes.'

'What did she buy?' Asked Hester, slipping off the blue jacket.

Edith was grateful that Hester could be so direct. She wasn't sure that she could ask a question that ought not to be any of their business. Still, it put the shopkeeper on the spot, and taken by surprise, she answered: -

'She bought that same jacket, in blue, as a matter of fact.'

Now it was Edith and Hester's turn to be surprised, although they each made an effort not to show it.

'They both bought the same blue jacket?'
Hester looked flummoxed.

'Yes,' said the woman, fiddling with her
bracelet uncomfortably. 'But don't tell her I told you
so. I don't think she wanted Miss Matthews to know.
She said she would never wear it at the same time
anyhow. I mean, so many of my customers *do* buy
the same item, but one simply learns, when dressing,
to check with one's friends before an event.'

'Mrs Wren bought the same jacket as Miss
Matthews after shopping together? They weren't the
same colouring or proportions at all. Did it actually
suit her?' Hester was astonished, but for Edith the
penny had dropped.

'Oh, it's alright,' Edith said to Hester,
reassuringly. 'I remember now that she told us
herself, didn't she sweetie?' She'd turned to face her
cousin. 'Caroline came back very early the next day to
buy the same jacket, didn't she? She must have been
the first customer.'

The shopkeeper acquiesced, uncertain if she
was giving away too much personal information. 'She
was on the doorstep when I arrived. She said that she
had to be quick, as she was expected in Arundel for
luncheon.'

Edith nodded. 'She bought the matching
gloves, too? And a tweed skirt?'

'The gloves, yes. But we don't sell country
clothes here. I directed her to the department store
down the road when she enquired.'

After dropping off a 'thank you for a lovely lunch' note for Detective Inspector Stevens at the Police station, the pair had driven back to Arundel talking of nothing else but the murder, and the significance of the two jackets.

'I can't wait to get back; we'll walk through the murder scenario,' said Edith. 'I think I know what happened. Poor, poor, Louise...'

Adrian Stevens was coming over for cocktails that evening, and she wanted to tell him how the murder was committed, although she had a strangely painful feeling and wondered whether she wanted to see him at all.

After a couple of gin and tonics and a swift lunch, Edith and Hester found themselves in the reception area of the Norfolk Arms, looking at the stairs which swept rather grandly up to the first floor, with a big vase of flowers in the stairwell, poking above the polished wooden rail, and a graceful black metal balustrade. The stairs were flooded with light from the large leaded window on the landing between the floors.

'Let's think back,' said Edith, 'Louise and Arthur were standing on the stairs about halfway up, looking over the rail, and Louise was all in blue. She had on the jacket, and the gloves, and a wide brimmed navy felt hat with the spotted veil pushed up. It was definitely them. They were standing so everybody got a good look at them and posing for snapshots.'

Hester grimaced. 'There were so many people

crowded around to see them off, I can't remember exactly, but I think the Wren couple were around then. I was aware of Mrs Wren after all that had happened. I can't remember seeing Peter Laine or not. Our attention was on the newly-weds.' Hester screwed up her face in concentration. 'Was the Bounder there, with Joanne? Trouble is, we didn't really know the other guests. It's hard to say who was there and who, if anybody, was missing.'

'I remember there was a slight reaction when the wedding car arrived, but nobody could really see it, because it came through the arch and drove behind the hotel, and all of the wedding party were still milling about the bride and groom taking pictures on the stairs. You could only hear the car and see the top of it go past the door, if you happened to be looking in that direction. Most people had their backs to it.' Edith went on, 'I think the Wrens took the tin cans and the 'Just Married' placard out to the car. They must of. It had to have happened this way. They handed the cases out of the door to the chauffeur, too, I'm pretty certain. It was natural they would, because they were the close friends of the Bride and Groom.

The relatives were too busy having their photographs taken with the couple.'

Hester nodded in agreement.

Edith continued, 'It was Mr Lamb senior who told everybody to stand on the Town Square to wait for the wedding car to pass, so the newlyweds could be waved off to their honeymoon. Perhaps Edward Wren asked him to say it? - a message from the chauffeur? There was no room under the arch, and the pavements were too narrow; we were quite a crowd. Of course, milling in the square would mean that we weren't close to the car.'

She paused, looking sombre.

'The Wrens must have accompanied Louise and Arthur to the car, where Peter Laine was waiting disguised as the chauffeur. I'm sure they were attacked straight away. There were three assailants against two victims who were taken entirely by surprise. They didn't stand a chance. I hope they died quickly, but I doubt it. They must have been put in the boot; it was a big car.'

Edith and Hester walked out of the hotel and turned right into the car park, walking slowly around the corner until they were out of sight.

'There was no one to help them,' Edith said, staring down at the gravel. 'The wedding guests were the only people in the hotel besides the staff - and even the staff came out the front of the hotel and stood in the square with us to wave the car off. Besides, you can't see this spot from inside the building.'

'If they were bundled into the boot, they could have cried out if they weren't dead?' Hester looked drained of colour.

Edith shut her eyes and tried to see the bride and groom's faces in her mind's eye. She winced and clenched her fists as her head buzzed.

'The two men cracked them over the head with metal car jacks and squashed them both into the boot - there was hardly room for the both of them, they couldn't breathe anyway - and then they rammed flannels into their throats for good measure. They suffocated.'

'Hester's warm brown eyes filled with tears,

'It's so cruel. All because of that blasted ring! Oh, why didn't Arthur just sell the bloody thing back to Laine!'

'Yes. They must have known they were being murdered - and by those they counted as their friends. Maybe they didn't even know why. They were only married for a day.'

'Then Caroline Wren put on an identical blue jacket and gloves... couldn't she have just used Louise's?'

'She knew they might be covered in blood.' Edith shuddered. 'And Louise's jacket was too big. Edward didn't need to change. His jacket was similar to Arthur's anyway. I think they pushed Arthur and Louise's hats off before they hit them, and then the Wrens clapped the hats on their own heads.'

The two women walked silently out into the Town Square, casting their mind back to that day some months gone. It had been such a happy day for most of the people there, who had been unaware of the tragedy unfolding.

'We were all standing in the Town Square when the car came out,' Edith said. 'The chauffeur had goggles, a muffler and cap, and an overcoat, and he was behind thick glass. There's no way you could recognise the man. Most of the guests didn't know

Peter Laine personally anyhow.'

'I know it was a bit windy', said Hester. 'It was a huge, very high car, and the hood was half up to protect the 'bride and groom,' - as we thought they were - from the elements. I seem to remember that they had to hold onto their hats. The bride's hat had a navy veil with spots, over her face.'

Edith sighed. 'Exactly. We could only see the hats and their general clothes, and those probably for less than a minute. A few seconds, really. I imagine the cases were in the front passenger seat, covered with a blanket or something. There's no way that anyone could see into that car from the middle of the square.'

'It's perfectly horrible,' Hester said, sobbing. 'We all waved off the car, with its tin cans and 'just married' sign fixed to the bumper, little knowing that Arthur and Louise were dying in the boot. D'you think they could hear everybody cheering?'

Edith nodded, tears on her cheeks, 'I'm crying too, now! Let's try and keep ourselves together. '*I kept painting cars*, she thought. *I was obsessed with cars when I got back to Cuckfield, but I simply ignored what the spirit world wanted to tell me back then. I've changed.* 'Shall we take a stroll to the station?'

They were still wearing their high heels and town clothes, and so Edith and Hester linked arms as they walked carefully along the narrow pavement, crossed the bridge over the Arun, passed the White Hart and turned along the main road towards the station. The London train had just arrived as they tottered heavy hearted, on the footpath under the road and walked across the forecourt to the main entrance of Arundel Station. The hotel bus was drawn up at the station front, and there was much high-spirited chatter and laughter as visitors, come to see the castle, poured out into the sunshine to look for taxis to carry their cases, or walk the short distance into town.

'The wedding car must have stopped right in front of the entrance for the lady in the ticket office to see them get out of the vehicle,' remarked Edith. 'They must have timed things, so they arrived with only a minute to spare before the Portsmouth train got in, so that it was assumed that they'd got on the train. They probably stopped unseen, just before the turning, to cut the timing so fine.'

'Yes.'

'The ticket lady remembered the clothes, but she'd never seen the couple before, so she couldn't know they were imposters. She saw the car pull slowly away to park, and she saw it drive out of the forecourt without the tin cans, but she didn't see what must have happened when Laine stopped at the side entrance, out of her sight.'

'What do you think happened?' Hester's eyes were red. 'The Wrens threw the cases back into the car onto the back seat?'

'Well, of course, they must have. Together with the hats, the blue jacket, and gloves, to be covered by the blanket. They walked along the platform and dodged out of the side entrance instead of taking the stairs. Peter Laine must have put the hood up on the car, which would mask them from the forecourt. The Wrens then stepped onto the footpath under the road, hidden from view by the stairs to the footbridge over the railway.'

'It all makes sense,' Hester said. 'Nobody forced Louise back along the path to Arundel. It was Caroline Wren who smoked the Sobranie cigarette. I expect she took the packet from Louise's handbag in the car. She must have been very shaken up to smoke in public.'

'She had just helped murder her good friend!' Edith said dryly. 'And we now know why she bought a frumpy tweed skirt and plain shoes - she had them on at the luncheon, but we only saw her top half in the blue jacket and hat, when she was sitting in the car. The ticket lady only remembered the bright blue colour. Caroline didn't want to be noticed as they walked back to Arundel, so she took the jacket off. She had a beige cardigan on underneath it. When the police started asking questions weeks later, nobody remembered her at all. Of course, it's why she was so upset at the reception and had been crying before the luncheon. She knew what was going to happen.'

'Let's get back,' said Hester. 'All this talk of ciggies makes me think of having a smoke a in the snug. It must be the cocktail hour somewhere in the world.' She adjusted her hat over her brown curls and straightened her pearls. 'I need a drink, darling, just to get this ghastly murder out of my mind. Reading about murder may be exciting, but not when it happens to people you know. It's dreadful.'

Twenty minutes later they were back at the Norfolk Arms.

'There you go darling,' Hester said, as they looked for a bar man. 'The Wrens were back at the hotel before you could say Bob's your uncle, and nobody knew they'd even left the town. Peter Laine must have parked the car not too far away, and walked back, too.'

She suddenly had an idea, 'Oh, I say! Good job he wasn't parking the car in Birmingham. He'd probably have got the boot broken into by one of those Brummagem gangs. They'd have got a dreadful surprise.'

'Now,' said Edith, as Nijinsky poured their drinks (he appeared to do everything at the Norfolk Arms,) and the wireless played a big band tune, 'What are we going to tell Adrian this evening?'

'And so,' Edith finished, 'that's how the murder was committed. Arthur and Louise Lamb never got further than the Norfolk Arms car park, let alone France. The wedding guests only thought they'd seen them drive off, and the ticket lady at the station only thought she'd seen them arrive and catch the train, but it was a carefully staged illusion.'

Edith and Hester were sitting in the hotel snug with Adrian Stevens, filling him in about the blue jacket and its role in the murder. The hotel wireless was still playing Count Basie, although the radio waves were occasionally lost, obliging the tuxedoed barman to fiddle frantically with the dial as thirsty guests hung around the potted palms looking at their watches. Two old ladies with matching ice blue Marcel waves came in, wafting cologne, and chatted to a tiny man towing a Pekingese. It was such a civilised English atmosphere that it was hard to imagine the brutal murder behind the hotel, which Edith had just finished describing.

Adrian crushed out his cigarette and looked from Edith to Hester and back again. He sat in his favourite green leather club armchair near the unlit fireplace, playing with his whisky glass. Edith studied him; she still found him just as handsome as ever she had; his eyes were just as clear and pale blue, and his body just as big and powerful. She touched his arm and felt a thrill. She was unable to finish the relationship even if she wanted to.

CHAPTER 21

'The thing that I find incredible...' he began, stretching out his long legs and making the Pekingese jump (Adrian hadn't realised that the little dog had crept silently closer to be petted by Hester). '...The thing I find incredible is how you always find the lucky clues instead of the police. I mean, the police have put in a lot of leg work in this case, but you just happened to pick up that cigarette filter, wander into the Arundel jewellers, identify the ring halves in Brighton, and now you've found a shop in Chichester which claims Mrs Lamb and Mrs Wren both bought identical jackets on consecutive days - not that it proves your theory, of course. What are the chances of you just hitting upon information by chance?'

Hester went crimson and gave an enormous hiccup. They had been sitting in the snug for hours.

Edith could see that her tipsy cousin was getting increasingly excited, no doubt fuelled by gin, and that she was working herself up to telling the detective about the séances and the redcoat spirit guide. Edith kicked her hard under the low oak table. She could endure the idea that the developing relationship with Adrian Stevens might either fizzle out, or come to an abrupt end, if she, Edith, was in control. However, when she looked at his manly face with its craggy nose, she felt a stabbing pain at the thought of the policeman storming out and breaking off their love affair if he knew the two cousins had been courting the occult to find clues.

'Hic! Whadya do that for?' Hester hissed, rather too loudly, making Bobby the Pekingese start yapping, and causing his owner to jerk him away from their table.

'Do what?' Adrian looked perplexed.

'Hic. Hic. *Her!* She *kicked me*. Ouch!'

'Edie? Whatever's the matter?' He was clearly bemused.

'Hic. She doesn't want me to tell you about *William.*'

'Who's Will...' Adrian started to say, but then he finished with 'not that it's any of my business, of course.'

He looked hurt, Edith noted, and he lit up a cigarette, took a deep drag and said, 'the trouble is, you may well be right about who committed the murder, and what the motive and the method were, but we'd never get a conviction because we can't prove anything beyond reasonable doubt. If it came to a trial, the Defence could argue that Arthur Lamb is either still alive somewhere in the world or committed suicide abroad, after murdering his wife. How can you prove otherwise? Scotland Yard thinks that the simplest explanation is generally the correct one and a dead wife was most probably murdered by her missing husband.'

'What about the ring in Brighton?' Edith was glad that Hester seemed to have decided not to talk about messages from the 'other side.'

'Louise's engagement ring was found in a

jeweller's shop linked to Peter Laine. How could Louise's ring end up there when she certainly had it with her at her wedding, and they had an appointment with Sotheby's when they returned from their honeymoon, to auction it?'

Adrian moved forward and clasped her hands sending a shiver down her neck. She gazed up into those blue eyes. The wireless was playing a bright jazz tune, and she wished it was something smokier.

'Lamb finished by selling it back to Laine after all? I do believe you, Edie - I do. I don't know how you manage to work these things out, that's all. The trouble is we can't just arrest these people on your hunches. The official police view is that we can get a certain conviction for jewellery theft. That's partly thanks to you! We wouldn't be able to get a murder conviction. After all,' Adrian continued, reasonably, 'if these people are convicted for the jewellery scams, they'll be in prison for a long time anyway. They'll be punished and away from society. Maybe we should be content with that? Forget murder! It'll never work!'

At the word 'murder,' the tinkling laughter of the blue rinse twins stopped, and the Pekingese began to yap ominously. The little snug felt as if it were all ears. Hester, over her hiccups by now, started to giggle. Edith and Adrian ignored her.

'Alright,' Edith said. 'What proof would it need to arrest the Wrens and Peter Laine for murder? For Arthur's parents and Auntie Alma's sake.'

Adrian appeared to be thinking deeply and the

whole room held its breath.

'Where's the car? Are there bloodstains in the boot?'

'The wedding car?' Edith's voice dropped to a whisper.

'Yes. Fingerprints on the wheel? Where did that car come from? Where did it go?'

Edith tried to visualise the car. To her surprise, the image that came to her was of the framed automatic drawing on the wall of the Honeytree cafe, rather than the physical car.

'Where does Laine live?' She looked at the detective.

'Worthing.'

'That's close enough. Edward Wren drove Peter to Worthing on the morning of the murder, whilst his wife went to Chichester by bus.'

The little room had returned to a hubbub of mellow conversation. Edith tried something she hadn't attempted yet; she visualised Willy the soldier. She hadn't 'seen' his face properly before, and her mind's eye gazed, fascinated, upon his 19th century features. A cordwainer's son. No grave. What was left of his teeth pulled before he'd expired to make dentures for the wealthy, and his body ground to make fertiliser for the Belgian farmers. He had a crude tattoo - it read *Annie*. And he wore his hair in little plaits with strong-smelling wax that trapped the lice. He was tied to Arundel because it was the last place he was happy before he began the march to Portsmouth to leave his native land forever. And now he was her spirit guide. Some people had angels to call on but as long as Edith was near the Norfolk Arms she had Willy it seemed.

'Edith? Edith?' Adrian looked worried.

'Don't be nervous,' said Hester. 'Her face sometimes goes an eerie blank like that...and then she has good ideas.'

Edith snapped out of her brief reverie:

'There's a man in Worthing Peter Laine is very close to. More than a friend. A lover, I would guess. He's a chauffeur to a Lady Stern. Go and question him. Maybe she reported her motorcar stolen? He had access to a saw. And plenty of petrol.'

'But it's all purely guesswork,' Adrian said. 'Even if a car were reported stolen, how could we prove it was the same car? Anyhow - suppose by *another* fluke you prove correct, and we do manage to find out where Laine might have got an outfit and a suitable car. Where is that car now? Answer me that.'

'Err,' piped up Hester. 'Scotland. '

Edith and Adrian both stared at Hester, momentarily taken aback. Scotland had to be a fair guess.

'Well done, Hess,' said Edith. 'The Wrens went straight to Scotland after the wedding.'

'Yes' said the detective, but with some uncertainty in his voice. 'Mr and Mrs Wren said they visited the highlands and went off the beaten track. However, they drove their own car and they volunteered all the information necessary to check them out.'

'Honestly,' slurred Hester. 'Don't you detectives ever read any crime novels? The guilty party generally gives the police plenty of information that checks out because they're proud of the complicated and watertight alibi they've constructed. But they might have driven up with two cars - and only explained to you the movements of one of them, eh?'

'We saw Mrs Wren on the bus,' Edith said, her grey eyes meeting Adrian's blue ones and smiling, 'but it doesn't mean she can't drive. Perhaps her husband had driven Laine to Worthing and driven back the means to cut up and burn a body? That's why Caroline Wren went to Chichester by bus - her husband took their car in the opposite direction. We're almost there darlings.'

Adrian leaned forward and ran his fingers through his sandy hair.

'I'm sorry. That car, the missing corpse, and Mrs Lamb's body parts may well be in Scotland, but how could we ever hope to find them unless the Wrens or Laine confess? Scotland is full of lakes, forests, and ravines. We wouldn't know where to begin to look. Personally, I think we should be content with jewellery theft as the main charge. I know I felt differently when we were together abroad, but the police view is to wrap the whole thing up now with what we can prove in a court of law.'

'What if there *was a* confession? And the Wrens led us to the car?'

Adrian stood up and bent all the way down to kiss Edith's cheek. 'Don't be silly love,' he said, 'Murder is a hanging offence, and those three will never confess; why would they?'

'They would never confess to the police,' Edith said. 'But perhaps they'll confess to *me*? What if I could get them to do it unwittingly in front of hidden police witnesses? Would that count?'

Hester had lit another cigarette. 'Why would they confess to you in particular' she asked blowing smoke at the ceiling and staring forlornly at her empty highball glass.

'If these people really *have* murdered their best friends, then they're very dangerous,' said Adrian. 'I don't want you to approach them.'

Edith stood up and looked down at him. 'Give me Mr Laine's address, and I'll write him a letter telling him everything I've just told you about the crime. I'll tell him that I haven't yet gone to the police because I intend to blackmail the three of them. I'll ask to meet him in a public place.'

'That's doubly silly,' said Adrian. 'How can you convince him you know everything about this murder when you may be wrong? It's just a theory. You have no proof.'

'Oh, I know what I'll do,' said Edith. 'I'll lie and pretend to be psychic - I think I can make him believe me.'

Hester got another fit of the giggles.

'Oh darling,' she said, 'That is just so funny'

When Adrian had left to get a taxi home, Edith

became despondent again. She hadn't accompanied him outside into a dark and quiet spot for a goodnight kiss and a cuddle, and he hadn't suggested she did. Perhaps doubts about their relationship had begun to creep in on the detective's side, as well as her own, following the Sunday lunch? Or maybe it was because she'd said 'psychic;' he seemed to have almost a phobia of the word. But she was still in love with him, and it seemed he was with her. Perhaps it was the mention of William, that had made him wary?

'You've got to be honest with each other,' Hester said. 'You can't carry on with him if you can't show him who you really are.'

CHAPTER 22

It had taken some persuasion on Edith's part to get Adrian to agree to her plan. And then some persuasion on his part, to get his superiors at Scotland Yard to allow him to carry out that plan. Then again Scotland Yard had to persuade the Chief Constable and the Superintendent to allow him to deploy extra constables drafted in from local towns along the coast.

'They're afraid the three of them will flee when Peter Laine gets your letter,' Adrian had explained when the pair were alone the next day, standing in the hotel reception of the Norfolk Arms mid-morning. The wireless played classical music, and they were glad that the sound hid their conversation from people passing by.

Hester was still upstairs enjoying a soak in the bath.

'I promise you he'll be curious,' Edith said. 'Laine'll realise I know details of the crime that no one else could know, and he'll fall for the blackmail story because if he's greedy for money himself, then why wouldn't *I* be, too?'

Adrian had hummed and hah-ed. 'Suppose you're wrong about the details of the crime?' He looked at her, doubtfully, pulling a face.

'I'm not.' She was firm. 'But if I was, you can still arrest him, and the Wrens, for the jewellery scams I'm also accusing them of. Perhaps you'll get a confession for those, too.'

'What happens if they try and murder you instead of paying you? - Supposing they *are* murderers.'

They certainly will think of that,' said Edith, 'but I'll ask to meet Laine in a public place, along with Hester as my wingman; it makes sense - I'd be afraid to go alone. All the other people in the place can be undercover police officers. We'll find a spot with a table near an area where you and another police officer can be hidden, and I'll lead Laine to incriminate himself.

Adrian had still been uneasy. He had to ensure he didn't lose these international jewel thieves, whose arrest would make glamorous newspaper headlines and be a feather in the cap for Scotland Yard. He also disapproved of Edith posing as a psychic, although she had made it clear that she would only be pretending in order to flush out the criminals and wasn't trying to tell him that she thought she was actually psychic.'

'Why are you so hostile to the idea of psychics,' she'd finally asked him, her heart racing and hands beginning to tremble. 'I'd like to know. Can we go and get a cup of tea? Not here. I'll get my hat and gloves.'

They sat in a café in the Highstreet. Edith started the painful conversation.

'You know that when I explain how the murder was successfully carried out, they'll have to believe that I really *can* find out things by contacting the spirit world. Or at least they'll have a doubt. That may make them afraid to run without checking me out first; they may think my psychic detection skills will find them wherever they hide. So... what makes you so dislike psychics?'

Edith waited, watching Adrian's face for a reaction. Her chest felt tight. His answer was important. Since she, herself, had finally accepted that side of her nature, she wondered if she could ever be with a man who obliged her to keep such a big part of her inner life secret.

Adrian toyed with his hat, looked sideways, looked up at the ceiling, and looked anywhere but at the auburn-haired woman sitting in front of him, rattling her blue willow teacup in the saucer.
'Well?' Edith grabbed the bull by the horns. 'You seem to be very against even a hint of talk of spiritualism. Why do you get so angry?"
Finally, his blue eyes met her earnest grey eyes. He had sensed that something depended on his answer.

He fiddled with his tie.

'I'll be frank with you,' the detective said. 'I once fell for that malarkey in the past, and I'm embarrassed to say that I lost quite a bit of money.'

'What happened?'

'It was after Minty died. I was having a rough time.'

Edith sensed that it was an understatement.

'I saw an advertisement in the local newspaper, placed there by a clairvoyant. She claimed to specialise in contacting soldiers who'd died in the war. I wondered if she could contact Minty,' Adrian said, looking ashamed.

Edith reached out and took his hand in a surge of pity, but he took it away. The memory was evidently still painful.

'Her name was Hilda Keith. A middle-aged woman with dyed black hair and too much rouge. She looked as if she was doing well, though. She had a very nice house, and framed photographs of celebrities on a whatnot, whom she claimed to have helped.'

'Go on.'

'We sat in her front room and chatted over a cup of tea and then she threw her head back and seemed to go into a trance. She started speaking in a strange voice. It was actually quite frightening. When she became normal again, she told me it was her spirit guide who spoke through her, and his name was Running Horse.' Adrian winced at the memory.

'Then, Mrs Keith told me that this so-called spirit guide had a message from Minty.'

Adrian was looking at the ceiling again.

Edith sat very still. 'What was the message?'

He shrugged in embarrassment and looked around the room. 'She told me that this Running Horse had said to go to my bookshelf and look for a book. I told her I didn't have a bookshelf, but she insisted that there was a book in the house and, eventually, we worked out it must be in Sophie's room. So, then she said that Running Horse was telling her that I had a daughter, and the message was for her, and she asked if my daughter was named Sophie.'

'You probably had just let that name slip,' Edith agreed.

'She told me the book was on the 1st row, third along, and then she started saying which numbered pages to turn to and what line down and what words to count along in each line - and to write them down to get the message. She got me to ring home and get Gwendoline to go into Sophie's room and do it - and then tell me the message. She called it a Book Test. That's the sort of rubbish these psychics use to swindle you.'

'I see,' said Edith carefully. 'What did the message say that convinced you then, that Mrs Keith was telling the truth?

Adrian drank down his tea. 'The message appeared to be the mumbo jumbo it was, but Mrs Keith helped me translate it, and then it all made sense.'

'That's why she didn't want you to look at the book by yourself.'

Adrian looked angry.

'It so happened that the message had the word 'horse' in it, and Minty and Sophie both loved horses as much as me. It would have been typical of her to send a message to Sophie about the horses. I was completely duped, and I thought the money was well worth the reassurance that Minty was still with us.'

Edith hardly knew where to look. The big man, with his craggy face, looked so vulnerable in that instant.

She reached out and patted his hand, but he stared into the distance, remembering.

'Of course, the book was Black Beauty, as Gwen pointed out, and so there were things to do with horses on nearly every page. Sophie had books about horses because she loves horses, and so it wasn't too difficult for so-called Running Horse to come up with this particular message.'

'Mrs Brown? What's she got to do with it?' Edith realised, ruefully, her reaction to the name 'Gwen' was spikey.

'It was Mrs Brown who made me see sense in the end.'

"But isn't she just a servant?'

'Oh, don't call her that, he said. 'She cares so much for the girls. She was really worried about the effects my visits to Mrs Keith were having on them, because after the first time I kept going back - and now I see how right Gwen was. It was such a relief to me to speak to Minty and know that she was with the family night and day, watching over us, so I kept going to see Mrs Keith, which went on for months. It was always Running Horse who arrived, supposedly. The methods of communication changed. There were no more books, but flames in the fire, or tea leaves, or a glass bowl she had, filled with water. And I'm afraid to say that the costs of the visits kept increasing and my Bank Manager became alarmed and then Mrs Brown put her foot down. She made me see just how Mrs Keith got me to give away information and then fed it back to me. It made me terrifically angry to see how these so-called-psychics exploit gullible people. I'd arrest all of them if I could.'

'Well,' said Edith. 'If an intelligent Detective Inspector can be taken in by false claims of clairvoyance, then don't you think Peter Laine and Edward and Caroline Wren, will be taken in too? Maybe I'll get them to give away information by the same methods.'

'I suppose so,' he sighed. 'Alright, here's the address; write Mr Laine that letter. There's a place in Littlehampton that would be perfect for the trap.' He was busy scribbling on some paper torn from his notebook.

'Tell him to meet you there in two days' time at eight o'clock. We can't leave it any longer if we're going to do it. I'll arrange to have the place closed, and I've already got permission to draft in some car loads of constables dressed as customers.' Adrian looked at her. 'Will I see you tonight or tomorrow night?'

He looked almost relieved when she said,' Hester and I talked about getting an early night tonight and going to the flicks tomorrow night.'

'I expect *Willy* wants to take you out,' he threw at her as a parting shot. 'Never mind.'

Hester mentioning the name had clearly raised doubts about her loyalty in his mind. It was probably why he hadn't kissed her good night the evening before.

When he'd walked her back to the Norfolk arms, she had to go to the Lady's Powder Room to wipe away the tears welling in her eyes. She knew she could never let on to him, nor his family, her natural psychic abilities, nor her own genuine spirit guide. The spirit world would forever be her secret refuge; never again would she shut it out as she had done before.

When she had redone her hair and face, Edith suggested to Hester that they compose the letter to Peter Laine straight away and post it that afternoon; there was no time to lose.

'The letter will only arrive tomorrow, and you're saying to meet us the evening after! There may not be time,' said Hester.

'If Laine doesn't turn up, the police will swoop on him and the others, in raids the next day,' said Edith. 'That's what Adrian told me. It's our last chance to get them tried for murder.'

They returned to the post office and bought some blank notepaper and envelopes, deciding that the hotel paper was not a good idea. For the same reason, Edith suggested they take a trip to Littlehampton to post the letter.

'We mustn't let them know our location by the postmark in case they try to knobble us before the sting,' Edith said. 'What say you that we drive to the coast, and check out this cafe to familiarise ourselves with it before we meet Laine there? We could have fish and chips on the Quay.'

'Goody! I want some whelks,' Hester said. 'It's a good idea to check out the café. I'm a bit nervous about this, darling - they may want to murder me too. Phillip wouldn't like it - although the children might find the prospect exciting. But I suppose the police are terribly used to this sort of thing. *I* have faith in them.'

Soon, the pair were dressed in their wide-legged trousers, pretty puffed-sleeved blouses and straw hats, heading for the seaside.

Adrian had written down the address of the cafe, which was easy to find. It was a long low building in white stucco and Edith saw immediately why he had chosen it for the trap. There was a large car park around it, which was used for fish markets, and where parked cars and the odd constable might wait unobtrusively in the shadows. There was also only one entrance in or out of the car park and building, which was easy to surveille.

Inside, the cafe was not luxurious, but it was respectable enough that two middle-class women such as Edith and Hester would not look inordinately out of place.

Simple as the place was, it still had fresh white tablecloths and black-clad waitresses with little frothy white aprons and caps. Hester squealed with delight when she saw fresh dressed crab on the menu. They sat at a table by the big picture window overlooking the sea and Littlehampton's long sandy beach.

'We can't sit here on the night of the trap,' Edith said. She looked around the room. 'We could sit at the table under the end of the curvy bar. There's room behind that to hide.'

It was a big cafe, which became more like a

bar in the evening and attracted tourists who didn't want to sit in the lounge of their grim bed and breakfasts, wouldn't drink in public houses, and couldn't afford the cocktail bars in the smart hotels.

Hester said, 'better not put any policemen too close to our table, or Peter Laine won't talk to you.'

Edith got the writing paper out of her handbag. 'Let's start on the letter,' she said, pushing her empty cup away.

'*Dear Mr Laine,*' she wrote. '*You won't remember me, but I was a guest at Arthur and Louise Lamb's wedding in Arundel this spring. It is such a sad thing that Arthur had to go and tell you that he intended taking that stolen diamond ring to Sotheby's when he got back from his honeymoon.*'

'Returned,' sounds better,' Hester said.

'*...when he returned from his honeymoon. The ring was stolen in Avignon by Edward and Caroline Wren. The police don't know that any of you are involved in the murder yet - but **I** do. I know you and Mr and Mrs Wren murdered the Lambs to hide your thieving. Everybody else still thinks the Lambs left for Arundel station, but I know the people who left in the car were you and the Wrens in disguise. I haven't told the police what I know **YET**. I think you have all made a great deal of money stealing diamonds, but **I**..*' Edith paused.

'Struggle,' Hester suggested.

'*...but I struggle for money. Perhaps if you give me £5,000, I won't go to the police at all, and you can*

carry on making more money?
How do I know what you did? I am clairvoyant. I
can see the future and contact the dead. There's
nowhere in the world where you can hide from **me**.
I suggest you bring me the cash in a suitcase this
Thursday (tomorrow) night.' She wrote down the
address of the café and the time. '*Make sure you*
come alone and don't think of trying any funny
business. The cafe should be busy, and I'll be with my
cousin as a witness. I will wear a fresh flower pinned
to my blouse and a green necklace, so as you know
me.
If you don't bring me the cash, I'll ask my spirit guide
whereabouts in Scotland the Wrens hid that car, and
you will all hang.' She signed the letter, '*your*
Impecunious Friend.'

'Gosh,' said Hester, 'that will really set the cat
among the pigeons. Can you imagine him reading
that when he thinks they've all got away with it?'
'Yes,' said Edith. 'The risk is they scarper. But the
police will be poised to arrest them if they do. It will
be good for the prosecution if they scarper because of
this letter. I think they might come to try and murder
us, but they'd be putting the noose around their own
necks if they do. The place will be crawling with
police.'

'Very reassuring, darling,' Hester said,
dubiously.

They left to find a red pillerbox, and to paddle
in the grey shimmering sea in their jazzy sunglasses
and rolled up trousers- the taste of sea salt on their

painted bow lips and the cries of seagulls overhead.

The time had never seemed to drag so long as it did the next day. Edith had rung Adrian to fill him in on the letter's contents and fix their plan, but she didn't arrange for them to meet before Thursday, and he didn't push her. One way or another, the denouement was near, both for the murder enquiry and their relationship. Frustratingly, it seemed there was nothing to be done except wait and see. Edith spent the day with Hester strolling along the river bank in the sunshine and sitting in the Black Rabbit enjoying a cream tea.

The day of the sting was even longer as they waited for the evening to approach, and the hour to arrive when they had to be at the Littlehampton café. They arrived around nine thirty to find the car park quite full. Edith and Hester sauntered into the busy café, both looking very pretty in their smart jackets and hats; Edith wore a rose pinned to the collar of her blouse and an emerald necklace. Both women felt ill at ease when they realised they were the only females there, although the plainclothes policemen sitting in groups at the other tables looked like ordinary enough customers.

A pianist played in the evenings, and the room was filled with gentle jazz tunes, although one of the ivory piano keys clearly needed fixing. The lighting had been lowered. The table under the end of the dark wooden and chrome bar was empty and waiting for them. The table directly next to them had been left vacant on purpose, so that Peter Laine would not feel as if any conversation could be overheard.

It *would* be overheard though. Two policemen had removed the lower shelf under the bar, directly next to them, and had bored a hole through which they could listen to the conversation.

'I'll crawl under with PC Crawford,' Detective Inspector Stevens said, showing her his shorthand notebook.' It's a squeeze, but we can just about do it. Thing is, with the way the bar curves, we can't be seen from the end of the bar. The barman's in on it, and he has instructions to mask us if Laine tries to look over the counter. Come out here...' Adrian led her out into the corridor towards the washrooms.

'There's a policeman stationed here in the passage, and another outside directly under the windows. There are two more in the car park. One's sitting in a car, over there next to the entrance, and another's hanging about the front of the building. There's no way anything can happen to you.' He pulled her into his arms and leaned down to kiss the top of her head. 'Just do your best and try and get him to talk. I expect he'll try and blame the other two.

These people generally turn on each other when they're cornered, but that just makes our job easier. If all three of them turn up, it might be even better.' He kissed her again and Edith melted in his arms.

Peter Laine arrived alone, in a taxi, at around ten to ten, and one of the plainclothes policemen sitting in the bar, near the front of the cafe, gave a prearranged signal by tapping on the window once.

The taxi dropped him near the big glass doors, then pulled over into the shadows at the side of the building to wait. The taxi driver turned off the big headlamps but left the engine running as Laine bounded up the steps in the fading light and sauntered into the café.

He was as good looking as Edith and Hester remembered him. Quite small, slim, and dark-haired, he oozed self-confidence. He wasn't carrying a briefcase, Edith noticed. He did have a roomy light raincoat on though, and a trilby hat, despite it being a balmy summer night.

Perhaps he has the money in his pocket Edith thought.

She fiddled with the rose corsage pinned to her collar. His eyes, sweeping the room, noticed her immediately. He didn't need to summon the barman, who had moved along the counter to serve him, trying not to trip over the bits of Adrian Stevens and PC Crawford which they hadn't quite managed to pull under the bar.

Edith and Hester stood up and stretched out their white-gloved hands to shake his.

'I'm the lady who wrote you that letter,' Edith said slightly flirtatiously, although she was aware that he was not attracted to women. Physically, he had an artistic actor-ish charm about him.

'Yes. I recognise you from the wedding. And the green necklace you mentioned in your letter. I always notice people's jewellery.' He laughed. Peter Laine went on, 'may I get either of you ladies another drink?'

'Mine's a double G&T.' Hester gave a charming smile.

'Did you bring the money?' Edith was also smiling in a friendly way. 'I'll have shampoo, please. I take it we're all celebrating?'

'I'm afraid they won't sell champagne in a dump like this. You should have suggested a decent hotel. Why would *I* be celebrating anyway?'

'I'll have a Bloody Mary. You should be celebrating because I haven't told the police what I know, and you've all got away with murder.'
Peter Laine laughed but stayed standing up. 'I really can't stay long because the taxi is waiting outside with the engine turning. I don't like driving in the dark you see. So, you're our psychic? You don't look like Gypsy Rose, I must say.'

'Yes,' said Edith. 'I can contact the dead, and I can see the past. That's how I can see what happened to the Lambs. I've got a third eye. I can find out where that car is hidden in Scotland. I'll get a map and I'll stick a pin in it. I'll get Arthur's spirit to direct me. Did you bring the cash? Is it in your pocket.'
'You really are Impecunious, aren't you? You have absolutely no idea what £5,000 in notes looks like and how much room it takes up, do you?'

'No,' Edith said.

'It was a stupid idea to ask me to give you that amount of cash in a grotty public cafe such as this one.'

As if on cue, the pianist hit the bad key.

'The money is in the Ladies Powder Room,' he continued.

'Don't be silly,' said Edith, 'How could it be? I used the Powder Room earlier and there's nothing there.'

'Check again. There's a window in the room. Open it, and you'll find the bag below the sill. Lock yourself in a cubical and count it all. All £5,000 of it. Then come back and talk. I have a proposition for you. Maybe there's a way for you to earn more of it.'

'How did you get the bag there? Aren't you alone? Why not bring it in?'

'Don't be ridiculous! I'm not handing over £5,000 in public. I tipped the taxi driver to put the bag under the window. He'll watch until you've collected it - he thinks you're my ex floozie and the bag contains some of your pathetic possessions which I'm returning behind your husband's back, and I'm inside the cafe now letting you know, surreptitiously, that it's all over between us.'

Edith stood up and headed for the door. She knew there was a policeman in the hallway, and another outside in the car park near the window. He would also be watching the bag - if it was there. She hoped Laine would open up to Hester whilst she was gone; Hester had a knack of getting strangers to confide in her - goodness knew why.

'Alright,' she said, 'we'll talk when I come back.'

'Miss,' Peter Laine said to Hester, with a clean white smile. 'A refill?'

Hester remained sitting down, but the minute Edith left the room, Laine's attitude changed.

'Tell your friend, when she comes back after counting all that toy money, that I'm not falling for that stupid story of psychics! I've got nothing to be afraid of, and neither have my friends. We've never murdered anybody, and her whole idiotic story is preposterous! What a silly little goose.' He motioned to the barman for a fresh glass, and set it down next to her last one and gave a sip of his own. 'Neither are we jewellery thieves. This rubbish is all a fantasy. My friend trades in rare stamps, and I make and mend jewellery for reputable firms - some in Hatton Garden, no less. Tell your friend we'll be taking her to court for slander if she makes any more false accusations. I thought I would come and warn you in person and have fun with the bag of fake money. Why on earth would I risk leaving it outside and not hand it to her here, if it really had money in it? She's idiotic.'

'We'll tell the police,' Hester said. She was afraid of his change in tone. He sounded rather menacing, and she was glad the room was filled with strapping men, ready to pounce if needed, to protect her.

'You're welcome to tell the police whatever you want. Your crackpot allegations have no foundation and I'm happy to answer any questions they haven't already asked. I'm afraid my old school friend, Lamb, murdered his beautiful bride and bolted. I hope your friend enjoys counting her Mickey Mouse money. It will take her some time. Now let me get that taxi. It'll cost me a fortune back to Worthing, and I don't have £5,000 to pay for it.'

Peter Laine sauntered back over to the double glass doors as the incognito constables looked desperately towards the bar, waiting for a sign from their officer to spring into action and arrest him. The sign never came, and the constables looked helplessly at each other as Laine stood at the top of the stairs waving at his taxi, which still had the engine turning. Soon its headlamps lit up, sweeping an arc over to the front door. Peter Laine ran nimbly down the steps and climbed into the car, which, very slowly, drove out of the car park.

Behind the bar, the bulky frame of Adrian Stevens was crawling out from under the shelf. He turned and helped up Crawford, and they stood there rubbing their limbs.

'I think I need a drink after that,' he said. He shouted to no one in particular, 'alright boys. you can relax now. It's all over.' He looked at Hester, 'You see, I shouldn't fall for this stuff. The Wrens stole that ring, and I'm sure other jewellery, but I don't even think it's certain Laine knew any of it was stolen - perhaps he bought items from them? It doesn't sound to *me* as if he had anything to do with the Arundel murder.'

'Edith thinks he was the mastermind behind it,' Hester said.

Adrian shook his head in seeming disbelief. 'You know how fond I am of her, but she's wrong.

And playing that psychic charade was wrong. No one would ever fall for it.'

Hester stood up. 'I suppose I better tell her it's not real money she's counting. I say...' she said hopefully, '...if it's counterfeit money, maybe you can arrest Laine for *that*?'

She walked out into the corridor. A young Constable stood there guarding the doors to the washrooms.

'Good evening, Sergeant,' she said, winking at him roguishly as she pushed the door of the Lady's Powder Room.

Hester stood confused for a moment. There were only two cubicles but, pushing them both, she saw they were empty. She went back out into the corridor.

'Did you see my friend with reddish hair?' She looked at the policeman, worried now.

'Yes,' said the Constable, bewildered at the question. 'She's in the Powder Room. I saw her go in and she didn't come out, so she must be still in there. I hope she's alright? She *has* been a long time... '

With a terrible sinking feeling, Hester went back into the room and examined the window. She saw that, although shut, it was unfastened. Opening it she saw the holdall laying on the ground, a little below her, in the gloom.

The building was set with its back against the dunes. The ground rose gently from the front of the building, and so while steps were needed to walk up to the cafe from the front carpark, by the time one walked around the side of the building to below the window of the Lady's Powder Room, the casement was barely two feet off the ground. There was no sign of the officer who was supposed to be guarding that area of the car park, and everything seemed dark and silent.

Brushing passed the confused constable in the corridor, with rising panic Hester ran back to find Adrian Stevens and promptly burst into tears.

CHAPTER 23

Edith felt crushed under the weight of two people, a woman and a man. Edward and Caroline Wren, she thought, horrified. Her imagination unwillingly conjured up an image of Louise's headless, burnt body. They were in a moving car, and she was being flattened under the couple - half in the footwell and half on the back seat. She could hear the voices of two men murmuring in the front of the motorcar. It was Peter Laine talking to the taxi driver, she knew. The others were lying flat on top of her so as not to be seen as the car moved very slowly out of the car park and then sped away.

Edith felt her ribs crushed. One leg felt bent at a strange angle, although it wasn't broken. The towel they'd held tightly over her mouth at first was loosened, and she could at least breathe. The feeling of being suffocated had been terrifying, and her lungs hurt. The inside of the motor car lit up with yellow light every time they passed the headlamps of another moving vehicle, but she couldn't move her head to see anything.

The car seemed to give a lurch every time it raced around the corners, and the Wrens bounced on top of her, knocking the wind from her.

At least they didn't crack my head and force me into the boot to suffocate, she thought.

Her initial panic had died down a bit as she realised that they didn't mean to kill her straight away.

Adrian Stevens and Hester would quickly realise what had happened when they examined the Ladies' Powder Room window and would be in pursuit immediately; they were probably already on their way. She prayed they'd be quick enough.

Her hopes looked like being dashed, however, when the taxi stopped in a secluded layby on a main road leading out of Littlehampton and the Wrens sat up, opened the car door, dragged her out into the air, and then pushed her into a different car which was parked there.

Peter Laine and the driver had gone to the boot of the taxi and, with difficulty, carried the torso of a shop window dummy over to the front seat. As a finishing touch, Laine rammed his trilby hat on its head. It made a passable silhouette of the passenger who had vacated the car, as the taxi quickly sped away toward Portsmouth.

It was Laine who, putting on a bowler hat, took the wheel of the Humber and turned the car back along the main road, pootling along in the direction from which they had come. The car was somewhat roomier, and Edith was allowed to sit up, although she soon realised that Edward Wren had a small knife held at her ribs. Its sharp point nicked her blouse, and she became afraid that even a pothole taken too fast might accidentally cause the man to stab her.

Several police cars passed them at breakneck speed, going toward Portsmouth, but there was nothing Edith could do as the Humber passed them on the other side of the road, sedately re-entering

Littlehampton.

Surprisingly, Edith's captors seemed genuinely quite amiable.

'Dreadfully sorry about that,' said Peter Laine, looking at her in the rearview mirror with a friendly grin. 'You couldn't possibly have thought we would allow ourselves to be blackmailed? It was a ridiculous trap. And, honestly, I've never seen a cafe or bar with so many very young, very tall men. They might just as well have had 'constable' tattooed across their foreheads. You and your friend were the only women in the place. But,' he continued, I really do have a proposition for you. That part wasn't a lie. Sorry about Eddie dragging you out the window like that, by the way. You'll probably have a few bruises. But really! You're going to have to be a bit smarter. Fancy opening the window and leaning out like that!'

'There was a policeman out there...' Edith protested weakly.

'Eddie knocked him out. I expect he'll live,' Caroline Wren said. She had a warm, engaging, modulated voice. Her manner was entirely different to when Edith had last seen her at the Norfolk Arms - and no wonder! 'We'll wait until we're safely on our way, and then we'll discuss it properly, but you're going to like it. If you're after money, you can have lots of it. I'll introduce you to simply the best designers in Paris. Champagne? You'll be able to take baths in it. You'll even be able to bathe in asses milk if that's what you fancy. No more struggling.'

'I must apologise for the necessity of the knife,'

Edward Wren said. 'We can't talk like this with police cars racing around, but we all want to be friends, and once we're aboard the boat, we can relax. Or rather, you three can; I've got to sail the yacht, and it looks quite choppy out in the channel tonight.'

Edith's stomach turned over, but she was determined to keep the calm atmosphere between them. She just needed to keep to the forefront of her mind that they didn't want to hurt her for the moment; they wanted to be pals. Nevertheless, she was petrified at the thought of being alone with them on a small boat, with no hope of escape and the possibility that nobody would know they had even left the country. She knew that Scotland Yard would have all the ferry ports covered and the main aerodromes in the South of England, but they couldn't stop every yacht or fishing boat in the Channel. She also feared that Adrian would lose his job because of her. Their relationship would be well and truly finished.

The Humber drew up at Littlehampton harbour by the yacht club, shrouded in darkness. There were few people around at night, but Edward gave a cheery wave to the nightwatchman, and Edith realised that they had either hired or bought the boat and nobody would report a stolen yacht.

'You're not going to take her across tonight, are you?' called the watchman. 'It's very rough out there. Better to wait until the morning. It'll be better weather by the looks of it.'

Edith became aware of the moored boats thumping together in the water and the clanking and jingling of the masts with their metal fixings and creaking wood. The yachts were just black looming shapes.

Edward Wren loosened his grip on her, but she felt the knife still digging in. Edith had no doubt that Wren would knife her if she attempted to cry out. The night was dark, and he'd carry her onto the yacht if he had to. She wondered if she *should* shout out or try and get away to alert help, but she hesitated, and the moment was lost. There was nothing to do but step off dry land and onto the rocking boat.

Caroline took her below decks as the two men cast off, and Edith's last hopes of somehow being rescued in the nick of time were dashed. The only hope of survival was to play along with the idea that she was joining their gang.

There was no light, but Caroline handed her a handheld torch and lit one herself.

The yacht had two cabins, a galley, and a water closet, but one of the bunks was piled with cases. The trip had clearly been planned in advance. The cabin was dark, but if Edith swung the torch, huge shadows loomed in the small space.

'We'll have to get you clothes in Le Havre tomorrow morning,' said Caroline. 'If you decide to come with us. It will be difficult because the ship is leaving tomorrow evening, and you'll need a lot of things for the voyage. It'll be ever so exciting, though! Have you ever been to America? I've been to New York before, but only for a holiday. This'll be completely different.'

'What do you mean?'

She felt the yacht move as it slipped out of the mouth of the River Arun, heading for France. She was well aware that she was in light summer clothes and the weather in the Channel would be very cold and wet. It looked like a rough crossing, and the night would be long.

'Well, we thought that if you *had* told the police everything you wrote in that letter, we had better move abroad. There are so many opportunities in America. It's so vast we can lose ourselves there and start a new life. And there are plenty of business opportunities for those who have the skills. We can have a great life.' She stopped. 'That stupid trap for Peter...We know you did tell the police. But it doesn't matter as they won't catch us, and with our wealth, America will be much more exciting than London. You don't need to worry about money. We've got bank accounts all over the world.'

'And I'm coming to America with you?'

'If you want to be one of us! It's up to you. Just tell us and we'll leave you in France if you prefer.' Edith knew they would throw her overboard. We're all booked onto a Liner crossing the Atlantic, leaving France tomorrow...If you're willing. We think you will be when you consider the money. Come on - you haven't got a husband or children...we did some snooping.'

'I don't have a passport with me,' Edith objected, 'they'll never let me onto a ship.'

'Don't worry. Peter made you one. He's

always making passports, and nobody has ever noticed. I've got dozens. He buys stolen original passports and changes the picture and the name. Peter's good like that. He's ever so clever, you know.' She took a passport out of a draw and showed Edith.

The picture was not perfect for a passport but she could make out her own features. She saw that the photograph's original had been cut from a close-up photograph of a group snapshop taken at the wedding.

'How did you know who I was?'

'Don't you remember? Your cousin spoke to me at the Norfolk Arms - I was about to go upstairs. She told me you're clairvoyant. Peter said he saw you with the necklace at the reception, too. I don't think he could pass the merest stranger without his eyes going automatically to their *bijoux*.'

The passport was in the name of Valerie Scadden.

'We'll make sure you wear that emerald necklace,' Caroline said helpfully, 'so it links to the picture. Fiddle with it at customs - It always works. Eddie and I speak french, so let me do the talking if they question you. Pretend not to understand. You will work with us, won't you? You'll have so much money and such an exciting life. You can have anything you ever dreamed of. Let your mother have that café.'

She was looking at Edith's left hand.

'You can look so wonderful you'll have men falling over themselves to woo you. You can pretend to be a wealthy English heiress.'

It crossed Edith's mind, for a second, that it would be no loss to wave Cuckfield good-bye - nor Gwendoline Brown, the Stevens girls, cats, horses, and all...but the temptation passed as quickly as it had come as she thought of the people she loved, the reality of a heartless double murder, and what theft meant to shopkeepers like the Tardys.

Edith suddenly noticed a porthole. She hadn't noticed it before because it was so dark outside. The ominous waves looked like black mountains, and the boat rolled.

'Have you got life jackets?' Edith asked.
Caroline laughed. 'Yes,' she said, 'up on the deck. But you mustn't worry. Edward has often sailed a yacht before. We rent one on the Med when the weather is fine.'

'Can we go up?' Edith was beginning to feel seasick.

Outside, the cold sea spray hit her. The lights of Littlehampton looked tiny on the horizon and were receding rapidly as a strong wind swelled their sails and pushed them further into the channel. There was no light on the deck or the top of the mast. Although *they* could see the shore, it would be impossible for anybody on land to see *them*, and nobody would be able to follow them even if it was realised they were on a yacht. Her only hope was that the Yard would telegraph France and that she'd have the opportunity to alert someone to her predicament - although she realised that Edward and Peter would make that very difficult if they didn't trust her. And if they didn't trust her, she might not even reach France. Her best chance was to play along with them and wait until they boarded the Ocean Liner.

Edith's thoughts went to poor Hester, and how devastated she must be that her cousin had been kidnapped. Given what had happened to Louise, Hester must surely be wondering if Edith would turn up as a burning, headless corpse in the morning. And poor Mama! Clara would have to be informed, and she was sure to be petrified. As for Adrian, she realised how upset he must be - and furious.

She spotted a life jacket on deck and put it on without waiting for permission.

Peter Laine struggled to help Edward Wren control the yacht as they tried to direct it through the waves. They were both clad in waterproof clothing and sou'westers. Peter Laine was wearing a lifejacket, too. He motioned to Caroline to take Edith back below decks.

'Keep out the way!' He was shouting. 'The sea's too rough to be outside. Get some rest. The wind will carry us to France quickly.'

Once below, the two women tried to dry themselves from the heavy spray and wrapped themselves in blankets from the bunks.

'I don't think we'll get any sleep tonight,' Caroline said with a laugh. 'I'd try to make some cocoa, but I don't think anything would stay still. Do you feel better? I feel rather queasy myself now.'

'You didn't tell me *why* you want to take me to New York?' Edith asked, 'What is the proposition

Peter was talking about?'

Caroline suddenly became excited.

'You're psychic, aren't you? That must be so useful! Everybody knows about psychic detectives, but have there been any psychic criminals other than fake mediums and fortune tellers? You're the real thing! What if you can learn to predict safe combinations? Or you can find where somebody has hidden their valuables? There must be a thousand ways you could help us that we haven't yet thought of. If it's money you want, you'll certainly get plenty of that with us - I told you! Believe me, you'll be rewarded. And it's such an adventurous and exciting life. Imagine driving your open sports car from your beachside villa in sunny Florida, covered in diamonds. That will be you.'

'How exciting! You're convincing me, but how do you know I'm real?' Edith waited for the confession. *But there's no policemen here to listen,* she thought.

'Your letter, of course,' said Caroline. You would *have* to be psychic to know all that. You might have been able to find out we cut up Louise - because we were seen by someone - but you couldn't possibly have known exactly *how we* carried out the murder, and the reasons why, unless you were psychic.'

Caroline Wren looked very sad for a moment, 'I didn't want to do it. I adored Louise. She was a very close friend. But we would have gone to prison for the diamond heists, and that would have been the end of our wonderful lives. I can't imagine *me* in

Holloway. It was dreadful murdering Louise. I've got sickening images of Peter cutting off a foot...I didn't see the rest because I couldn't watch any more. I have nightmares. It was Peter's idea. He said it would buy us time, and then the police would decide that Arthur killed her and close the case. I mean, what choice did we have? Honestly?'

'And Arthur?'

'He was so pigheaded - refusing to sell that ring back. Especially when Peter had only been trying to do him a massive favour in the first place. Arthur even tried to tell Peter that he preferred to take his chances at auction. Arthur thought Peter would admire him for being shrewd. And Sotheby's, of all people! I mean, they would be certain to see that the ring was French and check the lists. We ditched the car in Scotland, you were quite right. Edward drove the car up there with Arthur's body and Louise's head in the boot, and I followed him in our own car. We pushed the car into Loch Lomond in the night. You could barely see it. the water wasn't deep, but nobody will ever find it because it was a remote spot. The car doesn't have a number plate; it wasn't stolen because Peter bought it through his friend. Peter left a trail in France on Arthur's passport and caught the blue train back. That's all over and done with, sweetie, honestly. I must say I'm glad you're coming with us. Being friends and working with a real clairvoyant will be fun. And with Louise dead, I need a new female friend. I promise you won't regret it.'

'What about your stamp shop?'

'Eddie posted out all the rarest stamps a few days ago to some private buyers. I think he'll have to stick to the jewellery from now on.'

They could hear the men shouting to each other up on deck.

'I wonder what's up with the boys?' Caroline said, 'something's going on. I'm going up to see.

Edith looked out of the porthole. The waves were still rising high above the little yacht, and then dropping. But now, a dark shape, lit up like a Christmas tree, appeared a little way diagonally in front of them, frequently rising out of sight. It was evidently a fishing trawler heading back to Littlehampton to get out of the weather and it was getting nearer.

Staggering with the rolling of the yacht, Edith pulled herself up the narrow stairs after Caroline, both coming onto the deck and hanging on to whatever they could.

The fishing boat was much closer than a few minutes before.

The yacht was in darkness. It was merely a dark shape in the dark night whilst the bigger boat looked gay and twinkling against the starless sky.

The two men had their life jackets on and were battling to change the yacht's course, but the wind was in her sails, and she sped on directly towards the trawler.

Peter Laine turned to face them. He'd lost his calm for once - but you could only sense it. He was silent. He was an insignificant black shape against the vastness of the black swelling sea. It was impossible to make out his features. His self-importance had evaporated.

Edward Wren was searching for flares, but everything seemed even darker than it had before, contrasted with the big fishing boat growing ever closer.

'Put your life jacket on!' Edith ordered Caroline, 'Put your life jacket on - Now!'

She saw herself back in the Norfolk Arms, throwing up over the wash basin in her room, and remembered how she'd felt the woman's panic as she drowned so painfully.

Time slowed down.

She had glimpsed the future which she could only see if it was already decided. Were there any choices? *Can you change destiny?* She thought Caroline's destiny might hinge simply on whether or not she was wearing a life jacket if they collided with the trawler. Perhaps she *wouldn't* die in the water tonight, and Edith's role was to save her.

Swift wings you must borrow,
Make straight to the shore,

'Please put this jacket on!' Edith had grabbed another jacket from the store on deck. But Caroline either couldn't hear her or ignored her. She was looking for her husband.

We marry tomorrow,

And she goes sailing no more.

'Shout!' Edward ordered them. 'We've got to warn the fishermen.' He was lowering the sails in a futile attempt to stop the yacht.'

Peter Laine had given up.

Red Sails in the sunset
Way out on the sea

'Ahoy! Ahoy!' Caroline shouted in panic.

'Help! S.O.S!' Edith hollered. But the women's voices were thin, reedy, and lost in the night as the waves hit the yacht, soaking them to the skin. They were alongside the trawler now. In a minute, they would be able to touch her; they were so close. Caroline hadn't put her life jacket on. Edith linked arms with her.

'Caroline...please put this jacket on. Please do,' she sobbed. She knew what this woman's death in the water would feel like; she'd experienced it. But she also knew that if Caroline survived, she would be hanged for murder anyway.

'Help!' Edith screamed.

Without her sails, the yacht seemed to have stopped, but powerless, facing the swelling sea at a wrong angle, she was picked up by a wave bigger than the rest. Up and up, she was pulled, exactly like a fairground ride cranking to the summit of a rollercoaster until they seemed to be looking down upon the trawler from a vertical wall.

They all tried to hang on to anything solid on the deck, but as the wave crashed down, capsizing the sailing boat and dashing her against the trawler, all four of them were thrown into the sea. Caroline was wrenched away by the force of them hitting the waves.

Edith could hear the others shouting and screaming in the water.

She tried to scream herself, but every time she opened her mouth it filled with salty seawater.
The water was freezing, and her clothes clung to her like cold wet dishcloths. She was as afraid of hypothermia as much as of drowning. She might be picked up by a wave and thrown headfirst against the floating wreckage of the yacht, or it might land hard on her.

Edith could still hear the men calling desperately for help.

Panicking, she only wanted to stay afloat in her life jacket, but she knew she was a tiny speck in the vast black sea, and the men on the trawler might sail back to Littlehampton, never even knowing she was there.

It was then that Edith saw him.

An immense feeling of joy and peace swept through her, and she smiled and let herself float.
Michael! She saw his spirit, and he seemed real and solid, standing just above the water in front of her, dressed in his aviator's clothes. She knew then that everything would be alright. She didn't know if she would live or die, or even if she was already dead,

simply that everything would be alright because he was there. The sense of relief was overwhelming. How ironic that Edith had wished, prayed, and tried so hard to contact Mick from Cuckfield, but here he was out in the English Channel.

Mick was smiling, too. He was bending down and reaching out his arms to her. He was just a little bit ahead, a tiny bit out of reach. He was trying to give her his hands, and Edith rolled onto her side, kicked her legs, and stretched out her right arm to attempt to grab him, paddling with her left hand. She moved forward painfully slowly, afraid that at any moment he'd leave, or a swelling wave would snatch her away. But Mick stayed there, happy and reassuring, and she put her trust in him and kept moving calmly towards him.

She was aware that apart from the noise of the trawler's engines, a frightful silence had come over the sea, but she shut out any thought of why that was, and clung onto that joy she felt at seeing Mick so near and opening his arms to her.

With pure and utter elation, Edith finally reached the dashing young airman and felt his muscled arms and warm sheepskin jacket envelop her; she closed her eyes in relief.

She'd found peace and happiness at last.

CHAPTER 24

To Edith's great contentment, Mick didn't disappear but let her doze on in the cosy soft sheepskin flying jacket. She was lying against him. She didn't want to wake up, but to stay with him like this forever.

She felt safe, warm, and comfortable. But there were bright lights somewhere - probably from the trawler - and the light made her open her eyes.

It was a great surprise. She wasn't surrounded by cold black waves anymore but was floating against the ceiling of a long white room. Mick was still there, reassuringly beside her, and her feeling was still one of contentment.

As Edith grew comfortable with this new floating feeling, she began to look around her, curious. There were two rows of beds at ground level, and the one directly below her had curtains pulled around it. A man was sitting by the bed, with tears on his cheeks, and she saw it was Adrian Stevens. She looked at the person in the bed and saw with surprise it was herself; she recognised the copper hair. Her eyes were closed, and she had no colour and a drip in her arm. She wanted to tell Adrian not to cry because she was very happy and so warm and dry that it was a wonderful feeling to drift in peace. But she found she couldn't speak to him, and he didn't look up and see her hovering above the bed.

Without leaving the room, she realised that she could also see into the corridor outside, through the wall, and there were Hester and Phillip, with Clara and Alma. The women were also sombre and tearful.

Edith wanted so much to tell Hester that she was with her beloved Mick again, but she couldn't talk nor come down from the ceiling.

It became very confusing. Mick was there beside her, being such a comforting presence, and she was still floating. However, she felt a large warm hand take hers and she could see with her own eyes from above, that Adrian was holding the hand of the Edith who lay in the bed below her.

How could she be in two places at once?

Michael couldn't speak in words, but he could communicate in thoughts as she looked at him, and she knew that he was telling her that she had to make a choice. It was an easy choice she felt; she could follow Michael and stay with him, as happy and contented as she was now, or she could stay with those people she could see below, who loved her too.

She smiled at Mick. The decision was simple. She would choose to follow him. But then she felt other spirits in the room. She couldn't see them, and she knew they didn't have any physical appearance at all. Michael was telling her they were her unborn children. There were three of them. She knew that Mick meant she *could choose* to follow him, but the children wanted her to go back to her physical body or they could never exist. They wanted a life. Not only that, but if they were never born, then their own children could never be born, and so on.

She suddenly smelt a warm, soft baby's head with a milky orange blossom biscuity aroma that made her breathe in deeply as a little hand groped for her breast. Other little hands pulled at her body to get her attention, and she felt suffused with love.

Michael was nodding with understanding. She knew he hoped she would choose her children. The children whose father was Adrian Stevens, not anybody else.

It was an unequal choice.

I would have chosen you, Mick, she thought, *if it were only between you and Adrian, then I would have chosen you...*

Edith felt a terrible sadness as Adrian's warm hand kept caressing her own, pulling her down where she didn't really want to go. The choice was so unfair! If she chose to stay with Mick, could she ever rest in peace if she knew that she was surrounded by troubled spirits whom she'd denied their own physical existence and chosen destinies? It would be so much easier if Michael didn't make her choose but *made* her go back. Still, Mick was telling her that the choice had to be hers. He would watch over her, as she could now watch Adrian Stevens.

There was also a job she had to finish. The spirits of Louise and Arthur Lamb couldn't be here with them because they were trapped on earth. She knew they wouldn't be at peace until they were buried in a cemetery together, and the suspicion of murder was lifted from Arthur's name. She was the only person who could put them to rest and she had to go back.

She felt that big, warm hand pulling her down and back into that body in the bed as she started crying with a pain that was earthly and human.

I will always love you, Michael. Please wait for me.

'Edith? Edith? Edith!' It was Adrian's voice. He pressed a buzzer. 'Nurse. I think she's coming round! She breathed in loudly, and now she's started to cry!'

When her mother, Alma, Hester, and Phillip returned from drinking a cup of tea, they were astonished but delighted to discover Edith sitting up in bed, groggy but very much alive and able to talk normally, although she was slightly disorientated. She had herself asked for a sugary cup of tea.

A nurse was hovering around, looking delighted, waiting to take her blood pressure and temperature.

'You did give us a scare, darling,' Hester said. 'You've been out for two days. In a sort of coma, although I think they gave you tranquilisers to help you rest.'

'It was dreadful.' Clara was still tearful. 'I didn't think you'd survive. How d'you feel? Detective Inspector Stevens has been sitting by your bed day and night. He was distraught. He's been blaming himself. And I blame him, too! How could there be dozens of policemen, only one exit - Hester tells me - and they still managed to let you be driven off?'

'I've told him he shouldn't feel guilty,' Edith said. Adrian was holding her hand again. 'He took a lot of persuading to follow my own idea, and I was stupid enough to go alone into the powder room at the side of the building and lean out that low window. Is the policeman who was stationed at the side of the building, alright?'

'He got a nasty crack on his head, but he's recovering.'

'Laine? The Wrens?'

Edith drank her tea, although she felt rather weak and shaky.

'They didn't make it, I'm afraid,' Adrian said. 'The fishermen who got you out also rescued Peter Laine. He was still alive and made it to the hospital, but like you, he'd swallowed a lot of seawater and was unconscious. The fishermen broke his ribs while starting his heart. They went a bit easier on you because you're a woman, but they still saved your life. Laine died in this hospital, on another ward. He had water in his lungs and had stopped breathing - luckily you didn't. They found Edward Wren's body, but they couldn't find his wife. I'm afraid she's gone to the bottom. She's too far out to be washed up. I think...'

'She wasn't even wearing a life jacket,' Edith said. 'She wouldn't have stood a chance with the sea like that. I don't know how those fishermen knew we were there. We were calling but it was so windy, the sea was very rough, and the trawler had its engines on. They were inside the boat, and I didn't think they'd heard us shouting.'

'One of the trawlermen felt the yacht hit the boat and, luckily, he went outside to investigate. You were very fortunate. You were closest to the trawler, clinging to some wreckage, and although it was so dark outside, some light from the trawler was hitting you, and he saw you straight away - as if you were in a spotlight, he said. They pulled you out first. They had to search for the others.'

'Will you come to Horsham to recover?' Clara still looked worried.

'Not straight away,' Edith said. 'I want to return to the Norfolk Arms for a few nights. I think Adrian and I have some things we need to discuss. Phillip, you can take your lovely wife home! I'm going to be fine now - I don't feel bad at all, except I'd like this drip removed from my arm. I can remember everything, and I don't feel any different. It was so cold in the water, though...'

From when she awoke in her hospital bed, Edith made a rapid recovery, and since her time in the sea had done no lasting damage, she was discharged after a couple of days. Clara had been pleased to see Edith off at the station with the tall Detective Inspector. Edith looked at her mother with great affection, remembering the spirits of Clara's future grandchildren waiting to be born. Three of them! Clara was going to have the family she wanted to fuss over and spoil. Clara thoroughly approved of

Adrian Stevens - quickly forgetting how she had blamed him for her daughter's plight. Having seen just how distraught he'd been at her near drowning, she was obviously hoping that Adrian would become a permanent part of her family.

Edith's knowledge about her future made her look at Adrian in a different light. She didn't have that sick feeling of being in love and having to make decisions about the future of their relationship, but a calmer feeling that her destiny was already chosen, and she just had to go along with it. But on the train, Adrian told her what he hadn't wanted to say to her in the hospital. He had been temporarily suspended from his job. Three people were dead, Edith had been snatched and had very nearly died, and no arrests could now be made for the jewellery scams, nor the body of Arthur Lamb recovered if he had indeed been murdered.

Peter Laine had managed to fool a detective inspector and fifteen police constables and subsequently gave them the slip, sending the whole lot of them speeding off to Portsmouth like the Keystone Cops and making them a laughing stock. 'They're going to hold an enquiry, and I may well be demoted,' he said. 'This is the second time I've loused up. Remember when I believed Mrs Wren was the Arundel murder victim and didn't pursue other lines of enquiry?'

'I was right about that, though. Caroline Wren *did* die, and in water; it was just later than I expected, and she was also a murderess,' Edith couldn't resist pointing out.

Adrian grunted. He was so happy to have Edith back that he wouldn't spoil things by arguing the point.

'You know, when I was on that yacht, Caroline Wren confessed to me, and I asked her where they'd taken the wedding car? She told me it was Loch Lomond. D'you think the enquiry will go better if we find Arthur's body and Louise's head and prove that the three who are dead committed the murders? Caroline told me there was a witness, too. A witness to the mutilations of the body.'

'A witness?'

'I don't know who, for sure, but I've got a good idea. We must make sure the story of the yacht capsizing and the three drowning is covered by all the papers...hopefully the witness will come out of hiding. In the meantime, lets you and I go to Scotland. To Loch Lomond, and look for that car.'

'A trip to Scotland with you? Certainly, I think we should go. Darling Edie.' He leant over to kiss her, grasping her hands. 'Please don't ever go away from me again.'

Edith relaxed at the hotel and dressed very carefully because Adrian was taking her for supper, and he had mentioned a surprise. She rather guessed what the surprise would be so she was delighted when, instead of taking her into the snug, he led her to the castle gates in Mill Road, which were opened, allowing them into the grounds ('I used all my powers of persuasion as a police officer,' he said).

The detective was a big man, but he clambered to the ground and valiantly went down on one knee, with the castle as the backdrop. The castle grounds were shut to the public at that hour, and no one else was there. As they stood on the freshly mown lawn, there was a smell of cut grass in the air. It was evening, but the days were long, and it was still daylight. Edith could see the buzzards high in the sky, but all hints of anything threatening or magical seemed to have gone, and all that was left were beautiful birds who were part of Arundel's abundant wildlife.

'Will you marry me?' Adrian asked, taking off his hat, opening a ring box, and showing her the diamond solitaire he'd bought earlier that day in Chichester. 'If you don't like the ring, we can change it,' he said, 'and we can get it sized.'

'Yes, please.' She ruffled his sandy hair gazing down into his pale blue eyes. She put out her hand to help him up, but instead, he pulled her down onto the grass and kissed her tenderly as he felt for the right finger to place the ring on, pinning her down.

'So,' Edith told Hester excitedly on the telephone at the post office, 'we decided to get married at Gretna Green on our way to Loch Lomond because we'll only need one bedroom like that,' she finished coyly. 'We'll have a short honeymoon in Scotland.' There was a silence.

'Are you certain you're doing the right thing?' Hester asked over a crackling telephone line. 'I can understand what prompted him to propose; you're both in an emotional state after what's happened, but I think you should go back to Cuckfield and give it some time. After all, you've not known him very long. I think you should wait until you're both more clear-headed.'

'I'm sure I'm doing the right thing. I *will* marry him, and I don't want to wait,' said Edith firmly. For some reason she didn't want to tell Hester, nor anybody else, what had happened with Michael whilst she'd been unconscious. It was something very private, and she would keep it to herself.

'Darling...this is very difficult to say, but I have to...' Hester sounded very serious. 'I know you very well, and I only know him a bit...but do you think you have anything much in common? What do you talk about when you're not discussing the murder?'

'We've both lost the person closest to us. It's a bond.'

'Where are you going to live? Not in that house with all those animals? I can't picture you in that house.'

'Not *that* house. I told him I would only marry him if we could have a fresh start in our own home. I would like to live in Arundel. He's agreed. We will look for a house to rent tomorrow and move into it when we return from Scotland. We'll put his house up for sale and find something here that suits us both. He's going to let me furnish it how I like, and I can even put my own pictures on the wall. The animals will come too, of course. Although I'll put my foot down if they widdle in the house.'

'They will widdle in the house. What about his job? And the children's schools? The girls' friends all live in Chichester, too, I presume.'

'If he loses his job, he'll open a forge in Arundel. Otherwise, Chichester is really so easy on the train, and I'll teach him to drive. He's always telling me how to drive, anyhow.'

'The girls won't like moving. And you're not including them at their father's wedding?'

'No. We'll tell them when we get home. I don't want them to put a dampener on anything. They'll have to make the best of it if it's already done. Oh, but Gretna Green's so romantic! We'll marry in the old Forge, which is very apt since Adrian's a blacksmith. And Ma would simply take over if we hold it down here. And I haven't even met Adrian's brothers, yet.'

Neither of them had uttered the name, although it hung in the air. Hester said it now, 'And Gwen Brown?'

'Well,' said Edith, 'I couldn't be *too* demanding. I *have* got him to agree to move. I couldn't ask him to let her go just like that; after all, he's always told me she'll always have a home with his family. However, I can't imagine a glamour puss like her would enjoy it in Arundel. She might not like the idea of moving into a new house, where another woman is giving her orders, either. I think she'll hand in her notice.' Edith sounded very hopeful. 'We'll rent a house and tell them all once we get back from

Scotland. I'll leave Mrs Brown to supervise emptying the old house and putting things into storage - unless she's gone by then. I'll hire a char lady for the new house - and a gardener- and cook myself.'

Hester let out a very odd squeak, which Edith ignored.

The house they found to rent was a furnished cottage, with three bedrooms, at the bottom of the town and handy for the station. In red brick and flint, it had a beautiful wisteria on the front and a bank of delphiniums.

'The girls will just have to share a room until you've sold the house and bought a permanent home for us all,' Edith said as they paid the deposit and two months' rent in advance. Privately, she thought Mrs Brown would not be moving, and Sophie and Bella would get their own rooms.

They found a stable to take the horses temporarily, not far from Arundel. Edith hoped they might stay there indefinitely. Even if she had to pay for the stables herself.

She had decided to keep the Honeytree for the moment since it gave her an income and allowed her to rent out the rooms above it. She was within driving distance of Horsham and Cuckfield and could easily keep an eye on her mother and the café from her new home.

The trip up to Scotland was full of excitement. Edith drove the little Austin, and Adrian had tried to bite his tongue and stop back seat driving as he concentrated on map reading. It was a strange novelty for Edith to admire the new diamond solitaire on her engagement finger, which glittered in the sunlight through the car window. In many ways, it felt like the trip to Paris; it was wonderful for them to get away from other people and familiar surroundings and find themselves in love and alone together. Because she *was* still in love with him, Edith decided, and she wanted this marriage to work. Whatever she felt for Michael, he was dead and he wanted her to marry Adrian. She was confident that one day she would meet Mick again.

The pair had plenty to chat about on the way through England, with their impending marriage growing closer, they had booked the ceremony at the anvil in the Old Blacksmiths Buildings and arranged for witnesses to be found in advance.

They had slept in separate rooms when they stopped off on the way up to Scotland, and it had only seemed to heighten the anticipation of their wedding, knowing it was for the last time.

Edith wore the raw silk, sea green, jacket that she had returned to buy from the shop in Chichester, the same one as the bright blue version Louise had been murdered in.

'I feel it's like a promise to Louise,' she told her bridegroom earnestly. 'We'll find Arthur and give her back her identity - and we'll have the long marriage that she was denied.'

They'd stopped in a meadow near the bridge over the Sark and picked wildflowers for an impromptu bouquet, and Adrian put a cornflower in his buttonhole whilst Edith removed her hat and threaded a crown of daisies for her head.

The short ceremony with just the two of them was very moving; there were no guests, and the two professional witnesses were complete strangers. It was a private declaration, and there were none of the tensions that would surely have arisen had they married in Sussex and involved their two families.

'How on earth will we find the car?' Adrian had said as much to himself as to anyone. The Loch was huge, and it would be like looking for a needle in a haystack. 'Did they tell you the exact spot? What clues have you got? I'm sure I've asked you but I'm not sure what your answer was.'

That was because I didn't answer, thought Edith. She wondered how she was going to find the car. She couldn't ask Willy because he was somehow anchored to the Norfolk Arms back in Arundel. She needed to draw or paint, but she had to be on her own and not let Adrian see her.

'We won't be able to see it easily,' Edith said.

'Caroline Wren said the water wasn't deep. But she said nobody would ever know the car was there because the place was so remote. The loch must have been accessible by two cars, though, and one of them was big.'

Adrian turned to her. 'It might be a wild goose chase really. But I'm not sorry we came, Mrs Stevens. It's a lovely place for a honeymoon. I just hope that the police enquiry isn't too nasty.'

He was thinking of the enquiry into his conduct. 'If I have to go back to blacksmithing, I wouldn't be entirely upset. My brother has plenty of work. There're fewer and fewer skilled Smiths around, and it's not just horses you know... there's metal gates, bridges...'

'You won't lose your job,' Edith said. 'You'll wrap up this case and prove what an exceptional detective you are, sweetheart.'

'Going back to the bedroom seems like a very good place to start,' Adrian murmured contentedly, his blue eyes smiling. He kissed the top of her head.

When Edith finally got out of bed again, and had put on her dressing gown, she saw that Adrian was still fast asleep. Quietly, she took her box of pastels from her open case, and a sketch pad along with her toiletries and towel and crept along to the bathroom at the end of the corridor. Locking the door, she ran the bath very slowly and lay on the hard, cold, floor, trying to get comfortable, the pad and crayons by her side.

She willed the top of her head to go soft and then to open and her neck to release all tension. Then she let her arms go floppy, beginning with her hands and moving up to her shoulders, all the time counting backwards from one hundred. Next it was her feet and legs that felt heavy and useless, and her spine that felt soft and bendy and melted into the floor.

The sound of running water was relaxing. She was unaware of the rising steam. There was a buzzing in her temple.

She let her hand pick random pastels and move over the paper at will as she concentrated hard on an image of Louise and Arthur Lamb stood side by side. Louise was in her blue coat and navy hat, smoking a pink sobranie, a huge diamond cluster ring on her engagement finger. Arthur, tall and balding held her hand. But other images superimposed themselves unbidden. Poor Arthur. She suddenly knew that Louise had died first, squashed by his weight and bleeding and suffocating in the boot when they should have been on the way to France. Murdered by two school friends they trusted entirely. Caroline Wren was in her country tweeds; *She's hotter than Chicago's FIRE.* The big high wedding car with something unspeakable in the boot in the grey waters of the lake. But not on the lake floor. On a ledge at the edge of the lake. A shape hardly visible below the water, in a lonely spot. Pine trees. Logs. Log piles and piles of felled pine tree trunks. A timber yard.

The fear of the bath water overflowing brought her round. The sound of the water filling the bath had changed. Edith counted slowly to three before opening her eyes and dragging her stiff, cold body to her knees to turn off the taps. She sat back down to look at the damp paper with its rough pastel sketch. It was a long irregular ribbon shape with a wide triangular bottom: Loch Lomond. Edith thought it was rather impressive that she could draw the shape without looking, but it didn't help much at all.

As hard as she stared at the lake outline, she was no better off than she was before. Pine trees and logs in a lonely spot - that could hardly be unusual in about a sixty-mile circuit. She thought, though, it would be on the west side of the lake, with a view across to Ben Lomond. They might be able to see the car underwater if they found the spot.

Edith took off her nightdress and climbed into the warm bath, soaping herself and thinking. She needed to look at a map. The place would be outside of any town or village, and she was looking for a logging path accessible to two cars and leading down to the water's edge.

Logging; the pine trees weren't only used for small logs for fire places and stoves - It could be that whole pine trunks were cut for beams, planks, and boards, and you would need a lorry to transport pine trunks. It must be a track off the main road accessible to lorries. She wondered if there were many timber yards near Loch Lomond? Of course, the loggers might work for a business based in Glasgow or anywhere else, but it was worth trying local artisans working in pine. A local directory might yield a clue.

Drying herself off, she returned to the bedroom where a happy Adrian was standing naked, enjoying the Scottish mountain view from the window. She admired his long legs, like sturdy tree trunks themselves, and his wide buttocks, and slight freckles. He looked at home here, like a big, rugged Scotsman himself. She came up behind him and put her arms around him, and he caught her hand.

Hurry up and get dressed,' Edith said. 'I remembered some other things Caroline Wren told me on that yacht,' she lied. 'We need to consult a local directory to find timber yards. The car went into the loch from the end of a wide track through the forest used by lorries collecting pine timber. There can't be too many of them. Why don't you have a bath? I'll ask the hotel if they have a directory - we can look at it over breakfast and see if we can find where to go.'

But when Edith was alone, she had another idea, and dressing as quickly as possible in her navy diamond golfing sweater, slacks, and pearls, she raced down to the reception. The hotel did indeed have a directory, and to her surprise there was only one timber yard listed at any proximity to Loch Lomond, and that was at Stirling. She asked to use the telephone. The secretary at the Timber Yard was somewhat bewildered at the strange question of where exactly they got pine delivered from the banks of Loch Lomond. Still put on the spot and seeing no harm in giving out the information, the woman replied in a charming accent that she *didnae ken fo'sure,* but it was an area near Tarbet.

Edith sat down at the breakfast table and ordered a cup of tea, pulling out a tourist map and spreading it on the tablecloth to look for the spot. *If* this was the stretch of water, she'd narrowed it down to ten miles, more or less. Looking at the map, she knew it was the right place as she slipped straight into a reverie...

She could see a scene play in her mind as if it were a film by Mr Hitchcock, and her head vibrated: It was night; there were two cars. Edward Wren drove the wedding car. Caroline followed him in their own car. They already knew where to go because Edward had found the spot in the daytime and checked it out. Edward tried not to gag as he drove the car down the forest path; the boot had remained locked since Swanbourne Lake, but now, the smell of death had started seeping into the car. The stench of rotting meat. He opened the windows because it was night - he'd been unable to do so in the daytime because the car had filled with fat blue bottles every time he stopped (trapped, their corpses were strewn over the seats and footwells,) and besides, the unmistakable reek of death would attract attention. He didn't like to think about what was in the boot. It was the gruesome head and those pretty feet that got him. He couldn't stop his imagination from conjuring up a horrific image of green mottled flesh to go with the fetid stink. Louise had been a lovely girl and, secretly, he had always been attracted to her. He imagined kissing those lips now and shuddered. They parked up on the edge of the lake and Edward was frightened. He had had to turn his headlamps off as he moved the car as close to the edge of the loch as possible; he was afraid the lights would be seen from somewhere on or along the water's edge. Caroline directed him forward. He'd turned off the engine and left off the handbrake, and they'd pushed the car with all their force off the edge of the rocky promontory,

Caroline falling onto the muddy grass in the process. Then came a scary moment when they shone a beam into the depths of the water. What if the car didn't sink deep enough? Suppose you could see it? But it was *nearly* deep enough, and you couldn't see it unless you searched with a torch. Nobody would ever find that watery tomb unless they knew where to look.

'Edie. EDITH?'
She snapped out of her semi-trance to see her damp, handsome husband leaning over her, looking worried.

'Hello. Have you had your bath? Let's order breakfast. Would you like some tea? There's enough left in the pot.' She tried to sound normal.
'Whatever is the matter? You looked very strange - you looked in Nod. You didn't see me at all or reply when I first spoke to you.'

Edith knew from Hester's descriptions that her face would have been totally blank as if her own personality had been entirely erased; it usually happened when she slipped into a reverie.

'I was in a daydream, that's all.' She smiled and gestured at the map. 'I telephoned the only timber yard in the area from the hotel reception, and they told me that the pine comes from an area near Tarbet. It's going up the West side of the loch and we can look for the track. We'll find it, if it's big enough to get a lorry down. The Wrens found it, so we can.'
Adrian looked quite annoyed and somewhat hurt.

'You didn't wait for me? I'm the detective, and this is my case. You might have let me look for the timber yard and make the telephone call.'

CHAPTER 25

Edith was full to the brim with a hazy contentment. Not even Adrien directing her to slow down, change gear, check her rear-view mirror, or break, could dim her love for him as they drove along after a hearty breakfast.

He looked so rugged and handsome, she thought, hunched up in the front seat of her little motorcar. Maybe they would buy a bigger vehicle now it was going to be a family motor', although she was so fond of the green Austin.

The Loch looked navy blue today. The large angry clouds hung low over the mountains, and they drove in shadows, stopping only to buy some boiled sweets in the post office of a pretty little village. Adrian bought a postcard for his daughters, and one for Gwendoline Brown.

'I want to tell them we got married', he said, excitedly. 'They'll be thrilled! I hope they'll have time to get used to the idea before I see them, and I want Gwen to help them pack some cases and boxes to take to the cottage as soon as we get back. I don't ever want to spend another night without you.'

He put his hand on her knee, lovingly, and Edith turned to smile at him with adoration.

Adrian barked hysterically, 'Keep your eyes on the road!'

It was somewhere near Tarbet, but the unfamiliar route seemed never ending and none of the tracks they passed looked big enough to transport tree trunks down. There were few other cars on the road, even though it was the tourist season.

'The track will be somewhere near here,' Edith said, 'keep your eyes peeled for a likely place.'

'I don't think there're any turn-offs a car could use along here,' Adrian said. 'They're all for hikers or bicycle riders, nature watching at the loch.'

Edith knew where the turning was before she saw it. She felt the familiar buzz and her attention was attracted to a tall, slim, balding man who seemed to be loitering on the damp verge further along the road to Tarbet with a sorrowful air. His smart suit was entirely out of place in the mountainous outdoors. She only glimpsed the man briefly, but she recognised him as Arthur Lamb.

He's been waiting for me, she thought. *He's been wandering the forest and waiting for me since he was brought here.*

The Austin slowed to a crawl.

'It's coming up here on my right,' she said.

There was indeed a track off on the right, the entrance of which was half masked by fresh vegetation; no lorries had come down here recently. Edith turned, hoping the lush growth scraping along the paintwork would not scratch her motorcar too badly. Adrian told her not to worry; it was only a car, after all.

'How did you know the track was here?' He looked at her strangely as they bounced along over the flattened earth. 'The right track might be further along, even if you're correct about the car being in the loch.'

The edges of the track had widened out considerably into a series of clearings and plantations marked with wooden posts.

'I don't like it here,' the detective said, shivering.

There was no sound. There were no birds, squirrels, or signs of life at all, and the tops of the trees seemed to lean together menacingly.

This place is haunted, Edith thought. *There is a grave in the water nearby of a couple who died a violent and painful death. Their uneasy spirits are trapped here, near that tomb, because they want it to be found, and they want me to find them and take them home.*

'Look at that,' Edith said. She motioned at a large pile of full-length pines, stripped of branches, laying neatly like reddish telegraph poles.

'Further on we should see a pile of short logs, already cut up to fit in stoves.'

'It's very eerie,' Adrian said. 'That's all I can say. Caroline Wren described all this to you?'

'Yes,' Edith fibbed. She remembered Edward Wren driving past the logs, as she had seen him do when she lay on the bathroom floor.

The surface of the earthen track was hard and dusty, flattened by a roller, and no doubt countless lorries taking out loads of logs and upkeeping the forest, also allowing access to the water's edge. She saw Arthur Lamb ahead. He walked through the forest never looking from right to left or watching where he walked. He carried the weight of the world with him, and the canopy of the trees grew darker and heavier where he walked. There was also a lot of anger there, Edith thought. *He's not only sorrowful, but he's also angry and full of hate, and he can't move on.* He might as well have been chained to this place.

Edith drove carefully up the rudimentary road until she came to a fork. She carried straight on, pointing out the logs in a small pile by the side of the road, half covered with tarpaulin. Damp sawdust around the area indicated that many more logs had been cut here and already loaded onto transport some time ago.

'Well done,' Adrian remarked. 'For remembering the details of what she told you...'

'She also said there were no trees on the water's edge except for a lone pine left as a marker to be seen from the Loch to signal where this track ends. That's where they pushed the car over. You feel the atmosphere here? They can't rest until that car is found and they're given back to their families for a decent Christian burial? They want to rest together in a joint Catholic grave. We must ensure that Arthur's name is cleared when the inquest resumes, and the truth is printed in the papers. Mud sticks,' Edith said.

'Mumbo jumbo. They're dead, and they can't 'want' anything. If, indeed, Lamb's body is here, and he isn't a murderer.' The detective was looking over his shoulder and shuddering again. 'Let's be quick and then get out of this place. There's probably an axe murderer lurking in the forest somewhere.'

They had come to the water's edge and wide grassy banks, which had clearly been logged and upkept so that hikers could follow the edge of the Loch and admire the stunning views across the water to the slopes of Ben Lomond. A lone pine had been left standing at the end of the path where it met the hiking trail.

They got out of the car and walked to the water's edge and peered down into the depths. There was nothing to be seen. Black clouds gathered over the Loch.

'The car's down there,' Edith said matter-of-factly. 'Right near the edge; they rolled it over into the water.' She started looking around the area. 'Look,' she said, 'Caroline Wren was following him in their own car. She made a three-point turn to get the car in the right direction and drive back out. But the back of the car went onto the grass, and the earth was wet there in the spring. She churned it up. The earth is drier now, and it's grassed over, but look at the ruts.'

Adrian was looking at her suspiciously.

'Darling, you know I *couldn't* have been with them because you interviewed me in Arundel while the Wrens were in Scotland. Don't look at me like that! Let's smoke a cigarette and decide what we're going to tell the police.'

They decided that Adrian would show the police his warrant card whilst hoping they wouldn't check up on him with Chichester police, and discover he was suspended from duties. Adrian would present Edith as having been told particular information about the exact whereabouts of the car by Caroline Wren, during the time the two women were together on the yacht. The yacht and the story of the drownings had made the press, and Adrian had had the foresight to buy some newspapers to bring with him if they needed to explain the case to Scottish police. It wasn't too difficult to persuade the police to send down a diver, since crimes in the area often meant recovering evidence from water and divers were generally to hand.

A few days later, Edith and Adrian stood and watched as a police team slowly winched out the wedding car, water pouring from its open windows. It was lucky that the Wrens had not had the stomach to leave the boot open as they'd sunk the car, not wishing to view, and smell, the decomposing body parts as they were pushing it. The boot still held its grisly contents as they had been packed at Swanbourne Lake some months earlier.

That evening, the pair sat drinking whisky and Bloody Marys, watching the sun dip over the mountains from their hotel in Luss.
They had received a telephone call at the hotel to confirm that the boot had been opened and the contents returned to England for formal identification.

'We'll be able to match the cuts on the bones in her neck to the Arundel burnt corpse', said Adrian. 'There're also teeth. There were a number of personal items in the boot, too, including a blue jacket, watches, and monogrammed underwear.

Identification should be fairly easy. Then we'll reopen the inquest, although implicating the Wrens in the murder relies only on your testimony. Constable Berry, hidden in the café with me, in Littlehampton, heard Peter Laine deny the crime.' Adrian smiled at her, 'You will have to testify that Caroline Wren described to you in detail where they hid the body. I just hope it's sufficient to declare the case solved.' Edith fixed him with serious grey eyes and covered his hand with her own.

'Caroline Wren let slip that there was a witness,' She reminded him, putting down her glass. 'At Swanbourne Lake. That witness must have seen the newspapers by now and know that they're all dead. Will you do something for me, though?'

'I'd do anything for you,' he said. They'd returned from seeing the car brought out to a pleasant afternoon spent in bed, and Adrian was very in love.

'I need to speak to that witness alone, and I've got something I want to say to them that has nothing to do with this case. If you let me find them and speak to them first, then afterwards, I'll persuade them to come to you, make a statement, and testify at the inquest. It shouldn't be too long to wait if that witness knows they're out of danger now.'

He lit a cigarette and took a large drag on it.

'Who's the witness? Did Caroline tell you, then?'

'Oh, Come on!' Edith nearly choked. 'You're the detective! You can surely guess who! Nobody would need to be psychic to work that out.'

CHAPTER 26

Adrian was in high spirits as they drove to Brighton, two weeks later. As usual he seemed too big for the car, as he sat in the passenger seat, chubby fingers grasping a cigarette, his hand dangling from the window. This time, however, they also had his two sulky daughters crammed into the back seat.

Adrian was happy because Scotland Yard and the Chief Constable had been overjoyed that the Coroner would indeed rule that Louise and Arthur Lamb were murdered by Peter Laine, Edward and Caroline Wren, with the motive being linked to the international jewellery heists. Edith was safe and sound, and although three people were drowned, it would save them all the hoo-ha around hanging a woman and an expensive trial at the Old Bailey. The idea of an enquiry into Detective Inspector Stevens' fitness for duty had been discretely dropped, and he was entirely forgiven. Now, they were off to speak to the potential witness in the case, who would hopefully be the star of the inquest. Finally, the Chief Constable would be able to give a press conference where he could announce that the police had solved the murder in Arundel, taking all the kudos, and Adrian might even get a pay rise.

The detective was also very excited to be on a day out to the seaside with his new wife and beloved children. He had been living with Edith at the rented cottage in Arundel since their return from honeymoon, and this was the first time that his new family had come together since the wedding. He wanted everybody to find a bond they could build on for the future.

Edith had also hoped this day out would go well, but so far it hadn't. Firstly, both girls had moaned that they had been obliged to spend the night at the cottage and complained that they had each had to cancel plans to go riding and meet friends. It hadn't helped that the day was grey and covered over. They clearly did not intend to get to know their new stepmother, whom they treated as an insufferable bore.

Next, they had chattered incessantly in the back of the car about how marvellous Chichester was and how clever and pretty Gwen was. Adrian obviously thought this was just normal conversation, but Edith felt that Sophie was fifteen, not five, and was doing it on purpose to exclude her from the family and needle her about Mrs Brown. It had been unfortunate that Sophie had watched Edith's face as she had sat eavesdropping before that Sunday lunch.

The worst part had been when Annabella's new pet rat, St Peter, had escaped from Bella's pocket and run loose in the car to much mirth, including from Adrian. Edith had not been able to stifle a shriek before swerving to the side of the road and slamming on the brakes. The rat was used to running up Bella's body and perching on her shoulder, and Edith was scared it might do the same whilst she was driving or wedge itself under the pedals.

'Calm down, darling, he's perfectly tame and very friendly. Do you want to hold him?' Adrian had said, still amused. Edith had seen the glee in Bella's face and knew she would be seeing a lot more of St Peter, who had been named by Mrs Brown because, she said, with Satan in the house, the rat would never be far from the Pearly Gates.

Edith fantasised about buying a rat trap anonymously and where she might set it. She would definitely put one in the car, under her driver's seat, on future journeys.

The truth is things had not gone according to plan from the moment they'd returned from Scotland, and she and Adrian had moved directly into the cottage.

Edith had gone to Cuckfield to fetch some suitcases and look at the tearoom accounts and order books. She'd telephoned her mother, who, while sad at not being able to have a white wedding, was pleased as punch that Edith had tied the knot with such a suitable man, as she saw it, whom she'd met at the hospital. Clara was also ready to welcome Sophie and Annabella to her family with open arms.

Adrian, on the other hand, had arrived back from Chichester alone, carrying boxes, but rather dejected, and announced that the girls would not be moving in to the rented cottage.

He had flopped into an armchair.

'Mrs Brown doesn't think it's a good idea. We've agreed to wait until we've found a permanent home before they move,' he said.

'What do you mean?' Edith had not quite believed her ears. 'We've rented a place with three bedrooms, for us all to live in.' She sat down heavily on the chintz sofa.

'Actually, Gwen thinks that it's a terrible idea to move to Arundel at all. I told her that it was your idea and I insisted I wanted to make you happy, and we *are* going to move. She still thinks it's badly thought out, though. The girls will have to take the train to school now, or to see their friends, and that will be something that will make their lives a lot more complicated. They'll be much more tired on schooldays as it'll add travelling time onto their day when they could be outside in the fresh air on horseback, doing schoolwork, mucking out the stables, or learning to sew. Anyhow, I told her we're moving and I'm putting the Chichester house up for sale and that's that.'

'Thank you, darling,' Edith said, 'although,' she wrinkled up her nose, 'I wish you hadn't said it was *me* who insisted on moving; you want a fresh start too, don't you? You said you did.'
He leaned across from the armchair and kissed her. 'I do. With you. Still, I had to agree with Gwendoline that this furnished cottage isn't a good place for them to move into.'

He motioned around the sitting room.

'There're the animals to take into consideration, for one thing. Monty would be happy enough as dogs just like to be where their owners are, but the cats are territorial. The cats won't like moving once, but moving twice will make them very unhappy indeed. Besides, as Mrs Brown says, they'll sharpen their claws on the rented furniture, because you can't stop cats being cats. And we're too near the road. They'd have to be kept in until we moved to our new home, and then they'd wee around the cottage. Brutus would scent mark it. And it's hard to get rid of the smell. Of course, it's different when it's your own place...'

Edith was thinking of the beautiful new furniture she was intending to furnish their home with once she had found somewhere suitable.

'Brutus is the stray, isn't he? Those kittens are so big they'll be interbreeding soon. Perhaps we should look at finding homes for them?' She sounded hopeful.

'They're all females except for Brutus. Bella insists on bringing Brutus - we can't simply abandon the poor creature, I suppose. Then there are the horses. The stables are too far away from the cottage, Gwen says. The girls want to ride whenever they choose. The horses are fine in the paddock next to the house, and when we find a new house with a paddock, we'll move the horses straight across. You can't just move all these animals from pillar to post you know; it wouldn't be fair.'

Edith sat a moment in silence and then hunted for her handbag and took out her cigarette, lit it and took a long drag.

'Sophie and Bella won't share a room either,' he went on. 'They've always had their own rooms and, besides, Sophie is fifteen now and a young woman. Bella's room is always full of animals and they sometimes wee on the rugs. Sophie doesn't want to step in it.'

Edith thought of the three children she knew were waiting to be born to her. How many bedrooms were they going to need in the new house?
She did think of one idea, though...'I know! The girls don't need to share a room because we have three bedrooms. I agree they're growing up. They don't need a nanny, and I can run my own house. Maybe we don't need Mrs Brown?'

Adrian looked mortified. 'She's not really a nanny. I've told you before.' He sighed. 'She's part of our family. Of course she's coming with us - when we find somewhere big enough for all of us. Anyway, she thinks it'll be difficult for me with my job, my children, and my horse all in Chichester while we look for somewhere to buy, and we could save an awful lot of time and money if you came and lived with us over there. It would only be temporary. And there's Monty to think of, too - I can't cut him in half. Where's he going to live?'

'No.' Said Edith, 'I can't see myself fitting into your lives in Chichester. We need to all begin a new era, all of us together. I'm very happy with the cottage.'

Edith had been very content keeping house for her new husband and welcoming him home from work to a tidy home which smelled of fresh flowers and baking. She always had her lipstick and perfume on, and her hair done ready for him. But he got home later and later, and they hadn't been married a month.

'I've got to go and see the girls after work,' he said, 'however late I finish. I'm not abandoning my family. I respect your choice not to live with them, but don't complain if I'm late home because of your decision.' He put it so reasonably that Edith bit her tongue and smiled when he was late again.

He had put the house up for sale in the newspaper, but when Edith asked if Mrs Brown had made a start on packing up the house, he always said 'not yet.'

'The house has only been on sale a few days, don't worry about it darling,' was his response.

The worst day had been when Adrian came home so late that his dinner had been spoiled.

'We were playing board games with the girls; I always used to do that, and too much change isn't good for children,' Adrian said. 'Time went on and they tempted me with supper. Toad in the Hole, too, my absolute favourite. I'm sorry darling. They've wrapped you up a piece of it to try and see if you can make it the same way for me. Mrs Brown says she can give you some recipes.'

There was no telephone in the rented cottage, and so Edith had to go to the post office to telephone Hester. Just the sound of her cousin's voice made her feel better.

'I can't really complain too much,' said Edith, 'it's me who refused to move over there. He wants to live with both me and his children, and he's now forced to spend time separately with each.'

'Are you happy?' Hester's voice was kindly.

'When Adrian is home, yes, I am. I do love snuggling up with him,' said Edith, 'and I love living in Arundel, but we can't go on for a long time like this because he's being pulled in two directions. Otherwise, quite frankly, I'm quite glad not to have them here. Is that wicked of me, darling? And I have a lot of time for painting.'

'Find your new house first, and then have a frank talk with him about Mrs. Brown,' Hester advised. 'Are you sure you can't get one of your ghosts to start rapping and stomping about in her bedroom? I haven't told you this, but even I hesitated at being alone in the bedroom after those séances.'

After Edith had hung up, on the spur of the moment she asked the operator to get her the number of the Brighton art gallery. She'd telephoned a number of times since they had returned from Scotland but had never had any joy. This time though, was different. She listened a minute to the voice that answered, and without speaking, put down the telephone receiver. The next weekend they had collected the girls from the station and set off for Brighton.

Once in Brighton, Adrian took the girls off towards the pier, St. Peter perched on Bella's shoulder, his little pink nose and whiskers sniffing the salt sea air. The summer weekend crowds thronged the promenade, and the smell of candy floss, and the sound of the Punch and Judy show wafted up from the chilly pebble stone beach.

Adrian had given her a quick kiss and said, 'Do your best darling.'

'I will,' she said, feeling a surge of freedom as the girls walked away, 'it's much better that I talk to her woman to woman, besides I also want to talk to her about something else, other than the murder.' She held in her hand a leather satchel.

Standing outside the art gallery, Edith saw the Bounder through the window. He was stood behind the counter speaking obsequiously to a customer. She pushed open the door and admired the pictures on the wall, but one eye was searching the corners of the shop for the person she'd really come to see.

Joanne Forsythe was much thinner then when Edith had seen her last, and a terrible colour. Her hair was shingled, and she had tried to make herself look better by overdoing her powder and rouge. However, her orange blouse and lime green pyjama style slacks and black and diamante earrings rather suited her. Still, something had clearly happened to the woman since she'd last seen her, and not anything good.

Edith went over to see her where the woman was rearranging some antique pill boxes into an artful display.

'Mrs Forsythe?' Edith interrupted her. To her surprise Joanne obviously recognised her, although they'd only spoken once at the wedding. She evidently had the memory for faces that came with owning a shop.

'Hello,' Joanne said, warily.

Edith checked that David was busy, and said in a low voice, 'I need to talk to you. It's urgent. Can I buy you a cup of tea in Snows? You *do* remember me from the Arundel wedding? - I see you do.'

'What do you want?' Joanne sounded suspicious. 'Can't you talk to me here?'

'I need to ask you something, and I'll make it very worth your while. You know the three of them are dead?'

'Yes,' said Joanne, 'I read it in the newspapers. Why do you mention it?' Her eyes kept flicking over to her husband to check if he was watching. She hadn't needed to ask who the three were to whom Edith was referring.

Edith opened her satchel which was filled with pastel drawings and painted abstracts in oil on plywood. She saw the other woman's face light up with interest, and liked her instinctively.

'I'm an artist' she said.' I've spoken to your husband about my art before and he asked me to bring these in. He's busy, and you know as much as him about art, don't you? Tell him you're going with me to a café to talk about me presenting some pictures in your shop. Tell him very quickly so he can't object and tell him in front of his customer. He won't want to interrupt his pitch and lose a sale. Follow me out.'

Edith saw out the corner of her eye that David

Forsythe had now noticed her with Joanne, but she pretended not to see him looking and made rather a show of packing away her pictures. She saw Joanne go over to him as she'd suggested, but he was helpless to stop her leaving the shop without making a scene and giving his customer the time to think twice about his purchase.

Edith hadn't noticed how tall the other woman was before, as they wended their way through the weekend crowds. She was much taller than her pugnacious little spouse - tall and slender like a green and orange giraffe.

Soon the two women were sitting in the large tea shop and sipping from china cups.

'What do you want with me?' Joanne was evidently still wary. 'I remember you from the wedding in Arundel last spring. We were both powdering our noses at the same time, during the reception. Why did you mention the three who died in the yachting accident a few weeks ago?' She was fiddling with a large enamel jazzy necklace and looking round the room; anywhere rather than at the woman opposite her. But she wasn't unfriendly for all that. She was curious.

'First things first,' Edith said. 'Let me tell you what I could do for you if you let me help you. I'll tell you what *you* can do for *me*, in a minute.'
Joanne nodded cautiously.

'I know what David does to you,' Edith began.

'I know David is a controlling man who physically hurts you - doesn't he.'

Joanne looked at the tablecloth and her face became expressionless.

'No! Don't be embarrassed! It's not your fault. It really isn't. I overheard everything from the car park, when I arrived at the Norfolk Arms the day before that wedding, because you had your window open. He hurt your arm, didn't he? And you were so upset one morning you didn't want to show yourself at breakfast.'

Joanne's blue eyes met Edith's grey ones.

'What business is it of yours? What can *you* do about it?' She sounded bitter. Still, she didn't deny it. She was waiting and listening. 'Did you get me here just to throw this in my face? There's nothing I can do about it now. I've tried everything. He won't change and leaving is too difficult - I tried it.'

'I've got a solution for you.'

'*Nobody's* got a solution for me.' Joanne stared sadly out the window, listening to the mournful cries of the seagulls. She was watching the clouds drift by.

'One of your problems with leaving must be a roof over your head and money?'

Joanne nodded again.

'I've got a home for you, and a job,' Edith said.

'Where did you go when you disappeared?'

'London. I could only get very little work because I was living in hostels, lodging houses, or sleeping at the bus station. You can't live like that. People won't employ you without a permanent address, and you can't get a fixed address without a proper job. I couldn't even get a job in service at my age, with no experience. People are suspicious. Even my clothes were from charity, and I couldn't get my hair done - so I couldn't get a job in a shop, say, where I do have experience. Some days I didn't even eat, let alone afford cosmetics. Much longer and I'd have ended up a tramp. I had to come back in the end. There was no more point in staying away - once they were dead.' She was drumming her fingers on the table now. Her hands had modern style costume rings, but the nails were bitten to the quick.

I bet those costume rings were bought from Peter Laine, Edith thought. 'And your children?' She was relieved that Joanne hadn't been forced into prostitution, as far as she could tell; that would surely be the way out for other women fallen to her desperate situation.

Joanne shrugged. 'The children were fine. I don't know if they even missed me. David would never hurt the children and the two grandmothers spoil them rotten. It's *me*, David is always bullying - he's fine as a father, although he's poisoned the children against me. The family think it's my fault, and that I should just put up with everything because it's scandalous for a woman to walk out on her family and get a divorce. I've no support there. He's separated me from any friends I once had, too. I'm past worrying about scandal, but I've simply nowhere to go. I don't think I could survive being homeless again.'

'You must get out,' said Edith. 'I've a psychic

gift where I have intuitions about the future. He'll end up hurting you badly if you stay.' She had a thought...' Please don't tell *my* husband that I told you about my psychic gifts - he's a non-believer. My husband is Detective Inspector Stevens by the way. He was in charge of the Arundel murder case.'

Joanne didn't appear to question whether her companion could really see the future, or at least she didn't ask her about it. But then she didn't appear to be a conventional person at all.

'He wasted no time finding a lady friend when I was away, but it was a humiliation to him that it was me who walked out, though. They all kept it secret. I think they were angry at me for bringing shame on the family.' Joanne stopped. 'What's the job you mentioned? Why me?'

Edith explained to her about the cafe in Cuckfield.

'...So, you see,' she finished, 'I suddenly thought before I came to see you that as I've moved out to live with my new husband, my rooms above the Honeytree are free. I was thinking of renting them out to a family because there are four bedrooms and a sitting room, but then I had a better idea. What if you moved into my room and I advertised the other rooms to commercial travellers? You could make them breakfast and an evening meal when the café is shut and change the sheets. I wouldn't charge you for your room, or your food, and there're no bills. What's more, I'm taking all my pictures off the walls in the cafe to take with me, and you know all the local artists through your gallery. Why don't you arrange to sell pictures and objects downstairs, on your own account? I assume you can get a supply on sale or return? If you start making money, maybe you could get another premises in the Highstreet? I'll give you some of my own pictures back - I know you would understand them. Or maybe we can go into business together?'

Edith had decided that she liked Joanne Forsythe very much and wanted to be friends.

Joanne was circumspect. 'It sounds too good to be true.' She started gnawing her fingernails. 'You don't even know me.'

'Well, it's not,' Edith said. 'The room's free immediately but make up your mind quickly, as I need to make money myself.' Adrian was running two homes, and Edith felt guilty that his police salary was not enough to cover the cost for long (she had even agreed to make sandwiches for a day out recently, something she hadn't confessed to Hester.) Anyhow, if it makes you feel better, the reason I've come to see you is to ask you something in return. Will you testify at the inquests of Arthur and Louise Lamb?'

'What have I got to do with them?' Joanne was tapping the table leg nervously with her foot.' Arthur Lamb was David's schoolfriend, not mine.'

'Because,' said Edith, 'you were a witness at Swanbourne Lake, not him. Please, trust me. Admit it. The murderers are all dead anyhow. They can't get you now.'

Joanne Forsythe looked hesitant.

'Please, Joanne! I'll help you if you admit it. What harm can it do now?' Edith paused. 'Tell me about it,' she said encouragingly. 'Whatever were you doing out at that time in the morning?'

'May we order more tea, please?'

She waited until the waitress had brought a fresh brew.

'I'm often out at that time,' Joanne began, 'Sometimes it's David who throws me out of the house in the middle of the night if we've been fighting; especially if it's winter and I'm in my nightdress. Other times, it's me who leaves the house to avoid being hit. I've found that he's usually calmed down after a few hours and is generally very contrite when I come back.'

Edith took a sip from the pretty green china tea cup. 'What was it this time?'

'I managed to sneak out of the room with my clothes and shoes when he was using the water closet down the corridor. It was gone two o'clock in the morning. He was in a dreadful mood again. He'd been in a bad mood ever since we'd arrived in Arundel. He wouldn't let me get any sleep. And we'd been up late the night before at the wedding reception. He's worse when he's tired and can't settle.'

'Why take Mill Road? It's so dark and lonely. There're no houses. Only the dairy. I'd be too frightened to go there at night on my own. Why didn't you stay in town?'

Joanne gave a sour smile. 'In my long experience, It's people you've got to be frightened of, not foxes and badgers. I mainly saw ducks on Mill Road. In the Town, I'm always afraid to meet a tramp, or I'm scared that some strange man will look out of his bedroom window and see me all by myself. There was a collection of men on the road searching for jobs and sleeping rough in Arundel town..."

'So, you got to the lake...'

'Yes. I kept walking to keep warm and calm down. I didn't realise that anybody else was there until I crossed Swanbourne bridge and saw the two motorcars parked up near the kiosk. It was dreadful. I'll never forget it. I only saw what was happening for a moment, but it was lit up in the car headlamps as clear as day.' She shuddered as she relived the memory. 'It was a very big car parked in front, with the boot open. There was a second car parked a little distance behind it with the headlamps on, lighting up the boot of the first car. I could see that there was a person lying in the open boot, in a foetal position, but I couldn't see who it was. I could see who the two men standing next to the boot were, though; Peter Laine and Edward Wren.'

'Did you know them well?'

'Quite well, yes. My husband went to school with them and Arthur Lamb. David sometimes exchanged paintings or antiques for jewellery. Peter has been to the house many times. If you ask me, he had a bit of a crush on David. Peter has always been that way inclined in my opinion. David was a bit scared of him; Goodness knows what he went along with at school. I think Peter and Eddie bullied David mercilessly, but David was in awe of them and would do anything to please them. '

'Go on.' Edith said.

'I could see that Peter was doing something to a shape lying on a tarpaulin on the ground, and he was putting things in the boot, but I couldn't see what. Then I saw, very clearly, lit up by the headlamps, Peter bring down a meat cleaver hard and Eddie Wren hold up something by the hair.' She continued, 'Have you ever visited the wax works museum on Baker Street in London? The one that has the death masks of French revolutionaries sent to the guillotine?'

'Madame Tussauds.'

'She looked like a head from the Chamber of horrors, but I could still see it was Louise Lamb. There wasn't much blood, but she had a ghastly expression. Her eyes bulged.'

'She'd been dead for hours. What did you do? Why didn't you go to the police?' Edith shook her head.

'Can you imagine how shocked I was?' Joanne said, 'It really is the most horrific thing that has ever happened to me! I was absolutely petrified, too. Even more so when I realised that Caroline wasn't sitting in the motorcar with the headlamps on. She was smoking a cigarette at the side of the road, gazing into the trees; I don't think she wanted to watch her friend being decapitated. I bumped straight into her. She saw me and she even used my name.'

'More tea?' Edith was trying to picture the scene. She could see in her mind's eye where Joanne had come over Swanbourne bridge and had walked into a silent horror picture. 'What did Caroline do after she'd seen you?'

'I don't know. I left ever so quickly,' Joanne said dryly. 'I went down the steps to the footbridge, then down the path to the river bank and hid. Caroline must have run back and told Peter and Eddie that I'd seen them. They couldn't actually do a lot about it then and there. I mean...think about it. They couldn't move those motorcars very quickly up and down the road, raking the verges with their headlamp beams, because the clattering of the engines would eventually have woken somebody somewhere. There was the dairy house set back from the road. They couldn't drive on the river bank. They had to dispose of incriminating evidence very fast. So, in the end, they contented themselves with letting Peter run down the middle of the road brandishing the bloody meat cleaver promising, loudly, to kidnap and kill my children if ever I breathed a word of what I'd seen. He obviously knew I couldn't have gotten very far from the lake and would hear his threats wherever I was hidden. After I'd seen what he was capable of doing, I didn't trust the police not to inadvertently alert Peter that I'd spoken to them, and if the police didn't have proof to keep them in jail... well...'

'What did you tell David?'

'I promise you I didn't speak to David until I came home, after I read that Peter, and the Wrens, were dead. I thought they were bound to keep a watch on David to see if I went back to him. I stayed hidden, and I saw the cars eventually drive past. I'd some money in my purse, and some diamond rings on my fingers - ironically bought from Peter himself. After physically seeing what the three were capable of, I wasn't going to let them find me, and nor was I going to the police and risk my children having an *accident.* I'm sorry - they'd know it was me, even if I sent the police an anonymous tip off. I walked to Littlehampton along the river and caught the first train to London. I'm afraid it was cowardly of me not to get word to the police, or even David, where I was, but I have no doubt Peter would have been true to his word. That man was evil...to do what he did to Louise Lamb.' She shuddered.

'Did you know David was arrested for the murder, because you were missing?'

'No.' said Joanne. 'But I'd probably have been very happy. It would have been some sort of revenge on him and his rotten mother. I honestly think that I wouldn't have cared if they'd have hanged him! In fact, I could have come back and gone along with the police theory.'

'Please will you tell the inquest all that? - not the hanging bit of course... Your testimony is so important. Are you coming to live in Cuckfield?'

Edith touched her arm, sympathetically and

held her breath.

'Yes, to both.' Joanne said. 'I'll make sure you don't regret it.'

'Perhaps,' said Edith, 'it was simply our destiny to meet.'

Edith crossed the busy road towards Brighton's Palace Pier, while Joanne moved like a lofty and colourful exotic creature back towards the Forsythe Antique Shop and Gallery.

The entrance to the pier was thronging with people as Edith walked through the turnstile and looked out over the grey sea.

All at once it came back to her what it was like to be thrown into the cold turbulent water of the English Channel and how she'd been given a choice. The choice had been a cruel one, and she hadn't chosen the easiest answer.

She'd chosen to live out her life and to marry Adrian Stevens, for better - or for worse.

With a spring in her step, and renewed vigor, Edith Stevens strode over the wooden slats of the pier in her T-Bar shoes, her russet hair moving in the breeze, eager to find her very kissable husband and tell him all about her new tenant.

Epilogue

It was on a hot summer day that a large group of people dressed in heavy black clothes walked back down Arundel high street from the Roman Catholic cemetery and into the Norfolk Arms hotel for a late luncheon and some stiff drinks. It had been a very long morning.

Mrs Edith Stevens had walked up from her rented cottage for the funeral on the arm of her husband, Detective Inspector Adrian Stevens, and accompanied by their friends, Mr and Mrs Phillip Denney and Mrs Joanne Forsythe, who were staying with them since they had two spare bedrooms.
David Forsythe had not been invited.

The liturgy for Arthur and Louise Lamb had been held in the cathedral of Our Lady and St Phillip Howard, where the couple had been married such a short time before, although instead of walking in a gay gaggle up the road, the pair had done two laps of the town in a glass horse drawn hearse covered in lilies to arrive at London Road.

Edith could still smell the heavy scent of incense on her clothes, but it was a smell she liked. She looked down at the memorial card she held in her hand - an engraving of Jesus on his knees beside the empty tomb, being offered what looked like a fairy cake but was almost certainly meant to be a bread roll, and a large - and very full - goblet of wine.
Lucky him! Thought Edith, *Who could blame him?*

'Fiat Voluntas Tua,' the card proclaimed. 'Merciful Jesus Grant Eternal Rest' and, Edith thought, now Arthur and Louise had been committed to the ground together, near the big cross, they could rest in peace and would no longer haunt that lonely Scottish forest.

It wasn't yet time to go in to eat, and so Edith dragged Hester and Joanne into the snug and ordered up gin and Bloody Marys from a still charming Nijinsky...' who really has an incredibly trim bottom...' said Hester, after a double gin. 'I mean what's Adrian like...in the buttocks department?'

The Detective Inspector in question happened to be in the hallway in front of the snug and so Edith refrained from answering.

'We cannot ever, ever, thank you enough, Detective Inspector,' they overheard one of Arthur's uncles gushing to the detective. 'I mean without your dedication and determination to clear Arthur's name and bring him home, the police in Chichester would have simply given up. They're incredibly useless...So Thank You once again. We will make a donation to the police fund.'

'I was just doing my duty,' said Adrian, as the three women listened, glasses frozen in their hands. 'It was a tough case to crack, but I managed it in the end. Actually, My wife found a few clues, completely by lucky chance. She's quite bright, really! If I get another difficult case like that, I probably would ask her opinion again...'

Coming soon from

Ruby Vitorino Moody

EDITH
IN
CUFFS

When Edith reports a murder to the
police before it has happened, suspicions
fall on the Detective Inspectors wife.

Ruby Vitorino Moody

Ruby is a full time author, local historian, public speaker and tour guide. Her previous lives include being a Shephardess in Avignon, France, a waitress in Brittany, a jewellers assistant in Salisbury and a script writer.
She has an interest in historic crimes. She grew up in Cuckfield, Sussex and has lived in Brighton. With so many wonderful places in the UK to visit, Ruby and her husband usually prefer to return to Arundel.

Also by

Ruby Vitorino Moody

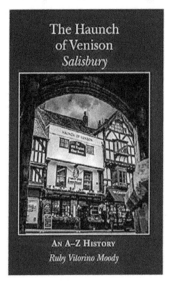

A non-fiction history of one of
Salisbury's oldest pubs, and Britain's
most haunted. Contains many first
hand accounts of the ghostly
experiences of customers and staff.
What did workmen find buried beneath
the fireplace? Who was the lady seen
on the back stair? What happened to
the real severed hand? The author
cannot say if ghosts exist, but many of
the customers and staff are now
certain that they do.

Published by Hobnob Press
ISBN: 978-1-914407-39-0

Milton Keynes UK
Ingram Content Group UK Ltd.
UKHW040912041224
3395UKWH00035B/243

9 781399 998260